RISE OF THE MYSTICS

BEYOND THE CIRCLE  TWO

TED DEKKER

Revell

a division of Baker Publishing Group
Grand Rapids, Michigan

© 2018 by Kiwone, Inc. f/s/o Ted Dekker

Published by Revell
a division of Baker Publishing Group
PO Box 6287, Grand Rapids, MI 49516-6287
www.revellbooks.com

Printed in the United States of America

Library of Congress Cataloging-in-Publication Data
Names: Dekker, Ted, 1962– author.
Title: Rise of the mystics / Ted Dekker.
Description: Grand Rapids, MI : Revell, a division of Baker Publishing Group, [2018] |
    Series: Beyond the circle ; 2
Identifiers: LCCN 2017061365 | ISBN 9780800729790 (hardcover : acid-free paper) |
    ISBN 9780800735043 (ITPE)
Subjects: LCSH: Quests (Expeditions)—Fiction. | Women prophets—Fiction. | GSAFD:
    Christian fiction.
Classification: LCC PS3554.E43 R57 2018 | DDC 813/.54—dc23
LC record available at https://lccn.loc.gov/2017061365

Author is represented by Creative Trust Literary Group, LLC, 210 Jamestown Park Drive, Suite 200, Brentwood, TN 37027, www.creativetrust.com.

18 19 20 21 22 23 24   7 6 5 4 3 2 1

Seeing, they do not see.
Hearing, they do not hear.

Yeshua
AD 32

You should read book 1, *The 49th Mystic*, before reading this novel. Think of it as season 1 and *Rise of the Mystics* as season 2, the completion of one overarching story, one that leaves behind the old, limiting confines of your mind. The ride is wild and sometimes bumpy, so hold on tight. There is no greater thrill than finding freedom from the shackles of a common existence. The old mind offers no life at all.

And so it continues . . .

Previously in
The 49th Mystic
Book 1

This is book 2 in the story of Rachelle Matthews, who came to be known as the 49th Mystic.

Born with sickle cell anemia in Eden, Utah, Rachelle became blind within months of her birth. She lived in that darkness for sixteen years, struggling with terrifying nightmares of the Shadow Man, who promised to blind her again and again even if she did recover her sight. Her father, David, desperately searched for a cure.

It was when he found one that the Shadow Man walked out of Rachelle's dreams and into Eden. He called himself Vlad Smith and he carried a Book of History, a mystical volume that allowed certain people to cross over into Other Earth, a dimension that mirrors Earth.

Without Rachelle's knowing, Vlad took her blood and applied it to the book, and she awoke in Other Earth with no memory of who she was. From that point forward, every time she fell asleep in Other Earth, she woke up on Earth, and every time she fell asleep on Earth, she woke up in Other Earth.

But a man named Justin, who was far more than just a man, came to her in the desert and healed her blindness, and when she awoke in Eden, Utah, she could see. That's how Rachelle learned that both realities had to be real.

And she learned much more.

She learned she was a Mystic in Other Earth. Unlike the Albinos and the Horde, who numbered in the millions, there were only a few dozen Mystics. Seen as the worst kind of heretic, they were despised by all.

More, she was the *49th* Mystic. Her mission: to fulfill an ancient prophecy that foretold of a child to be born in Other Earth who would divide the world to expose the shadow of death. Only then would the lion lie down with the lamb, meaning that fear would yield to love in the hearts of all. But neither Albino nor Horde interpreted the prophecy this way. Each race was convinced that if the 49th succeeded, they would be subjugated by their enemies. Thus, she was the enemy of all.

Rachelle also learned that, as the 49th Mystic, she could only fulfill the prophecy if she overcame her own fear. And the only way she could conquer her own fear was to find the Five Seals of Truth before the Horde or the Albinos found and destroyed the Realm of Mystics.

If she failed to find all five seals before then, all would be forever lost in Other Earth. And Earth would face a terrible threat, yet unknown.

Stunned by the revelation that so much hung in the balance of her quest, Rachelle learned that a powerful Leedhan had been sent from Other Earth to Earth with the sole mission of preventing her from finding all five seals before the Realm of Mystics could be destroyed.

He was Vlad Smith, the Shadow Man who'd haunted her dreams and entered Eden in an attempt to prevent her from finding the seals.

Facing what felt like insurmountable odds, Rachelle began her quest with the help of Talya, a wise sage who'd been tasked with helping her discover the five seals. They weren't five amulets or medallions but five truths, and when she discovered each, a seal appeared on her shoulder as a three-dimensional tattoo.

She found the First Seal in Eden, and it branded her shoulder with a luminescent white circle. *White: Origin is Infinite.* Meaning Elyon, who was God, could not be threatened or disturbed by anything finite. Nor could he suffer fear, least of all the fear of loss, on any level. He was the light in which there was no darkness.

She found the Second Seal in Other Earth, and it branded her shoulder as a green band of light. *Green: I am the Light of the World.* Inchristi is me and also in me. Meaning she was made in the fabric of her Father, one with Justin and so as safe as Elyon.

She found the Third Seal on Earth when she saved Eden by bringing down the synthetic sky, and that seal appeared on her shoulder as a black circle. *Black: Seeing the Light in Darkness is my Journey.* Meaning her journey during this life was a journey of transformation that allowed her to see who she was as the light of the world, joined as one with Justin.

But not all ended well from her limited perspective, even in the wonder of finding the first three seals. For starters, the seals she had could be rendered powerless until she found all five of them, Talya said. Against the Fifth Seal there was no defense, but unless she found the last two before the Realm of Mystics was destroyed, all would be lost.

Furthermore, Vlad Smith, the Shadow Man, proved to be a deviously manipulative adversary who accomplished his objectives in Eden and returned to Other Earth to prepare for a final assault on the 49th Mystic.

Most disturbingly, although Rachelle saved the town in a demonstration of great power, she was forced to write her father into Other Earth, where he now remains a slave of Vlad—to what end, she does not know.

On Earth, her heroic rescue of Eden was heralded by the world as a wonder that defied the mind.

But in Other Earth, she found herself captive to the Elyonites, imprisoned alone in a dark dungeon far beneath the city.

As she shivers deep in the dark Elyonite dungeon, the light she once felt in such staggering fashion grows dimmer each hour. The armies of the Horde and the Elyonites are gathering for a war that will tear the world apart. In that war, they will surely find and destroy the Realm of Mystics before Rachelle can find the last two seals.

Samuel, the Albino son of Thomas Hunter, might save her. He's smitten with her. Jacob, the Horde son of Qurong, might save her. She thinks she might be falling in love with him. Thomas Hunter, supreme commander of the Circle, might save her. Talya's gone to find him. She can only hope and pray.

At least she's safe and secure on Earth.

These are Rachelle's thoughts as she tries to be brave in the Elyonite dungeon.

But Rachelle is wrong. Very wrong.

1

I ONCE KNEW who I was.

More precisely put, I once *thought* I knew who I was, but four months of intense therapy aided by psychotropic drugs slowly showed me who I *really* was. Even more precisely put, all that therapy helped me see who I *wasn't*.

I wasn't the girl who'd saved the residents of Eden, Utah, by bringing down the synthetic sky as I once thought I had. That was DARPA, as part of its experimental process.

I wasn't the girl who could travel to other worlds in her dreams—those were all implanted memories, one of the unfortunate triggers that had led to my schizophrenia. I hadn't dreamed in months, and the dreams I used to have were lost in a distant fog.

I had confronted a man named Vlad Smith, but he was only a part of DARPA's programming, designed to test us all to a breaking point. He was a phantom implanted in our brains, they said. He didn't really exist, which is why he'd vanished.

That's what they've told me, and I believe them.

So who was I as I sat there in the lab across from Charlene Morton, one of the therapists who tested my brain to monitor my progress? I was Rachelle, a girl who'd just turned seventeen. I was one of the survivors of Eden who was well on her way to healing, though I can't say I loved the process. Then again, no pain, no gain, right? It had taken me a few months to accept the truth, but at least I was finally on the road to a full recovery.

"Are you ready, Rachelle?"

"Always," I said. The wireless cradle on my head, called a Mindflex, had been custom fit to my head. Its twenty-four sensors read all of my brain activity and displayed the data on both Charlene's monitor and the screens behind the one-way glass to my right. I was a bit of a celebrity at DARPA, and I can't say I didn't find all the attention comforting. My dad and I were the only two residents from Eden at the facility—the rest were in other "integration centers," adjusting to a new reality. But my dad and I were special to DARPA.

Charlene moved her coffee cup to the side and smiled at me. One of the voices in my head—the one I associated with Charlene—whispered, *Poor girl, she has no clue.*

My thoughts were often a bit fuzzy due to the drugs, but my auditory and visual hallucinations cut through all that fog with amazing clarity. I'd learned to mostly ignore them, knowing they were simply misfiring neural connections.

She studied me with warm eyes, preparing the numbered cards that she would quickly flip through before asking me to recite the numbers I'd seen. I'd done the same exercise dozens of times. It was designed to measure my ability to recognize and recall images the way a normal brain does.

"You're having auditory hallucinations," Charlene said, glancing at her screen.

"Just a little," I said.

"What did you hear?"

I hesitated. Some of what the voices in my head said could be embarrassing, and I often changed what I actually heard. The voice might say anything, no matter how inappropriate. I used to attribute those voices to the people around me, thinking I could hear their thoughts.

"I heard, 'Poor girl, she has no clue,'" I said, then grinned. "I guess I'm feeling sorry for myself today."

Charlene held my gaze. "Are you? Or is that just a stray, uncontrolled thought you associated with me?"

"One associated with you. But really me."

"That's good, Rachelle." She tapped a few keys, then faced the deck of cards toward me so I could see the first card clearly—9. "Focus on the cards."

I already was.

Using her thumb, she fanned the cards so they landed facedown on the table, giving me a very brief glimpse of each one. I can't say I was consciously seeing the number on each card, but a string of numbers popped into my mind as the deck of cards fell in about four seconds.

"What did you see?"

"9, 23, 24, 52, 4, 11, 21, 27, 2, 12, 32, 45 . . ." I continued on, because I could see the numbers there in my head, floating across a white horizon the same way I always saw numbers or any other image they showed me. She let me recite what I was seeing, and somewhere in there the voice spoke again.

Amazing. Never get used to it.

Again, Charlene's voice, but really just my mind speaking to me, telling me how impressed I was with myself.

"How'd I do?" I asked when my mind went blank.

She lifted her eyes from the screen. "Good."

"Better?"

"Let's just say your brain is lighting up like a Christmas tree. Slowly but surely we're forcing it to make typical connections. So, yes . . ."

I didn't hear the rest because I was seeing her elbow bump her black coffee cup off the table, and I bolted from my chair, acting from pure instinct, not wanting to see the cup shatter on the floor and make a mess. Three steps and I was there, catching the cup before it had fallen more than a foot.

I held it there for a moment, then stood up and set it down, grinning at her. "Close one."

"Close indeed. Thank you, Rachelle."

"You're welcome."

That was one thing I was really good at. Moving quickly. Project Eden had messed up my brain, but all that rewiring had somehow formed new neural connections that allowed me to perceive and react to motion with catlike quickness. I couldn't exactly catch bullets, but I could move like a ninja, as Steve put it.

Steve Collingsworth was the young DARPA scientist who'd been the first to reach Eden when they dissolved the sky and brought us all out safely. Next to my dad, he was my closest friend now.

Ninja practice, he sometimes called the physical tests they put me through. I sometimes thought Charlene knocked stuff off the table on purpose, just to see how quickly I would react.

They wanted to cure me, I was sure of that, but they also wanted to understand how my brain and body could operate in such a unique way. That's why I was special to them. At times I wondered if they were actually more interested in studying me than helping me, but even so I didn't mind. I, too, wanted to know how I could do the things I could do. If that meant being their guinea pig, so be it.

No one had ever encountered a mind quite as gloriously messed up as mine. If they could figure out what was happening to me, they might be able to re-create the good without the bad. I was playing my part in the evolution of the human mind/body connections.

I returned to my seat, feeling accomplished.

Who are you, dear daughter?

They had told me that was my mother's voice, speaking from the grave. Just an old memory fragment from Eden.

Re-member your true name.

They knew I was hearing things—no hiding that with the Mindflex on my head. They also knew I was getting much better at ignoring the voices.

Charlene stood, retrieved a clear glass from the cupboard, filled it with water at the sink, and set it down on a silver disk five feet in front of me. The nickel-plated sensor would read even the slightest change in the atoms contained in the glass and the water.

"Ready when you are," she said.

We'd done this exercise twice in the last week. Focus on the glass and imagine boiling the water. Impossible, naturally, but that was the point.

My brain had learned to see the water boiling with my intention to see it in that state. A hallucination I could control.

"Why, if we already know what I'm going to see?" I asked.

"For two reasons. The first is as a simple exercise in retraining your brain. See if you can observe what's really happening."

"The water *not* moving."

"That's right, even though you think it is. Can you think of it boiling but still see it as it really is—not moving? That's what we still haven't achieved. Fair enough?"

"Fair enough."

I stared at the glass of water and focused all of my thoughts on seeing it bubbling, boiling, changing, heating, as if I really had that power, like someone from a comic book.

Return to the truth of who you've always been, dear daughter.

The auditory hallucination of my mother's voice distracted me. I dismissed the interruption, drew a deep breath, and began again.

Focus . . .

Less than five seconds passed before I saw the water's surface shimmer, as if the glass was vibrating and agitating the surface of the liquid inside. Small bubbles formed in the water and rose.

Within ten seconds the water was bubbling.

"There," I said, looking up at her.

"You're done?"

"I'm done."

"You saw the water bubbling?"

I glanced at the water and saw that it was still again. But I already knew that I'd only imagined that boiling.

"Well?" I asked.

"Well, what?"

"Did your sensors pick up any change in the water?" It sounded ridiculous to me, but they seemed to think it might be possible, so I was a little disappointed when she shook her head.

"No."

"All in my mind."

"But what a beautiful mind it is. Want to go again?"

STEVE COLLINGSWORTH stood next to DARPA's director, Theresa Williams, watching Rachelle through the one-way glass, arms crossed. Next to them: Bill Hammond, leader of the now-defunct Project Eden.

It would be an understatement to say that Steve had developed a profound interest in the girl wearing blue jeans, a black shirt, and a new pair of red Converse tennis shoes. Everything about Rachelle fascinated him— the way she flipped her black hair when it hung in her eyes, the way she walked, light as a feather, the way she read her surroundings like a book.

The way she could transform the physical state of water through thought alone.

Real. All of it.

"She moved before Charlene bumped the coffee cup," the director said. "Ten seconds and the water boils. She's getting stronger." Eyes on Steve. "Why wasn't I told?"

"It's nothing new."

"What is new is the ease with which she's doing it."

"Which is why you're here, watching what we're watching."

Theresa looked at the data on the monitor as if to convince herself that what she'd just seen had actually happened.

Steve nodded at the screen. "You see the energy readings. Her operational field extends at least ten feet from her body." Charlene's field extended the mere six inches typical of most humans. "We're still no closer to understanding where all that extra energy comes from."

They'd long ago developed instruments sensitive enough to read a person's energy field in the same way a less sensitive monitor could read a light bulb's energy from a distance. Human beings, like all matter, were made of energy—99.999 percent of flesh and bone consisted of empty space charged by energy fields that held atoms and subatomic particles in a perceivable form.

Humans "saw" matter, when what really existed was collapsed energy.

Part of what the human eye couldn't see was the energy field extending beyond a body, a field that changed dramatically depending on the body's brain activity. Fear limited the frequency of that field, retracting it to within an inch of the typical body. Feelings of gratitude and love operated at a different frequency and expanded the field to several feet in most human bodies.

Most. Not Rachelle's. Hers was much stronger and extended much farther.

Theresa nodded at the monitors, voice tight. "I'm not sure you fully appreciate the danger a person with her abilities poses to a world that essentially runs on information. She proved as much when you put her on television four months ago."

Steve had allowed Rachelle one field interview on an ABC affiliate the same day she'd collapsed Eden. He'd asked her to keep it simple, so she had. She said nothing about Vlad Smith.

His motivation had been split. In part he wanted to protect himself from DARPA's backlash—any firing of him, the man who'd rushed in to help save so many souls, would only raise suspicions among the public. In part he hoped to put Rachelle in the nation's consciousness, thereby protecting her as well.

The brief interview with the blind girl who could now see had gone viral. As had the few seconds in that interview when she'd told the reporter, Robert Martin, that he didn't need to worry about his daughter because she was in a better place now. The camera caught his stunned reply: How could she have known that he'd lost his unborn daughter when his wife was killed in a car accident three months earlier? They hadn't told anyone about the pregnancy. Rachelle offered no response.

Speculation ran rampant as social media and news pundits ran with the story. She became the face of Eden, DARPA's mind-blowing memory-manipulation experiment.

Alarmed, DARPA spun their own version of the events: All in Eden had signed up for the project in full knowledge of the experiment's parameters, designed to measure the effects of memories on both physiological and psychological behavior. What all of the residents, including Rachelle, believed was radically subject to alterations made to their memories within the context of the experiment. Whatever they thought had happened hadn't necessarily happened at all.

What had happened was classified. End of story.

Still, conspiracy theorists made their hay for a couple of months before the story finally died. Everyone wanted to know: How could Rachelle have known that Robert Martin had lost his daughter?

DARPA went silent. They sequestered Rachelle along with her father, David. They simply couldn't allow someone who could read thoughts to roam free.

Within a week of sequestering her, the director concluded that the only way to protect both Rachelle and DARPA was through a radical, drug-induced recontextualization of her memories. And of her mind-reading skills. And of her dreams of another world, from which she claimed all her skills had come. Memory wipes wouldn't work with her—they'd tried—but old-fashioned brainwashing might.

Despite Steve's strong objections, they proceeded, first by dosing both Rachelle's and David's water with Rexpinal each night to suppress their capacity to dream. Dreams gone, they'd wiped David's memory entirely using a procedure called MEP, or Memory Editing Protocol.

In 2017, using engram cells to trace the specific location of memories, MIT had first discovered the mechanism for short- and long-term memory storage. At the outset, memories were simultaneously recorded in both the amygdala and the prefrontal cortex as previously theorized. The amygdala stored short-term memories. It took two weeks for the brain to decide whether the memories in the prefrontal cortex were worth holding on to. If so, the memory became long-term, stored there. If not, the memory was deleted.

All DARPA had to do to wipe a brain of all memories was replicate the brain's process of purging itself.

But the process that worked with others didn't work with Rachelle. Unable to reformat her brain, they'd begun systematic sessions of deconstruction. Old school. The administration of both psychotropic and hallucinogenic drugs had scrambled her mind, leaving her to finally accept that her memories of Eden weren't real.

Over the course of three months, she'd embraced the only diagnosis that made any sense: severe schizophrenia triggered by the trauma of her experience.

Nothing could be further from the truth, but there it was.

Steve turned to Bill Hammond. "I've never doubted the danger she poses. I'm also aware of the danger to Rachelle."

"An unfortunate consequence," Bill returned. "You know as well as anyone that she's a liability."

"A liability? She's the single greatest opportunity for consciousness research this or any organization has stumbled on. I agreed to go along only because it gave us access to a mind that's clearly operating outside our best models. Rachelle understands that much and is agreeable. But I've never liked the deception."

"And what precisely have we learned about consciousness in the last four months? We have to weigh the danger she presents with these parlor tricks."

"There's clearly a field outside of her mind that she's able to access," Steve shot back. "We don't know how external consciousness can be accessed, but we're just getting started. I think—"

"Consciousness outside the mind? We all know consciousness is generated by the mind. Our brains make us conscious."

"So says prevailing science, but from what I'm seeing, Rachelle defies that science. We have to figure out how and why. Isn't that what we're doing here?"

A slight grin of disbelief crossed Bill's face. "Need I remind you that spirituality isn't science? The brain isn't receiving consciousness from a higher source as if the mind was some kind of antenna. It's generating it between the neurons."

Steve peered through the window where Rachelle was on her third or fourth successful attempt to stimulate the water using her thoughts alone. To his left, Theresa watched in silence, letting them go on.

The water was boiling.

"And I suppose you have a logical explanation for how she can affect water at a distance of seven feet," Steve said. "Any of your models allow for telekinesis?"

"Clearly there's a quantum field between them. 'Spooky action at a distance,' as Einstein called it. But the brain's creating it, not receiving it. Regardless, I doubt our research into one subject's ability to influence the quantum field is going to redefine science. Particularly a subject who presents such a risk."

"A risk due to her ability to hear thoughts, which also defies our understanding of consciousness. She's far too valuable to treat with such low regard. We should at least reconsider our approach," Steve insisted.

"And what approach would you suggest?" Theresa asked, turning.

"Bring her in. Tell her everything we've done and why. Ask for her help in decoding her own mind. If she can boil water with her thoughts, maybe she can solve problems not even our best quantum computers can."

"You want to tell her that she's not, nor ever has been, schizophrenic?" Bill cut in. "That we've deliberately scrambled her brain with drugs? That we shut down her dreaming to hamstring her? You can't be serious."

"You mean the dreams of a world that at least offered an explanation for Vlad Smith? The dreams that somehow manifested her sight and the tattoo on her shoulder? We still have no explanation for Vlad, and we all know Eden had no access to holographic dye technology."

Bill looked stunned. It was probably the bit about her dreams offering an explanation for Vlad Smith. An explanation, maybe, but not one that could be taken seriously.

Steve continued in a more measured tone. "Okay, so we don't tell her we've cut off her dreams. The rest, yes. I think I could bring her in gently. Nothing would surprise her anymore."

The director crossed her arms and paced, eyes still on Rachelle. "From the beginning our process has been to use a sequential regimen of drugs that systematically impairs her brain functions, hoping to isolate the neural regions responsible for the skills she demonstrates. That would prove useful to us, no question. Unfortunately, other than shutting down her dreams, we've been unsuccessful. Meanwhile, her power is increasing. You can understand how that might concern some people."

"Concern who? The military? The administration? Fear of the unknown, I get that, but—"

"Some risks overshadow any potential reward, Steve. DARPA's own history has proven that much. Which is why I'm ordering the initiation of the new MEP."

Steve felt the blood drain from his face. Rather than replacing old memories with new ones, the new Memory Editing Protocol was designed to essentially reboot the brain, retaining only those systems integral to motor and logical functions. It had been tested on three volunteers, all of whose minds were reduced to those of young children in adult bodies. Two died within weeks.

"Please tell me this is only a stray thought."

"We've been preparing for it all along," Theresa said.

"Who's 'we'?"

"We!" she snapped. "Surely you knew it could come to this."

"I knew we would eventually find a solution short of eradicating the finest brain since Einstein's. There's no telling what the MEP will do to her!"

The director shook her head. "I'm sorry, Steve, this one's over my head. In a perfect world, I'd give you all the time you need, but it's out of my control."

He pushed back the fear lapping at his mind. It was the first time she'd admitted that someone else was pulling the strings.

She looked at him, eyes soft. "If it helps, I can have someone else—"

"No, she needs me by her side. Just because we've drugged her into oblivion doesn't mean she can't detect threats."

"You sure she won't pick up those threats from your mind?" Bill said.

"She probably will, but my presence will mitigate them. She trusts me."

It felt like betrayal because it was. On the other side of the glass, both Rachelle and Charlene were laughing about something.

He swallowed. "When?"

"Tonight."

2

WHO WAS I, lying on the ground in the Elyonite dungeon, alone and afraid? For the hundredth time I rehearsed what I knew, hoping it would calm my fear.

I was Rachelle, the 49th Mystic, destined to bring the sword of truth to the world. Then the lion would lie down with the lamb, as foretold. I knew that I could only bring the truth as I re-cognized myself as the daughter of Elyon, already one with him Inchristi. To this end, I had to find the Five Seals of Truth, and I had to find them quickly or the Realm of Mystics would be destroyed.

Against the Fifth Seal there was no defense. Until all five were a part of me, their power was limited. Three seals already branded my right shoulder.

Two seals to find, and time was marching on without me. Vlad was now in this world, determined to stop me before I could accomplish my mission. My father was captive somewhere in this world. The thought left me numb.

I'd been in that deep hole for a week. Days and nights were indistinguishable in a darkness broken only by the coming and going of torches, when the Elyonite guards brought me slop that passed as food and emptied the bucket I used to relieve myself. Other than those guards, I'd neither seen nor heard anyone.

Not Jacob, not Samuel, not Talya, not Justin. No one.

The last time I'd dreamed was that first night, after they took Jacob and left me alone. I wasn't dreaming because they were lacing my water with the rhambutan fruit, which prevented dreams. In that last dream of Eden, Utah, I'd found the Third Seal and brought down the synthetic sky that blinded the town. The Elyonites had blinded me after sentencing me as a heretic, but when I found that Third Seal, I'd regained my eyesight in both worlds.

After five or six days in the darkness, all I seemed to have were the three seals on my arm to remind me of a mission that had begun to feel hopeless.

That's who I was as I lay in the Elyonite dungeon on Other Earth.

At least that was one me.

The other me was on Earth, and I had no idea where or what was happening to me there, if anything. Neither did I know how much time had passed on Earth. Talya said that if I wasn't dreaming in either reality, there would essentially be two of me, one in each reality, each living her own separate life, oblivious to the other's circumstances until one of us dreamed again.

I knew I wasn't dreaming in the dungeon. And I had no reason to think that I wasn't dreaming on Earth, but somewhere in those long dark days and nights, the fear that something had happened to me on Earth entered my mind and stuck.

For all I knew, I wasn't dreaming on Earth either, and a whole month or year had passed there.

I stood up from the blanket and crossed to the bars. I looked down the dark passageway, hoping for light. None. Of course not. There never was. So I crossed my arms and began to pace to ease the aches in my knees and hips and get my blood moving.

One thing about such a cramped space: pain and stiffness.

I paced back and forth, lost in thought again, stepping the minutes away, wondering what was happening beyond my cell. During the first several days, I would count my short laps in the cell, back and forth, back and forth, up to four hundred once. Counting helped keep my mind off all the things I didn't know, but it wasn't working these last few days.

The counting no longer interested me enough to replace the endless stream of questions.

Where was my father? Was he in pain? I could imagine him with Vlad, being manipulated to some terrible end. He had the book with him, right? Was Vlad going to force him to—

Follow the finger under the moon, precious daughter.

I dropped my arms and gasped. The familiar voice in my mind was tender, but in that solitude it might as well have been an orchestra in full crescendo.

I was too stunned to speak. I'd heard it, right? It wasn't just my mind speaking. No, it was audible, just like before.

Follow it to the moon until you can follow no farther.

My heart pounded and I wanted to scream with gratitude, because now I had no doubt. I'd heard! And if I'd heard, it could only mean that something was going to happen. I couldn't follow the moon in here because there was no moon in here!

I blinked. "Follow what moon? Am I okay? Is my father okay?"

Follow the finger under the moon, dear one. Follow it until you can follow it no farther.

My mind swam in those words as meaning settled. The seals. I was being given a clue. A finger that came before each Seal of Truth, like riddles that pointed the way. This was a riddle?

No, it must be a direction that would take me *to* the next riddle.

I finally found my voice again, broken and scratchy. "What moon?"

Silence answered me.

"Is someone coming for me?" I asked.

I waited for a few seconds, but nothing came and I knew it wouldn't. Not now. Not until it was needed. And I knew from Talya that my earthen vessel self didn't know what was in my best interests or what I truly needed. For that I would have to trust.

Still, I tried again.

"Hello?" A beat. "Are you there?"

I am everywhere, dear one.

That infinite voice came like a whisper that shook my bones.

I dropped to my knees, hung my head and wept.

26

WHILE RACHELLE wept in the Elyonite dungeon, oblivious to the fate of her other fractured self on Earth, Thomas Hunter faced a shallow desert canyon lined by three thousand of Elyon's followers. Each had drowned in the red lakes to rid their bodies of the scabbing disease that covered the skin of all Horde.

They called themselves the Circle.

To Thomas's left stood his wife, Chelise. To his right stood the old man Talya. And on a hill behind Talya, his lion, Judah. The man had come from the desert speaking of the age to be ushered in by the 49th Mystic, a girl named Rachelle who dreamed of the other world.

Of Earth, where Thomas had come from in his own dreams so long ago.

"I hope you know what you're doing," Thomas breathed.

Talya's gaze over the gathering remained steadfast. "Justin always knows what he's doing."

"I wasn't talking about Justin."

"He's all that matters."

However cryptic, the man's authority was undeniable. Thomas's flesh prickled with both anticipation and anxiety.

His mind spun back to his first meeting with the mysterious man who'd haunted his dreams, calling him into the desert. After seven nights of this, he'd finally gone and been surprised to find Talya there, exactly as the dreams had shown. For that reason alone, he clung to the prophet's words.

"Call your tribes to a Gathering celebration at the Bhodista canyons in the eastern desert," Talya had said. "You will find a red pool there. In four days' time, I will address all."

A red pool at the Bhodista canyons? He'd never heard of it.

"To what end? The eastern desert is exposed and dangerous."

"And more so now, for the Horde army marches east to the Great Divide, beyond which more than a million Elyonites make their home. Albinos like you."

The revelation stunned him. "It's true then."

"As is the prophecy of the 49th Mystic. She's there, in their dungeons. She needs you. As does your son, who's there of his own choosing."

"Samuel?" His son had been gone for more than a week, but the boy always returned. "Across the Great Divide?"

"Don't worry. He's as safe as your Circle for now. But that will all change if you don't do as I say."

Thomas sat on his stallion, wondering what kind of madness would draw his son to the Great Divide. He'd lost his mind!

"The 49th Mystic drew him, as she now draws you," Talya answered, as if Thomas had spoken his thoughts. "He rescued her from the Horde a week ago. I would venture to say he's smitten with her." He dipped his head, eyes on Thomas. He was already turning his horse. "Gather all you can, conduct your ceremony of the Gathering, and present me to your people in four days. I will meet you there."

The old prophet had left without another word, leaving Thomas conflicted and frustrated. Frustrated because he knew he couldn't ignore the old man's directions despite the danger. And so here they were.

He'd told the council only what Talya had told him.

Standing before the people who were now lost in the song of the Great Wedding to come, he had no clue what to expect. A hundred questions had peppered his mind over the last forty-eight hours as they rode east, joined by smaller tribes to whom he'd sent word.

The 49th Mystic had the same name as his first wife, who'd been killed by the Horde long ago. Was there a connection? Did she have access to a Book of History? What was happening in that ancient Earth? Did the dreams work for her as they had for him, without the correlation of time if she ate the rhambutan fruit? How would the Elyonites receive other Albinos, beginning with Samuel? Why were the Horde marching east?

Thomas set his mind back on the Gathering still lost in song. The sweet, yearning voices of six maidens filled the valley as they cried the refrain in unison, faces bright with an eager desperation.

Ten years ago, most had been Horde, enslaved by Teeleh's disease. But Elyon made a new way to defeat the disease: any Horde simply had to drown in one of the red pools, and the disease would be washed away, never to return. Those who chose to drown and find new life were first

28

called Albinos by the Horde, because their skin, whether dark or light, was smooth.

Thomas glanced at Chelise, who was watching Talya with bright eyes. She glanced at him, brow raised. Thomas offered her a shallow nod.

A raging bonfire cast shifting shadows over intent gazes in the dusk. To his left, the red pool Talya had promised they'd find glistened, nearly black in the dim light. Guards lined the top of the hills, keeping a keen eye on the desert for any sign of Horde.

An echo followed the last note, and silence fell upon the Gathering as the maidens backed slowly into the crowd. Thomas lifted his chalice, filled to the brim with Elyon's red healing waters from the pool, as was customary at all Gatherings.

As one, three thousand followers of Elyon lifted their chalices to Thomas. Their eyes held his, some defiant in their determination to stay true, many wet with tears of gratitude for the great sacrifice that had first turned the pools red.

He let them wait.

The leaders stood on a ledge beyond Chelise. Mikil and Jamous, her husband, side by side, goblets raised, staring at Thomas and Talya. Suzan, one of the many colored Albinos, and her lover, Johan, who had been a mighty warrior—*was* a mighty warrior—held each other's hands and watched with curiosity.

They all wore the symbol that represented their own history, a medallion or a tattoo shaped like a circle, with an outer ring in green to signify the beginning of life. Then a black circle to remember the darkness of evil. Crossing the black circle were two straps of red, the drowning that brought life in the red waters. And at the center, a white circle, because it was prophesied that Elyon would come again and rescue his bride from Teeleh, the enemy who pursued her day and night.

Still the Circle waited for him. He let the silence stretch.

Marie, his daughter, stood beside Vadal, the dark-skinned warrior she was to wed. Marie, dear Marie. What a stunning beauty she was—a warrior to the core in her own right. Where had all the years gone? The last time he'd taken a breath, Marie was sixteen; now she was twenty-five. A hundred boys would have wed her years ago if Thomas hadn't been so stuffy, as she put it. Two years ago, Marie had taken up hunting Horde with Samuel after his fiancée was killed. Marie's betrothal to Vadal occurred only after she'd abandoned her more violent passions.

Samuel, on the other hand, still pursued his, with enough eagerness to throw them all in danger.

The fire crackled. The Gathering watched him over raised goblets.

Thomas startled, suddenly aware that he'd experienced this before. Not in the same detail, but he was certain he'd stood here thinking these same thoughts once. In his dreams, maybe. Or in another time and place. The déjà vu stilled his breathing for a moment. No—it was more than just déjà vu.

But that was impossible.

Or was it? No. Talya's claim that Rachelle, the 49th Mystic, was dreaming of ancient Earth had triggered the awareness.

He collected his thoughts and returned his focus to the ceremony. They couldn't see Elyon, hadn't seen him for many years, but he was near. Soon, Thomas thought. Justin had to come soon.

"Lovers of Elyon who have drowned in the lakes and been given life . . ." His voice flooded the canyon. "This is our hope, our passion, our reason to live."

"It is as he says," Chelise said in a soft but clear voice.

Together the three thousand responded, "He speaks the truth."

Thomas recited the Gathering tenets with more intensity. "He has rescued us. He has wooed us. He has lavished us with more pleasures than we can contain in this life."

"It is as he says," Chelise said.

Their reply washed over Thomas like a wave, gaining volume. "He speaks the truth."

"Now we wait for the return of our king, the prince-warrior Justin, who will bring justice."

"It is as he says."

"He speaks the truth."

"Our lives are his, born in his waters, made pure by the very blood we now raise to the sky!" Thomas lifted his chalice high. As did Talya his own, honoring their customs.

Chelise cried her agreement now. "It is as he says."

"He speaks the truth." Their voices spilled over the canyon walls for any within a mile to hear.

"Remember Elyon, brothers and sisters of the Circle. Live for him. Ready the bride, make a celebration ready for his coming."

"It is as he says."

The volume rose to a crushing roar. "He speaks the truth."

Silence.

"Drink to remember. To the Great Romance. To Elyon!"

This time they whispered their response in reverence, as if each syllable was something as precious as the red water in their hands.

"To Elyon."

Thomas closed his eyes, brought his chalice to his lips, tilted it back, and let the cool water flow into his mouth. The healing waters weren't nearly as strong as the green lake waters that had once flowed with Elyon's presence. And they didn't contain the same medicinal qualities of the fruit that had hung from the trees around the pools, but they lifted spirits and brought simple pleasure.

"To Justin!"

As one, the Circle pulled their goblets from their mouths like parched warriors satisfied by sweet ale and roared at the night sky.

"To Justin!"

Thomas turned to Chelise, drew her to him with his free arm, and kissed her wet lips. A thousand voices cried their approval, chased by undulating calls from the unwed maidens and their hopeful suitors. Chelise's laughter filled his mouth and he spun back to the crowd, goblet still raised.

But before he could speak again, Talya stepped forward. Just one step, and with that step the crowd began to quiet. They fell to a hush when he casually lifted one hand.

"Now, Thomas," he muttered without turning.

Now what?

"Now give me your authority to speak," Talya said.

Thomas faced the Gathering. "You are wondering who this man is. What stranger I would invite to stand beside me at a Gathering called so suddenly. His name is Talya and he comes with his lion, Judah. He claims to be from beyond the Great Divide where the Elyonite Albinos live. Samuel, my son, has crossed the Divide in pursuit of a woman said to be the 49th Mystic."

Whispers of concern filled the valley, and Thomas held up his hand for silence.

"It was Talya who persuaded me to call you here to the eastern desert. We will hear what he has to say. Know that my son's life may depend on it."

He turned to give Talya the floor, but the man was already speaking.

"When you look upon a forested valley many years after it has been consumed by a raging fire, what do you see?" he called out. "A lush valley. Beauty, blooming with new growth and flowers so that one would never know a fire had ravaged that place, yes?"

A few agreed audibly, though all knew it was true.

"But during the fire, all caught in its flames might assume that reckoning, that judgment, to be a terrible thing. They can't see that new beauty is being born by the burning of so much undergrowth. This wrath of fire is simply nature, purging the old and moving forward to higher beauty."

He paused for a moment.

"A similar wrath now comes to this world, like a sword to divide the old from the new. It is a reckoning of the old ways of law and the new way of love and peace. In this fire's judgment, many bodies will perish through war, both Horde and Albino. But even in that death, there is only good for all."

Thomas felt Chelise take his arm, moving closer, but his mind was swallowed by Talya. Not by what he'd said as much as how he was. His presence. Thomas could feel his words as much as hear them.

"On whose authority do you make such claims?" Vadal demanded, stepping away from Marie, who cast Thomas an apologetic glance. "The rumors of Albinos beyond the Divide have never been substantiated," Vadal continued. "Much less these Mystics."

"And yet you gaze upon one now," Talya said, brow cocked.

"How do we know this is true?"

"Because I tell you it is."

"Yes, but why should we—"

Talya lifted a hand toward the bonfire, and the roaring flames suddenly winked out, leaving only glowing coals. For the space of several breaths, they all stared, stupefied. Talya snapped his fingers and the flames erupted again.

"You should listen, Vadal," Talya said softly. Thomas had no idea how he could know the man's name.

Talya addressed the full Gathering. "We don't have time for argument. The end of this age calls to us all. Among all Albinos, you, the Circle, are most prepared for what comes because you've given yourself to Justin without yet knowing the extent of his love. The Elyonite Albinos number in the millions. They too have drowned in the red pools, and they, like you, claim to follow Justin. They, like you, know little of who they are."

"What do you mean, we don't know who we are?" Vadal pressed. The same stubbornness that had earned him Marie's hand was on full display. "You're condemning our way?"

"Let him speak, Vadal," Thomas said. He turned to Talya. "We've given ourselves to love the Horde. Isn't this the way of Justin? The woman you just saw me kiss was once Horde."

"Yes. Chelise, daughter of Qurong, sister of Jacob, who joins Samuel in their pursuit of the 49th. I am well aware."

"You've seen my brother?" Chelise asked, stepping out.

"I have. He, like Samuel, thinks he loves the 49th. And herein, the mystery." Talya faced Thomas. "Albino and Horde alike think they know love. But do you?"

Silence.

Broken by Vadal.

"Love, yes, but we also seek a light that will rescue us from the Horde when Justin returns," he said. "His return is our greater concern."

"And Justin will return, though perhaps not in the way you expect. You only have to ask yourself, is Justin also Elyon?"

"He is."

"Is he then limited like you are, able only to be here or there?"

Thomas answered for them all. "No."

Talya turned his bright eyes to him. "He's everywhere at once. Yes?"

"Yes."

Talya looked at Vadal with kindness, like a father leading his son into truth. "If Justin is like Elyon, everywhere, is he not here already?"

Vadal hesitated.

"Yes," Marie said.

"Ahhh, so then you already know. Justin never left. When you sing 'come to me,' or when you invite his Spirit to fill you, you're really asking for your *awareness* of him to come or to fill you. He never left. How can he return as you think of returning, if he's already here?"

"But . . ." Vadal glanced at Thomas, seeking support. "He's coming again—all Albinos know this."

"He *will* come again for all to perceive," Talya said. "*And* he never left. So now we seek the one who never left while we still draw breath in these earthen vessels. In our seeking, we awaken to who we are now, glorified and complete. And in this knowing all will discover true love."

The idea was new to Thomas. His skin tingled with fresh anticipation. This was the Mystic way?

"To this end," Talya said, "Justin has called the 49th Mystic. She comes like a sword to divide the old way from the new way. She asks all to surrender that old way of being in fear, so that she can lead you in the way of love, which knows no fear. Her name is Rachelle, and she is currently held in the Elyonite dungeons by Aaron, son of Mosseum."

He cleared his throat. "If the 49th succeeds, the shadow blinding this world will lift. Then the lion will lie down with the lamb. I urge you to go there, beyond the Great Divide, where you will find true life. All of you."

Talya swept the gathering with steady eyes. "You should also know that the Elyonites have taken Qurong's son, Jacob. The Horde marches east to wage war as we speak, some not far from us."

Thomas scanned the hills. No sign from the guard. "How far?"

"We can't just up and leave for the Great Divide!" Vadal cried. He faced the council. "You know this, Jamous. Mikil. Our home is west, where we know every watering hole, every forest, all that we need. Going east is madness! We must know more!"

"He's right," Mikil agreed, stepping forward. She faced the crowd, her long red-and-blue tunic bright in the firelight. "At the very least, we must hold council. We have no idea how these Elyonites would receive us."

"They're Albino," Johan said, staring at Talya. "They have an army?"

"Equal to the Horde's."

Johan regarded Thomas, right brow raised. His thoughts were clear: an Albino army would tip the balance of power in their favor.

But Vadal was more deeply invested in the Circle's pacifism than most. "What good is their army if they see us as the enemy? I refuse to go anywhere near war."

"My son is among them!" Chelise cried. "We should go!"

"Samuel's only concern is revenge!" Vadal shot back. "He's always been—"

"Enough!" Thomas stepped forward. "Mikil, Johan, Suzan. Quickly, gather the children and send them up the back canyon under the guard of a hundred warriors, then return to us."

Mikil hesitated.

"Now!"

She whistled, initiating the evacuation order for the young and weak. A hundred fighters moved with practiced precision, calling the children to them. Within seconds a stream of children and a third of the adults flowed around the boulder Thomas stood on, hurrying up the narrow canyon behind them.

Thomas studied Talya, who seemed to have no qualms about imminent war. How many Albinos had been slaughtered by the Horde over the years? Too many to count. And each time, the Circle celebrated their dead's passing into the higher realm. But the joy of that passing had been replaced by weeping these last few years.

"Only remember that if you live by the sword," Talya said, voice low, "you will die by the sword. The choice is yours, either way."

"You're condoning the use of the sword?"

"I neither condone nor condemn. I merely point out that in this plane of existence you reap whatever you sow."

Talya paced to his right and addressed the fifteen hundred who remained. "Follow Thomas across the Great Divide to the Marrudo plateau. There you will find life."

"You've already told him you'll go?" Vadal snapped at Thomas. "We must know more!"

"I've said nothing."

"Thomas will go," Talya said. "He'll go because the 49th needs him. And you'll follow Thomas, because you know that what I've said is true. You live in as much fear as the Horde. The Realm of Mystics awaits you. It's time to come home."

A shrill call cut through the air—the all too familiar cry of an enemy sighting. Thomas spun south, eyes peeled for a sign. A second call joined the first, this one from the hills to the west. For a brief moment, nothing more. Then the distant, muffled rumbling of a thousand horses, felt more than heard.

"Horde!" voices cried.

And on the heels of the warning, "Swords!"

They all kept weapons but used them only to defend, never to kill, despite their training in the Roush arts. Except for some on the fringe, like Samuel, the fighting arts had become more like a dance than a means of survival.

The Circle ran for the horses in the side canyon, throwing themselves into saddles, snatching up their blades.

Talya grabbed Thomas's shoulder and spun him back. Then stepped in front of Chelise so that he faced both of them with his back to the scattering Circle. Without warning, he spit—a fine spray that lighted on Thomas's face. Then Chelise's.

"So you might see what is to be seen when the time comes."

Chelise blinked, wiping her face and eyes. "What—"

"Take the Circle to the plateau beyond the Great Divide at all costs, Thomas," he interrupted. "Camp there under the north star and have the Circle wait. Then go with Chelise to the Mystics five miles south. You'll know the Realm when you see the colored forest. The survival of all depends on the 49th. She needs you."

Thomas could hear the Horde's battle cry now, a deep, throaty rattling of rage. It was too late to run.

"There are other considerations! I have three thousand souls here alone, another seventeen thousand in the other tribes."

Talya glanced between them. "Come, and come quickly."

Without another word, he stepped around them and strode toward his lion.

3

THEY TOLD ME that DARPA subcontracted nearly all of its projects to private firms like Boeing or MIT, so they didn't have large labs and facilities to handle multiple projects. Project Eden had been special, as was the White Center, where my father and I were being helped.

We called it the White Center because it was mostly white. The rooms, both halls, the recreation area, the dining room, the three labs—all white. Only the large black tiles on the checkerboard floor and the furniture added color and contrast. The furniture was a soft green, and the covers on the beds in both my and my father's rooms were pink. Not a girly pink but a fuchsia pink.

After finishing up with Charlene I played chess with my father in the rec room. Thanks to the MEP he'd forgotten everything that happened in Eden. He'd also somehow forgotten how to play the game, so I took it upon myself to teach him. Being so smart, he was a quick learner—better than me after only a couple of months.

That's what we did most of the time—took tests, ate, slept, read approved novels, and lounged in the rec room, talking, watching old 2-D movies or playing games. We had a soda machine, a foosball table (my dad always won when he was trying), a coffee and tea dispenser, two small card tables, a 60-inch panel television, the green couches, and on one wall a cool water feature that changed color.

You might think I would be bored most of the time, but the hours seemed to float by and be gone before I knew it. Some of the drugs they were giving me messed with my short-term memory, so sometimes I couldn't clearly remember what had happened even a short time ago. Like the effects of cannabis, Mary told me.

Mary Newman was our caretaker, a nurse who usually wore green scrubs. She sometimes played games with us and was always willing to talk. I found conversations with her interesting because, although older than me by more than ten years, she hadn't grown up in Eden. She offered me an insider's look at the world I would soon be entering, after my brain could handle it. In the meantime, I was full of questions.

If the population of the world had already passed twelve billion, where did they grow all the food? Did people still hold hands and kiss? What about dating—did she think anyone would want to go out with me?

One of my greatest wishes was to meet another girl my age or younger. I wanted to know how ordinary people lived. What was it like to be a seventeen-year-old girl not living in Eden or in the White Center?

I asked and listened for hours as she told me all about her life, her husband, Chuck, and her two children, Johnnie and little Milly, short for Mildred.

Another thing that fascinated me to no end—her description of virtual reality movies, which were like games that you could interact with. When you were in them, you had to keep reminding yourself that it was only holographic or you could easily get lost in another world.

"Like Eden in some ways," Steve explained to me. "Only in Eden we changed your brain itself, not the external world you were in."

You see, that was what fascinated me. How did we know we weren't living in a holographic world now? I mean, I'd been fooled in Eden for so many years. What if we were all fooled?

He chuckled. "Nice try. I don't think so."

But still . . .

Steve was the other person we spent a lot of time with. He was a genius intensely interested in our progress, and he was kind to me. Though he was only twenty-eight years old, I saw him as a kind of second father. The one who cared for me and would protect me.

He said the world's technology would be far more advanced than it currently was if not for the Cyber War of 2021, which had set the world back by at least a decade, maybe more. The internet had been radically corrupted, and world commerce had come to a near standstill for a month before being slowly rebuilt with new security measures, which Steve still didn't trust.

Once each week, Steve took me to church at Washington National Cathedral, a twenty-minute drive from DARPA. They thought my going to a controlled religious setting would help to ground me, because I'd grown up with deep religious roots. I could go as long as I behaved myself and didn't talk to anyone. I didn't care that much for the sermons, but I quickly grew to love the weekly ventures into the real world. We always sat at the back, and I never gave the therapists a reason to change their minds about my going.

In a nutshell, that was my world, and I didn't dislike it.

After playing chess with my father, I spent most of the afternoon lounging in the rec room, scanning the hundreds of approved movies, looking for something interesting that I hadn't watched. We didn't have access to any streaming content from the outside world, so this was it. I couldn't find anything new, so I settled for watching an old movie called *The Matrix* again—at least my twentieth time, but my brain couldn't remember how many. Maybe that's why I watched certain movies over and over: I couldn't remember the details, so every time I watched, it was almost like the first time.

I was lost in the scene where Neo was stopping bullets with his hand, thinking I'd seen something like it before, maybe not just in this movie, when the voice I associated with Steve spoke to me in a distant whisper.

She's watching it again.

Maybe Steve was behind me, but I had to learn how to ignore the voices. Practice makes perfect.

She knows, I heard.

This time the draw was too much, and I turned my head, half expecting to see Steve. Instead, I saw glowing writing etched into the wall, like someone had carved it deep, and light from behind was seeping through. A visual hallucination. Sometimes I saw doors, other times the wall moving. The writing on the wall was a new one.

I turned back to the movie, but now that writing wouldn't leave my mind. So I looked again. Still there, plain as day. And now my curiosity was getting the best of me.

I slipped off the couch and walked up to the wall, thinking it just might be real this time. Even though I knew it couldn't be, my pulse quickened.

I stopped in front of it, waiting to see if it shifted or wavered like some hallucinations. Nothing. Just what looked like real words carved into the wall.

What is seeing beyond what you think should be, daughter?

It made no sense to me. A riddle? Or maybe I was seeing it because I thought I shouldn't be schizophrenic, and my mind was telling me I needed to heal. Which was what DARPA was helping me do. Or maybe it wasn't a hallucination. Maybe it was real, carved into the wall right here.

I'd just lifted my hand when I heard a soft cough. I jerked my hand away and turned. Steve was watching from behind the couch.

"Sorry, didn't mean to startle you."

Glancing back at the wall, I saw the words were gone. Just a white wall. Figured.

"What do you see?"

"Nothing. Just some words," I said, returning to plop back down on the cushions.

"Words, huh? What words?"

"'What is seeing beyond what you think should be,'" I said. "Something like that."

"Interesting. Does it mean anything to you?"

"It means I should stop seeing things," I said. "Have you seen my dad?"

"He's in his weekly health check."

"What time is it?"

"Almost seven."

The time had flown. Seven already and no dinner yet? That was odd.

"Mary's wrapping up with him," Steve said, walking around the couch and sitting next to me, eyes on the movie. Neo was recognizing his power. Re-cognizing—once again knowing. *Re-cognize yourself.* Clever thought. It's what I was doing.

"About the words on the wall—"

"An illusion," I interrupted, nodding at the movie. "And maybe the wall's just an illusion too. Everything's perception, right? If my brain can tweak things so that I'm seeing what isn't there, maybe yours is too. In fact, how can anyone know that what they're seeing is really there the way they see it? What if they're just seeing another illusion? What if everyone is blind and doesn't know it?"

She knows . . .

"I know that I know," I said.

"You know?"

"Sorry. I was just speaking to the voice in my head. See, it's not only a visual matrix but an auditory one. All five senses."

"If you know that, why are you so agreeable to us helping you hear and see what everyone else is hearing and seeing?"

I looked over at him. "Because I can't function in a society where I see one thing and everyone else sees something else, even if what they're seeing isn't really what they think it is."

His brow arched. "You think that what others see isn't real?"

Back to the movie. "No. But you can't fault my logic."

"You're right, I can't. I guess you'll just have to trust me when I say that what I'm seeing is at least reasonably accurate. Although emerging science now suggests that the whole world is in gravitational quantum entanglement and is actually malleable. But we'll leave that dimensional exploration to others."

She's our best chance of doing just that, but I have no choice.

"What's up?" I asked.

He stood and took a deep breath. "We think we've found a way to speed your recovery. It's not a quick fix, but it might stop your hallucinations."

I sat up. "All of them?"

"All of them. You think that would be a good thing?"

I didn't need to think about it. "Very."

He paced with one hand on his hip as if concerned. "It's not guaranteed, and it does come with some risks."

"What risks? What's the procedure?"

"We've decided to try a newer version of the memory protocol to reboot your mind."

"I thought the MEP didn't work with my mind."

"This isn't the old MEP. Something quite different. If we can neutralize your unconscious memories, your neural connections will lose their habitual patterns and be free to form new ones without the old-school drug therapy."

I got it. One thing I'd learned: most people don't know that over ninety percent of their thoughts are unconscious. They don't even know they're thinking them. These thoughts determine our perception of the world more than anything else, which is why people have such a hard time thinking positive thoughts when they've subconsciously programmed their brain to think negatively. Ninety percent of their brain is thinking negative thoughts even while they're trying to think positive thoughts.

Clearing the mind's unconscious patterns was the key to healing.

"I'll do it."

He looked at me, surprised. "Just like that?"

"Why not? It's not easy being a schizophrenic. Besides, I'm guessing I don't really have a choice, do I?"

"You always have a choice. But they're quite eager for this."

"You mean the director."

"The director."

"So what are the risks?"

"Well, for starters, you could lose what's so wonderful about that brain of yours. Your personality might also change. There's a slight chance you could lose all of your memory."

"All of it?"

"'Course, if that happened you wouldn't know it. Your memory of having a memory would be gone."

"Like being born again with a brand-new mind," I said. "Like being transformed by the renewing of your mind."

He blinked. "Yes, like that. Those are religious terms that express a process of spiritual awakening. You remember that from Eden? Doesn't sound like something Simon would have taught."

I didn't know where I got the thoughts. Most of what Simon had taught in Eden was now foggy to me. For all I knew, Simon wasn't even real. No, that was going too far. Or was it?

Confusion swirled through my mind whenever I tried to think about what was or wasn't real relating to Project Eden.

"Maybe," I said. "Either way, I'm okay with it. As long as you think I'll be safe. When?"

He hesitated. "They're prepping now."

I stood up. "Now? Tonight?"

"Tonight. It's why you haven't eaten. Better on an empty stomach."

My stomach began to do flip-flops. But that was just my brain as well.

"Okay," I said.

STEVE PACED in the control room, chin in his hand, staring through the glass at the Memory Editing Protocol scanner. Similar to old CAT scan machines in its dimension and positioning, but the MEP connected directly to the subject's skull at thirty-seven points. Rachelle lay sedated on her back, head already wired, MEP in place.

The tech, Sandra, spoke into her wireless headpiece. "Check electrodes seven and eight, Charlene? I'm getting a calibration error on the fourth array."

Charlene pushed a button and the MEP whirred, pulling back from Rachelle's head to grant access. Charlene flipped a switch that engaged recalibration. A magnetically charged fluid, Diosomium, had been intravenously administered to Rachelle an hour earlier. The MEP had already coaxed the marking fluid into every neural connection in her brain. One of the monitors displayed a perfect map of that brain, at least what could be seen by a human eye.

The quantum computer saw far more—all of the 100 billion neurons that made up the average human brain. In Rachelle's case, 112.4655 billion neurons, according to the screen. Each neuron was now isolated and could be manipulated.

"Readings are right on my end," Charlene said. "You?"

"Stabilized."

The machine whirred again and Rachelle's body slid back into position.

"I think that does it." Sandra glanced up at Steve. "We're ready when you are."

"I'm never ready."

"Sir?"

He took a deep breath. If not for Rachelle, he would have left DARPA as he'd planned after Eden's collapse. But he saw clearly during that first week that without a guardian, she wouldn't stand a chance. If the MEP successfully wiped her mind as designed, he would build it back up with her, step by step, this time without any deception. She deserved at least that much.

"Go ahead."

"Initiating phase one."

"Initiating phase one," came Charlene's reply.

Sandra tapped a key on her board. Other than a slight hum, nothing seemed to change, but the work was already under way. Specific neurons were now being switched on and off, some stripped of their charge completely, others overcharged to deepen their connections. Once initiated, the two-hour process couldn't be stopped without risking permanent brain impairment.

Steve watched, pacing, rubbing his chin, eyes on Rachelle. Always eyes on Rachelle. Sandra reminded him that he didn't need to stay for the entire procedure. He thanked her and sat down. Eyes still on Rachelle.

For the first twenty-two minutes, all went as expected. No errors, no anomalies.

At twenty-three minutes and eleven seconds, Rachelle jerked violently and began to scream.

4

THOMAS SPUN to Chelise as the Horde's distant thunder closed in. "Head north, two children to a horse. Ride!"

She grabbed his arm. "Sound the retreat! It's not too late!"

He flung off his ceremonial robe and sprinted for his stallion. Talya had already vanished with his lion.

"Thomas!"

"If we all retreat, they'll follow," he snapped, spinning back. "We distract them here to give you time. Run! Go!"

She dropped onto her mare beside the boulder and slapped its rump.

He leaped into his saddle and jerked the reins free of the tree. "No blood!" he shouted, spurring his mount. The pale beast bolted. "No blood!"

The order was relayed by Marie and Jamous, then by a dozen others, making it clear that, as was their customary way, they would engage but not kill. Their close-fitting leather armor stopped most arrows and all but a direct blow by a blade. Their necks, heads, arms and legs were bare, but they'd learned to maneuver in ways that favored their armor.

Thomas took the stallion over the boulder he'd conducted the Gathering from. The horse landed on the sand below with practiced ease and galloped into the shallow valley. Already, half of the fighters who remained were mounted and streaming up the hills. They knew what to do. Buying time for the children and elderly would be their primary objective.

"High ground, Marie!" he cried. His daughter was ahead of him, calling to those fighters just now mounting the last of the horses they'd corralled in the side canyon. If the Scabs reached them before they could reach the hills on either side, they would become caged in to be plucked off.

Not today.

The warning cries had sounded south and west. The children were north. They would be safe.

"East!" he roared, pulling his mount abreast of Marie's as they tore up the slope. Neither of them had withdrawn their swords from their scabbards. They would if needed, but only to defend blows or discourage with a nonlethal wound. At least to the best of their ability. Even so, more than a few Horde had died at their hands.

If you live by the sword, you will die by the sword. Talya had quoted Justin. You suffer the same fate you inflict in all walks of life. Give and it is given. Take and it is taken.

Marie reached the crest two lengths ahead of him and pulled up hard, eyes fixed on the desert. His mount stomped to a halt three paces from her.

"Elyon help us," she breathed.

No fewer than three thousand Horde thundered toward them, heavy with armor, battle axes, swords, and hammers. Rising dust from their horses fogged the deep dusk.

Thomas quickly surveyed the desert. A rocky hill to the east; beyond that, open sands. The guards they'd placed on the eastern hill were gone, but they'd issued no warning. So . . . the east was open.

He reined his mount around. The valley was now vacant—they'd all made it out. Of fifteen hundred warriors, roughly five hundred were grouped across the valley on the western flank. The other thousand spread out on this crest with him.

"They're too many, Father!" Marie cried, eyes wide.

Vadal pulled his horse abreast of hers.

Thomas turned his mount to face the approaching Horde. "Johan?"

"She's right. Too many for engagement without bloodshed."

"Then we split them. Right down their throats with guns blazing." None in this world knew of guns, but they knew what he meant by the term he'd brought from his dreams of ancient Earth, where he'd been Thomas Hunter from Denver, Colorado.

"Guns blazing or not," Johan said, turning, "they're twenty deep. Better to draw them into the canyon where—"

"Too risky. We drive ten abreast and split them up the middle. Once we break through, we lead them south, away from the children."

Thomas trotted up to Johan, staring past the thousand fighters waiting for orders. Marie was now twenty paces to their rear.

Still the Horde army thundered for them. Still the Scabs cried full-throated. The earth shook with their intentions. They would be upon them in under two minutes.

"We could circle around behind them," Johan said.

"We could, but they're familiar with our old tactics. As soon as we move, they'll do the same. Talya says they're marching to the Great Divide east. If we go north, they may not follow."

"Talya, the one who led them to us, you mean."

"No, Talya, the one who drew me out here because it's halfway across the desert, far from our home. The Divide is only two days from here."

Johan frowned. "Crafty old man. Will you go?"

Thomas hesitated. "I have the tribes to consider."

"Father?" Marie, behind him.

He lifted a hand without turning back. *Hold.*

"So then, what is it?" Johan asked. "Up their throats with guns blazing, as you say? Or east, the safer route?"

Thomas considered Johan's preference. Nodded. "You're right. Signal the far hill to join us. We draw them east and—"

The distinct sound of a blade thudding into flesh cut Thomas short. He twisted in his saddle.

Marie had dropped her reins and was clutching at her neck. He saw the butt of the blade when she turned to face him, eyes wide in terror, mouth stretched in a silent scream. Blood ran between her fingers.

Vadal stared, dumbstruck.

Thomas jerked his mount around in a blind panic, slamming his heels into its flank. He was halfway to her when she slumped over and slipped from her saddle. He dropped to the ground and ran.

Three strides and he was there, and in those three strides, he saw the line of Horde on the crest beyond Marie. A side party of several hundred had circled around from the east.

He slid to his knees and pulled his daughter into his arms. "No, no, no! It's okay, Marie! I have you. Your father's here. Just breathe . . ."

But she wasn't breathing. And she wasn't moving.

Vadal dropped to his knees, weeping, clawing for her.

"Back!" Thomas shoved him aside, numb. He knew they had to move. The raiding party was holding, waiting for the rest of the army to close. They'd been boxed in. He knew that, but his body had stopped responding. His mind told him it was all a mistake. Her throat hadn't been cut. She wasn't dead.

He wanted to say something. Scream his objections. Reverse time. Give her the chance to live and wed and bear children.

But he could only hold her in his arms, grasping for reason. Stunned.

Rage seeped into that dead space and slowly settled over him, pushing aside his initial shock. Anyone but Marie. Why? Dear Elyon, why now?

"I am Campous!"

Thomas slowly lifted his head and looked at the Scab with long dreadlocks and heavy armor twenty paces distant. He sat atop his mount with arms spread wide, holding his ground.

"Slayer of Albinos!" he roared.

It was he who'd thrown the blade.

"Master of Hunter, who defiles our children and wives!"

Thomas let Marie's body slip from his arms and staggered to his feet, returning the man's stare. Hunter. Him. Marie had caught a blade meant for *him*. True or not, it no longer mattered. His only daughter had been slaughtered by this monster.

Vadal was tugging at Marie's body. Hefting her up. Sliding her onto his horse. Thomas was locked on the man who'd killed her. Those gray eyes.

That sickening morst paste slathered on scabbed skin. The warrior was a foot taller than him.

"I avenge Jacob!" the one named Campous rasped. "Son of Qurong, taken captive by Samuel of Hunter beyond the Great Divide. Now, we water the desert with the blood of all Albinos!"

Someone was calling to him. Johan. Saying something . . . But Thomas was hearing Talya's voice.

If you live by the sword, you will die by the sword. The choice is yours, either way.

He could feel his fingers trembling. Hear the pounding of his heart. Smell the scent of blood on the ground.

Marie, who hadn't lived by the sword, had still died by the sword.

Thomas stood with his hands by his sides, blind to everything but vengeance without remorse.

Talya's teaching returned to him. *I condemn no one.*

"But I do," he breathed.

He reached for the scabbard on Marie's mount. Placed his hand around the hilt of the sword fashioned after his own. Pulled the blade free and let it hang to the desert sand, light in his grasp.

He took a deep breath, lowered his head, and roared for all of the Forest Guard to hear.

"Blooooood!"

For a moment none took up the cry as his fighters assimilated the first such charge to them in many years. Campous the Scab slowly lowered his arms, reconsidering his enemy.

But for only a moment, because now the Circle Guard took up the cry as one, like a parched army reaching the shores of a life-giving pool. Only this pool did not hold water.

"Blooooooooood!"

Thomas grabbed the horn of Marie's saddle and swung into it, staying low and to one side as he took the mount into a full gallop, directly toward Campous and his line of Scabs.

With catlike quickness, Campous bounded for his mount. Not to run, but to attack with the rest of his men who were already charging past him. Running wasn't in the Horde mind. Their pride was in victory or death, either or both.

A horn was signaling the fighters on the far ridge. Johan was crying out his orders. Hooves thundered as the bulk of his warriors launched themselves south, at the main body of the Horde. Up their throats, guns blazing.

Behind Thomas, archers would be covering his charge. If they did not, he would die. Either way, many would die. Many Albino. Many Horde.

But all of this remained distant in Thomas's mind. He knew only one aim. Reach the one named Campous.

Kill Campous.

He was only a horse length from the Scabs' forward charge when the first Guard arrows slammed into them. Two of the arrows sliced into throats; the third sank into the right eye of the closest warrior.

Each was thrown back, dead already, toppling from their mounts with axes still raised into the path of those behind. Thomas nudged his mount left, toward the gap created by the falling Scabs. Immediately a volley of arrows from behind followed his lead, firing into the same side, widening the gap.

Typically the archers would have aimed to wound.

Today the arrows found vital flesh—heads and throats of both horse and Horde.

Thomas drove deeper into the wedge made by his archers, ignoring the impulse to engage the line himself. He would trust his fighters. He had only one objective.

Campous.

Who was now three horse lengths away and roaring. He meant to take Thomas with a raised battle axe heavy enough to fell a horse. But Thomas had agility on his side.

He released his reins and his sword as one, planted his right palm on the saddle horn, threw his legs up and behind his body, and twisted as he vaulted high.

The move came too quickly and too late for Campous to react with more than a slight shift upward. His axe slashed the air under Thomas's twisting body, now vaulting over the Scab warrior's head.

A head heavy with long dreadlocks, the same locks Thomas grasped as he completed his half twist. Using the much larger man's weight as an anchor, he bent at the hips, tucked his body, and landed on the beast's rump behind Campous, facing his back.

Jerking the Scab's head back, Thomas palmed the man's own blade from his waist and slashed at his throat through to his spine. The man's massive body went limp.

"You live by the sword, you die by the sword," Thomas muttered in the man's ear. He shoved him off the mount. The Scab's body landed heavily and lay dead, left behind.

Thomas found the mount's reins, brought the troubled beast to a stop, and stared at the unfolding battle, head pounding.

A familiar shrill cry ripped through the air. Mikil had rejoined them and taken the head off a warrior who'd been knocked off his horse.

Vadal was mounted on a Scab's stallion, screaming, swinging his blade like a man possessed, eyes red with anguish and rage. He took down two Horde in the space of as many breaths, one through his breastplate, another by cutting off his right arm.

Ahead, the archers raced, standing tall in their stirrups and firing at will. Seven Albinos lay dead already in this small skirmish. Dozens of Horde.

He shifted his gaze south. Johan and a thousand fighters tore toward the brunt of the army head-on. Hundreds of arrows were already in the air, cutting down the Scabs' leading edge.

Pushing back dread, Thomas whistled for his mount, met it halfway, and reacquainted himself with his familiar saddle. He dug his heels into its flanks, bent low over the mount's mane, and raced toward the Horde army.

Live by the sword, die by the sword. All that remained now was the reaping of living or dying in the Circle's first battle in over a decade.

"So be it."

THE FUNERAL PYRE roared as its flames consumed the bodies of seventy-eight of Thomas's loyal. *Never break the Circle* had been their cry. Now the Circle had been broken for them.

Nearly three thousand stood around the massive fire, fueled as much by bodies as by the wood they'd gathered at the edge of the northern forest late into the night. Not a soul stirred. No one wept, not even the children who'd rejoined them. The only sound came from the fire.

They did not weep, but glistening tears lined the faces of many in that somber moment.

Tortured by screams of pain and rage, the battle had lasted an hour before tempering the Horde's passion with enough bloodshed to turn any stomach. The Forest Guard had killed at least four hundred Horde, but there was no glory in it. No value even. Only the trading of flesh in an agreement called war. A weak and useless way.

Talya was right, Thomas thought. The Circle had placed their hope in a better life to come while living in fear in this one. Who was to say that running from a storm was any better than joining it? In this life, the way of the Albinos was no more powerful than the way of the Horde.

The way of the Mystics was to find power in this life. Peace in this storm.

Ten years earlier, Thomas and his people would have already begun the dance for the dead, celebrating the union each would experience as the bride reunited with Justin, who had left. That celebration of hope had been waning for years. Now in the midnight hour, no one appeared eager to sing those words of promise, much less dance at the deaths of so many sons and daughters.

His own among them.

They had been pretending for a long time.

What if Talya was right? What if Justin had never left? What if they, the bride, were only oblivious to their true union, blind to their own light as the bride?

What if Justin's "return" was a return to an awareness of their identity as the bride, one with Justin *already*, as much as a physical return?

The thought was staggering.

It also had the ring of heresy. And Johan's assertion that Talya had deliberately led them into harm's way had a ring of truth.

Though it was unlikely, Thomas couldn't shake his anger at the thought. If not for the man's powerful presence and his pronouncement of love, Thomas would have agreed with Johan.

He had no idea how being one with Justin already was possible, but this much he did know: they had been pretending far too long. And he would be the first to stop.

Thomas stepped away from Chelise and approached the fire, in full view of all. He didn't look down, he didn't look to his right, he didn't look to his left. He stared at the flames and walked toward the fire.

Marie's fire.

Smoke was ascending to the heavens as if it was her spirit—isn't that what they'd always celebrated? But now all he could see were the angry, fiery coals left behind.

A fist of anguish rose in his throat and he yielded to it, stopping halfway to the funeral pyre. Waves of heat from the fire lifted his shoulder-length hair. His eyes burned. Tears slipped down his cheeks.

"The man with the lion who called us from our homes told us that we would find true life beyond the Great Divide." His voice rang out for all to hear. "He told us of a reckoning in which we would trade fear for love, shown to us by the 49th Mystic."

His throat ached, choked by sorrow, and he breathed deep, calming himself as best he could.

"I have decided that I will follow Talya and seek the 49th as I would seek my own daughter. I will go because I hear her calling to me through Talya's words. I will be joined by all who so choose."

He let the statement stand, eyes still on the fire, unblinking.

"But tonight . . ." His voice trembled. "Tonight, I feel no love. No peace. No desire for song or dance."

His words cut through the night air.

"Tonight, I feel only sorrow. Tonight . . ."

But he couldn't say more because that grief erupted from deep in his bowels and shook him with terrible pain. Then more—bitter anguish from a deep well, unstopped. And to the rising of those dark waters, Thomas lost himself.

He ripped his tunic at the breast, lifted his face, and sobbed at the sky.

The wails began behind him with Chelise. Then with a hundred more, accepting permission to express their gut-wrenching truth. Within seconds, the entire Circle was undone.

Thomas sank to his knees, doubled over and wept.

5

THE SOUND of Rachelle's first scream had flipped a switch somewhere in Steve's mind as he watched, powerless to stop her trembling in the MEP three hours earlier. It wasn't her last scream. She spent half of the procedure in agony, and no amount of correction made the slightest difference.

Now he sat in a lounge chair outside the recovery room while David spent a few minutes with his daughter. It was critical that those few anchors to reality Rachelle still had be reinforced—the director had agreed to at least that much. David tied her more firmly to terra firma than any other influence, despite the fact that most of his own memories had been stripped.

The MEP had failed. Her mind simply wasn't compatible with the algorithms that other minds aligned to. She'd survived and returned to consciousness without any memory of the treatment. Which was good, because if anything had happened to her he would . . .

Steve didn't know what he would do. But he couldn't just stand by while they methodically destroyed her.

One way or the other, they were intent on silencing her. With the failure of the MEP, he wouldn't put it past whoever was pulling DARPA's chains to consider removing her from the equation altogether.

Which raised the same questions he'd asked himself a hundred times: Who was pulling DARPA's chains? Who was so threatened by her?

There was something more threatening about Rachelle than her ability to expose the truth about Project Eden. Something more concerning to them than the fact that she could read minds.

What?

David opened the recovery room door and poked his head out. "She's asking for you."

"How is she?"

David grinned. "See for yourself."

He followed David into the recovery room where Rachelle lay under covers, propped up in a hospital bed. Wearing a faint, pale smile under tangled black hair, she looked like a brave doll that had been dragged around by a dog.

"Hi, Steve."

"Hi, Rachelle."

Her fingers were still trembling. He glanced at the monitor. "Vitals still in line. You sure you're okay?"

"I can't stop all this shaking, if that's what you mean. But the doctor said it was normal. My body's reacting to the treatment."

It wasn't normal. But Charlene wouldn't have left her if she had concerns.

"Well, I think you came through like a champ."

"You think so?"

"I know so," Steve said.

"I'm still hearing voices. So . . . there's that."

He nodded. "I guess your mind's just too broke to fix the normal way. And by broke, I mean brilliantly broke."

"So it seems."

Her father grinned wide. "That's my girl." He eased into the bedside chair. "Nothing can shake her."

David was wearing his blue flannel nightclothes with slippers. Hair combed neatly, T-shirt pressed. He'd come out of his reconditioning with a clean streak.

He too had come out of Eden talking of dreams, but the team determined that the dreams were psychosomatic, and they were in such a rush to cover their tracks that they wiped his brain before any serious study could be made of it.

Clearly, science wasn't interested in anything beyond its self-imposed materialistic firewall. If it couldn't be measured within the material system, it wasn't science. There was nothing beyond the observable universe. Dreams of another world were like fairies—nice conversation for children, but absurd, like any hallucination.

Steve looked at Rachelle. "So how are you feeling, really?"

She shrugged. "Tired, like I got hit by a train, maybe. I'm imagining you talking about dreams and science. And I'm hungry."

"Right. We'll get you some chicken, how's that sound?"

"Sounds yummy."

"Good."

"I've already eaten," David said.

"Dinner any good?"

"The steak or the dessert?"

"Either."

"The steak was tough and the ice cream was too cold. Makes the mouth so numb you can't taste anything."

"Good to know. You tell Mary?"

"Naw. She's got enough to do besides microwaving my ice cream."

Sweet man. Not the same man who'd lived in Eden, but so sweet. Simple. Rachelle knew he'd changed, naturally, but her own drugs kept her amenable. In some ways, she was like the parent now. At the very least they parented each other.

More accurately, neither parented. DARPA was now their parent. Sad.

Steve crossed to the wall and flipped a red switch.

"What's that?" Rachelle asked.

"I'm making sure no one can hear us."

"What for?"

He returned and sat on the edge of the bed. "Because I want to ask you a few questions, for our ears only. Is that okay?"

"Sure."

He glanced at her father. "You, David?"

David lifted his thumb and forefinger and zipped his mouth. "My lips are sealed."

"Good." Steve stood and paced, choosing his words carefully. Both father and daughter were in a delicate place. Popping their carefully constructed bubbles could throw them into a tailspin. "David, you don't remember any of your dreams, right?"

"I don't dream. Not that I know of."

"And you don't remember any of your dreams from when you were in Eden."

"Right. Or is that left?" He glanced between them, grinning. "Right or left, get it?"

"Don't be silly, Dad. He's trying to be serious."

"I get it," Steve said. "Very funny. What about you, Rachelle? Remember any dreams?" He already knew the answer.

"I don't dream anymore either, but I do remember dreaming. Why?"

"So you can or can't remember the dreams you had in Eden?"

"Not really, no." She looked slightly uneasy. "Why? I don't want to remember those dreams. They were all a part of some fantasy you created in Project Eden. Why would I ever want to remember the dreams that messed me up?"

Neither of them knew that their water supply was dosed with Rexpinal to actively suppress subconscious brain activity like dreams. The only way to find out if there was any validity to those dreams was to allow them to dream again. A single dose of Kinazeran would negate the effects of Rexpinal and allow either to dream for a night, but Steve couldn't even think about activating their subconscious minds without their consent. In strict confidence, of course—doing this would put him in breach of his operating agreement. If anyone else found out, he would likely be dismissed.

For Rachelle's sake, he couldn't risk that.

"Maybe you wouldn't want to remember those dreams," he agreed, "but would you ever want to dream again? New dreams, unrelated to those old dreams."

She looked away, concerned. "Not really. What good are dreams?"

"You're afraid you might dream the same kinds of dreams you did in Eden?"

"I can't remember my dreams from Eden, like I said."

"But part of you is afraid that if you did dream—tonight, say—that dream might stir up old memories. Something like that, right?"

She thought about it for a moment. "Something like that."

He decided not to press the matter further. "Sounds reasonable." Steve looked at David. "What about you?"

"You're asking me? Because I wouldn't mind dreaming, not at all. I just can't. However that MEP machine of yours works, it messed with that part of my brain. But heck, yeah. I think it would be cool to dream again."

"You sure?" Rachelle asked him.

"Why not?"

She shrugged. Nothing more.

They sat in silence for a moment. *David, then,* Steve thought. He'd give David a dose of Kinazeran when they retired, and either David would dream or he wouldn't.

If he did, he just might dream of that world. The world Rachelle had once claimed gave her the same clairaudience and telekinesis she now had. The world that had given sight to a blind girl.

Steve had considered the possibility a hundred times but backed off, hoping DARPA's methods would ultimately allow Rachelle to stabilize and return to some semblance of normal life.

But with the introduction of the new MEP, the game had changed. He had to start somewhere. Allowing David to dream might be that start, if only to see if that dream world might, just might, open to a mind cleanly wiped. However absurd it sounded, even to him.

"Well, if you do dream, David, make me a promise. Tell only me. Not a word to anyone else. Deal?"

"Deal. But like I said, I can't dream anymore."

6

VLAD SMITH rode high on his black stallion and peered down at the city of Mosseum, east of the Great Divide. The 49th was there, deep in an Elyonite prison.

Chained to the mount behind him, naked to the waist, rode his leverage, David Matthews, the father of the 49th in that ancient world. They'd left Ba'al's Thrall in Qurongi City five days earlier, on the same day both he and David had awakened in this world.

Although only five days had passed here, four months had passed in that other world. The world where those he'd set in place were surely doing as instructed—his persuasion was thorough. They awaited his return.

He knew all of this because, although the 49th wasn't dreaming in either world, David was dreaming here and informing him of his experience in that world.

Both David and Rachelle were mere shadows of who they'd once been. Blinded. And that blindness would soon deepen. The 49th was more easily hindered in that other world than here, which had been the whole point of his going there so long ago.

She still had only three seals. His aim to prevent her from finding all five before the Horde and Elyonites found and destroyed the Realm of Mystics was now almost a foregone conclusion.

Her guide, the old sage Talya, couldn't be underestimated, but he was confined to this world. Vlad would crush the 49th in the other.

"It's the perfect day to wreak havoc, is it not, David?"

Only the clopping of the man's mare answered his question. He turned back and glanced at the slouched man, barely awake in his saddle, mouth bound by cloth. A part of him almost felt pity for such a hopeless soul.

"You should be proud of the service you will offer me during your short visit to this world. Though I must say, dragging you all this way hasn't been the most convenient of my tasks. You've cost me at least two days, Daddy."

David lifted his head and studied the city ahead with bloodshot eyes.

"Today is the day," Vlad said, facing the city again. "My legion tells me that all is in place for our little party. All the guests have arrived, awaiting only you and me, although they don't know it yet. Aaron, Jacob, Samuel. The three sons of the three great leaders, all in one place. I couldn't possibly have hoped for more."

Clop, clop, clop. After so many years in a different world, he found traveling by horse a terrible bore. Which is why he kept David bound and gagged except to feed him and coax details of his dreams from him each morning. Amusement could be found in many forms, most satisfyingly in another's suffering.

"You know, they say that the second generation learns from the mistakes of the first generation. I'm glad to say this isn't the case, or everyone would be water walkers by now. The sons are as blind as their fathers, and I intend to keep it that way. You'll see, David. You'll see."

He let the horse amble on.

"Or maybe you won't see anything."

And then that was enough of talking to the gagged slab of meat. It was time to set his mind on the simple task ahead in the hall of fools.

Vlad nudged his stallion and felt the rope tied to David's mount jerk as the beast kept pace. The clothing Ba'al had offered him would do the job—black pants and tan shirt with a dark jacket, all woven of the finest cotton and silk. Tall riding boots. No need for weapons, but he'd accepted the sword in his scabbard if for no other reason than it looked impressive in the eyes of small minds.

As Leedhan, Vlad could appear to be Horde or Albino, whichever suited his purpose best. Today, he rode as Albino, approaching the great Albino city of Mosseum.

Half an hour and he was at their gates, facing four of their black-clad Court Guard who blocked the way. As if they could.

Vlad cleared his throat. "Send word for Aaron, son of Mosseum. Tell him Marsuuv of the first order brings an ally in his war against the Horde. I will speak to him and the other two sons in private quarters immediately."

The first man glanced at the second guard, who was grinning. "That so? Leedhan, is it?"

"Are you deaf?"

Undeterred, the man took in David behind him. "And I suppose this wretch is the ally you bring?"

"Both deaf and blind. Can't you see that he's my prisoner?"

The guard's mouth fell flat. "No one enters without proof of citizenship or express approval."

"Which is what I'm seeking."

The guard studied him, unsettled by his tone. "You'll have to wait here." He shoved his chin at one of the rear guards, who took off at a jog. "And you should know that any insult of the Court Guard is an insult of Aaron."

"Now you annoy me." Vlad nudged his horse and rode forward, eyes on the bustling city beyond the gate. "If you keep talking, I may have to cut out your tongue."

The guard withdrew his blade and stepped up to stop him. "You will wait until word—"

Vlad grabbed the man's hair, lifted him off the ground at arm's length, shifted the color of his eyes from green to a bright amber, and drilled him with a penetrating stare.

"I don't have time to wait. Neither do you. My audience will be in place before I reach Aaron's chambers or I'll take the time to hunt you down and remove your bowels. Is this something you can comprehend, or have they taken your mind with your eyes and ears?"

The man grasped at his hair, wincing. He tried to nod—good enough.

Vlad released his grip. The guard landed hard and stumbled back, glancing at the other two, who'd also found wisdom in backing away.

"Run," Vlad said. "Make sure I'm properly anticipated."

The man took off at a run, chasing the first guard.

Satisfied, Vlad took his prisoner into the city.

He rode leisurely, allowing them time. No one took much notice of an Albino riding with a second in tow.

He'd only spent a few hours among the Horde before leaving, but from what he could gather, there was little difference between this Albino city and the Horde city. Different skin, different colors, different flags, different architecture, yes. But human behavior in the world of polarity was still just human behavior, which wasn't so different from any animal behavior.

Here, mothers chased their children off the streets and traded their wares in the market, just like in the Horde city. Boys and girls kicked around balls of tightly wound grass. Here, like there, men sawed wood and laid bricks; horses were shoed; dinner was served; some kissing and cuddling and sleeping took place before they all rose to do it all again, over and over for years and decades and centuries.

Humanity lost in polarity.

He should know. He'd watched the other world over the course of three hundred years and saw no real shift beyond humanity's desperate yet hopeless attempt to improve life through style and technology.

But that wasn't entirely true. A few had indeed shifted beyond polarity—devout women and men of faith. Most of these had lost interest in the world's self-absorption and remained humble, out of the limelight that seduced most religious leaders.

Here, like there, religion blinded most followers to their own true power. Various forms of fear and judgment enslaved the faithful to polarity in this life, in large part by shifting the conversation to the next life.

The 49th could change that. Fortunately for him, they'd branded her a heretic.

"You like their stench, yes, David?" The man was fully awake, staring.

"That's right, you can't smell it like I can. It's the stench of fear. Found not only among the Shataiki but in nearly all humans, Horde and Albino. Love, love, love that smell. In this way we all smell the same, including you and me. Take it in, it's who you are."

Vlad took a deep breath and blew it out slowly.

"*Fear.* Love, love, love."

A terrible terror washed through him and his fingers trembled. Truly, fear was all he knew.

It took him twenty minutes to reach the massive domed palace. As he'd hoped, the guard who'd gone to announce his arrival awaited him.

"Aaron waits in his chambers. You may leave your horses here."

"Good." Vlad swung his leg off the mount and dropped to the cobblestones. "Do me a favor and help our friend from his horse, will you?"

"Of course, sire."

The man dragged David off his mount and led him by his restraints. Vlad took the chain and nodded at the man.

"This way."

Aaron's chambers were well appointed with many bookcases, comfortable seating, a desk, woven rugs—but these didn't interest Vlad. Neither did Aaron's battle dress, the way he'd groomed his dark hair, or the authority with which he held himself.

The moment Vlad stepped through the open door and gained the man's eyes, he knew Aaron would do his bidding. This is what interested him.

"Your guest, sire," the guard said before bowing and taking up position at the door opposite another guard.

The other two sons were also present. Samuel, son of Thomas, Albino. And Jacob, son of Qurong, Horde. Samuel, unbound, was dressed in a tunic and sandals. A guest here. Jacob stood in tattered undergarments, arms chained behind his back. A prisoner here.

They looked at him in silence, all curious. Slightly unnerved except for Jacob. Vlad's legion had informed him they'd been here a week.

It wasn't the only thing they told him.

"So," Aaron said, stepping forward. "To what end does an Albino who claims to be Leedhan appear at my gates, demanding an audience with me? I was occupied."

"Pleasures of the flesh can wait. The world needs us, my friend." Vlad shot his prisoner a harsh glare—*stay*—dropped the chain, and walked toward them, leaving David near the guards.

To Aaron, indicating the couch: "Please, my friend, take a seat."

"I don't know you as a friend, and we sit if I say we sit."

"Stand if you prefer. But I see you followed my orders to have your two guests join us. I think that settles the question of who's in charge here, don't you?"

Aaron glared, but he was too seasoned to squabble. A good sign.

"Who are you? What do you want?"

"Better." Vlad crossed to a high-backed chair covered in sheepskin, sat to face the three sons, and folded one leg over the other. Then shifted his eye color again, answering the better part of the first question with one look.

"I am the Leedhan Marsuuv, better known across the worlds as Vlad Smith. So you will call me Vlad. Before I tell you what I want, do you need me to persuade you further?"

"Dear Elyon, it's true!" Samuel breathed. "I thought they were rumors."

Aaron's jaw clenched.

Jacob looked unaffected.

"Why are you here?" Aaron demanded. "Who's your prisoner?"

"My prisoner is the father of the 49th Mystic. My legion tells me you have her in your dungeons."

"How did you come across her father? Mystics are ghosts in this desert."

"I also understand that you've fed her the rhambutan fruit to keep her from babbling about other worlds."

"I know nothing of other worlds." Aaron paused. "You're well informed."

"But of course. I have eyes unseen by you. And though you may know nothing of other worlds, you will. Tell me the prophecy that concerns the 49th."

Aaron glanced at Samuel, gauging the other's reaction. They'd become comfortable with each other. Also good.

"'A child will be born, the 49th Mystic, who will divide to expose the shadow of death,'" Aaron recited. "'Then the lion will lie down with the lamb.' So?"

"So . . . the Horde believes this to mean that if the 49th succeeds in exposing this shadow of death, they, the lion, will be subjugated by the Albinos. Your people believe the opposite. And so you both have your reasons for wanting her to fail, which indeed she must. But it's much worse than what either you or the Horde believe."

"Nothing could be worse than being enslaved to Horde," Aaron said. "I prefer death, as would any true follower of Elyon."

"Of course. And the Horde would say the same about being subjugated by Albinos. But you both have it wrong. In truth, if the 49th completes her mission, she would expose the shadow of death, as the prophecy states. If the shadow is brought forward, it will blind all. The lion and the lamb will lie down together. Both Horde and Albino will be forever lost in a darkness not yet known."

He let his claim set in for a beat.

"You see how devastating heresy is? Indeed, the Realm of Mystics should be called the Realm of Heretics. The 49th will be the death of all."

It was a lie, naturally. But those in fear knew no better than to fight fear with more fear. Fear was their god. They were compelled to protect themselves from a perceived threat, as they always had been.

"This can't be true," Jacob said, speaking for the first time.

Vlad drilled him with a piercing stare. "Isn't this what the prophecy states? 'A child will be born, the 49th Mystic, who will divide to expose the shadow of death.' Both Horde and Albino live in so much fear of each other that they no longer see the far greater threat of the shadow of death that looms over all."

Jacob evidently thought better than to advance his argument.

"So you see, we are at a time of great reckoning. In the end, either the 49th and her Mystics will complete their mission and release the shadow of darkness to enslave all Horde and Albinos, or the 49th will betray the Realm of Heretics so we can destroy it and break the curse looming over our world. Do I have your understanding of this?"

"Why have none of our theologians interpreted the prophecy in this way?" Aaron demanded. "Or the theologians of the Horde, for that matter?"

"Because you are equally blind." That much was true. "I'm here to give you sight." That was stretching things a bit. "You must know by now that if you torture any scripture long enough, you can get it to say whatever you want." True and common in both worlds. "But I present you with a truth you cannot afford to dismiss for fear it might be right."

None of them replied, but Vlad knew he had Aaron's attention. The other two . . . Well, at least one of them would eventually come along.

"What is your role in this matter?" Aaron asked.

"I am Leedhan. My only concern is to save this world for my kind. To that end, I was dispatched to the other dimension, which the 49th also seeks to blind. My role was and is to undermine her there, for the simple reason that if she succeeds there, she will also succeed here, and we can't have that. You don't want to live in hell, do you?"

David, who'd remained obediently silent thus far, staggered forward, issuing gagged cries at the mention of his daughter in the other world.

"Silence him," Vlad ordered.

The guard behind David hit him with the hilt of his sword, hard enough to drop the man to the floor, unconscious.

Vlad looked at Aaron and continued. "Following her birth in the other world, I learned that her mind couldn't be compromised like other simple minds, at least not using the means available there. I require the help of . . . shall we say, 'elements' from this world. Which is why I went to so much trouble to make my way back. I won't be here long. I only need you to understand your most critical role here so that I can play my role there." He flashed a grin. "Capisce?"

It was the first time he'd laid out his mission to humans in such plain terms, all of them true. He felt a bit naked. An interesting feeling.

"Capisce?" Aaron said.

"A term from the other world. To understand."

"This is madness," Aaron snapped, crossing to the mantel where his glass of burgundy wine sat. "There are no such worlds."

"You don't need to believe that there are. It's none of your concern. Finding and crushing the Realm of Heretics before the 49th can fulfill her mission, on the other hand, is."

Aaron turned back, glass in hand. "My concern is to protect my people. To this end, the Horde are the most immediate threat." He took a sip of his wine.

"Of course, and you'll get your war. Qurong marches east as we speak and will be joined by the Eramites. Frankly, I don't care if you all kill each—"

"The Eramites? The half-breeds from the north?" Aaron had lowered his glass.

Vlad was losing his patience. "Will you question everything I say?"

No response. Aaron was stubborn, he'd give the man that much. A good quality, if properly channeled.

"As I said, you will get your war. But in all the bloodshed, you must remember what you hear today. The Mystics are by far the greatest threat our world faces. All of them. Not one can be allowed to remain living."

Aaron stared at him. His capture of Jacob could only mean he was baiting the Horde, eager to end them in one final conflict.

"How far out?" the son of Mosseum asked.

"Two days. Now, the more urgent matter."

"You're suggesting I execute the 49th."

"No," Samuel said, stepping forward. He caught himself and quickly offered his reasoning in a thinly veiled attempt to throw them off. "No, she must betray herself."

"Very good, son of Thomas. The 49th is the only one who can betray the Realm of Mystics. So, no, execution won't do."

Vlad unfolded his legs and stood. It was time to move things along.

"The 49th must be allowed to escape. To this end"—he faced the son of Qurong—"Jacob will break her out."

"Out of the question!" Aaron snapped. "I have him as bait and leverage."

"Your bait has already drawn the full attention of Qurong. As for leverage, Qurong isn't so easily manipulated. Jacob's release, on the other hand, will make the Horde think twice and weaken their resolve. This will be to your advantage."

He let the logic sink in.

"What matters far more is that Jacob will be led by the 49th to the Realm of Mystics, which has been hidden from you for so long. When he returns with the location, you will be free to destroy them. Do you not understand the gravity of your situation?"

"You trust a Horde to reveal what he finds?" Samuel objected. "Why this beast?"

"Because the 49th is falling for him."

The statement settled between them. Jacob stood impassively in his chains. Samuel, on the other hand, could not hide his offense.

"She trusts Jacob," Vlad continued. "Which is why it must be him and no one else." He held Jacob in a long stare. "But we know he would never betray his own people. Allowing the Realm of Mystics to survive would endanger Horde as much as Albino."

Silence settled in the room. Aaron was torn between a war against the Horde and the destruction of all Mystics. Jacob was eager to liberate the 49th. Samuel was still trying to decide if it was possible that the 49th could love a Scab.

Surely.

Aaron faced Jacob. "What say you?"

The Scab hesitated, then offered a single nod. "His logic isn't flawed."

"You agree to this?"

"I do."

Aaron returned his glass to the mantel. "So be it. When?"

Samuel stood like stone, face flushed.

Vlad ignored him for the moment. "Tonight."

"I'll need my armor and weapons," Jacob said.

Vlad dipped his head. "Naturally. I suggest you prepare. You may go. Samuel, stay for a moment."

Jacob glanced at Aaron, who nodded.

The Scab looked at Vlad, held his gaze for a moment, then strode for the exit. The guard opened the door and allowed two others to escort Jacob from the room.

"How can you know this?" Samuel snapped the moment the door closed. "That she loves this beast?"

Vlad cocked his brow. "Do you doubt me?"

"It's impossible! She loves all, but not him, not as a man!"

"Why do you care?"

No response. Which was answer enough.

"But you're right about one thing, son of Thomas. Jacob cannot be trusted."

"Of course not. He's Horde."

"Not because he's Horde. Because he's falling in love with her."

Samuel looked gut-punched. "You're saying that they're both party to this madness?"

"I'm saying that you must follow them without being seen. They will lead you to the Realm of Mystics. You, my friend, will be the one who saves all Albinos from the shadow of death."

Vlad faced Aaron. "Kill every last rotting Scab if you must. But remember what I've told you today. The annihilation of all Mystics must take precedence! I have eyes everywhere."

"And yet not even you know where the Realm of Mystics is."

"The Mystics have surrendered polarity at a very high level. Like all Shataiki, Roush, Horde, and Albino, we Leedhan are bound in polarity."

"Meaning?"

"Meaning, their Realm is beyond our purview. If we knew where they were, they would already be dead."

Aaron frowned. "So be it."

"Good. Now show me where you have the 49th. I have a gift for her before I leave you all."

7

DAVID bolted up in bed, sheets soaked, heart hammering, confused and disoriented. Confused because he'd just dreamed—only it wasn't a dream. Or was it?

Disoriented because he'd just been in a room with a man named Vlad and three other people after riding across a desert as a prisoner. He'd awakened here when they knocked him out there.

So was this place the dream? No. No, that couldn't be.

He flipped on the light, flung his legs from the bed and sat still, listening. Staring at the white wall. The details of his dream spun through his mind in perfect clarity. Rachelle was there, they said, a prisoner in their dungeons. She was called the 49th Mystic. Vlad wanted her dead.

Steve had asked him if he wanted to dream. But it felt so real . . . Was this how he'd dreamed in Eden?

The question tripped through his mind. What if Rachelle really was in some kind of danger? And what about him?

He shoved himself from the bed and crossed to the door. Twisted the knob. Locked from the outside. Of course, it was after hours. He could press the button beside his bed, but that would bring Mary. Mary couldn't know about the dream—he'd given his word to Steve.

Regardless, it was just a dream, had to be. A nightmare.

He turned and glanced around the small room. No windows. One bed with a reddish, pinkish cover, one white dresser, one bedside table with a green lamp.

Safe. Familiar. Home.

Slowly, his heart returned to an even pace. The clock on his nightstand read 2:12 a.m. He'd slept only a few hours. What if he forgot the dream in the morning?

Returning to his bed, David opened the drawer on his bedside table, pulled out his notepad and pen. There, on the first page, he scribbled himself a note.

Dream: Another world. Desert. Vlad. Mystic. Captive.

He stared at his writing. Enough to jog his memory. He returned the notebook to the drawer, slid back under the covers, and turned off the light.

Strange how he'd awakened here when he got knocked out there, in the nightmare. But that's how dreams worked. Even more strange—how he was so worked up about something his mind had only imagined. Unlike him, Rachelle still had some memory of Eden, even though it was mostly suppressed. Maybe this was why she didn't want to dream.

Maybe she knew it would be a nightmare.

David let his mind drift. Tomorrow was what? Saturday, so pancakes for breakfast. He wasn't sure how the MEP had altered his mind, because he couldn't remember anything before the treatment, nothing at all. They'd given him subconscious memories, which affected his preferences, like his craving for pancakes, which Rachelle claimed he used to hate.

A part of him wondered if having his memories wiped should upset him, but he didn't have any reason to be upset about something he couldn't remember, like how he'd once been. He was just . . . this.

After the first couple of weeks, Rachelle had stopped telling him how things used to be. The MEP didn't work with her for some unknown reason, but she was on her own path of healing. Memories that were fake to begin with were slowly being washed from her so she could focus on that healing.

Sleep pulled at him, and his mind returned to the other world again. What if believing in another world was like believing in religion? The thought got him thinking about Rachelle's Sunday excursions to the church. He'd never gone, but maybe he should. She always returned with a smile. It was the music, she said. That and seeing other people looking beyond themselves to something greater. God. She said she'd always had a deep faith in God, and she was working through that somehow.

Good for her. She was so beautiful. Such a gentle and bright spirit. So loving and smart. Maybe he should go with her. Maybe it would do him some good too . . .

Those were the last thoughts that crossed David's mind before he fell asleep and opened his eyes in another world.

He was on the ground. Someone had just kicked him. He grunted and tried to get up, but his hands were chained behind his back.

A familiar panic coursed through his veins. He'd been here, crossing the desert with the one called Marsuuv, who was Vlad Smith. They had Rachelle. Dear God . . .

"Cover his head."

Someone shoved a hood over his head and hauled him to his feet.

"Bring him."

VLAD SMITH peered through the open cell door, studying the small form sleeping dreamlessly in the stone hole. The guard stood behind him, holding a torch in one hand and the father's restraints in the other. He'd taken the liberty of placing a hood over David's head. No need for a commotion before its appointed time.

Looking at her frail form, he knew that commotion would be significant. Wonder filled him to think that this woman curled up in a filthy, tattered tunic—black hair disheveled, skin bruised—presented the greatest risk to the shadow, excepting Justin himself.

He stepped up to the cell. Wrapped his fingers around one of the iron bars. Was it wonder or fear he felt? He could hardly tell the difference anymore. Because there was no difference to him. He could only feel fear, regardless of what he called it or how he pretended to be.

Her chest slowly rose and fell with shallow breathing. Her eyes were no longer blind, he knew that. She'd brought the sky down in Eden and gained the Third Seal. All three were there, on her bare shoulder.

White. Green. Black.

Seeing them now, he took a calming breath. He couldn't fathom how the world would be if they all discovered who they were. But it wasn't going to happen.

Here lay the 49th Mystic in all her puny glory. That a single human could cause such a disturbance in the valley of shadow made him ill. He'd given so many years of his life in the other world, preparing. All was in order there, waiting for his return to end what he'd started.

And yet . . . three seals. If she found a way to recover her strength there, in the other world, despite all of his preparations . . .

A chill washed down his back.

"Set the torch."

He heard the guard maneuver the torch into its bracket on the wall.

"Leave us."

"Sire . . ."

"Now!"

A beat.

"As you wish."

He didn't bother turning as the guard's footfalls retreated down the stone passage. Behind him, David's breathing was labored under his hood. Before him, the girl's breath came easy in deep sleep. That would now change.

"Stay where you are, David."

He stepped into the chamber, withdrew the twine and muzzle from his jacket pocket, and lowered himself to one knee beside her head. Here she lay cradled in peace, totally ignorant of the violence coming to both worlds because of her.

Vlad slipped one end of the twine around her neck, then slowly eased the mouthpiece over her lips. With sudden force he pulled the muzzle tight, swept her arms down behind her back, and cinched the noose at the other end of the twine tight around her wrists.

She jerked, eyes wide in the torchlight, struggling. He would have relished the opportunity to have a conversation with her, but he couldn't risk her talking, plying her father with reason.

The 49th had evidently recognized him and was jerking around in panic, screaming through her muzzle.

"Now, now, Rachelle. It's pointless."

The father, recognizing his daughter's cry, began to holler as best he could through his gag. It was all a bit pathetic sounding, daughter and father screaming. She didn't even know who the hooded man outside her cell was yet.

Vlad slammed her up against the side wall, fed the rope through the bars behind her, and cinched the bonds tight. Then a second rope, this one binding her neck to the bars.

He stepped back, satisfied. She calmed, knowing well that there was no escape, but staring at him in raw terror.

"There we go." David was still trying to scream. "Shut up, David!" He did not.

To the 49th: "Did you miss me? You didn't think this was over, did you? No, no, my little peach cobbler. I promised to blind you again and again, and I'm going to blind you permanently, right here, unless Daddy saves you."

Her eyes shifted to her hooded father.

"Do you like my gift? I'll give you a better view, yes?"

Vlad retreated from the cell, hauled the father over to the cell door, and chained him to the bars. "So you don't do anything stupid." He jerked off the man's hood.

The moment the father laid eyes on the daughter, both disintegrated into a pitiful display of tears and desperate, muted cries.

"Okay, I think that should do it."

Vlad crossed to the 49th and shoved the hood over her head. Nonverbal communication between the pair no longer served him. He pulled the twine around her neck tighter, so she could barely breathe.

"See how your daughter struggles, David?" He stepped in front of the father and lowered his voice for him alone. "Thing of it is, this is all just a dream. A test of sorts to see how much you love her. That's why you've joined her nightmares. You remember all those nightmares, don't you, David? This world isn't even real."

The man's bloodshot eyes strained to see the 49th over Vlad's shoulder.

He grabbed the man by his neck, lifted him clear off his feet so that the chain was stretched tight, and shoved him against the wall. "Eyes on me, David. I need your full attention."

A quick, desperate nod.

He set the man back down.

Leaning in: "Now, there's only one way she lives more than a few minutes. And if she dies, I'm going to keep you alive with her dead body for a long time, so you can remember what you failed to do."

He withdrew the same Book of History David had previously used to return him to this plane. Also, a pen. Only humans could write their history, or Vlad would have used the book himself. And only the 49th or a human who'd traveled through the books before could activate them.

The 49th would never write Vlad back to Earth.

But after five days of considerable stress, the father was hanging on to his sanity by a thread.

"These are the words you will write into this book to save your daughter. I've written them on a piece of paper here." He showed him the slip of paper tucked into the cover. "'Marsuuv to Earth with his legion in one minute.' Only that, exactly that, yes? Simple. Write it and I'll be gone to leave you with your daughter. At least you'll both be alive and together. And I'll be forever gone, because there's no book there to send me back."

The 49th was standing on her toes so she could breathe. Sobbing quietly.

He shoved the man down to his knees, spread the book open on the ground, and pressed the pen into his trembling fingers.

"I'm going to count to three, one for each seal on her arm. Nod so I know you've understood my instruction."

He nodded, frantic.

"Good." Vlad palmed his knife, crossed to the 49th, and pressed the blade against her neck. "One . . ."

The man bowed over the book, writing so furiously that Vlad wondered if he might write the wrong thing.

"Two . . ."

But it was the intention behind the writing, not the actual words, that mattered.

David dropped the pen and shoved the book toward Vlad. The torchlight showed the writing on the page—messy but readable.

Vlad stepped away from the 49th, surprised by the simplicity of it all. Damage done. Game over. At least for the next minute.

David knelt, sobbing as his emotions overwhelmed his body.

"There, there, it's okay." He walked to the man. "Simple, right? It's all over now."

David remained on his knees, bowed over, rocking.

Vlad's legion was six. And those six could do more than a thousand lesser beings. He withdrew a vial of Shataiki blood from his inner pocket and looked at its contents.

"Again and again, 49th," he muttered to himself. "Again and again."

He opened the vial, jerked the man's head back, and shoved the bottle between his lips. Half the contents . . . Enough to kill his body within ten seconds.

David gasped; his body began to shake.

Deed done, Vlad straightened and tossed the vial to one side, where it landed and shattered. It would have been easier to just slit the man's throat, but Vlad needed his death to remain a mystery in that other world. If he cut his throat here, his throat would be cut there.

David quieted and slumped over like a toy doll switched off. Dead here, dead there.

The 49th must have figured out what was happening, because she uttered a deep, gut-wrenching sob under her hood. Unfortunately, she wasn't dreaming in the other world, so she wouldn't recall any of these details when she awoke there. Pity.

The book and all those like it in his possession would be left behind when he vanished from this world. Unlike humans, he couldn't coexist in both places, and the book only traveled with their kind.

He straightened his coat, took a deep breath, and nodded at the 49th strapped to the cell bars. "See you on the other side, 49th."

The world began to fade.

8

I WOKE with a start, barely aware of a fleeting memory, like a ghost shifting out of my awareness. Not just any ghost, but a black wraith. As if a darkness had invaded me while I slept and then flown off just as I woke up, leaving me with an ominous dread.

My first thought was that I'd had a nightmare. We'd talked about them last night and something in my subconscious had been triggered. If so, I couldn't remember it.

No, the sensation was probably tied to the MEP that had failed. With all the different drugs they'd tried, whittling the concoctions down to just the right combination for me, I was used to wild emotional swings, especially in the early days.

But this . . . This felt different.

I climbed out of bed, trying to shake the darkness. The last time I could even remotely remember feeling something similar was in Eden, when they'd played games with our heads. It made me regret having agreed to the MEP. Not that I'd really had any choice.

Steve would know what to do.

It took me fifteen minutes to shower and pull on my jeans and shirt. And by then the dread had passed, leaving me in a somber but reasonable state of mind. I didn't bother drying my hair.

The doors had automatic locks on them that engaged at midnight and disengaged at 7:00 in the morning. It was now 7:30. Saturday. Dad would be looking for pancakes. Funny how simple his tastes were now. My fuzzy recollection of him in Eden was of a man always looking for a solution to some problem, most often my blindness, which had been caused by a disease that switched off the visual center at the back of my brain.

The hall was empty when I left my room. My dad's room was two doors down to the left, and I thought about checking to see if he was up. But knowing him, he was probably already in the cafeteria.

I headed down the hall to the rec room. No one there. Poked my head into the cafeteria. Mary was behind the counter, pulling syrup and whipping cream from the refrigerator.

"Morning, sweetheart. You ready for some pancakes?"

"Sure." No sign of my dad. "You see my father?"

"Not yet. You beat him for a change."

"'Kay, I'm gonna go get him."

"I'll be here."

Seventy-three steps, that's how far it was to my father's room. I knew how many steps were between all the rooms. In fact, I could walk the whole complex with my eyes shut and pretty much get where I wanted to go.

My brain had developed echolocation skills in Eden, part of all their programming—that much had been real, Steve said. But I'd lost the ability due to the drugs, he guessed. I sometimes walked with my eyes closed, maybe hoping the echolocation would return just for fun.

Seventy-three steps, but today it was seventy-four. I was getting sloppy.

I knocked, and when I got no answer I turned the knob and cracked the door.

"Dad?"

No response, so I pushed the door wide. He was still in bed, lying with his back to me. "Dad? It's time for breakfast. Pancakes."

He still didn't move. That was the first sign something was wrong. Even with drugs on board, my dad was a fairly light sleeper.

Heart pattering, I hurried to his bed and tapped his shoulder. "Wake up, Dad." Not a move.

Now worried, I shook him. His skin was cold.

Adrenaline crashed through me and I jerked him toward me. "Dad? Wake up!"

His body rolled over, but his chest wasn't moving and his lips were purple. I stood still, unable to move. Confused. My mind wasn't making the connections yet. He'd passed out?

Then I was on his bed, slapping his face, jerking his body, pounding his chest. "Wake up! Wake up!"

He wasn't waking.

He's dead, a voice in my head said, and at first I thought it was an auditory hallucination. But it was my voice, telling me what was happening.

Now in a full-fledged panic, I fled the room, slamming my shoulder on the door frame just as I was calling out for help. The blow sent me to the floor, but I didn't feel the pain. I was screaming for help as I scrambled to my feet.

"Help!" Sprinting for the rec room. "Help! My dad's not breathing! Steve! Mary!"

"Rachelle?"

I whirled and saw that Steve had entered from the hall that led to the labs, looking like he'd just woken up.

"What's wrong?"

I ran back the way I'd come. "Hurry! My dad . . ." It was all I said. He was already running, me right behind, begging myself to be wrong about what I thought I'd seen. Praying for it to be a hallucination.

Steve was already at the bed, bending over my father, ear to his chest, when I spun into the room, breathing hard. I pulled up there, afraid.

He began to pump my father's chest with his palms. Then breathe into his mouth, trying to bring him back. I knew then . . . I knew but refused to know.

I flew for the bed. Slammed into Steve, knocking him out of my way. With hands balled like battering rams, I slammed my fists on my dad's chest. "Wake up!" I screamed. "Wake up!"

"Shh, shh, shh . . ."

Steve was trying to comfort me, but I wasn't shushing. I was slamming, now with anger as much as desperation. He couldn't leave me! I didn't know how to live without him! I was his daughter!

His body shook a little each time I hit him, but he didn't move, didn't breathe, didn't even know I was hitting him.

He couldn't because he was dead.

"Wake up! You have to wake up!"

"Rachelle . . ."

"No! Don't you dare leave me here like this!"

A hand was on my shoulder, easing me back. "It's too late, Rachelle. He's . . ."

He's dead. I knew that. And his body was cold, which meant he'd been dead for a while. But that didn't stop me.

"Wake up!" I beat him again.

"I'm so sorry, honey." Steve's voice was weak. "I'm so, so sorry."

Anguish like I had never known boiled up from my belly and sucked the life out of my mind. I flopped over on my father's chest and began to sob.

STEVE PACED OUTSIDE the infirmary, glancing through the window at Rachelle, who was curled up on a chair pulled close to the hospital bed. Her head rested on the white sheet pulled over her father's body. She hadn't moved in half an hour. His gut churned.

Four hours had passed since they found David in his bed. Cause of death: massive internal hemorrhaging. There were no signs of external trauma, no traces of poison in the preliminary toxicology report, no marks on his body, no indication of cause.

Only the note he'd found in David's drawer.

Dream: Another world. Desert. Vlad. Mystic. Captive.

He'd ripped out the page and crammed the note into his pocket, fearing the worst. The Kinazeran. He'd given David a dose of the drug last night with his other medication. It had killed him.

Between doing his best to console Rachelle, ordering blood panels, and making the calls to the project leader and the director, he checked and double-checked the literature on Kinazeran. There was no way. At most, Kinazeran could put a smile on your face. It was often prescribed with the same mild psychotropic meds they were giving David, if only to ease the brain fog that often presented with those meds.

It wasn't the Kinazeran that had killed David.

It was his dream.

Dream: Another world. Desert. Vlad. Mystic. Captive. David had woken up having dreamed, made the note to remind himself, then gone back to sleep. Back into that same nightmare.

The nightmare of Vlad in a desert.

For the last two hours, Steve had scanned the recordings made in Eden during that last week. Vlad had disabled the digital video feed, but they'd retrieved some local audio from the rubble, including some made in the courthouse and Rachelle's home. It was the recordings from her home that contained what little information they had of her dreams.

Yes, the sky had been vaporized; yes, she could read minds; yes, she was no longer blind. But he'd never really believed that whatever was happening in her dreams had actually manifested in a tangible way.

Steve had convinced himself that Vlad was more likely than Rachelle to be responsible for the sky coming down. Rapid epigenetic mutations explained how a blind person could be cured. Her mind reading had something to do with her ability to access quantum consciousness beyond space and time. It was all plausible.

But this? Dreams of another reality where Vlad Smith had taken David captive? Not so much. They'd all agreed the dreams were mental projections.

Regardless, the effects of whatever had happened in David's and Rachelle's minds could not be denied. All dreams aside, Rachelle *did* have her gifts. And David *was* dead.

According to Rachelle, she was the only one who could have saved Project Eden. Without her, all would've died. *She* was the one fighting for the survival of her father and the others in Eden. Fighting what, or whom?

Vlad Smith.

Which once again raised the question, who was Vlad Smith? Could he really have come from another reality, however absurd that sounded? And was he there now, as David's note seemed to suggest?

They'd convinced Rachelle that Vlad had been nothing more than a figment of her imagination, but they all knew that wasn't true. Vlad had forced their technicians out, set the perimeter explosives, and brought the cliffs down—that much was documented. And Vlad was still out there somewhere.

David's dream wasn't the cause of his death. Vlad was. Vlad, who evidently wasn't done. Vlad, who'd been stopped by Rachelle in Eden.

Rachelle was the key. Maybe the key to far more than just saving Eden.

A chill snaked down Steve's spine as the thought slithered home. What if?

Steve quietly opened the door and stepped into the infirmary. Rachelle kept her eyes closed, cheek on the mattress. He walked up to her and set his hand on her arm.

"You okay?"

Stupid question.

No response.

Hiding the truth from her felt cruel in the wake of David's sudden death. The bubble they'd fabricated to "protect" her from herself was as suspect as the drugs they'd been feeding her.

His phone buzzed. The director. He stepped out, closed the door, and tapped the green answer button.

"Theresa."

"Steve."

Gentle voice. "How is she?"

"Out of it. I've upped her meds, that's part of it. Her father just died, for crying out loud."

"I know." A pause. "We've made a decision. I know you'll object, but I think it's our best course at this point." Another pause. "The engineers have made some adjustments to the MEP that we think will give us—"

"You've got to be kidding!" Anger washed over him. "Again, now?"

"We have to get the memory of David's death out of her. She's in a tailspin, Steve, you know that. We've successfully taken her this far. The last thing we can afford now is for her to begin questioning the program. Any risk the MEP might present pales in comparison to her well-being, wouldn't you agree?"

She had a way with words. "Her well-being? Or yours?"

"Without a memory of so much trauma, she'll find peace. Surely you can see that."

"No."

"No?"

"No, because the MEP won't work with her. Period. You'll just traumatize her more."

"You can't know it won't work. We have to try."

He peered at Rachelle through the glass. She still hadn't moved.

"It won't work. It has never worked."

"Be that as it may, the decision is final. Top down. This goes beyond me, Steve, you have to know that."

There was that claim again.

"Who's the top, Theresa?"

"The people who keep our doors open."

"But *who*, specifically? And why does Rachelle threaten them so much? This can't simply be about her abilities."

A long pause this time.

"I'm not sure I really know, Steve. All I know is that the decision is final."

There it was. Nothing short of blowing the place up could stop them now, and even if he had the mind to counteract DARPA, doing so would only put Rachelle in more danger. Without him to watch over her, there was no telling what they would do.

"When?"

"Tonight. The sooner the better."

Dear God. He had to buy some time.

"She's under too much stress. Look, just give me a couple days with her. Let her grieve. I'm the only tether to sanity she has left. Let me talk to her. Take her to the church tomorrow. Reassess on Monday. Give me that much and I won't buck this."

Silence.

"Two days, that's all I ask. For the sake of all that's decent, give her at least that much time."

"Monday. I can live with that. But come Monday, I don't want to hear this again."

"Fine."

The line went dead.

Steve took a deep breath, slipped his phone into his pocket, and looked at Rachelle through the glass window.

He had to find out more about the desert world in David's note. The dreams, not the MEP or the drugs, might hold the key that unlocked Rachelle's recovery. If she showed some kind of significant change in the next two days, Theresa might capitulate.

He would give Rachelle a dose of Kinazeran tonight.

She would dream again.

Decision made.

9

VLAD VAN VALERIK. That was one of his names.

And this . . . Vlad stood on Pennsylvania Avenue, staring at the White House rising from its manicured lawns . . . This was his game. Corny, yes, but he preferred mixing human slang with more formal structures of communication.

Here, for the time being at least, beat the heart of the fourth pillar of power in this world, as he saw it. Beijing, Brussels, Moscow, and Washington, the latter arguably still being the most powerful of the four. But not for long, not unless significant changes were made.

He was that change.

Or so he'd successfully argued five years earlier, three years before Calvin Johnson was elected to the highest office in the land. The 49th Mystic had just turned twelve when Vlad first made his proposal to the then-senator from Oklahoma. Vlad had far more in his purview than haunting the 49th in her dreams while he waited for her to come of age.

He'd known within a year of her birth that he would likely need to return to Other Earth for a refined power this world's technology couldn't yet deliver. Her mind was too strong.

Now he had that power.

It was Saturday, and he'd arrived to discover that President Johnson intended to play golf. A brief call to his chief of staff, Karen Willis—did she still wear her dark hair short?—altered those plans. Now the politicians both waited for Vlad in the West Wing, nerves rattled, no doubt.

As they should be. Johnson's presidency had been bought and paid for by none other than Vlad van Valerik, through the most ingenious means. Money. Funding well hidden from all their limiting laws. The wealth that came so easily to Vlad was not so easily transferred. Nonetheless, here they were, as planned.

But this wasn't the primary reason for their rattled nerves.

The real cause: StetNox malware, the most powerful weapon in what would soon become another cyber war, launched and won in a single, massive attack. This was his gift to them. StetNox—meaning "perpetual blindness"—was now dormant but could be activated by him. Only him.

Perhaps Rachelle also rattled their nerves. More specifically, his instructions to them regarding her treatment at DARPA. But this was far above their pay grade.

He rolled his shoulders, easing the form-fitting suit he'd helped himself to at Michael's Elegant Wear, five blocks east. Black. He'd opted for cowboy boots because he thought they made at least a small statement—Texas was by far the wealthiest state in their shaky union. For now.

"And so it begins," he muttered, and he headed down the sidewalk.

It took him ten minutes to reach the main entry, fully in form as the Russian diplomat called to meet with the president regarding trade. Another fifteen to wait for and clear their security. Another five to reach the Oval Office.

He'd been here on only two other occasions. Most of his dealings had been off-site with Karen Willis, the hardnosed and overconfident staffer. He'd insisted Johnson select her as chief of staff long before the election.

Two Secret Service agents stood in the hall leading up to the door. Vlad ignored both.

The staffer who escorted him knocked lightly, opened the door, and announced him.

"Show him in."

Vlad was already walking through when she turned to usher him in. Calvin Johnson stood in front of the desk, one hand in his pocket, more gray than when Vlad had last seen him. Tall and solid, dark trimmed hair, navy blue suit with a yellow tie. One look at his steely gray eyes and Vlad saw through his rigid mask. The man was deeply religious and nearly fanatical in his beliefs that some kind of end was drawing nigh. Vlad had helped him along with those beliefs because he was right—just not in the way Johnson thought he was.

Karen stood by one of the two couches. Yes, dark hair still short to match the president's, a black business suit, black heels.

The president pulled his hand from his pocket and stepped forward, smiling cordially.

Before he could offer any customary welcome, Vlad strode to Karen.

"So good to see you again, princess." He took her hand, lifted it to his lips, and kissed her knuckles. "Always so good."

Color flushed her face. "Hello, Vlad." He had this effect on all the women he'd chosen to seduce. In the case of Karen, seduce and then reject, leaving her confused and off balance.

"You really should forget the makeup, you know. Pale skin suits your dark eyes."

"So you've said."

"And I'll say again, assuming you're alive to hear."

He turned to Johnson, who appeared slightly flummoxed by his lack of decorum.

"I see the office has gone to your head, Calvin." He shoved his hands into his pockets and walked to the window. "It's time to remember where you came from, Mr. President."

Behind him, silence.

"Remind me," Vlad said.

"We both know where I came from," Johnson replied.

"And where you'll go if I let the cat out of the bag. So humor me. I want to know how well you understand the situation."

"Excuse me?" Karen, impressing her boss. "You vanish four months ago after giving me instructions about DARPA and the girl from Project Eden—instructions which, by the way, make no sense—and now you suddenly reappear and walk in here as if you own the office? Show some—"

"But I *do* own this office," he said, turning. "I owned it the moment you agreed to my release of StetNox five years ago. By now the malware hides on virtually every computing device in this country, if not the world. You pay nearly half a billion dollars for the development of a piece of software to work precisely as you need it to, and it had better. Trust me, it has and will. It is also strictly prohibited by a hundred privacy laws. As was my funding of your campaign. Are we forgetting?"

No, they weren't.

"So tell me why I did all of this for you. I've come a very, very, very long way, leaving all but six of my friends at home, and I want to hear you say it."

Karen looked at Johnson, who hesitated before answering. "All our algorithms confirmed your own, which predicted a ninety-seven percent likelihood that the United States would collapse as a viable economic society within seven years." He stopped.

"And?"

"The problem is, most of our country is more worried about terrorist attacks and personal privacy than their own failing economy, propped up by overwhelming debt."

"And?"

"You offered a way out. A threat that would allow me reasonable cause to introduce new controls and make the corrections I think are appropriate."

"What kind of new controls?"

"We both know!"

"Say it. Don't worry, I'm not wired this time."

Hard stares. This was news to them.

"Tell me."

"Once activated, the StetNox malware will give my team unrestricted access to and control of all activity on the web. The world will be blind to the source behind the systematic redistribution of wealth. When pushback comes, we finger terrorists."

"You will have power to liquidate any personal or corporate account you wish at your whim. Untraceable and without recourse. At the touch of a few buttons, millions of rich and middle-class will be bankrupted overnight. Welcome to the digital age. I can hear the wailing and gnashing of teeth already. They should have stuck with silver coins." A beat. "And the outcome?"

The president hesitated, but he couldn't hide the enthusiasm in his tone. "A major correction that levels the playing field by stripping individual wealth for the good of national reconstruction."

"Under martial law."

The president gave a curt nod. "If needed."

It wouldn't be needed for the simple reason that the collapse would come without their help. All great nations rose and fell like the changing of seasons, and it was this country's turn. The only question was who would be in power to rebuild. Beneath all of Johnson's altruistic bravado, the ambition for control justified by sacred beliefs motivated him far more than idealism.

Not unlike the Elyonites.

"Now tell me what I get out of it, Karen."

She held his stare. The stronger of the two.

"Clearly, you have this office by the tail."

Bold but honest choice of terms.

"True. But as I recall, there's more."

"Our full cooperation with what was Project Eden and all those who survived its collapse. Which has never made sense."

"No." Vlad walked to the president's desk and leaned back against the edge. "But today it will. Tell me you've carried out those instructions that made no sense to you."

"Of course. The drugs have worked as you said they would. The MEPs failed . . ."

"As I said they would. Not to fear." He crossed his arms. "Tell me about her. How has she been getting along these last four months?"

Johnson settled on the couch and sat on the edge of the cushion, still uncomfortable. "What is it with her?"

"She's the 49th Mystic," Vlad answered.

"A mystic . . . What do you mean, mystic?"

They were uncomprehending and he had no desire to make converts of them. "Just tell me how she's been getting along."

Karen followed her boss's lead and sat across from him. Crossed her legs, folded her arms. "Based on reports from the director—"

"Theresa Williams."

"Correct. There are still a lot of unanswered questions, but DARPA isn't pursing them. They know someone named Vlad Smith is responsible for Project Eden's collapse, but they've spun the evidence." She cocked her brow. "I'm assuming that was you."

"I'm not interested in what I did. Back to the girl. Is she strong? Does she remember?"

"She thinks she's schizophrenic. It's a bit monstrous, if you ask me. They have her so doped up she hardly knows who she is anymore. They say her memory's still there, but she's discounting most if not all of it." A pause. "Her father died in his sleep last night."

"Yes, of course. I killed him."

"You?"

More news. "Never mind. Does the girl still have her . . . gifts?"

"You mean her auditory hallucinations?"

"They aren't hallucinations. But I was referring to her more physical skills."

Karen's left leg swung on her right. "She developed some interesting epigenetic mutations in Project Eden. Exceptional hand-eye coordination, reaction speed, that sort of thing."

"This is all well and good," Johnson interjected, "but I still don't see her connection to StetNox."

"And as I said, you will." Back to Karen. "How did she react to her father's death?"

"She's devastated."

"Yes. Yes, of course she is!"

They both looked at him as if he'd lost his grip on sanity.

"I would be as well," he said, easing his tone. "She's been attending church as I instructed?"

"Every Sunday."

The president set his hands on his knees and pushed himself up. "Look. I didn't agree to all of this so you could play whatever sick game you have going. This is absurd. We've specifically delayed plans of our own to facilitate *your* plan. Meanwhile, we have a meltdown steaming our way, and all you've given us is a list of unfulfilled promises and ridiculous demands concerning some poor girl who's been through—"

"Sit!"

Johnson glared at him.

"Now, before I rip out your tongue and shove it down your throat."

The president eased back down, face flushing with rage.

Vlad stood from the desk, tired of the man's arrogance. "Listen carefully. I will only say this once. That innocent little girl you call Rachelle Matthews is the most dangerous human alive on the planet."

He spoke with the authority of one who knew far more than they could, which was true.

"There's a great darkness coming to the worlds. A far greater danger than any of your own paltry concerns. Forget what you think you know about me. In the end, you'll be grateful for the gift of her demise. Do you understand this?"

"If she's so dangerous, why didn't you just kill her?"

"That's not how it works!" he snapped. Then relaxed. "I'll deal with her my way, which includes your participation as I see fit."

He paced.

"The World Security Summit is scheduled in four days' time. My work with the girl ends there, while the world watches. If I succeed, I will activate the StetNox malware and you will have your power. What you do with that power, I don't care. Announce yourself supreme ruler, reduce every American citizen to rags, and rebuild your utopia if you so desire. But if I fail, your crimes will be exposed for the world to see. Do I need to be any clearer?"

Understanding slowly darkened the man's mind. No one liked being a puppet.

Vlad loved puppets.

"The girl is my only concern now, which means she is yours as well," he said. "I strongly recommend you do precisely as I say."

The president sat back. Wiped beads of sweat from his forehead with his forearm. He finally nodded. "Go on."

Satisfied, Vlad withdrew the small test tube of yellow fluid he'd withdrawn from one of his legion only an hour earlier. It was new blood, unlike his own, which had been defiled by hundreds of years in this plane. Fastened around it with a rubber band was a note with simple instructions.

"You will give this to the director at DARPA." He handed it to the chief of staff, who took it between her thumb and forefinger.

"What is it?"

"Something you don't want to touch much less ingest. Please put it away."

She placed the glass tube in a tissue and set it gently in her handbag.

"Tomorrow," Vlad continued, "both of you will attend the services at Washington National Cathedral."

"That would be a considerable—"

"I need the media there," Vlad interrupted. "I also need the world to see her with you. And it will help to have a crisis to distract the public before the main event. A major distraction that will whip the world into a frenzy before you unleash your own economic Armageddon."

Johnson was cagey. "What kind of crisis?"

"One that begins with your giving the fluid I just handed you to DARPA and attending the services at Washington National Cathedral tomorrow morning."

"And then?"

Vlad strode to the sofa, lowered himself onto the firm cushions, withdrew a folded piece of paper from the pocket inside his jacket, and handed it to the president.

"And then this," he said.

Johnson glanced at Karen, then took the instructions. Slowly opened the paper.

Vlad leaned back, crossed his legs, and waited for the man's response, already knowing that he would agree.

One way or the other, the world was about to change.

10

HOW CAN a person go from such a lofty air of security and gratefulness to the darkness of hell itself in the space of only one day? That was me as I lay in the dungeon below the Elyonite city after Vlad had awakened me in my cell, bound me, then killed my father with his poison. I knew death was a shadow, but that shadow was an abyss so deep I would have gladly given my life to be saved from it.

Follow the finger to the moon, daughter. Follow it until you can follow it no farther. When I'd first heard the voice before Vlad's coming, my heart had soared. I knew something was about to happen. Something that would free me from imprisonment—how else would I follow the moon?

But that something wasn't my freedom. It was the death of my father.

Guards came a few hours later, cut the ropes that bound me, and took away his body without letting me touch him, regardless of my pleas.

For hours I lay on my side, curled up tight, sobbing, begging to hear the comforting whisper that had guided me so many times before. But all I could hear was my own weeping.

Part of me wanted to dream so I would wake in the other world. Maybe I would find my father still alive there. Though I knew he wasn't.

Devastated, I slowly surrendered to sleep.

How long I was in that dreamless sleep before I heard the tender voice again, I don't know, but it came to me like a warm breeze over a frozen wasteland.

Follow the finger under the moon, precious daughter.

I was still asleep. And suddenly crying.

I'm precious? Tell me I'm precious again. Tell me my father's okay. Tell me we're safe.

Follow the finger under the moon, dear one. Follow it until you can follow it no farther.

I was being given the direction again. The one I'd guessed would take me to the next riddle. Which meant something else was going to happen. The last time I'd heard the voice . . .

The memory of Vlad appearing like a demon in the night with my father smothered me again, and I felt my tears flow, unrestricted now. My father was gone.

No, precious daughter.

The voice was hardly more than a whisper, but at those words the darkness of my dreamless sleep vanished in a blinding light. The next moment I found myself standing in the night desert, staring at a bright moon on the horizon.

But what took my breath away was my father, standing ten feet from me. He looked the same as I'd known him in Eden, but with a slight glow coming from his skin.

I blinked, unsure that I was there, in the desert. Unsure that this could be my father. I was only imagining it. I had to be. But it felt real—I could feel the gentle breeze stroking my cheeks and neck. I could see the moon.

I looked down at the ground, saw my bare feet in the sand. I was here. I had been set free? I was dressed in the same tattered tunic the Elyonites had given me to wear, still bruised and battered from my ordeal in the dungeon. This was me, in the flesh. Right?

I jerked my head up. I was here and my father was here, looking as surprised as I was! And the moon behind him had to be the moon I was to follow. Had I only dreamed he'd been killed? But how had I gotten here?

"Dad?"

He beamed like a young man who'd just returned from a long journey having found a great treasure.

"It's real," he said, lost in wonder.

A knot filled my throat. "I . . ." My voice cracked. "I thought you were dead."

He lifted his hands, turning them to look at his fingers in amazement. "But I'm not dead." He looked at me again, eyes bright. "It's real, Rachelle. I was wrong. It always *has* been real!"

I couldn't contain myself another second. I rushed up to him and threw my arms around him and held him tight with my cheek plastered against his shirt. "I was so afraid. I thought I'd lost you. I . . ." Emotion choked me.

He was chuckling, delighted, strong arms wrapped around my body, lifting me from the ground and spinning me around. "It's real! It's more real than you can possibly imagine."

Only then did it occur to me that he wasn't talking about us. I pulled back as he set me down, my hands gripping his shirt.

"You're not dead, right?"

"There *is* no death! It's only a shadow!" He looked around. "Death, suffering, darkness—they're only shadows that reveal contrast. They allow experience in the world of polarity. Without up you can't have down. Without darkness you can't experience light. Don't you see?"

I did, but I was still wondering if he was actually here, alive.

He gripped my shoulders. "I was foreknown!"

"Foreknown?"

"I was known and knew God before this life. It's like my whole life only lasted a few seconds. In some ways, my memory of it doesn't even feel real, not compared to this." He spread his arms, looking around again. "This . . . *this* is real!"

I followed his eyes, wondering if I was seeing what he was seeing. "What's real?"

"You are! I am! Life is, but not the way you think of it." He reached for my face and tenderly stroked my cheek. "You don't need to be afraid, sweetheart. Never again. It's okay. It's more than okay."

I immediately recalled my encounter with Justin when the serpent had blinded me. The light. *I am the light. Inchristi is me. Inchristi is in me.*

He gave me a nod. "You remember now?"

I blinked, unsure if we were thinking the same thing. And with that single blink, he was gone, and I thought, *Oh no, what happened? What did he mean that life is real but not the way I think of it?*

A loud clank cut through the silence and I jerked up, gasping, half expecting to see my father again.

"Dad?"

A form rushed toward me, muttering curses. I would have recognized him anywhere.

Jacob. Jacob, but where was my father? Had that been real?

He dropped to one knee, hand on my cheek, but I was still disoriented, caught up in what I'd just seen.

"By the fangs of Teeleh, what have they done to you? Are you okay?"

For a moment I just stared at him.

"Rachelle, I beg you . . ."

I threw my arms around him, unable to stifle a sob.

"Please forgive me," he whispered. "I would have come sooner but they've kept me chained. I'm so sorry."

Follow the finger, precious daughter.

I slowly pulled back, orienting myself. Jacob was dressed as an Elyonite guard with his own armor over their clothing so that he looked half Elyonite, half Horde.

He snatched a bundle from the floor and set it gently in my arms. "Dress quickly."

"I . . . I saw my father," I said.

This didn't seem to surprise him.

"He . . ." I started, but what could I say?

"I know. I'll explain on the way."

"You do? We're leaving?"

"Hurry."

I hurried, pushing away my questions. Adrenaline coursed through my veins as I scrambled to dress. Pants, tunic, riding boots. And as I dressed, courage filled me once again. My father was alive, just not the way I wanted him to be, but did I know what I really wanted? Either way, I was still the 49th Mystic and I had to find the moon.

Within a minute I looked like an Elyonite guard, however feminine. Jacob, on the other hand, looked and smelled like a Scab dressed in an Elyonite uniform. There was no hiding his face and dreadlocks.

He rushed to the wall and grabbed the torch he'd brought. "Stay close behind me."

"There's a better way," I said. "I lead. You follow."

He stared at me as I plucked the torch from his hand. "What are you doing?"

I smothered the flame against the wall, and the room was thrown into pitch darkness. "I have the gift of seeing in the dark, remember? Torches will only lead them to us. We find the darkest hallways, the blackest alleys, the places in which only the blind can see."

"It's safe, Aaron knows I'm here. But he doesn't know my loyalties."

"You're meant to free me?"

"Yes." He glanced down the corridor. "He believes I'll inform on you."

The connections fell into place. But Jacob wouldn't inform on me, because his loyalties were with me. They were because he loved me.

"Do all of his men know?" I asked. "We can't afford an arrow in the back. It's better to be safe."

I clicked with my tongue and the room came into my blind view—shapes and sizes. Part of me missed seeing in this way. Either way, seen with eyes or with sound, the world wasn't as we saw it through such limited senses. Eden had taught me that lesson well.

I took his hand in mine, filled with confidence. "Try not to trip."

"Where are we going?"

"To find the moon," I said.

THE MOON sat on the eastern horizon, beyond the great wall that circled the Elyonite city, kissing the top of a plateau that ran north and south as far as I could see. I saw it the moment we emerged from a sewer drain at the perimeter of the palace.

Heavy black clouds covered the sky above us, like a slate ceiling. Deep darkness enshrouded the city.

Two thousand years earlier in the world of my dreams there would have been streetlights, but in a land that had no electricity, flames illuminated only the main streets leading up to important buildings.

We ducked into an alley and ran east, me clicking when I needed to, Jacob close on my heels. *Follow the moon.* So I did, working my way east as best I could, keeping to the darkest route possible.

I knew by now there were at least four reasons Talya had allowed me to be taken by the Elyonites. The first was so they could see my power as one who could heal. The second was so I could encounter their ruler, Mosseum, and his son, Aaron, and deliver my warning as the 49th. The third was for my benefit—to be put in a situation that would allow me to surrender to the light.

The fourth was so I could learn to love the Horde through my encounter with Jacob.

It took us two hours to reach the city's eastern wall, make our way onto the roof of a tall building built into the wall, and drop twenty feet to safety beyond. From there, it was only a short run to the edge of the forest.

"And now?" he asked.

"I follow the moon, east."

"To where?"

"Until I can go no more," I said. "It's all I heard."

He eyed me, silent for a moment.

"This voice you hear. Elyon . . ."

"Yes." I turned my eyes to the distant moon, filled with the memory of my father's death. But he wasn't dead. He was intoxicated with love and joy, and I would never want him to be any other way.

But in this life his body was dead. A heavy fist of sorrow filled my chest and throat, and I closed my eyes.

"Then we follow the moon," he said.

"You came to take me captive—"

"No." He paused. "Not now."

"No? Does this mean you're turning your back on your own high priest?"

"I don't know what it means. I only know that life has delivered me here, to the side of a young woman who will change the world. I can't very well leave her to fight the wolves on her own, now can I?"

"You're trying to say that you love me." Not even I had anticipated those words spilling from my mouth so freely, and I quickly clarified. "Not as a woman as such. But you know . . . love."

He hesitated. "It's a warrior's privilege to honor his equal in battle," he said. "Between the two of us, not even a battalion of the wretches back there stand a chance."

"I doubt that's true. And that's not why you love me."

"What's not to love?" he asked, deflecting.

"My skin."

"Skin . . . Yes, there is that. Does mine bother you?"

"No," I said, and took his hand again. "Let's go. We have horses to find."

It took us another hour to find our way back to the farms we'd seen upon coming into Mosseum City. We took two horses from a barn. Finding two saddles proved to be more challenging, but once mounted, we left the city behind us at a full gallop.

The way was clear to me. The terrain rose gradually to the base of towering cliffs that supported a massive plateau. We'd lost sight of the moon as dark clouds gathered over the cliffs, but a single dip along the plateau marked its place. We rode for that dip, speaking only when we slowed to give our mounts a rest.

"You seem different," he said the first time we slowed.

"You think so? In what way?"

"You seem . . . more sure."

It was true and it wasn't true. I had the Third Seal. My father was dead. *Follow the finger to the moon.*

We let the horses walk longer.

"Something happened to you?"

I told him then. How I'd found the Third Seal in another world, how my father had crossed over and been killed by Vlad. How he'd come to me as I slept. All of it. Jacob listened with rapt attention. When I finished, he let out a long breath.

"This Vlad . . . He met with Aaron, Samuel, and myself. Your father was with him, in chains."

My heart leaped. "You saw him?"

"Yes. I too was in chains. It was Vlad's position that I should free you and return with the location of the Realm of Mystics."

"How did my father . . . Was he in pain?"

A short pause. "He was tired."

I didn't want to know more. The idea that he was gone but not gone . . . I couldn't process it properly. Could anyone? And there was still a chance he was alive in the other world, something I would know soon enough. Without the rhambutan fruit in my water, I would dream the next time I slept.

What would I awaken to?

"Vlad's there, in the other world," I said. "And I have no clue how I am or how much time's passed. What I do know is that he'll do anything to prevent me from finding the next two seals before he destroys the Realm of Mystics. We can't let them find it."

"We won't. How can we if you don't even know where it is?"

True, but I would, right? At some point.

"I have to find the Fourth Seal, Jacob. I feel totally lost. Time's running out!"

"So we follow the moon."

I nodded. "Yes. We follow the moon."

It was all we said for a while.

"This Yeshua from so long ago," Jacob said. "He actually lived? He's recorded in the Books of History?"

"He lived. He lives still. He is Justin."

We rode deep into the night, pushing the horses to their limit, putting distance on that place of death as much as being drawn by the moon. My destiny lay ahead, beyond the cliffs. The closer we came to them, the less interested I was in talk. Sensing my preoccupation, Jacob remained silent.

The gathering storm broke over our heads just as we reached the bottom of the cliffs. It was as if the skies themselves knew I was coming and had gathered in darkness to stop me. But nothing was going to stop me, not now. Never mind that we could see only a rising stone wall before us. Never mind that there seemed to be no way up the cliffs.

To the moon. Until you can follow no farther.

Jacob rode to the base and sharply reined his horse. "It's the end!" Lightning flashed and his horse whinnied. "There's nowhere to go from here."

Rain began to fall in sheets. I rode past him, studying the cliff. *Until you can follow no farther.* How literally was I to understand that direction?

There was a fissure in the cliff to our right, and I headed for it. Then urged the horse into the three-foot gap.

"It's too narrow! You'll never turn your mount around if it ends."

Concern edged into my mind, and I pulled up. He was right. A pile of fallen boulders ahead of me was impassable on horseback.

"Then we leave the horses," I said, leaping over my mount's head to land on the sand. The horse frantically backpedaled, then turned and galloped away as soon as it cleared the opening.

Jacob watched it go. Dropped from his mount and slapped its hide.

"Very well. Lead on."

I scrambled over the boulders and pushed on, following the narrow passage as it began to rise. It was dark and I had to click to see my way. Jacob came behind, breathing steadily.

"How far?"

"Until we can go no farther."

I expected the fissure to play out, because all do. But this one did not. Every time we came to what appeared to be an end, I would quickly find another way, up the side of a steep wall or over towering boulders. I doubted anyone had ever made it as far as we did, even a third of the distance up the cliff's inner passageways.

We were protected from the storm in that cliff, but the pounding of thunder punctuated with brilliant flashes of lightning made us all too wary of its fury.

For a full hour, scrambling over rock and crag, we climbed. And then we climbed what we were sure was the last short wall, fully exposed to the wind and torrential rains.

I shielded my eyes and peered ahead. The way was blocked by another jagged wall of stone at least fifty feet high.

I ran up to it, searching the face for anything that might give us a foothold. "Find a way!"

Unlike the rock we'd climbed, the surface here had been worn smooth by the elements. Even with ropes and tackle, the climb could hardly be made in such weather. Regardless, we had none. As far as I could see, north and south, there would be no scaling this cliff.

Until you can go no farther . . .

"There's no way up?" Jacob called.

"No. No, I don't think so."

"Then come! We stay here tonight."

I turned back. "Stay where? The storm—"

"In the cave! Hurry!"

The small opening he'd found was shrouded by mist and rain.

Jacob pulled me into the darkness, and I clicked to see that it extended ten feet before ending at a wall. I stood still, thoughts crashing through my head.

We could go no farther. But surely this wasn't it!

"It's the end," he said. "Unless you have wings, we go no farther in this weather."

He was right, of course. The floor was sand. Soft. But we had no fire and the wind brought a chill with it. We could retreat back down the cliff we'd just climbed, but that wasn't what I'd been told to do.

The cold cave would be our home for the night. Without the rhambutan, if and when I fell asleep, I would dream. I wasn't sure how I felt about that.

I heard a cracking sound and turned to see that Jacob was bent over a few sticks of wood. He reached into his dreadlocks, withdrew a small pouch, and took some pitch and a piece of flint from it.

"No Horde wanders far from home without pitch in his locks," he said, striking the flint. A single spark and the resin flared to life. "Whether dried horse dung, wood, or the clothing off a man's back, fuel can be found almost anywhere. But without pitch it's useless."

The small fire lit up the walls. Several dried-out shrubs withered along the smooth stone. Jacob sat on the sand and crossed his legs, satisfied.

"The fuel won't last long and it will grow cold, but even a small fire will lift the heart. Rest."

I sat across from him, gazing into the growing flames. Not so long ago I'd faced Talya across many fires, listening to his tales and watching the flames' reflection in his bright eyes. Where was he now? Finding Thomas. Why Thomas?

"You said you were with Samuel," I said, looking up at Jacob. "How was he?"

"He was Samuel. The impetuous one who is taken with you."

"Is that so?"

"It's impossible for him to hide."

"Well, that's good. I'm taken with him."

"You are?"

"Of course. And with Aaron. And with as many as I can be. Not the way you mean it, but they're all just lost. Isn't that why I'm here?"

"I suppose so."

I stared at the flames. "But there's something unique about Samuel, don't you think? I don't know . . . Maybe because he once saved me from you." I grinned.

Jacob did not.

"In all seriousness though, there's a quality in him that draws me. He's like a boy, full of wonder and unbridled passion. It's a part of humanity that I never noticed. Or at least can't remember."

"Ba'al's poison is a terrible thing to know," he said.

And then neither of us said anything for a while.

THREE times, Samuel had all but given up on following through a rain heavy enough to wash away the tracks of their horses. If not for the fact that his stallion was well trained in picking up the scent of Horde, if not for the favorable direction of the wind, he would have lost the trail.

All the way he cursed under his breath. The Leedhan was wrong, naturally—no offspring of Shataiki and Horde could possibly speak truth or deal in anything short of deception. It was in their blood.

Yes, he'd seen how favorable Rachelle had been toward Jacob during the trial and after, in Aaron's chambers. But she'd been as gentle with Aaron. They mistook her gentle nature for more.

The fact was, Rachelle, whom he'd rescued from the Horde, could not love any Horde as women loved men. To think of it bothered him.

What bothered him even more was that he cared so much whom she did or didn't love.

Why had he followed Jacob and Rachelle to the Great Divide in the first place?

Why had he surrendered himself to the Elyonites, knowing they held her?

Why had he remained as a guest of Aaron for a full week, after the man had given him permission to leave, unharmed?

Why had he betrayed his obsession with Rachelle to the Leedhan and Aaron?

But he knew why, and he gave himself clear answers for every question. He had followed Jacob because he'd vowed to protect all Albinos from the Horde. He'd surrendered himself to the Elyonites because such a vast body of Albinos was unknown to the Circle, and he would be the one to make this first contact for his father. He'd remained in the Elyonite city to save Rachelle, an innocent Albino. He'd betrayed his obsession with her to the Leedhan because the foul beast's eyes had confounded his mind.

He wasn't obsessed. Of course not. And the only reason he'd gone along with the plan to follow Jacob and Rachelle was because he had no intention of returning to Aaron with what he learned.

He was going to save Rachelle from Jacob. His mission was to keep her from falling into a trap.

These were the stories that occupied Samuel's mind as he pushed his mount toward the towering cliffs, close on their heels with rain and wind in his face.

He pulled up sharply half a mile from the cliffs when one of their mounts pounded past him, headed back toward the city. They'd abandoned their horses? But his own was still intent on the cliffs, aware of Horde scent.

Samuel gave the stallion his head and let him trot the last half mile to a fissure in the cliffs, the only conceivable passage up the rock surface. No sign of the second horse.

He dismounted, tied his mount to a shrub, and started a slow climb, careful not to catch them and be discovered. They could easily have taken refuge along the way. Not once did he hear them, which meant they were either well ahead of him or holed up.

He was forced to make his way slowly, silently cursing the cold and rain. So be it.

The rain had stopped and the clouds were gone by the time he finally reached the plateau to discover yet another lip ahead, rising fifty feet. Surely they couldn't have scaled the sheer face without tackle. Not here.

Moonlight cast the wide ledge in cold gray. He picked his way south through the rocks, crouching low. But the farther he went, the higher the lip rose. So he doubled back, past the fissure, and headed north.

He'd only gone fifty paces before he saw the dark hole. A cave. And from that cave, a thin haze.

Smoke. He was surprised he hadn't smelled it earlier. They were in the cave . . . Or was that a passage to the far side? No, a cave. If a passage, they wouldn't have stopped and built a fire. Then again, it had been raining when they'd reached the plateau. Maybe they'd decided to rest for the night.

The Leedhan seemed to think Rachelle would take Jacob to the Realm of Mystics, but she'd told him she had no memory of her past. Where was she going? Was she following some sixth sense, like a bird that knew its home?

Heart pounding, Samuel crept to the cliff, then edged his way to the mouth of the cave. Held his place for a few long, careful breaths.

A soft grunt from inside spiked his pulse. Then nothing. The beast in his sleep.

Samuel peered around the edge of the cave and let his eyes adjust to the deep shadow. He blinked.

There on the ground next to a burned-out fire lay the Horde's body. Jacob was on his side with his back to Samuel, lost to the world. But no sign of Rachelle. He could see the back wall, but no one else was in the cave. He'd abandoned her?

He wrapped his fingers around the butt of his blade, considering the option of ending the man's life now. Yes, his purpose was to follow them to this Realm of Rachelle's, but . . .

The beast shifted his leg, and doing so revealed another leg. A much thinner leg. Rachelle's leg. She was sleeping in Jacob's arms with her back to him.

Samuel pulled back, mind spinning for reason. Jacob offered warmth, yes, but she'd suffered through much colder nights. And with a Scab? How could she stomach the scent of his rotting flesh? Was she restrained? No.

She'd accepted his warmth willingly.

The Leedhan's claim whispered through his mind like a hissing snake. *She's falling in love with Jacob. And he with her.*

Samuel leaned back on the cliff face and swallowed deep, closing his eyes. Had he been so blind? If so . . . If in a confused state of shock due to Ba'al's poison Rachelle didn't know better than to fall in love with Horde, the state of the world itself would soon rescue her from that madness.

Jacob was Horde. All Horde were destined to suffer in this life and the next. It was in the defiled nature of Scabs to take advantage of all humans, including one as innocent and confused as Rachelle.

Ba'al had poisoned her in his Thrall.

Jacob defiled her by his presence.

Once again, Samuel considered taking the beast's life—cut his throat while he slept. But he knew this wouldn't go over well with Rachelle in her current state of mind. She was under the delusion that the fool had rescued her, oblivious to the fact that he intended to betray her.

No. Not now. He'd come this far for her; he would go as far as required to save her from Jacob. From her delusions. From all that would harm her in any way.

In the end, she would see the truth for what it was.

Samuel retreated, feeling ill.

11

A POUNDING on my door woke me and I jerked up, gasping.

I'd just dreamed!

"You okay, Rachelle?" Steve's voice penetrated the door. "We have to leave soon." It was Sunday. We were going to the early service, he'd said, not the later one like normal.

"Okay," I called.

But my mind was on that dream. I blinked. It was a little fuzzy and slipping quickly, because on my meds everything did. But for the first time in months, I'd dreamed. And in that dream, I knew who I was. I was the 49th Mystic and I lived in Other Earth, where Jacob had rescued me from the Elyonite dungeons. Vlad Smith had come there and killed my father. That's how he'd died.

He'd written Vlad back into this world.

My heart was pounding. So it was real!

"Coming!"

"I'll be in the rec room."

"Okay."

I flew out of bed and lurched for the bathroom, nearly stumbling because my thoughts were on the dream, not the floor. It was real, and so was what had happened in Eden. Maybe not all of it, but enough. Vlad was something . . . I couldn't remember the name . . . He'd come to stop me, just like I'd once believed.

I was the 49th Mystic, and I was searching for the Five Seals of Truth before the Realm of Mystics could be destroyed.

I stopped in front of the mirror and yanked up my sleeve. Three of those seals were now a part of me. If my dreams were real, then DARPA had lied to me. Even Steve!

If they hadn't prevented me from dreaming, I might have found a way to save my father.

A terrible bitterness settled over me as I stared into the mirror. My mind was fuzzy and I couldn't hold on to my thoughts for long, and that too was their fault. The details of the dream were already fading. If I only pretended to take my meds, that would clear up, right?

I reached for my blue toothbrush, squeezed on some toothpaste, turned on the water, and brushed my teeth, raging.

But then another thought hit me. Not taking the meds would only make my symptoms worse. My delusions would take over my life. All the work we'd done would be set back and . . .

I stopped and stared at the mirror, foamy toothbrush sticking from my mouth. No, that was the meds talking. I wasn't delusional at all, was I? If I was, it was being caused by the meds, not the dreams.

But within seconds, confusion pushed aside the certainty of that as well. In dreaming, my mind could easily have tripped back to what it thought was real in Eden. I was relapsing and dreaming of things that weren't real again.

Or maybe not. So which was it?

I rinsed out my mouth and splashed water on my face—no time for a shower, but I'd taken one last night. Dressing quickly, I made the one decision that made sense to me, regardless of what was really happening. I wouldn't tell them what happened, not even Steve. If I told them how upset I was, they'd only increase the meds.

Maybe that would be a good thing. Maybe not. But until I figured some things out, I'd just be who they'd made me to be.

The me whose father had died.

A deep sorrow overtook me as I finished getting ready. He'd come to me in my dreams, but that part was fuzzy to me now. I suddenly felt hollowed out, nearly dead myself.

I brushed my hair and applied some deodorant—getting ready for church never took long because I didn't use makeup. There was no one to impress. We always sat at the back of the church and slipped out early. Some of the regulars recognized me from all the media coverage following Eden's collapse, but Steve kept them at a distance.

I gave myself one last look in the mirror, took a deep breath, and headed out to the rec room.

Steve was at the door, keys in hand. "You good?"

"As good as can be expected, I suppose."

He opened the door and put his hand on my back, ushering me through. "Maybe church will help."

Maybe it would. I always loved the music and the reverence. Steve said the opportunity to recontextualize what had once hurt me was good therapy.

"See you soon," Mary called, sticking her head out of the cafeteria. "Eggs, bacon, and French toast for brunch."

"'Kay. See you, Mary."

And then we were gone, up the elevator to the ground level, into the parking garage, out into a dreary day. At least it wasn't raining.

We drove for a while in silence. Normally I was a talker, asking questions about how the car worked without input, why there were so many drones, what other countries were like—anything and everything, because the technology was quite different from what I'd known in Project Eden, and I found it fascinating. They'd kept us locked in a time bubble while the rest of the world advanced.

But this time it was Steve who broke the silence.

"So how'd you sleep last night?"

"Good."

"Good." But I heard more as I sometimes did. I heard, *Did she dream?* Before I thought to stop myself, I answered. "Yup."

"Yup, what?"

Oops. I'd decided not to tell Steve. But suddenly I was.

"I dreamed."

"I didn't ask you if you dreamed."

"Well, that's what my mind asked me, so, yes. I dreamed last night." I faced him. "I dreamed about Vlad and the other world. How's that possible?"

He set his hands on the steering wheel, which all cars still had as an option. "I don't know, likely buried memories. Tell me about it."

So I did. I talked the whole way, telling him everything, including how Vlad had poisoned my father and was back in this reality coming after me. My story came in bits and snatches because my memory of the dream kept going in and out. He didn't correct or suggest, he just listened like he always did. That's another reason I liked him.

By the time the car parked itself in the lot behind the church, I'd told him everything I could remember, wondering how much I'd forgotten or butchered with meds on board.

He faced me, one arm on the wheel. "Do *you* think that's how your father died?"

"I'll answer if you answer a question first."

"Fair enough."

"Were you going to ask me if I dreamed?"

He looked ahead, and I already heard an answer in my head.

"Yes," he said.

"So these thoughts I keep having . . . they're not all auditory hallucinations."

"Honestly, Rachelle, I don't know what's really happening. Or how. That's what we're trying to figure out."

"We or you?"

He hesitated. "I'm not sure. Me, at least, and I've got your back."

"You were going to ask, and I did hear that. So it's possible I can do that."

He nodded and let out a breath. "It's possible, yes. Actually, more than possible."

It was the first time he'd said that to me, and a dozen thoughts swirled through my mind. I was right: they'd forced him to mislead me. If about the voices, then what else?

"Thank you for being honest."

He nodded, concerned. "The dreams are another thing. Who knows, seems far-fetched to me. We'll talk more on the way home, okay? Just promise me you won't say anything back at the center."

"Promise."

We'd parked in a new garage at the back, so we didn't see all the extra security until we were around the side, in front of the massive towers that rose high over our heads. Steve stuck out his arm and stopped me.

"What's happening?" I asked.

"I don't know. Someone important. Just stay by my side."

"Maybe we should go."

He frowned at the commotion. Red ropes blocked off the main entry into the back of the sanctuary. "Maybe."

"Steve?"

We turned to the voice on our right. A woman with short dark hair had opened a side door.

"Steve Collingsworth?"

"That's me." Then under his breath to me, "She's the president's chief of staff, Karen Willis."

The woman stood to one side of the door, smiling. "This way."

"You know her?" I asked.

"Not personally, no."

He took my hand and led me toward her.

"Karen Willis," she said, holding out her hand, which Steve shook. "And you must be Rachelle."

I shook her hand without responding. I wasn't used to strangers.

"You'll forgive all the fuss, but the president's in attendance today. He can't meet you personally, you understand how it goes. He'll be leaving for another engagement before the end of the service."

I could see reporters with cameras through the hall behind her.

"He asked me to extend the country's respect for you and all the residents who braved Project Eden," Karen was saying to me. "He also asked me to pass on his condolences for the loss of your father. We're so sorry."

I looked up at her. They knew?

"They've roped off a section to the side for special guests." And then she was drawing us in, leading us down the hall and into the church.

That was strange enough. But even more so, the moment we entered the formal sanctuary, we were surrounded by cameras.

Steve pulled me back. "What's this?"

Karen turned on her heels. Now it was her with a ring of media people, and me with Steve, surrounded. "You don't mind, do you? We thought it would be appropriate to get a word from you." She winked at me. "You have a lot of fans out there, young lady. It's been a long time since anyone's heard from you."

"Out of the question," Steve snapped. "Rachelle's under strict protocols that prohibit—"

"It's all right, Steve. Theresa's given her consent." Karen held his eyes for a moment, then nodded at a blonde woman who held a microphone. "This is Cynthia Rupert for *World News*. Do you mind taking a question or two? Just a hi-and-bye kind of thing."

I glanced at Steve, who looked like he'd been caught flat-footed. The last thing I wanted to do was answer any questions. What was I supposed to say? That they've been lying to me about the voices in my head and my father just died, so leave me alone?

But then Cynthia was there, holding a microphone while a cameraman filmed.

I could see that half the auditorium was filled. Security was heavy at the back, where I guessed the president would be sitting. Which meant we wouldn't be sitting in our usual place. Bummer.

That's what I was thinking when Cynthia spoke.

"Hello, Rachelle." She smiled and her voice was warm.

"Hi."

"I understand religion was a big part of your experience in Eden. We're in a church today, though I'm guessing it's a lot fancier than the one you attended. What do you think of religion after going through what you have?"

It was the worst kind of question she could have asked. I was confused about religion, but saying that would sound dumb, wouldn't it? Heat from embarrassment rose up my neck.

"You don't have to answer," Steve said quietly.

I glanced at the arched ceiling, the huge stained-glass window over the entrance at the back. Like Eden, only in Eden's church the stained-glass circle was over the platform: Memories flooded my mind, and I was speaking before I had the good sense to think through my words.

"I think most religion preaches a form of false law, blinding people to who they actually are as the light," I said. "The law's a system of fear and control based on punishment, because fear has to do with punishment. It's like the sky in Eden. Something has to give or people will never be free to know who they really are."

They'd all gone silent, and I could tell by Cynthia's look that my answer had taken her off guard. I thought I'd spoken well, right? But on meds, my thoughts were never crystal clear. Maybe more explanation would help.

"Well, that's an interesting way to put it," the newswoman was saying. "Are you saying you disapprove of religion in general, or just the kind of religion you experienced in Eden?"

I don't disapprove, but I think it could do a better job of helping people see themselves the way the Father sees them, I wanted to say. But another thought interrupted me. A word.

StetNox. It was so loud and so strange that I blinked, losing track of the question. I looked at Karen Willis, who was staring at me. The word had come from her. And I heard more.

She's just given us more than we could have possibly hoped for.

"What's StetNox?" I asked, forgetting where I was.

She didn't react. She didn't even blink.

"I'm sorry, Rachelle. Maybe it's too early for an interview." Karen turned to the reporter. "Let's try another time, Cynthia. Bury this, will you?"

Cynthia nodded. The cameras winked out. Someone else tried to ask a question, but Karen shut the man down with a hard glance.

She shook our hands again, smiled, and told us to enjoy the service. She had to get back to the president. A man named Charles would show us to our seats.

I sat next to Steve, halfway down the long sanctuary, eyes fixed on the choir filing in as the organ played. "How'd I do?" I whispered.

"You did just fine," Steve said. "Although I'd refrain from mentioning anything about religion or politics in the future."

"I thought I said it well."

"You did." He patted my hand. "I'm not a religious man, and I don't know what you mean by the law, but—"

"It's a term from the Bible. The law of sin and death that the early church wanted to return to. And for the most part have, like a dog to its vomit. Christians will get it."

He stared at me. "You remember all that?"

I shrugged. "I guess so."

The choir stood in perfect order dressed in white robes, and their director led them in a hymn. The sounds of the organ and harmonizing voices filled the grand auditorium. I actually liked the liturgy of the Episcopal church—it was different enough from Eden to give me some distance.

The service continued with more songs, some readings, communion. President Calvin Johnson sat near the back, head down in reverence when I glanced back. Steve nudged me. Not appropriate.

But I couldn't resist casually glancing again as Reverend Galloway seemed to be wrapping up his teaching on the grace of the cross. This time when I looked, the president was gone. They must have slipped out during the choir's performance halfway through the sermon. They didn't usually sing during the sermon, but the song illustrated a point the pastor had just made. Or maybe they'd done it knowing the president had to leave. A song was always a good time to slip out.

My head was still turned and Steve was nudging me again when a thundering explosion at the front of the sanctuary shook the building.

119

I spun back, ducking. Dust billowed, sweeping toward us as part of the ceiling above the platform fell. Huge chunks of concrete slammed onto the stage. The huge wall behind the pulpit was gone. Screams filled the air.

I crouched in my seat, stunned, thinking of the choir and the reverend, who'd been on that platform. Bloodied bodies lay in the rubble. Someone had blown up the front of the church!

Steve was pulling me by the hand, practically dragging me to the aisle. He was following a man in a dark suit who was waving us to the same side door we'd entered through.

"This way! Hurry!"

I stumbled on a fist-sized hunk of debris but caught myself on a chair. Steve tugged me forward.

"Out, we have to get out!"

His panic made mine worse. I covered my nose and mouth with my arm, squinted so the dust wouldn't get in my eyes, and ran. The air in the hall was clear, but we didn't slow down. Not until we burst from the building.

I sprinted out onto the lawn and spun around. The whole front of the cathedral had caved in. People were still running from the main entrance, crying out. Somewhere far away, sirens were already blaring.

"In the car! I'll take her."

I turned to see that the dark-suited man was motioning me to a large black sedan. Steve grabbed my arm and turned to me.

"It's okay, Rachelle. That's Tom. He's DARPA security. They're always with us when we leave, just to be safe. Go with him. I'll be right behind in my car, okay? Just go."

So I went, sliding into the back seat of the black sedan, still wondering what had happened to the reverend, the choir members, visitors on the front rows. People had been killed! How many? More than twenty, I thought.

Maybe it wasn't a bomb. Maybe a furnace or something had blown up.

Within a minute we were winding our way through streets I'd never seen before. Tom was at the wheel, adjusting his course based on information he was getting over a headset. From what I could gather, he was avoiding blockades, which were already going up.

It was all surreal to me, the girl on meds in the back of a big black sedan, being raced to safety.

All I could think about were all the people who couldn't have survived such a huge blast.

Maybe someone had tried to kill me. But no, that was ridiculous. Who was I? This wasn't Eden, and even if it was, Vlad wasn't . . .

I caught myself. Vlad had forced my father to write him back into this world. What if this was tied to that? But that seemed absurd.

The president, then. Someone had tried to assassinate the president? But that was pretty far-fetched too, right?

Or was it?

The drive seemed shorter than usual even though we went the long way. Somewhere along the way, Steve's car had fallen back. Or maybe he'd gone a different route.

The moment the black sedan lurched to a stop in the underground parking structure, Tom was at my door, throwing it wide.

"This way, hurry!"

I clambered out and followed, running because he was running. Down the steps, not the elevator. We passed the rec room door walking fast and headed down the hall to the back of the center.

Only then did I think something might not be right, and I pulled up.

"Where are you taking me?"

Tom turned back. By the long look on his face I knew he didn't like whatever he was thinking. And then I heard his thoughts.

Poor girl . . .

Something sharp stung my neck and I cried out, grasping for it.

"Sorry, sweetheart," a voice whispered behind me. An arm wrapped around my waist. "Time to sleep."

Then I was falling from consciousness.

Into another world.

12

FOR THE FIRST time in many days, I had dreamed. I'd fallen asleep in the cave close to Jacob, who offered me warmth and comfort, and woke at DARPA as Rachelle, a mere shell of my former self. They'd fed me drugs for four months. I didn't know who I was anymore.

But this me in the cave, slowly emerging from that dream, had a clear mind, unaffected by DARPA's treatments. Physical effects and skills transferred between realities, but not state of mind, or I would have lost my memory here as well.

But there, it was worse than I could have imagined! I was completely lost, back in a kind of blindness, maybe even deeper than before.

I was reeling from the loss of my father, angry and desperate. Worse, totally naïve. Details filled my mind. My words at the church, the explosion, the frantic return to DARPA, where they'd stuck a needle in my neck.

Who had? I didn't know. What were they going to do to me? Who'd blown up the church? What was happening?

My eyes fluttered open, and the stone ceiling came into view. I was in Other Earth. We'd escaped from the Elyonite dungeons and followed the moon to this cave.

Follow the finger to the moon.

I jerked up and searched the cave. Light streamed in from the entrance, ten paces away. I twisted and saw that Jacob stood at the rear wall with his back to me.

Jacob, who'd saved me. Who was protecting me. Jacob, who was Horde, and who I maybe loved even though I didn't really know how to love a man in that way.

He turned. "You need to see this."

My dreams began to fade as my waking reality took over.

"What do you mean? What is it?"

"See for yourself."

I scrambled to my feet and hurried to the back wall as he stepped aside. The markings came into view.

"I could swear this wasn't here last night," he said.

"Or we missed it in the darkness."

"Regardless, the writing makes no sense."

I stepped closer.

What is seeing beyond
What you think should be?

"It's the fourth finger!" I whispered.

"Pointing to the Fourth Seal."

My heart was hammering. "Yes."

What is seeing beyond what you think should be?

Jacob reached for the wall and pushed with his hand. Nothing.

He faced me, speaking quickly. "What is seeing beyond what you think *should* be? I think this wall should be solid. It *should* be, but maybe it's not." A pause. "You try it."

I lifted my hand, and the moment my palm touched the cold stone surface, the entire wall began to shimmer with light.

I gasped and jerked my hand away as what had just been solid rock vanished, leaving a tunnel that reached a hundred feet through stone before opening to a bright sky. And under that sky, a wide, grassy ledge that abruptly ended at a cliff.

Jacob stood aghast. "Teeleh's breath . . ." He looked at me. "What did I tell you?"

I took his hand and started to walk. "Come on."

"Inside?"

"Until you can go no farther. So we go, because we can."

Déjà vu flooded my mind as we walked through that tunnel. I'd been here before? The sensation nearly swallowed me when we stepped into a shallow meadow, crossed the grass, and looked over the cliff to the vista below.

We'd come to a massive circular sinkhole carved into the high plateau. Cliffs ran the full perimeter, falling three hundred yards to a gnarled and twisted desert landscape at the bottom. In every other respect, its similarity to the sinkhole in Eden, Utah, left me breathless.

The meadow we stood on was a wide, fertile ledge that ran a third of the perimeter before petering out. A hundred paces to our right, a grove of pine trees rose around a small pond. A red pond.

"This is it?" I asked. "It's just an ugly hole in the ground."

"Not the Realm of Mystics, surely. What are you looking for?"

"I don't know. What am I looking for?"

"That's the question, isn't it?" a voice asked behind us. I spun around to the familiar timbre of Talya's voice. He stood, staff in hand, beside his pale steed, not twenty paces from us. His lion, Judah, stood at the top of the cliff above us, staring intently at a group of boulders north. "What are you looking for?" He stepped forward. "Or more pointedly, what are you seeing?"

My heart was in my throat, and I ran for him without thinking. The emotions of the past week crushed me, elevated me, screamed through me, and when I reached him I didn't slow. I threw my arms around his neck and clung to his body as if I were a young child and he my returning father.

Talya dropped his staff and wrapped me in his long arms. There were a thousand things I could have said, but none of them could have possibly expressed my experience since he'd left me to find myself at the Great Divide.

"Easy now." He chuckled. "This jar of clay is much older than yours, you know."

I released him, suddenly unsure if my response was inappropriate. What did I know of the Mystics' traditions?

"On the contrary, dear daughter," he said, sensing my thoughts, "you will soon see that you're only just beginning to behave in your true way." He kissed the top of my head and stood back, blushing.

"Sorry . . . I just . . ."

He reached for my sleeve and pulled it up. Saw the three bands of white, green, and black now a part of my flesh. Tears misted his eyes, and the fingers that held my tunic trembled, if only slightly.

"Good," he said, releasing my sleeve. "Very good. Tell me what they mean to you."

I searched my mind and put the seals in my own terms.

"The First Seal is white: Origin is Infinite. He is light and can't be threatened or disturbed because he's infinitely complete and all-knowing. Nothing can bother or compromise him or what he knows. He isn't subject to polarity."

Talya gave me a nod. "And?"

"The Second Seal is green: I am the Light of the World. Inchristi is me and in me." I stopped, recalling my encounter with Yeshua and Justin when the Elyonites had blinded me. "I saw him," I breathed, flooded with emotion. "I'm the light, made of his fabric. He told me I had the same glory he had. Like Justin, I can't be threatened or harmed. That's who I am, and I'm only temporarily in this earthen vessel, which is made of . . . dust. I'm *in* the world of polarity but not *of* it."

"And?"

I felt like a student who'd just received her doctorate at a very young age.

"The Third Seal is black: Seeing the Light in Darkness is my Journey. I'm here in this world, the valley of the shadow of death, to see who I really am as the light. Seeing is a new perspective of the mind. Metanoia. And what you see is the kingdom of heaven, which is everywhere."

He smiled. "Well done, 49th. You are learning through your own experience in the valley of shadows. Awakening to who you've always been is a beautiful journey."

"Yes." But part of me didn't think my journey had been that beautiful.

"You will when you find the Fourth and Fifth Seals." He cleared his throat. "You'll forgive me for allowing you to experience those shadows so deeply and so quickly. Life typically teaches us the futility of the law through years of suffering, but we don't have that kind of time. I had to . . . rush things somewhat."

"There's nothing to forgive." I lifted his hand and kissed his knuckles.

"I trust you'll thank me with as much grace in the coming days. The seals are easily forgotten until you have all five." He looked over my shoulder. "So this is Jacob, son of Qurong."

Jacob was staring up at Judah. Talya followed his eyes and clicked. The lion rose and leaped from the cliff, then quickly made his way down to the meadow.

I stepped out and dropped to one knee as Judah trotted toward me. Laughed when his large tongue licked the side of my face. Wrapped my arms around his huge head. "I missed you."

Talya nodded at his lion. "Greet our new friend, Judah." To Jacob: "Don't worry, he won't bite you."

The lion sauntered toward Jacob, who stepped back, unsure. Judah stopped five feet from him and looked back, just as uncertain, tongue hanging.

"Go on. Give the boy a hug."

Judah closed the distance between them, rose on his hind legs, and set his large paws on Jacob's shoulders. Had it been me, the lion's weight would have knocked me flat, but Jacob was as strong as Judah, and he held his ground, though clearly none too comfortably.

The lion licked him once, then dropped back down before returning to Talya's side, where he lay down, panting, staring off at those boulders again.

"You see, Jacob," Talya said, "the lion perceives no threat in you, Horde or not. But teach him differently and he would as likely tear off your head as give you a kiss."

"This was a kiss?" Jacob grinned wryly.

"From his perspective, yes." Talya picked up the staff he'd dropped and approached Jacob near the meadow's edge. "From another perspective, it might be called a lick. Which is it? What do words really mean? It all depends on perspective, doesn't it?"

Jacob glanced between us, then gave Talya a nod. "Indeed."

"Like your perspective of me," my teacher continued. "In one moment you might see me as an enemy. But in that same moment, seeing with different eyes, you might see me as a savior. Yes?"

"Yes."

Talya walked past Jacob and stopped at the edge of the sinkhole, gazing at the vast vista before him. "And what if I could teach you to see no threat? No anxiousness over the lack of food in the coming day, no fear of loss, no anger at having been struck on the cheek. How do you suppose you would experience life then, son of Qurong?"

Jacob and I stepped up to either side of Talya and followed his eyes to the gnarled landscape.

"I suppose it would be like a blissful haven. Impossible, of course."

"But if you *could* see the world in this way? Even for a moment?"

"It's not possible."

"But if you could, Scab! If you *could*."

Strong words for a strong man, but they were meant as much for me.

"Then I would have found peace without fear," Jacob said.

"You would be abiding in love," Talya said. "And in joy. These are the fruits of the tree of life rather than the tree of the knowledge of good and evil, which you cling to as a god of your own making. Judgment of yourself and others—I am naked, naked is bad, she is cruel, he is Horde—casts you out of the garden, blinded to the tree of life. Eating of the tree of the knowledge of good and evil, which is judgment rather than love, is the fall of mankind and the source of all suffering."

For a while Jacob only stared at the sinkhole, lost in thought, and I with him, recalling my own experience of seeing. When Jacob finally spoke, his voice had softened.

"Love without judgment isn't possible. But if it were—"

"It is possible," Talya said, and the authority in his voice seemed to shake the air. "In fact, it is crucial, as written by the ancient Mystic."[1]

"Who?"

"Paulus."

"Paulus." Jacob looked at me. "The Elyonites claim his writings to be heresy."

"Because it was he who wrote that any confession of belief, any loyalty to correct doctrine and knowledge, gains one nothing without a love that makes no account of wrong.[2] To make no record of wrong is to see the light in the darkness. The Elyonites don't know this kind of love. They can't imagine that without it, their drowning means nothing, so they call Paulus's teachings on the matter heresy. They do the same with his teaching that we're glorified beings."[3]

Jacob frowned.

"Tell him, 49th."

I glanced at Talya. His eyes remained fixed on the sinkhole.

"He speaks of seeing the way of Justin," I said. "Perception is the lamp that determines your experience of life in this body. If your perception is clear, you'll experience light and love, not darkness and fear. If your perception is unclear, you'll see a world of darkness and fear. Judgment is making record of wrong. The choice is ours: to release grievance and see light, or to judge and walk in darkness."[4]

Hearing myself say it, I realized that I was speaking more to myself than to Jacob. Was I seeing in this way? Only at times. I suddenly felt overwhelmed.

The Elyonites believed that Elyon did hold record of wrong and that Paulus's writing, which claimed love held no such record, was therefore heretical. Believing that Elyon held record of wrong, Elyonites also held record of wrong and called it love. But it was a false love that was weak and useless. What kind of love was I extending to myself and the world?

"Thus we come to the crux of the matter, son of Qurong," Talya said, speaking as much to me. "We journey through this life to see with a new mind rather than with the eyes of the earthen vessel, which are prone to see with judgment. Seeing with a new mind, we see the kingdom of heaven, now at hand and within. To believe in Inchristi is to hold no record of wrong. This is eternal life, which isn't a destination in some future, but a dimension now. Lift your eyes, change your perception, and you'll see that the kingdom of heaven is already here."[5]

"What of the next life?" I asked, thinking about all those sermons back in Eden. "And what about other people in the next life?"

"The next life will show you more than your human brain can possibly imagine. There is no language for it on Earth, only metaphors that have led many who don't understand metaphor back into the law."

He stepped closer to the cliff and looked down, holding himself steady with his staff. Then he turned back at me.

"As for the fate of others, this is their Father's business, not yours. Trust him. To say that he knows what he's doing is a vast understatement. Your path is to abide in the vine of love that holds no record of wrong."

I wasn't sure I knew how to do that.

"But you will know how," he said. "The question is, will you do it? Seeing with a new mind is your prerogative, chosen every moment during this life. So tell me, what mind are you seeing with right now, 49th?" He nodded at the huge sinkhole behind him. "Tell me what you see."

I looked. "A wasteland."

"Really? It's not what I see. You must be blind."

Jacob took a step forward and peered down. "You really mean to say that we're blind and don't know it?"

Talya dropped his staff and spit in the palm of one hand, ignoring Jacob.

"It's only a two-degree shift, daughter. Like a radio dial. You're tuned to a station that offers you the static of polarity. Adjust your tuning only two degrees, and you will find beautiful music. This is how you hear if you have ears to hear, and see what is otherwise unseen."

"A radio dial?" Jacob looked confused.

Talya's analogy struck a chord deep within me because I knew that the human brain could only pick up a fraction of what was in the air, both in sound and in vision. I held Talya's eyes, too caught up to give Jacob an explanation.

"Metanoia," I whispered. "Change your cognitive perception."[6]

"See with the mind of Christ."

"How do I turn the dial?"

"You surrender the old station of static in order to hear the new."

"Surrender?"

"Yes." He spit in his other hand. The air prickled my skin. "You let go of the old mind to see the kingdom of heaven with the new mind." He stepped up to us. "You have the power. But today, I offer a hand."

The breeze fell off. Silence settled over us.

He winked at Jacob. "Would you like to see what is unseen?"

"Yes," Jacob said without a second thought. And before I had a chance to speak, Talya reached for our faces and flattened his palms over our eyes.

"May Justin give sight to the blind."

A hot wind hit me full in the face, carrying on it the distant sound of children giggling. Talya's hand darkened my sight, but new sounds filled my ears. Falling water, like a distant downpour. Faint music . . . A high-pitched tone, pure and light.

I'd been here before! On the cliff when I'd first seen beyond this world.

The tone grew and expanded, as if angels were singing in long, unbroken notes that vibrated through my body. My bones resonated in perfect alignment, like a tuning fork that vibrated in perfect pitch.

A nearly irresistible urge to join in that song pulled at me like an ancient memory begging to be re-membered.

Talya's hand fell from my eyes, and a flash of light blinded me to one world and opened my eyes to another.

The sinkhole beneath us, only moments earlier a desolate wasteland, now brimmed with forests and green meadows sprinkled with brilliant patches of red and yellow and blue flowers. Once again I saw the village nestled at the center. Once more, the tall Thrall that was its prized jewel.

All of this I saw in a single glance. But again it was the color of the houses and the trees that pulled my focus. A colored forest, enchanted with wonder and beauty, the same one I'd seen the last time. A dozen large white birds soared through the air far below us. Not birds as such, though. Roush, like Gabil and Michal.

My eyes were drawn to the large waterfall on the far cliff, cascading down the sheer rock face like oil that shone in colored hues as the light reflected off its surface. At the bottom of that waterfall: a lake with a sandy white shore.

Even more than before, I knew I had been in those waters. I had come from this valley.

This was the Realm of Mystics!

Talya pressed his hands together and dipped his head at me. "Welcome home, dear daughter."

My body felt electrified.

Jacob was on his knees, staring aghast.

"If this amazes you," Talya said, "you should see the upper lake that feeds the waterfall."

"It's . . . It's been here all along?"

"Hidden to blind eyes," Talya said. "One day all may see it everywhere on this plane. A new millennium. For now, others can only see it when you're here."

WAKING FROM a dead sleep, Samuel of Hunter had rushed to the cave to find it vacant save the remains of their fire. Fearful that he'd allowed them to escape, he'd run along the cliff wall, searching for signs.

They wouldn't have gone back down the cliff—that would make no sense. Nor could they scale the wall here without tackle.

A tall tree half a mile north had been his salvation. He'd scaled its dead branches and made the precarious leap to the cliff's lip, only just managing a grip on the edge. Hauling himself up, he'd run back the way he'd come, scanning the large sinkhole beyond the cliffs. No sign of them. Nothing but this wasteland.

Maybe they hadn't gone over the cliff.

He was about to double back when he saw the lion looking down at a wide meadow above the sinkhole.

The old man's lion!

He ducked behind some boulders, heart pounding, then saw what the lion saw. The old wizard with Jacob and Rachelle, staring into the wasteland.

But that wasteland had now changed into a colored forest with a lake.

He blinked to clear his vision, but the sight remained fixed. They'd found the Realm of Mystics!

But how . . . how could this be, that something could appear as if by magic? It was sorcery of some kind. Witchery that drew him with its power.

The Horde beast was on his knees.

Confusion tore at Samuel's mind. That this was the Realm of Mystics was certain. That Mystics were indeed heretics who practiced sorcery, nearly as certain.

Why, then, was he so drawn to the sight?

Samuel settled to one knee behind the boulder and tried to understand.

13

JACOB WAS STILL on his knees, rocking now, muttering under his breath. Tears streamed down his cheeks. The sight divided my mind—half on the sight below me, half wondering at the undoing of such a powerful warrior as Jacob.

A person might look at him and think he was in pain, but I knew better. His mind and body just didn't know what to do with such a stunning and jarring reversal of perception. Talya had already told me how Paulus first saw the light. The experience left him blind for three days, then he went into an Arabian desert for many years, where he was caught up in seeing far more. Talya had known Paulus in that desert as a boy, a long story he would tell me one day.

"They know me?" I asked, staring at the village.

"They wait for you."

I could see tiny figures walking in the village now, and I wanted to rush down to meet those I'd known. "How do we get down?"

"We don't. Not now."

And then I understood.

He nodded. "As the 49th, you, my dear, are a thin place. As long as you're here, any Horde or Albino who comes will see what we see. Once they know where it is, they will bring their armies. If they destroy it before you have all five seals, all will be lost in this plane."

"But . . . I was here before, right? Why didn't anyone find it when I was here then?"

"You weren't the 49th until you came of age a few weeks ago while captive of the Horde. Before then, the Realm could only be seen by those who've awakened to their true identity. Mystics. The Leedhan knows you're the key to finding the Realm and has prepared. Even now, eyes see."

Leedhan—Vlad.

"Do you know what's happened to me in ancient Earth? They've made a mess of me. I can't remember who I am there, and Vlad's back. What if he gets to me before I find the seals? I don't even know what I'm doing there anymore!"

"Now you understand why he was sent."

My heart was pounding. "You have to help me find the last two seals!"

"Is that what you want, 49th? To know the Fourth and Fifth Seals?"

"I'm running out of time!"

"Is that what you really want? To awaken to that stunning power?"

"Yes. Of course, yes."

"Will you count the cost, 49th? Will you surrender all that you think you know for the Fourth Seal?"

Jacob suddenly staggered to his feet, staring at the village below, hands clenched into fists. Uttering a sob, he turned back the way we'd come.

"Jacob?"

Talya held up a hand to stop me.

Jacob lurched forward, then began to run, sobbing in great heaves. Veering to his left. Sprinting toward the grove at the far side of the meadow.

I was already moving. "Jacob!" Tearing across the meadow behind him. I wasn't sure what his intention was, what pushed him at such a breakneck pace.

"Jacob!"

He was halfway to the grove when he began to strip off his clothing, first his shirt, then his boots, then his pants, stumbling as he ran.

He was going to bathe in the cleansing pool.

I pulled up halfway, breathing hard. I knew I'd drowned, but I couldn't remember the experience. What if it didn't work for him? What if in his frenzied emotional state he only threw his life away? There had to be some protocol or teaching that went with it.

"Jacob, wait!" I began to run again, frantic. "Wait!"

He did not wait. Silent now, he ran like a world-class sprinter, head down, arms pumping, oblivious to all but the water. Hooves sounded on the ground behind me. Talya had mounted and was coming.

I was only thirty paces from the shimmering red waters when Jacob reached the shore, planted his right foot on a fallen log, and dove headlong into the air.

His hands parted the water and his body followed. Scarcely a splash disturbed the surface as the red pool swallowed Jacob, son of Qurong.

And then he was gone, into the depths of those red waters.

I slid to a stop on the shore, staring at the ripples that spread across the pond's surface.

My first thought was to dive in after him. But I didn't even know if I could swim. I spun back to Talya, who was dropping to the ground.

"He's gone in!"

"I can see that." He strode up to me, staff in one hand, a bundle of clothing in the other, eyes twinkling like stars.

"It's okay?"

"I suppose that depends on one's perspective."

"I mean . . . he'll live, right?"

"Of that there's no question. Assuming he drowns, that is. The waters will heal his body and invite him to see the kingdom of heaven as it is, within and at hand. Like all Albinos, however, he may continue to embrace judgment and grievance. If he does, that law will blind him once more to the true nature of love."

The water had stilled. No sign of life.

"How long does it take? What if he hit his head on the bottom? Are you sure he's okay?"

Talya was chuckling. "So many questions, 49th. These are things you once knew like you know how to breathe. It takes as long as he lingers in the beauty past death. And he didn't hit his head because the red pools have no bottom." He winked at me. "Would you like to join him?"

But I'd already drowned.

135

"True. And yet you walk in darkness most of the time. You cannot experience Justin and come away the same. Love awakens to replace the law, but the cares and concerns of the world often choke out that love. Fear smothers love. As you've seen, the Elyonites have reverted to the law of fear. We Mystics have taken a journey of abiding in true love. Jacob will chose his own journey."

Judah had sauntered up to the pool and was tentatively lapping at the water.

"He'll become a Mystic," I said. "I'm certain of it."

"You must always remember, 49th, even knowing the truth, you will remain powerless if you don't follow the way into that truth. You are re-learning what you have forgotten. The forgotten way. In that way, the first two seals are those simple truths of who the Father is and who you are, but they cannot save you in the storms of this life unless you follow the way of experiencing those truths yourself."

"And the other seals?"

"The Third and Fourth Seals are the way to experience the eternal dimension in this temporal life. As it is written, no one can experience the Father except Inchristi. We call the way 'seeing with new eyes.' Water walking. Being saved from fear in the storms of life."

"Salvation in the storm," I said. "Unless one is reborn he can't see the kingdom that's here. Yeshua taught this. But I already have the Third Seal: seeing. I can see who I am."

"Can you?"

Jacob was still under.

"Sometimes."

"To find salvation in the storms of this life, you will need the Fourth Seal. Each struggle that comes your way is simply an opportunity to experience who you truly are, or to remain in darkness. Think of each of those troubles as opportunities for salvation. You have many such opportunities ahead of you in both worlds."

The wonder I'd felt back at the cliff was nearly gone. The path ahead of me suddenly felt impossible. In the other world, I didn't even know who I was.

"And you will need to find the Fourth Seal there, in that other world. Discovering it will require far more than the first three. And then the end will come, because the Fifth Seal is immediately bound to the Fourth."

I faced him. "There? You don't understand—"

"But I do. And it will get worse. They are erasing your mind now, using Leedhan blood. It's why Vlad returned. When you next awaken there, you will know far less than what you know now."

I stepped back. "They . . . The MEP is going to work?"

"You won't have a clue who you are. Neither will you dream of this world, which means you'll be completely separate from each other." He arched his brow. "Didn't the shadow promise to blind you again and again?"

"Yes, but I defeated him in Eden when—"

"No," Talya interrupted, finger raised. "Justin did that a long time ago. Can a human defeat a shadow? Can you sweep a shadow from a room? No, you simply light the room and the shadow is gone. In the same way, you don't defeat the shadow; you awaken to who you are as the light. As you awaken, you will witness the light in which there is no darkness. To witness means to see. So see. Become a witness. You will show them Justin's way by witnessing the light in and as yourself."

It was all too much for me.

The pool's surface was like glass. Jacob had been under for several minutes.

"Meanwhile, here you should know that the Horde army is only a day's march from the Great Divide. The Circle has already gathered at the Marrudo plateau. The Eramites have agreed to join the Horde's campaign. A war unlike any seen gathers. All but a few despise the 49th and her Mystics. Jacob's drowning will make matters worse." He smiled.

"This isn't good news! Why is everything getting worse? It's too much . . ."

Talya turned to me and gently took my face in his large hands. "How else are you going to learn that bad news is only misperception, dear daughter?" His eyes searched mine. "Do you feel the fear?"

I swallowed. "Yes."

"Think of the shadow as an evil man. Do you feel that evil man coming against you?"

"Yes."

"As written, do not resist the evil man who comes against you.[1] In resisting, you only give the shadow authority by honoring it as a threat against you. Don't honor what has no true power except that which you give it."

He held my gaze.

"Do you feel the fear?"

"Yes."

"Do not resist. Enter that fear with love, which casts it out. Work out your salvation from the storm *through* that fear. It's the only way to finally see fear for what it is, a shadow."[2]

I felt like such a failure. The moment understanding came to me, it slipped from my grasp.

"No need to condemn yourself, daughter. Condemnation is only your earthen vessel's way of operating in polarity. Instead of condemnation, offer your earthen vessel love. A love that holds no record of wrong is the only form of resistance that casts out fear. Only then will it flee."

A calm settled over me in those warm hands.

"When Jacob rises, I will take both of you to meet the Horde. You'll understand why when we do. Yes?"

I nodded. "Okay."

He lowered his hands. "Tonight, you will dream. When you awake in the other world, you won't remember any of this. You'll operate only out of what you do know, as all do. In the end, you will be given a choice, and I believe the pupil I see before me will rise to her glory."

My eyes were misted, but those tears were now from gratitude, not sorrow. Talya was a master with me. I loved him.

He smiled. "You are doing well, daughter of Elyon. Justin's heart soars with pride. To the extent you can in this world, re-member. Always re-member."

I swallowed the knot in my throat.

The lake began to boil with light, bubbling up as if a fountain deep within had broken loose. Jacob's head broke the surface first. His eyes were closed as the water streamed over his face.

I watched in stunned fascination as what had died in the bowels of that pool came to life before me. His chest and his arms, bound in muscle, cleansed of the scabbing disease. His skin was bronzed, as new and as smooth as a child's.

The sight took my breath away. But more, the cry of elation that shattered the air as the fountain of water propelled him from the deep and summarily dropped his body facedown on the shore. His torso landed on the sand with his legs still submerged in the shallows.

Jacob did not rise. He did not look at us. He lay with his arms by his head, trembling in the ecstasy of his encounter with Justin.

And then he began to sob.

Talya dropped the clothing by Jacob's head and winked at me.

"Follow your heart," he said. "We ride in an hour."

I dropped to my knees beside Jacob's body and began to weep.

IT WAS THE drowning that broke Samuel. The sight of the beast running for the pool. Of him stripping naked to defile the air with his disease, then diving headlong into the red waters. He spat to one side, cursing, begging Elyon to take the life of this one infidel, regretting that he hadn't done it himself already.

All of this crossed his mind before he thought to ask himself why he was so disturbed. Wasn't the conversion of Horde to Albino the hope of the Circle? Wasn't this Justin's charge to them?

Samuel sat back against the boulder, listening to the distant, indistinguishable murmur of their voices, confused by his rage. The wizard had conspired against him, first by snatching Rachelle from his grasp, now by turning the enemy who'd slaughtered his bride into an Albino. Nothing would protect Rachelle from the beast now.

He caught himself again, aware of his obsession with her.

But no . . . This wasn't about his love for her. Yes, he was drawn, but there was far more at stake. The Leedhan had made the case plain.

The Horde were marching and would be joined by the Eramites. Albinos faced extermination. He'd come intent on rescuing Rachelle from Jacob, but what if his role was far more important than he'd imagined? Thomas had always warned him of his impetuous nature, rushing here and there in search of himself. Like a fox chasing its tail, he'd once said.

So here he was, far from home, a fool or a savior—which was it?

What if the Elyonites were right in their fear of the Mystics? Hadn't the magic he'd seen proven that? What if the prophecy was true, meaning the lamb would surrender to the lion Horde?

It would make the 49th the most dangerous human alive. And he the one who could stop her.

He stared at the horizon, lost in a stupor, grappling with conflicting thoughts, powerless to stop them.

When he heard the distant splash of water, he knew the beast had emerged and he couldn't bring himself to look. But he couldn't *not* look, so he peered around the boulder, hoping the Scab had failed to drown.

Jacob lay facedown, smooth skin glistening in the sunlight. And there, Rachelle kneeling by his side, weeping over him.

The deeper bitterness came then, like hot tar from deep in Samuel's bowels. He could feel it rising, feel it heating his face, feel it hardening his mind, and he felt powerless to do anything but surrender to it.

She'd made her choice. Samuel had found what he'd come for. The Realm of Mystics was here.

Aaron waited.

14

STEVE KNOCKED ONCE on the director's door, then turned the knob without waiting for a response. It was Sunday. Theresa rarely visited the White Center on Sundays, and yet they said she was in, meeting with Bill Hammond.

The door swung open and he took in the room with a single glance. The muted television on the wall was tuned to *World News*, flashing with chaotic images of the church bombing. Theresa was at the glass wall behind her desk, pacing. Bill sat in one of the two leather chairs facing her. They both turned as one.

For a moment, Steve tried to make sense of their blank stares.

"What's going on?" He stepped in, suppressing the outrage that heated his face. "You told me you wouldn't initiate another MEP attempt until Monday. It's Sunday."

"Good morning, Steve. You were there, you know exactly what's going on. I'm glad you made it out."

"That bombing has nothing to do with Rachelle or any decision to put her through the Memory Editing Protocol! If I didn't know better, I might be tempted to guess you never intended to wait until tomorrow. By the time I got here, Rachelle was already under and prepped for the procedure. So please, what's going on?"

Bill reached for a remote on the desk. The television's audio blared to life. Sirens, smoke, video of people running from the damaged cathedral. Cynthia, the same *World News* reporter who'd interviewed Rachelle, was in a small callout box, exchanging reports with the anchor desk in New York. All indications pointed to terrorists, but no claims of responsibility had surfaced yet. The president had left the church five minutes before the bomb went off and was now in a secure location. Had the target been the church or the president? The scene was a frantic mess.

"I know," Steve said, crossing the wood floor. "I was there. But again, this has nothing to do with Rachelle."

"On the contrary," Bill said, nodding at the television. "She was there."

"So was I. So were a lot of people."

"True. But they didn't say this." He pressed another button, and the images on the television rewound to a cutaway that had been aired earlier. Cynthia's brief interview with Rachelle. The camera was close on her face.

"I think most religion preaches a form of false law, blinding people to who they actually are as the light. The law's a system of fear and control based on punishment, because fear has to do with punishment. It's like the sky in Eden. Something has to give or people will never be free to know who they really are."

Bill paused the image.

Surely no one could think Rachelle had anything to do with the bomb.

Like toppling dominoes, other details fell in line. At first Steve refused to give them any significance.

"Rather abrasive comments, don't you think?" Bill asked.

"Yes, that was unfortunate and unplanned. They've taken her comment out of context. Either way, I don't see—"

"I received a call from Karen Willis an hour ago," Theresa cut in. "She said Rachelle divulged classified information she had no way of knowing." The director drilled him with a hard stare. "Not only did she read Karen's mind, she spoke that mind."

Steve threw up his hands. "She was expressing her struggle with religion. It has nothing to do with classified information!"

"I'm not talking about what was aired. I'm talking about what wasn't aired. A comment about a program called StetNox. Sound familiar?"

His mind spun back to the question Rachelle had asked Karen: *What's StetNox?*

"You're saying Karen Willis ordered this MEP?"

The director turned to the glass wall and stared at the view of the city, cautious. When she spoke, her voice was tight, quiet.

"I'm saying I was given no alternative."

"I don't think you appreciate just how dangerous Rachelle is," Bill said.

Steve shivered. *It's a setup. They're going to pin this on Rachelle.* The whole thing was a setup, not by DARPA but by someone else who feared far more than a bloodied nose from a girl saying inappropriate things. And he knew only too well that with the right spin, even the most absurd story could be made to sound perfectly reasonable.

Rachelle had been attending the cathedral for months now, at Theresa's suggestion. They could say that Rachelle's experience in Eden gave her ample motivation to hate religion. They wanted her to be filmed at the church, seated well out of danger. They'd fished for her views on religion, already knowing how she felt. They'd known when the bomb would detonate and what the damage would be.

And who were *they*? Vlad Smith?

He could be wrong, but it all fit into a frame that explained how and why they'd treated Rachelle as they had this whole time.

The only thing that didn't fit was the MEP. Why attempt yet one more brain wipe now, immediately following the church blast? What did Theresa and Bill know?

Steve took a deep breath and sat heavily in one of the leather chairs, eyes on the television's frozen image of Rachelle. He couldn't betray his suspicions, but he had to know more.

"Okay, so let's say the new MEP works. Her motor memory remains but she loses her historical memory, and with it, you hope, her psychic abilities. No more reading of minds."

Theresa nodded. "She opened the wrong can of worms this time."

But it had to be more than that.

"And if the MEP fails?" he asked.

"We cross that bridge if and when we get to it."

Steve barely heard her. His mind was on Vlad. More precisely, what Rachelle had told him about how Vlad first poisoned David in the dream, then returned to this world to go after her.

Fact: Vlad Smith had penetrated Project Eden and was still at large.

Fact: While in Eden, his primary focus had been Rachelle.

Fact: In her confrontations with Vlad, Rachelle had regained her sight and found a way to vaporize the canopy over Eden.

Fact: David had died in his sleep while dreaming of the other world.

Fact: Rachelle had dreamed last night and awakened with details of that death.

Fact: Rachelle could read minds and make water boil from across the room. She was arguably the most valuable subject science had ever encountered. But rather than work with her, the powers that be insisted on wiping her mind.

Why? Because Vlad was pulling the strings and he wasn't done with Rachelle. At least that's how Steve was seeing it.

"Tell me again about the variance between this new MEP and the MEP from last week," he said.

The answer was belated, from Bill. "The team is testing a new agent, still classified."

"So now she's a guinea pig?"

"Hasn't she always been?"

Steve ignored the comment. If he did nothing, Rachelle would continue to be at their mercy. Knowing what he did now, he could no longer sit by.

"How long will the new protocol take?"

"Two hours. Another hour before she's awake."

Steve nodded. "Okay."

The director studied him. Exchanged a glance with Bill Hammond. "This isn't going to be a problem, is it, Steve?"

"My only concern is that she be treated as humanely as possible. She just lost her—"

"Her father, I know. In two hours she won't have any memory of her father. It's the most humane thing we can do for her."

"Maybe. Assuming it works. Either way, I want to be the first face she sees."

"Of course." Theresa offered him a tired smile. "I know how close the two of you are. It's the least you can do."

No, it's not, Steve thought. *Not even close.*

15

I COULD NOT LIE—I loved Jacob with smooth skin, cleansed of the scabbing disease. In spite of Talya's insistence that our bodies were only our earthen vessels, I found myself captivated by the change of his body. I did not resist the temptation to touch his skin. Even Judah, the lion, took an interest in the changes to his new friend, perhaps because the old smell was gone, replaced by the scent of fresh skin.

I laid my cheek on his back as he lay on the grass, and I draped my arm over him when he rolled over, laughing with delight. And when he stood, I threw my arms around his neck and held him tight, afraid to let go. Maybe I thought he might revert. Maybe I just wanted to be close to him, because I'd never felt so attracted to any man as I was to Jacob.

It was as if a thin layer of gray mud had been washed from his body to reveal strapping muscles, which now clearly defined his broad chest, his arms, his belly, his thighs. He still had his dreadlocks, but even they were washed clean of any odor. And his eyes . . . Dear Elyon, how his eyes shone, green now rather than gray.

I felt like a woman next to him, holding his face and looking into his gaze, tracing his shoulders with my fingers, lifting his hair and smelling the sweet scent of . . . I couldn't say what the scent was. Just clean. Maybe the smell of spring.

His personality was the same as before, naturally—he was still Jacob in every way. But his spirit was soaring, and I with it. He tried to explain what had happened deep in the water, but he kept stumbling over his words because there were no words.

"Love!" he cried, spinning on the meadow with arms stretched wide. "More love than I imagined a heart could feel."

"And colors?" I asked, side-skipping around him. "Did you see the light?"

"Colors and light and the sky and the sun!" He grabbed my arms and we spun round. "The kind of light I see in your eyes now."

We laughed.

"Justin! Did you see him?"

He pulled up, thinking. "I don't know. I heard him. I felt his love. But I didn't see a man."

Talya chuckled, and we turned to where he sat cross-legged under a leafy tree heavy with red fruit, picking at a splinter in his foot.

"What is it, old man?" Jacob said. "Tell me what I saw."

"Do you think Justin is still in an earthen vessel? He can appear as he wishes to whomever he wishes and to as many as he likes without the restrictions of space or time. And he has, millions of times throughout history."

"So I did see him?"

"Of course. More importantly, you feel him now. You are one with him." He lifted the splinter, now free of his foot. Flicked it into the grass and looked at Jacob. "It's called the first love, a foretaste of what you may know."

"And this?" I asked, slipping my arm through Jacob's. "What is this called?"

"I would say this is mostly one earthen vessel clinging to another in delight." He winked at me. "A wonderful sight to behold. Enjoy it while you can."

He'd told me he was going to take us to meet the Horde. Then what, I didn't know, but I fully embraced his permission to enjoy my time with Jacob while I could. We talked and we laughed and we danced, and the lion joined us like a dog at play, rushing this way and that.

Talya said we would leave the high ledge overlooking the Realm of Mystics within the hour, but two passed before he led us to a brown stallion and a black mare he'd tied to a tree beyond the pool. The way down the southern cliffs was long and treacherous on horseback, but neither Jacob nor Talya seemed to notice any difficulty, so I let my mare have its head and follow their mounts.

That being said, I felt much more at ease when we finally reached the base of the plateau and headed southwest. We would take the southern route over the Great Divide and reach the Horde encampment from the southeast in the morning.

As the day passed, the wonder of Jacob's drowning slowly faded, dimmed by my concern of what awaited us both.

"Talya?"

We rode through the grasses of the plains, three abreast with me in the middle. He turned his face, and in his eyes I saw a depth of wisdom and knowledge that I had only begun to know. It made me wonder what stood between me and his wisdom.

"What will happen to us? When we find the Horde?"

He looked ahead. "You will know tomorrow. Today, enjoy the banquet of love you've found."

Jacob, who hadn't breathed a word about what he might expect among the Horde, seemed to have caught my concern like a contagious disease. "My father's there?"

"Qurong is the supreme commander of all Horde. They are all there."

"I can't imagine what he will say."

"Then don't," Talya said. "Being anxious for tomorrow will only cast you out of the garden today."

Jacob nodded and looked around, breathing deep. For half a minute we rode in silence, a stillness that Jacob shattered when he impulsively stood in his stirrups, threw his arms wide, lifted his chin, and thundered for all living things to hear.

"Life!"

A dozen birds fluttered from the grass and took to the air.

"Love!"

I couldn't help but laugh with delight.

"Attaboy." Talya chuckled.

We made camp in a small ravine on the Divide far south of the main crossing. As I had seen him do many times before, Talya retreated to a high ledge, where he bowed to the heavens before standing and swaying to unheard music. To that radio station I couldn't pick up yet. Soon, he was singing a high tone.

"What's he doing?" Jacob asked.

"Aligning," I said, mesmerized yet again.

"Aligning to what?"

"To Inchristi."

"Who is she?"

"She isn't a she or a he. Inchristi is the light of the world."

He didn't seem to know what to make of that.

"Have you met this Inchristi?"

"Yes. I am Inchristi." Saying it, I felt some of Talya's wisdom. "So are you."

Finishing his practice, Talya wandered behind some boulders and returned with a rabbit no more than a minute later. He started the fire by breathing on the wood I'd gathered, a feat that left Jacob terribly impressed.

We slept close that night, lost in the newness of whatever love had consumed us, both in spirit and in earthen vessel.

As we slept, I dreamed. In that dream I was asleep, not in the way I thought of sleep, but in a kind of coma, being drained of memory as if someone had pulled the plug at the bottom of my brain.

It was almost as if I could watch my memories leaving me. Memories of my father's death, memories of going to a church that blew up, memories of Steve, my only true advocate in that place. All of it, leaking out of me, replaced by empty space.

My hard drive is being deleted, I thought. *Oh no! How will I know how to brush my teeth?* But that wasn't the memory that was being wiped. It was the story of my history that was going, going, and then gone.

I was becoming a nobody on Earth. Talya had warned me, but sensing those memories slip away, I felt hopeless.

When I woke, Jacob and Talya were already saddling the horses. No fire, no food but some fruit Talya had collected near the pool. I scrambled to my feet and caught a red plum Talya tossed at me.

"We leave now."

The heavy fog from my dream pressed into me. "Talya?"

"Later, daughter. Later."

Jacob approached me, smiling. "The old man's in a mood." He winked. "Places to go, worlds to conquer, you know the drill." He took me in his arms and held me for a moment. "We surrender, Rachelle. Life is too short to fight."

I assumed that was something Talya had told him, which meant it was also for me, although I wasn't entirely sure what he meant.

Beaming like a boy, Jacob pulled away and showed me his arm. "Have I showed you my skin recently? It's as smooth as a child's. Touch it!"

I took his hand and kissed his forearm. "You're too beautiful for mortal eyes."

"And you, my dear." Jacob kissed my forehead. "And you."

"Exchange your pleasantries on the way," Talya said. "Qurong's army awaits."

IT TOOK US most of the day to reach the high place overlooking the Miggdon valley, west of the Great Divide. We sat on our mounts staring down a long grassy slope that ended in the desert. There, on white sands, the Horde army spread over miles of land that butted up against forests to the north and a large muddy lake to the south.

No tents but the large one at the center of the camp. As far as I could see, there were as many horses as men. Maybe more, some on the slopes feeding, most near the water. I'd never seen such a gathering of flesh and beast. Their stench was on the wind, faint but distinct at this distance.

Judah the lion trotted up to us from the north. Where he'd been, I had no idea, but he looked unconcerned. Maybe in going ahead he'd led us around Horde or Elyonite scouts, which was why we hadn't seen any.

Jacob stared at the valley, eyes wide, jaw set.

"What do you see, son of Qurong?" Talya asked.

"They've come. All of them. Six hundred thousand, at least."

"At least. To be joined by three hundred thousand Eramites by morning."

"You're sure? They came to agreement so quickly?"

Talya didn't need to respond. Of course he was sure.

"The Elyonites know?" Jacob asked.

"Aaron is prepared. The two Throaters Qurong sent to demand your release were returned dead this morning, necks cut. And so you see, Jacob, the die is cast."

"It'll be a bloodbath for both Albino and Horde! I have to talk some sense into him."

"Of course, you must try. But you can't reach him without me. His warriors won't recognize you." He paused. "The 49th might have the power—anyone else would be cut down by an eager blade long before they reach Qurong."

I doubted I had whatever power he was talking about. But I had shown power when I spoke plainly to Mosseum in the Elyonites' court. I was struck by how quickly that confidence had slipped away from me.

So what had I gained?

"Then you'll take me to him," Jacob said. "I have to speak to him."

"Of course. I only have one condition."

"For the man who opened my eyes to wonder and starts a fire with his breath, I would cross a hundred deserts."

"Good, because it might come to that," Talya said.

A beat passed.

"So?" Jacob said. "What's your condition?"

Talya turned to him. "If your father refuses to soften his heart, you will return to your home alone, win the confidence of your mother, and bring her here, to the Miggdon valley."

Alone? The thought of Jacob leaving filled me with dread.

The idea sat no better with him. "Here? To what end?"

"To the end of this age." Talya paused as his words sank in. "Trust me."

"Hold on," I said, searching for reason. "Are you sure?"

"You will take another path with me, 49th. One that begins when we reach the first of these Scabs."

"Yes, but after what Jacob and I have gone through, do we really have to be separated? I'm just beginning to—"

"Who are you?" he interrupted.

I said the first thing that came to mind. "The 49th Mystic."

His brow arched and I saw my mistake immediately.

"I'm the light, an aspect of the Creator manifested in this earthen vessel for a short time. My journey is to see who I am as Inchristi."

"And by what names do you know yourself in this earthen vessel?"

I spun through the experiences I'd had in finding the first three seals. Peace settled over me and my confidence soared.

"I go by the names woman, human, Rachelle, Albino."

"And?"

What else? There were so many.

"Intelligent, the dreamer of another world, daughter, the 49th Mystic, victim, white . . ."

"Among a thousand others," he said. "These are the masks you wear in this life, yes?"

"Yes."

"These names are what you put your faith in as you walk the earth. If they are taken from you, your earthen vessel feels threatened."

"Yes. But I don't put my faith in them. Not like I used to."

"No, because your journey is to see who you are without the masks, isn't that right?"

I knew he was setting me up, but I wasn't sure how. The clue to the Fourth Seal filled my mind. *What is seeing beyond what you think should be?* What were the things I thought *should* be? I was supposed to be intelligent. I should be good. I should be respected. Was that it? If so, what was seeing beyond that?

"Isn't that right, 49th?" Talya repeated, pulling me out of my thoughts.

"Yes. Yes, that's right."

"So then, are you willing to be seen without the masks you wear?"

Was I? Of course I was.

"Yes."

"Splendid."

Judah rose and trotted forward without a word from Talya.

"Then it's time for Qurong to meet his Albino son and the 49th Mystic. We ride in silence. Not a word before we reach him, no matter what happens. Agreed?"

"Agreed," I said.

Jacob nodded.

Judah led us, staying only several horse lengths ahead, followed by Talya, then Jacob and me. My heart beat with anticipation and confidence. Anyone who could literally walk on water was one who couldn't be threatened by any Horde, any Shataiki, any human, no matter the size of their blade or the sharpness of their tongue.

The stench of Horde grew stronger with each step. We were descending into the valley of the shadow of death, the disease of humanity, the blindness that brought fear. But we were the light.

I glanced at Jacob a dozen times, curious to see how he, an Albino now, was affected by his return to the Horde. Here rode the greatest of all warriors, son of Qurong, slayer of Albino. Now stripped of the scabbing that marked them all.

Defiled in their eyes.

He returned my looks with nods of assurance, but less frequently as we crested a small rise and found ourselves fewer than fifty paces from the first group of Scab Throaters.

They'd mounted and faced us, a hundred abreast, having seen our approach a long way off. Their eyes were on the lion as much as on us.

Still Judah sauntered forward.

Still Talya rode without concern.

Still we followed, two servants surrendered to the leading of our master, though I saw the sweat on Jacob's forehead now.

We were within twenty paces before three heavily armored warriors Jacob's size and larger nudged their mounts forward. Immediately the others withdrew their weapons. The sound of metal clanged through the air—broadswords, battle axes, skull hammers, sickles.

Neither Judah nor Talya slowed.

The three leading Scabs flipped bows from their backs, slung arrows, and drew on Judah.

"Halt!"

Talya did not halt.

"Halt or the beast dies!"

I thought Talya would say something then, but he didn't. In answer to his silence, the leading Scab released an arrow aimed directly at Judah's head. I saw it leave the bow, heard the twang of the bowstring and the whistle of the razor edge cutting through the desert air. My heart forgot to beat.

Only then did Talya react, and only with a casual flip of his right hand. The arrow stopped midair halfway to its intended target, hung still for a beat, then fell to the sand.

Two more arrows followed in rapid succession. Both fell to the sand like useless twigs.

"Dear Elyon," Jacob muttered.

Talya lifted his arm as if commanding the air they breathed. Immediately the Scabs lowered their weapons, stunned and confused. Their horses backed up, whinnying, then parted to make a path through the ranks.

"Do you believe in the name of Justin, 49th?"

I was overwhelmed by the show of power. "Yes," I whispered.

"So then you won't mind letting go of your other names."

We were abreast of the first warriors now, all staring with round eyes as first Judah then we three Albinos passed through them. Not a soul spoke. Only the heavy steps of our mounts could be heard.

I was so enraptured with the sight that I hardly heard Talya's last comment. The putrid stench of this sea of Horde was so heavy in my nostrils now that I could barely breathe. The sounds of six hundred thousand warriors filled the air like a low murmur, but as we moved toward the second group, they too went silent and made a way as if pushed aside by an unseen shield.

And then we were in the thick of the army, surrounded by campfires and loitering warriors and horses and steaming pots. Without exception, the Scabs grew quiet and stared as we approached then passed.

I could not have been more honored to be an Albino in the service of Talya, riding next to Jacob. Jacob, whom I loved. What a grand statement we were making with such a triumphal entry.

That's when I faced Jacob, soaring in pride. That's when his expression of wonder turned to shock. That's when I followed his stare and glanced down at my arms.

My skin had changed.

I gasped, horrified. My smooth, pale skin was gone, replaced by the flaking, gray scabbing disease! And I knew it wasn't only in my mind's eye, because Jacob saw it as clearly. Even more, I could feel it, like a million ants on my skin.

I yelped and swatted at my arm, which only intensified the discomfort. "Talya!"

"Not now, 49th."

"But I have—"

"A new mask, I know. Only an opportunity for salvation in the storm."

"But—"

"Not a word!"

His saying "mask" prompted me to reach for my face, and I felt the rough skin there as well. My cheeks, my lips . . . The stench was so strong because I was now wearing it as my own skin, in my own nostrils, on my own eyes. Were my eyes also gray?

I knew they were.

Talya had turned me into a Scab. I'd said I was willing to let go of my masks . . . but this? I knew it was an object lesson, but none of that softened my horror.

It was one thing for Jacob to have been Horde, but me? Wasn't being Albino at least part of the whole point of drowning? So how could Talya strip me of that healing?

In my panic I wanted to demand answers. I didn't care that this was an opportunity to find salvation, I only wanted him to reverse what he'd done.

But we were surrounded by the Horde, riding through them uncontested, like Moses passing through the Red Sea. We were all of that, but my eyes were on my trembling scabbed hands holding the reins. My cracked knuckles. My gray fingernails.

I hardly noticed the Scabs we passed now. I only saw me. And I hated me.

Judah sauntered forward. Talya led us. We followed him through thousands of silent warriors muted by Talya's power. But my pride was gone.

I realized that I was failing Talya's test by hating my skin. Having found the first three seals, I should know better than to be so affected by the onset of the scabbing disease, right? But I still hated it. Then I began to condemn myself for hating myself when I should know better, which only deepened my self-loathing.

What is seeing beyond what you think should be, dear daughter?

Tears filled my eyes. I felt like a victim, abused by a condition I'd neither asked for nor deserved.

I dared not look at Jacob, not after telling him how beautiful his new skin looked. But I had to, so I did. He offered me a smile, but I saw pity and confusion in his eyes. I'm sure he meant well, but in that pity, I felt only rejection. If I were him I would pity me too. I *did* pity me.

A hot tear slipped down my cheek, and then I hated myself for crying as I rode through the Horde like a prisoner led by two Albinos. I had already failed. And what if the disease was permanent? Maybe this was what was supposed to happen to the 49th Mystic.

Talya didn't even look my way. I think a small part of me hated him in that moment.

I was so wrapped up in trying to adjust my thinking and judging myself for not being able to that I hardly noticed we'd reached the center of the Horde camp. Qurong waited outside a huge canvas tent, dressed in white tunic, battle pants, and tall riding boots. With him stood five fully armored commanders and a scrawny man wearing black robes.

The lion stopped and sat on his haunches, tongue lolling, ten paces from the supreme commander, whose eyes were locked on him. Behind

us, a thousand warriors closed ranks, sealing us in. We faced the Horde command, smothered by silence.

Qurong was the first to speak, arms crossed. "Unless you come with news of my son, Jacob, I will return you in the same condition you returned my men." Meaning dead.

"I don't think you understand," Talya said, voice gentle. "We don't come from the Elyonites."

"Then who?"

Beside Qurong, the robed one was trembling. "Sorcerer," he hissed, spitting to one side.

"No, not that either. We are Mystics, outcasts and heretics among all Albinos. You may call me Talya. The woman to my right is the 49th Mystic, who brings this great crisis to divide truth from shadow. Beside her rides Jacob, son of Qurong."

For the moment, I forgot I was a Scab. Qurong's eyes shot to Jacob and he stared. Recognition dawned and he slowly lowered his arms.

"This can't be . . ."

Jacob slipped off his horse and rushed forward. "It's me, Father! I'm safe. It's not what you think, I swear it isn't—"

"Away!" Qurong roared, drawing back. "This isn't possible! What kind of trick is this?"

"Father." Jacob sank to one knee. "I beg you, listen to him. Ask the men and they'll explain his power. You must stop this madness. War will only turn this valley to blood!"

"I bring the war to save my own flesh and blood!" Qurong thundered. He was still struggling to believe. "What sorcery is this? Tell me what you've done with him!"

"I *am* him! I drowned and was healed of the disease. And more, I saw Justin. I experienced a new love just like my sister Chelise, your daughter, did. Everything they say is true, and I kneel here before you to prove it. You must not wage war on the Albinos, I beg you."

"It's true!" the robed one cried, stepping back. "The prophecy is as I, Ba'al, servant of Teeleh, swore it to be. The lion has surrendered to the

lamb, seen here as the firstfruits. The son of Qurong has surrendered to the Albino and intends to lead all Horde into damnation!"

This was Ba'al. The one who'd first poisoned me. Did he recognize my face?

"It's a lie," Jacob said, rising to his feet. "The prophecy speaks of peace for all, not suffering."

"And yet you come in heresy and deception." Ba'al lifted a crooked finger to me. "She's the 49th turned into Horde to blind us to her deception! I see her face now, from the pit of hell itself. By sorcery and the twisting of minds she's blinded the son of Qurong as only a sorcerer can."

"Don't be ridiculous," I said.

My words stopped them all. So I said more.

"It's true, I am the 49th Mystic, but I didn't deceive Jacob. I love him. I loved him while he was still Horde."

"And now you seek to deceive us!" Ba'al cried. "You come to trick us with clever words." He spun to Qurong, who stared unblinking at Jacob. "The Elyonites have sent you your son, diseased and lost to us forever. We must prevail, or this"—he stabbed his finger at Jacob—"this will be the fate of all Horde!"

"No!" Jacob snapped. "Do I look diseased to you?"

"See there," Ba'al returned. "The disease has blinded his mind as well. He doesn't even know he's diseased. We must take the 49th and force her to betray all Mystics, all Albinos, all that would force us into a submission of death."

Talya chuckled. "How blind you all are, Horde and Albino both. Freedom stares you in the face and yet you run back to the prison, thinking it will protect you from the shadow."

He took a deep breath and let it out slowly.

"So I will say what I have come to say and we will be on our way. Jacob will go to see his mother as any son has the right to do. The 49th will go with me to face her greatest fears. And you are free to wage your war. But you must know what I told the others. If you live by the sword, you will die by the sword. You reap what you sow. If you sow in fear, you will

reap more fear. If in love, then love. The choice is yours—remember that when the blood reaches your ankles."

"Liar!" Ba'al cried.

My eyes were on Qurong, who may not have heard a word. His eyes were still fixed on Jacob.

The ruler suddenly dropped to his knees, eyes misted with tears. At first I thought he might be yielding to Jacob, but in the next moment he grabbed his hair, threw his head back, and wailed.

Jacob stepped forward. "Father . . ."

Qurong clawed at his shirt, ripped it open and wept in mourning, a father who'd just lost his only son. The sound of his anguish made me shiver.

"Father, please—"

"Away from me!" Qurong's eyes were red with rage. He shoved a thick finger at the desert. "Away!"

"We must take them!" Ba'al snapped.

"Leave!" Qurong roared. He slumped over his knees and shook with sobs.

Ba'al glared, resolute. The commanders stood with firm jaws, hands on their swords. Jacob stumbled back to his horse and swung into his saddle.

Talya dipped his head. "As you wish."

Judah rose and trotted west, toward the deep desert. Without a second look, Talya followed. Jacob and I fell in behind, torn by mixed emotions.

None of us spoke for the next half hour as we passed through the Horde untouched, or when we'd left them behind.

I was Horde and didn't know what to make of myself.

Jacob was Albino and didn't know what to make of his father's sorrow.

Talya was Mystic and didn't make anything of our confusion, which annoyed me even though I knew I wasn't supposed to hold a grievance.

What is seeing beyond what you think should be?

I let the finger point but couldn't see what it was pointing to. How could I, when I was blind again?

"But of course you are," Talya said, pulling his mount to a halt. "And your journey is now to see light in that darkness. Isn't that what the Third Seal on your arm tells you?" He shoved his chin at the mountains to the north. "To this end, I will take you where few dare tread." He looked at me with a raised brow. "The Fourth and Fifth Seals call to you."

I didn't want to go where few dared tread. Jacob was staring west, face set. When he turned to me I saw the marks left by tears on his cheeks.

"Say your good-byes," Talya said. "Both worlds await you, 49th. Time is short."

Ancient Earth was so distant in my mind in the wake of becoming Horde. When I slept that night, I would awaken there in my dream, stripped of identity by the MEP.

And if I died there?

I would die here.

But I slipped from my horse, eager to offer Jacob whatever comfort I could. He was already on the sand by the time I rounded my mount. He wrapped me up in his strong arms. Bound together, we let ourselves cry.

Only two days ago our conditions had been reversed and we'd loved each other. Now we did the same, oblivious to my condition for the moment. In his embrace, I had no disease.

Jacob took my cheeks in his hands and kissed my cracked lips. "I have to go, you understand? I'm called to my mother, but I'll return, I swear it. Promise me you'll be here when I return."

"I will," I whispered through the ache in my throat.

He lifted my sleeve, and for the first time I saw that the seals were still on my arm, unaffected by the flaking skin. "Do whatever you have to do. Find the seals. If that means you must surrender me, then surrender me. But please, I beg you, come to me alive."

"I'll never surrender you, Jacob."

To this he said nothing. Instead he kissed me again. "I love you. I love you as life itself."

16

I WAS FAR too familiar with the dense fog that normally clogged my brain whenever I woke from sleep. The ever-present drugs had that effect—a tiny price to pay for the benefits they brought me.

This time it was different. I was in a dreamless sleep one moment, and the next awake. But even to say that I was familiar with the fog of drugs or that my waking this time was different is misleading.

I awoke with no recollection of anything. No drugs, no name, no memories at all, and no idea that I should even have memories.

I was simply . . . well . . . I was.

It was an awareness more than a thought, and it lasted for what felt like a very long time.

I was staring at a bright light above me, powered by electricity. I was in a body. A female body that was lying on a bed with light blue sheets in a room with humming machines.

Something was in my arm.

I turned my head and saw a man with an instrument—a syringe—stuck in my arm. His eyes met mine and he pulled the needle out.

"There we go. Sorry for waking you so quickly," he said, looking over his shoulder. "But we don't have much time."

"Hi," I said, amazed to be seeing a man attending to me. His hair was blond and curly and his eyes were blue. There was sweat on his forehead.

"Hi, Rachelle." He smiled at me. "Rachelle, that's your name. My name's Steve. Do you remember?"

I tried to, but nothing came to me, so I shook my head.

"Not a problem, there's nothing to worry about. You just need to do exactly as I say, okay?"

"Okay."

"Good." He grabbed a stack of clothes from a chair next to him. "Hurry, put these clothes on."

Without any concern, I sat up, took the blue jeans, and pulled them on. Then the black T-shirt and the socks and shoes as he talked in a hurried voice.

"Remember everything I'm about to tell you, okay? You're in the recovery room at DARPA. They erased your memories, so everything will seem new to you, but you've actually been here for four months. Not all your memories, only personal memories. That's why you don't know who you are. Does that make sense?"

Did it? "I guess." None of it alarmed me.

"Do you know what danger is?"

"Danger?" I said, pulling on my right shoe. "Of course I do."

"Do you feel any danger now?"

"No."

He paced as I pulled on my left shoe and laced it up. A perfect tie. They were Converse shoes. I liked them. A lot.

"No, of course you don't. But I need you to. Cruel, I know. Normally you would be eased out of innocence, but I need you to understand that staying here will end very badly for you. There's someone out there named Vlad who wants to stop you."

"Stop me from what?" I asked, standing. Steve wanted me to go with him before someone named Vlad stopped me.

"That isn't important right now. We have to get you out of here. If anyone tries to stop us, we have to get past them. Okay?"

"Okay."

He picked up a green apple from the cart next to the bed and tossed it to the side. "Catch."

I flew to it and snatched it from the air just before it hit the ground. Fast, faster than lightning. I grinned at him. "Like that?"

"Like that." He seemed pleased. "If anyone tries to stop us, move quick, like that. Stop them from stopping us, okay? Distract them or something. If you have to, hurt them."

I tossed the apple into the trash can. "Hurt how?"

"Stop them. Just make it so they can't hurt us."

"Why would they hurt us?"

He peered through the blinds before turning back. "Think of it like a game. A rough one. Don't worry, they won't be hurt for long." He rolled a wheelchair up to me. "Sit here."

When I sat down, he threw a blanket over my lap and chest, adjusting it so most of my body was covered.

"We're going down the hall to an elevator. When we get to the garage, we'll leave the wheelchair and run to my car. I need you to hide behind the front seat. Once we're clear of the facility, you can climb up front. Okay?"

He was breathing hard. Excited.

"Sure."

"Can you still read minds?"

"What do you mean?"

"Never mind." He took one last glance through the blinds. "Don't say anything to anyone. In fact, pretend you're sleeping, it's better that way."

"Close my eyes?"

"Until I tell you to open them."

"Okay."

He grabbed the chair from behind and wheeled me backward toward the door.

"Now?" I asked.

"Now what?"

"Close my eyes now?"

"Yes."

I heard him open the door. Felt the chair roll as he spun me around and hurried down the hall. I did peek through my eyelashes once halfway down the hall, but that was it. I could feel us turning a corner and hear

163

distant voices from another room. Then the sound of elevator doors opening. *Ding.* He rolled me in.

"Can I open—"

"Shh," he said. "Wait."

So I did, wondering why I should keep my eyes closed in an elevator.
But when the door closed he tapped me on the shoulder.

"Okay."

"Now?"

"You can open your eyes."

I smiled up at him. "Well, that was easy."

"We're not out yet. We have to get past the guards."

The bell dinged again and the metal doors slid open to a parking facility. I saw the guard as soon as we exited the elevator, a man dressed in
black with a gun on his belt. He was leaning against the wall to our right,
reading something on his phone.

But I didn't feel any concern or fear. That was just a man with a gun
reading a phone.

Steve wheeled me toward a line of black cars.

"Steve?" the guard called out. "What's going on?"

"Hey, Curt. Taking her to evaluation in the east building. Crazy business out there, huh?"

"They have DC locked down." He paused. "The east building? You'll
have to take the tunnel. Director's orders, no one leaves these premises
without her authorization."

"Seriously?" We stopped halfway to the cars. "It's faster to swing around
the block with the construction. Last time I was down there, the train
wasn't running."

"Running now. I'm sorry, you'll have to head back down. I could call
if you want."

Steve turned the chair to face him. He left me there and walked up to
the guard named Curt. "Look, she's just been through a horrible ordeal. I'm
sure you heard we were at the church bombing. We had to sedate her—"

"The whole world knows she was there. All the more reason. I'm sorry, man. Orders."

I could see that the guard's mood had shifted. He was glancing between us now, concerned. Maybe now was when I was supposed to stop him from stopping us, though I had no idea how I, a person half his size, could stop him from doing anything.

"You have the latest feeds?" Steve asked, nodding at the man's phone.

"'Course."

"What are they saying?"

Curt looked at his phone and when he did, Steve rushed him, slamming him back against the wall.

The startled guard grunted and grabbed at his gun, but Steve was too quick. He slapped the gun away, clamped his hand over Curt's mouth, and shoved his head back into the concrete. The guard swung back wildly, only missing Steve's head by a smidge.

I watched it all as if it was happening in slow motion, captivated by the movements. What if Curt had pulled his gun and shot Steve?

The first stab of fear I could remember hit me with that thought. And then Curt got his teeth around the fingers at his mouth and bit down hard. Steve roared.

I didn't consciously think about what I was doing. I just moved, as if I had always known exactly how to deal with a situation like this.

I bolted from the chair and ran low, leaning into each flying stride, and reached them before either one knew I'd left my chair. From there, it was simple. I just brought my hand up into Curt's chin as I straightened.

My palm connected with the underside of his jaw, snapping it back with enough force to knock him out. With a grunt, he went limp and dropped to the concrete.

I jumped back. Stared at Curt's crumpled body, surprised by my handiwork.

"Stop him like that?" I said.

"Run!"

Steve ignored his bloody hand, spun me around and ran, half dragging me until I caught up. "Will he be okay?"

"He'll be fine." He crashed into his car and threw the back door wide. "In! Lie on the floor!"

So I crawled in and lay facedown. The door slammed shut at my feet. Then he was around and sliding in. The electric car whirred to life as we backed up.

But I was still thinking of Curt, who was on the ground, hurt. I'd done that. Steve said to pretend it was a game, but how could it be? If it was, Steve wouldn't have a bloody hand, right? Did people play those kinds of games?

The car flew over a bump and I bounced a foot off the floor. Muffled voices were yelling outside the car. We smashed through something but kept moving, faster now. We took a corner at full speed and my head plowed into the far door.

"Ouch! Slow down, I'm getting hurt back here."

"I can't slow down!" he shouted. "Hold on!"

We flew around another corner.

"We're in one of the company's clean cars and I've disabled the private link so it's untraceable, but we have to get clear of sight." He was short of breath and scared, and suddenly I was too. "We're gonna make it, just another minute."

I hunkered down for another minute, but I didn't like the feelings running through me. What if I'd hit Curt too hard? What if he was dead? Steve wanted me to feel danger, and I did, I thought. But I didn't like it.

"Okay," Steve finally said. "We're clear for now, but every patrol in town probably already knows we're on the run. Maybe it's best for you to stay where you are."

I popped up and looked between the seats. "Why? They already saw the car, right?"

"True. Okay, jump up."

I clambered over the seats and dropped into the passenger's side.

"How do you know Curt's okay?" I asked. "I think I hit him pretty hard."

"There's a lot more at stake here than Curt. I'll explain as soon as I can, but I have to get out of the city. Friend of mine's father-in-law has a cabin near Shenandoah National Park. No one lives out there. I know where they hide the key. I have to get you there so we can stop and figure this out."

"Figure what out?" I looked out the front windshield. We'd pulled onto a large highway, surrounded by dozens of cars, some with drivers, some without. "I don't like this. Why can't you explain now?"

He kept looking in the mirrors, hands gripping the wheel as if he was afraid it might get away from him.

"Steve?"

"Sorry. I was just . . . I just hope I'm doing the right thing."

"Why would you be doing the wrong thing?" I asked, looking over my shoulder. No one was following us that I could see. But my heart was now pounding like a drum.

"I'm not. They're gonna pin the church bombing on you. I should have seen something like this coming!" He slammed the steering wheel and I flinched.

"What church bombing? And why do I know some things but not other things?"

"Like I said, your history is gone—your declarative, episodic memory that stores contextual information like time and place and the things that happened in those contexts. But your procedural and semantic memory are still intact. You have your learned skills and can speak. You know facts, like the car, but you have no memory of ever being in one. Assuming whatever they gave you works like the MEP."

"What's MEP?" Now I was truly alarmed.

"I'm so sorry, Rachelle." He was shaking his head, looking at me with sympathy, which only made things worse. Then looking forward again.

"MEP, Memory Editing Protocol. It's a cutting-edge technology that erases and replaces memory. In your case, hopefully only erase. Normally a few weeks of controlled acclimation are required with a clean wipe because a new mind has no context for danger or fear. Like a child. You can fear but have no context for it. These things are learned. Learning too quickly can be devastating."

I stared at him. My fingers were shaking. I was like a child who didn't know fear yet? "But I do feel fear."

"It's easy to learn, trust me. And for us that's a good thing."

"Because we're in danger." I looked behind me again. "Who's Vlad?"

"I don't suppose you remember anything about Project Eden?"

"No. Is that a fact or something contextual?"

"Contextual." He punched a button on the dash, and the six-inch screen switched to an image of ambulances around a huge cathedral. Half of the church was missing. Two small pictures were set into the image at the bottom, and under them the words "Authorities Searching for Fleeing Suspects" ran across a red banner.

I leaned forward, not sure that what I was seeing could be true. The two pictures were of me and Steve.

He tapped the screen off. "That was fast."

I stared out the window, mind clogged with confusion. A picture began to form. One I didn't like. Did not like at all.

"Please," I said, voice shaky. "Just tell me. Everything."

He nodded. "Okay. Okay then." He blew out some air. "You were born seventeen years ago in a small town called Eden, Utah. But Eden wasn't just any ordinary town."

Then he told me everything. About DARPA's Project Eden. About me being blind since a few months old. About my father, who'd spent his life trying to help me see.

About Vlad Smith, who took over the town and tried to force me to write him into a book—at least that's what I'd claimed before the MEP, though Steve couldn't be sure. What he could be sure about was that I'd regained my sight and found a way to bring down the synthetic sky that hid Eden from the world. In addition to my sight, I gained certain skills that I claimed were from another world in my dreams.

Skills like the ones I'd used to put Curt out of commission.

With each additional detail, my heart beat faster. It got worse about ten minutes in, when he started to explain what DARPA had done to me after I escaped Eden. They'd convinced me I had schizophrenia. They'd lied to me and wiped David's mind. David, my father, though I had no memory of him. Steve said my father and I had been close.

But it wasn't until he told me what had happened in the last few days that I really began to lose my grip. How my father had died. How we'd gone to church that morning. How they'd caught me on camera, saying some things about religion that they were going to twist. How the bomb had gone off . . .

How Vlad had to be behind all of it.

"My father was killed in another world?"

"I know it doesn't make any sense, but I have some theories. I'm so sorry, Rachelle."

I stared ahead, numb. "And *I'm* from that world?"

"No. Heavens no." He paused. "Actually, I'm not sure how it's working, but you've evidently tapped into another realm of consciousness. Like I said, I have some thoughts I'll explain once we get to safety."

"But I'm safe as long as I don't dream, right? That's what got my father killed."

"I don't have the drugs to keep you from dreaming. And maybe dreaming is exactly what you need to deal with Vlad, assuming this is his work."

My mind spun, working fast.

"But if that's true, he wouldn't *want* me to dream." I was having no trouble believing that another world was possible because I had no context that told me it couldn't be. And if I was someone trying to hurt me, and my powers came from those dreams, I wouldn't want me dreaming.

"Maybe. We'll find out next time you sleep whether you can still dream. I don't know any details about the new agent they used in your MEP."

"But . . ." I faced him. "I have to dream! How else will I know what's really happening?" Something else came to me. "Why does he want me dead?"

"I'm not sure he does. He could have killed you in Eden but didn't."

"Then what does he want?"

169

"Maybe to finish what he started. And whatever that is, it's big. Assuming this is all Vlad, he's pulled a lot of strings that aren't easily pulled."

My breathing became shallow as I sat there in the passenger's seat. The world was flying by, but my mind was in another place. A horrible place filled with images of a wraith from another world coming for me.

"Do the words *49th Mystic* mean anything to you?" he asked.

"No. Should they?"

"It's something you used to think you were in Eden. Evidently, so did Vlad."

It was all too much for my new mind, and I began to panic. "We have to hide!"

"That's what we're doing." His voice had softened. "You're safe with me. As safe as you can be, which is why I broke you out, remember? We're in this together now, nothing's going to change that."

But I was feeling the horror of being in terrible danger and not knowing why. It was too much! I was just a girl who'd woken up in a white room! Why was this happening?

Overwhelmed, I folded over in the seat and began to cry, then sob until my whole body was shaking.

"It's okay." I felt Steve's hand on my back. "We're going to figure this out together, you and me, I promise."

But I knew better. I knew that Vlad was going to find us and finish what he'd started.

17

"YOU'RE SURE this treacherous path is the way? It was dark when you came."

Samuel spat and hoisted himself up between two boulders, found a place for his foot, and pushed himself onto a small ledge that hugged the cliff for fifty feet before widening.

"It's the way. Trust me."

Aaron scaled the trail easily enough, complaining only because his armies awaited his command. In every way, the son of Mosseum was Samuel's equal. It had taken some convincing to persuade Aaron to make the six-hour journey to the Marrudo plateau because the high wasteland had been surveyed many times.

There was nothing but a sinkhole on the south end of the plateau and plains to the north.

Yes, but that had changed. Samuel had seen the transformation with his own eyes. And Jacob, son of Qurong, was now with Rachelle in that so-called sinkhole beyond these cliffs.

"If I didn't trust you, I wouldn't be here," Aaron said. "But you can't deny that this is most unusual. My commanders await, the Horde is gathered, and I find myself crawling up a cliff with an Albino from a group of renegades called the Circle. If it wasn't for the Leedhan's insistence, I wouldn't be here."

"So you do believe him, the Leedhan, when he says the Mystics are the most dangerous threat to this world?"

171

"Of course I do. I'd be foolish not to believe the words of a shape-shifter who vanishes from my dungeons. What good would it do me to destroy the Horde army only to discover the heretics in my own lands will bring our order down?"

Heretics. Yes, heretics—he had to remember that word whenever he courted doubts about his decision to betray the Realm. Which he still did, far too often for his liking. But once he'd marched into Aaron's quarters with the announcement that he'd succeeded, there was no turning back.

As Samuel saw it, what mattered more than the Mystics was the war against the Horde. Their slaughter would fulfill the prophecy and release all Albinos from their perpetual fear of their enemies. The key to ending the Horde threat was Aaron and his army. By proving his value to Aaron, Samuel and the Circle would be trusted.

He was doing this for the Circle then. For his father, really. And for Justin.

It didn't sit entirely square in his mind, but that was only because he'd made the mistake of falling for Rachelle. Emotion had clogged his better judgment. Wasn't love always that way? Up one day, down the next. Safe one night, dead the next.

The Horde had killed his bride two years ago. In the coming days he would show them the full wrath of Elyon.

They'd left their horses tied off below. The sun was high in the sky—plenty of daylight hours left to confirm the location of the Realm of Mystics and return to the city before dark. They would come back with a regiment at night, take captive or kill all who lived in the Realm, then set their minds on the Horde.

He hadn't mentioned Jacob's drowning and had no intention of doing so now. Better for them to think of Jacob as Horde. Regardless, he wasn't here to end the life of Jacob or Rachelle but to save all Albinos, which included the Circle.

So he kept telling himself. So it had to be. It was too late to change his course.

"Just over this ledge," Samuel said, bounding up the rocky slope. "When we reach the top, we go left to scale the final cliff."

"Another cliff?"

"A short wall. I'll have you at the top in five minutes."

It took them maybe twice that, but then they were at the boulders from which Samuel had last peered into the Realm.

"Here." He ran in a crouch with Aaron walking behind. Grabbed the side of the large boulder, heart pounding. Peered into the sinkhole.

Gasped.

Aaron walked past him, taking none of his precautions. He looked down at the wasteland and set his hands on his hips.

"This is it?"

"THIS MUST BE IT," Thomas said, urging his mount to a trot. "Just ahead."

Mikil pulled up, craning for a view beyond the cliffs that dropped off fifty paces ahead of them. "I thought you said it was a realm of some kind."

"Eden," Chelise said, spurring her horse. "He said we would know it when we see it."

"A common sinkhole?"

To their right, towering boulders blocked the western horizon. A sinkhole, Thomas thought, but not common. Larger than any he'd seen by far, hidden in the high plateau. As uncommon as Talya himself.

The rest of the Circle was camped a few miles north, lost in arguments about what their next course of action should be. Marie's death had left Vadal embittered; the death of so many others had left the whole gathering divided, searching for understanding.

Maybe they would find some answers now.

Thomas slowed his stallion and approached the drop-off with some caution, unsure of its stability. Mikil and Chelise had drawn abreast.

Slowly the depths of the sinkhole came into view. Steep, jagged cliffs on all sides cut into sheer rock hundreds of feet deep. Red cliffs. By what force of nature such a hole had been made, he had no clue. The cliffs weren't the kind to easily fall, even if the bottom had given way and . . .

Chelise's gasp cut his thoughts short.

"Dear Elyon!" she breathed, pulling her mount back. "What is this?"

"What is what?" Mikil demanded, leaning forward in her saddle. "I see only wasteland."

But Thomas saw more. Far more.

And what he saw took his breath away.

SAMUEL stepped up to Aaron's side, peering down. "I don't understand. I swear it was here. I saw it this way, and then I saw it transformed. It's here, I swear it's here."

Aaron gave him a dubious glance, then scanned the tall cliffs falling into the massive sinkhole. "Tell me again what you saw, exactly as you saw it."

"That's it!" Samuel paced, running his hand through his hair as realization dawned. "She has to be here!"

"I think your emotions for her are getting in the way. She isn't here. Jacob betrayed us as the Leedhan said he would. They—"

"I mean the 49th has to be physically present for the Realm to open," he blurted. "When she's not here, it's unseen, which is why you've never found it." He shoved a finger at the cliffs. "It's here, I tell you! I saw it with my own eyes. The old wizard, Rachelle, and Jacob, all here with a lion. When they were here, the way was open. Which only means they're gone. Don't you see it?"

"Actually, no. I see only wasteland. You expect me to believe we're actually staring at lush forests but can't see them?"

"As much as I expect you to believe the Leedhan vanished from your dungeons. Is that any more possible?"

Aaron didn't answer quickly, so Samuel pushed on.

"It's obvious. She has to be brought here. The Leedhan knew the gate would be open when she was present. It's why he wanted her released and followed. Knowing what we do now, it's only a matter of finding her again!"

Aaron crossed his arms and frowned. "All of this wizardry unnerves me.

First the Leedhan and now the Mystic. Wounds healed, bodies vanishing, realms appearing and disappearing." He spat. "Heresy is wicked business."

"So you see it?"

"The Realm, no. Your logic, yes." His frown deepened and he gave a reluctant nod. "So yes, I will believe you." He eyed Samuel for a moment. "Tell me, how deeply are you connected to this woman?"

Samuel wasn't sure where the man was headed. "In what way?"

"You seem quite taken with her. If the Leedhan hadn't insisted you be the one, I would have sent someone else to follow her."

"Elyon forbid! I had no idea she was a heretic when I rescued her from the Horde. How dare you question my motives?"

"On the contrary, I do believe your connection to the 49th could now serve us. So tell me, how deeply does she feel for you?"

He hesitated, disliking what Aaron was suggesting. "She trusts me, if that's what you mean. Maybe more."

"And you love her?"

"I was taken with her before I knew who she really was."

"But you must love her now. It's the only way she'll trust you. In my experience women are far more intuitive than men in matters of romance. So if you're scolding yourself for having fallen for her, don't."

"You want me to find her and bring her back. I have no idea where to begin."

"And I do."

"How?"

Aaron shoved his chin toward the north. "My scouts have watched a large gathering of Albinos cross the Divide and make camp north of here on the plateau. Perhaps three or four hours at a jog around the sinkhole and north. I instructed my men to stand down because I assumed them to be your Circle."

Samuel spun to the man. "My father? You're sure? How's that possible?"

"You tell me. The point is, they're here, roughly ten thousand."

"All of them?"

"And if I were one of these Mystics searching for support, I would entertain approaching them."

Two thoughts collided in Samuel's mind. The first was reuniting with the Circle. If they were here, they knew more than he would have guessed. Regardless of how they knew, he was now in a position to argue for joining with the Elyonites against the Horde.

The other thought was that Aaron could easily be right. Rachelle wasn't here because she'd gone to the Circle with her new Albino in tow. For all he knew, the old man Talya had been complicit in convincing his father to bring the Circle across the Great Divide.

He studied the northern lip of the cliff, too far away to see any detail other than groupings of massive boulders. There could very well be Circle scouts there now.

"You said there was another way into the sinkhole," Samuel said, peering down again. "Where?"

"On the other side, if I recall." Aaron nodded at the eastern cliffs, a few miles away as the buzzard might fly, but another day's march around. "It's the only opening large enough to accommodate an army. Short of that, I'm sure an enterprising person might find a crevasse through which to descend. But that's not where you'll go."

"You knew that if we didn't find the Realm, you would ask me to reach out to my people," he said.

"Of course." Aaron uncrossed his arms. "More than reach out to them. Be my hand among them."

"I'll go. Even if she isn't there, no Albino has as much experience against the Horde as our Forest Guard. While you've been sitting in peace, hunting stray heretics for sport, we've been learning the strategies of the Horde."

"You haven't seen us in war," Aaron said.

"No, and I mean no disrespect. But we know the Horde in ways you can't. We live in their lands, for the love of Elyon."

Aaron nodded. "I realize that. But it's the 49th I want more than your fighters. Don't get me wrong, I'll gladly accept whatever guidance you can offer. But the Leedhan is right, she's the greater danger."

"Either way, you will wage your war."

"Of course. Better in the Valley of Miggdon than marching halfway across the world to rout them. One way or the other, I intend to see the end of Elyon's enemies. All Horde, all heretics, and if need be all Leedhan. The way of Justin must be honored at all costs. Unless a man willingly drowns and follows the only way, he belongs in hell. We will give them an early departure for their final destination."

The logic, however different from his father's, brought Samuel comfort. A world without enemies could only be realized by force.

"Then we're agreed." Aaron grasped his arm, then turned to leave. He took two steps before pulling up short. "Speaking of heretics, you don't think your Circle will have a problem with sound doctrine, do you?"

"Not when you help them see its wisdom." A task more difficult than Samuel would care to admit.

"Good. Then be my hand among your people, Samuel. Bring me the Mystic, bring me your seasoned fighters, bring me the power of Elyon if you can find it. The new age awaits us."

THOMAS DROPPED from his mount and walked forward on numb legs, spine tingling. A forest unlike any he'd seen in a long time filled the bottom of the sinkhole, broken by large meadows of brilliant green grass and colorful flowers.

The leaves on most of the trees were green, but the trunks were golden and blue, some orange, others yellow. A scattering of white Roush glided over the trees, oblivious to the humans peering down on their Realm from above.

Talya's Eden.

"What is it?" Mikil demanded again. "Horde?"

Chelise turned to Thomas, eyes wide. "Are you . . . Do you see this?"

"I do," he whispered.

"For the love of Elyon, will someone please tell me what I'm supposed to be seeing!" Mikil cried.

Thomas was too overcome to respond. There was more than the colored forest. There was the village near the east side. Several dozen square huts, each glowing with a different color, rested like children's playing blocks in concentric circles around a large pinnacled structure, which towered above the others at the village center. The sky above the dwellings was spotted with Roush that floated and dove and twisted in the afternoon sun.

As his eyes adjusted to the incredible scene, he saw a door open from a dwelling far below. He watched a tiny form step from the door. And then he saw that others dotted the village.

A powerful sense of déjà vu hit him. He'd been here before, stumbling upon a scene just like this a long time ago when he'd first awakened in Other Earth. The memories were dulled by decades of desert dwelling, hiding from Horde, but he'd been in a village like this. Maybe even this one.

When he looked past the village to the east, his heart bolted.

The lake! And feeding that lake, the waterfall cascading down the distant cliffs. He couldn't see what source fed the waterfall, but he was sure he'd been to that source. Was it there now?

"Do you know this place, Thomas?" Chelise asked.

He hesitated. "Yes . . ."

"It's the place you told me about?"

"Yes, like that place."

"Here? But . . ." She jerked her head and stared at him with round eyes. "I thought the Shataiki blackened the land with the Fall."

"They did. I . . . I was there."

"And yet it still exists!" she cried, scanning the village again.

"You're seeing forests down there?" Mikil asked, now far less demanding. "How is that possible? I can only see sand and rugged hills strewn with dead shrubs."

Chelise grabbed her arm, excited like a child. "He spit in our eyes!"

"Who spit?"

"Talya! He opened our eyes to see this."

"It's a perception, not a destination," Thomas said.

"The old man spit in your eyes and now you're seeing what I can't see." Mikil peered down as if by chance she too might suddenly see. "That's what you're telling me? Then for the love of Elyon, at least describe it."

"A colored forest as bright as a box of crystals in the sun!" Chelise returned. "Large white birds floating in the sky. A village with people. Living souls, hidden from the world."

"Roush?" Mikil asked. No one had seen a Roush in years. Many doubted they'd ever existed. "Do you mean to tell me you see Roush?"

Thomas's wonder was now joined with an excitement he hadn't felt for a long time. He began to pace, thinking through their options. Then he stopped and stared at the sight of this Realm called Eden. Here it was, undeniable, drawing him like honey drew the bee. A terrible analogy—the draw was far greater than something that could only be tasted. It was . . .

"Thomas!"

"Yes?" He spun to Mikil, who'd been talking.

"Should we?"

"Should we what?"

"Bring the others."

He paced again, hand in his hair, casting glances to the Realm below. "Dear Elyon, no. No, no, they wouldn't see a thing, and even if they could, Talya told us to wait for him in the plains. Only Chelise and I can see this."

"But to what end?" Mikil demanded. "We have thousands of frightened souls hidden on the plain north, far from safety. Vadal is swimming in misery and leaking whispers of revolt. We have to give the people something! What will you tell them?"

"Nothing," Chelise interjected. "Thomas will tell them nothing because he isn't returning."

"Don't be absurd! He's the only one they'll listen to."

"Well, they'll have to listen to you this time, Mikil, because Thomas is taking me down there. I have to see it! Talya wanted us to see it."

"Apparently, you are seeing it."

"I mean up close. I have to be in it!"

"While the rest of us—"

"Enough!" Thomas lifted his hand. Chelise's excitement wasn't only infectious, it was demanding. "She's right. Talya wouldn't have wanted us to find this Realm if he didn't want us to enter it. To what end, I don't know yet, but this will change everything! Can't you see that?"

Mikil studied the sinkhole, only a wasteland in her perception. They were asking her to believe what could not be seen—a tall order for any rational human.

"I suppose I can," she said. "If I imagine seeing what you say you see."

"It's there, Mikil. I swear! All of it!"

Mikil softened and looked at him quizzically. "You say the old man spit in your eyes. Perhaps if you spit in my eye—"

"My spit means nothing."

"And his does?"

"You saw how he quenched the fire with nothing more than a raised hand. Yes, his spittle evidently does mean something. Only Chelise and I can see, so we have to go. And so do you, back to the Circle. Surely you can all survive without me for a few hours."

"Hours? It'll take half the day for you to find a way down there."

"Then a day or two. I don't know. Whatever's needed."

Mikil finally nodded. "Okay. You're right."

"Just don't let Vadal prevail."

"We can handle Vadal." Mikil scanned the mountains. Between where they stood and that Great Divide lay a city of Elyonites none of them had yet seen. And beyond the Divide, the Horde were gathering for war.

"Maybe the old man will come to us," Mikil said. "Maybe with this 49th Mystic he spoke about. For our sakes, I hope so, and soon."

Thomas wondered where the 49th was now. If Talya was right—and Thomas was now certain of it—this world teetered on the balance of her journey.

"He'll come."

Mikil was staring down again. "Roush, huh? Do you suppose they might be everywhere, and us only blind to them?"

Thomas looked around. There were no Roush outside of the Realm that he could see. But Mikil made a good point. The only difference between her and them was that they were seeing differently. Talya had changed their perception.

"It's possible," Chelise said.

"Wouldn't that be something?" Mikil said.

Thomas stared down at the incredible sight. "It would be," he said.

And then they didn't say anything for a while.

18

IT TOOK Thomas and Chelise two hours to find their way down the narrow crevasse, along broken ledges, and finally to a meadow that butted up against the red cliff at the bottom of the sinkhole called the Realm of Mystics. They stood on a flat rock, three feet above a thick carpet of vibrantly green grass. And there, only twenty paces ahead, trees. Colored trees that glowed.

"This is it," Chelise whispered, staring at the trees. She was breathing heavily from the climb down. "This is it!"

They were maybe a mile from the village, due east, where the Mystics lived in houses made of wood from the colored trees.

He glanced up. No Roush that he could see.

"Come on." He took her hand. "Just hop down."

They took the three-foot drop together, landing lightly on the thick grass. He released Chelise's hand and stooped to feel the grass. Rubbed the blades between his fingers. Grass, just like any grass. Smelled his fingers. Grass that smelled like lilacs.

Chelise gasped. "Thomas?"

"What is it?" He stood and turned to see that she was looking back at the cliffs they'd just descended. Only there were no cliffs.

He blinked. The meadow they were in ran a hundred paces before running into more trees. He spun around, stunned. No cliffs. None anywhere!

"How's this possible?"

Thomas reached for her hand, took it in his, heart hammering. Gently rolling hills filled with trees extended in every direction, as far as the eye could see.

"The Realm is a dimension," he said. "Not a destination."

The moment he said it, a warm breeze wafted through his hair, bringing with it the scent of roses. And when the warm air hit his lungs, a gentle power lit his nerves, sending tingles through his arms and legs.

Chelise lifted her hand and stared at her fingers. "Did you feel that?"

"I did." And he'd felt it before. "Everything here is charged."

The air stilled and the scent faded, as did the subtle power they'd felt.

"Come on!" He pulled her toward the colored forest, headed east. The village still had to be east.

The thick grass silenced his footfalls. The carpet didn't thin out under the trees but ran heavy and lush right through. Violet and lavender flowers with petals the size of his hand stood knee-high, scattered about the forest floor. No debris or dead branches littered the ground.

Thomas lifted his eyes to the tall trees shining their soft colors about him. Most seemed to glow with one predominant color—like red or blue or yellow—accented by the other colors. How could the trees glow? It was as if they were powered by some massive underground generator that delivered fluorescent chemicals in large tubes made to look like trees. No, that was technology from ancient Earth.

He ran his hand gently across the surface of a large ruby tree with a purple hue, surprised at how smooth it was, as if it had no bark at all. He took in the tree's full height. Breathtaking. He'd been here before . . .

Thomas spun around, grabbed Chelise's hand, and pulled her into his arms. He kissed her mouth before throwing his arms wide and turning in the shafts of light piercing the canopy above them.

"This is it!" he cried. "I've found my home!"

She laughed and spun with him like a ballerina. "Home!" Then to him: "This is your home?"

"I don't know, but I hope it is. Our home. To think it's been here all this time. Mikil was right! We were blinded by the Fall! Our perception was distorted!"

"It's only her theory."

"True, but how else is this possible? Hurry, we have to reach the village!"

He walked fast, like a schoolboy headed home to play, with Chelise right there, skipping once or twice to keep up. They broke into a meadow and Thomas took to a jog.

"Hurry!"

She tore past him, then turned, skipping backward. "Hurry, you say? Do you think I look like the kind of girl who needs to hurry to keep up with you? If my memory serves me correctly, I beat you in the race at the last games."

He took after her full tilt, but she was fast. Faster than him if only by half a step when they entered the forest again. They were both still clothed in battle dress, and their thick boots didn't help.

"Hold on!" He pulled up, dropped to his seat in the grass, and tugged his boots off.

"Whatever for?" she asked.

"I want to feel the ground under my feet," he said, scrambling up and leaping into the air. "I want to touch the trees and breathe the air and smell the flowers and kiss my bride!"

Her eyes flashed with excitement. "And I want to eat the fruit and . . ." She caught herself and looked at a branch heavy with a red fruit. "Can we do that? Eat the fruit?"

A flutter of wings from above and behind turned both of them. Thomas watched, heart in his throat, as a white Roush swept down from the treetops and alighted next to him, plump face grinning. "Are you hungry, Thomas Hunter?" He held up one of two blue fruits in his spindly fingers.

Thomas blinked. Here, before his eyes, a real, living Roush with thick white fur and round green eyes.

"You know my name?" he stammered.

"But of course. We've known each other a very long time, though I will admit that it's been a long time since you've had the good sense to see me." The Roush paused. "You do see me now, don't you? You do recognize me? Or do you think you're dreaming again?"

"That will be quite enough, Gabil," a voice said above them.

Thomas watched as a second Roush floated to the ground and alighted next to Chelise, who took a step back.

"That's Michal," the first Roush said. "Be careful, he can bite."

"Don't be childish," Michal chided. "Pay him no mind. Do you know the one named Talya?"

Gabil. Michal. The memory of being rescued by these two at the Crossing flooded him.

"Gabil? It's you!"

"It's me!" the Roush cried, throwing his wings wide and nearly tipping over.

Thomas dropped to his knee, wrapped his arms around the furry creature's exposed body, and lifted him up, twirling around. The Roush giggled and flapped his wings. "Ooooh, that tickles! Hehehe, ooooh, that tickles!"

Laughing, Chelise impulsively mirrored Thomas, wrapping her arms around Michal.

"Oh yes, well, easy there. Easy now . . ."

Thomas set Gabil down as Chelise stood, beaming. For a long moment they all stared at each other.

"Michal is getting old, so you shouldn't be alarmed by his strange behavior," Gabil said, hopping over to Chelise. "You can hug me. And if you like, I can show you how to fight like I showed Thomas. You're in love with him?"

She glanced at Thomas, delighted. "Well, I would love to hug you!" She bent over and gave him a gentle squeeze. "And yes, I am in love with Thomas."

"All very well," Michal said, waddling away from her, "but we do have business to attend to. Talya sent us here, far from our home. He doubted you would remember much because the scabbing disease once fogged your older memory, but he thought our familiar faces might help. We're only to guide you to the village, that sort of thing. It's quite easy to get lost if you don't know the way."

"Food?" Gabil said, holding the blue fruit up to Chelise. She took it in her fingers and Gabil tossed the second one to Thomas, who caught it.

"This is very good fruit. A blue peach. Look." Gabil reached for the fruit he'd given Chelise, took a small bite, and showed them. The juice glistening in the bite mark held a green, oily tinge. "Delicious," he said, shoving it back up to Chelise.

Thomas took a small bite and felt the cool, sweet juice fill his mouth. A flutter descended into his stomach and warmth spread through his body.

Gabil grinned wide. "You see? I'll get more!" With that the short creature trot-waddled a few feet, leaped off the ground, and flew back into the canopy.

Michal chuckled at his companion and headed into the forest. "Come. Come. We must not wait."

With a nod at Chelise, Thomas followed. Through the forest, across a wide meadow, into more colored trees, heading in a more northerly direction than they would have taken alone.

Chelise had just finished the blue peach when Gabil brought them both another fruit, a red one this time. With a swoop and a shrill laugh, he dropped it into their hands and took off again. The third time the fruit was green and required peeling, but its flesh was perhaps the tastiest yet.

Gabil's fourth appearance included an aerobatics show. The Roush screamed in from high above, looping with an arched back, then twisting into a dive. Thomas threw up his arms and ducked, sure the Roush had miscalculated. With a flurry of wings and a screech, Gabil buzzed his head.

"Gabil!" Michal called out after him. "Show some care!"

Gabil settled on a high branch and looked back at them, smiling bashfully yet obviously impressed with himself.

"Mighty warrior indeed," Michal said, stepping back along the path.

Less than a mile later, the Roush stopped on a crest. Thomas and Chelise stepped up beside the furry creatures and looked down on a large green valley covered in flowers like daisies, but turquoise and orange. Nestled far below was the village, laid out in a circular pattern, sparkling with color.

Thomas caught his breath. He was sure he'd been here before, not just here at this village, but standing *here* with Gabil and Michal, seeing the village so close for the first time.

Beside him, Chelise stared, speechless.

The square huts glowing in different colors, the large pinnacled structure that towered above the others at the center, the Roush flying above. And humans here and there, going about their business without hurry.

These were the Mystics?

"Does it jog any memories?" Michal asked.

"Maybe. Yes, but they're not clear. It's smaller somehow."

"Oh, but this isn't the village you first came to. There were hundreds of dwellings then. Only forty-nine live here now. They've rebuilt the houses."

"So it was destroyed? When did the colored trees come back?"

"With Justin's rising, naturally. After his drowning. But only those with eyes to see can see."

"So . . . our drowning doesn't necessarily mean we can see?"

"Well, I think you already know the answer to that question."

"If I knew I wouldn't be asking. I can see now."

"That was Talya's doing. It's temporary, I think."

Gabil hopped forward and lifted eager eyes to Thomas. "What Michal is trying to say, and what I'll now say with perfectly chosen words, is that most Albinos are as blind as bats." He strutted to his right, finger raised like a little furry prophet. "As written in the Books of History, unless a human is born once more they cannot see the kingdom that's already here. The realm of love without judgment. If you don't experience it . . . well, that must mean you're blind. At least somewhat blind."

He lowered his wing and grinned ear to ear. "Simple." Then looked at Michal for approval. "How was that?"

"Too many words," Michal replied. "At any rate, I don't think it's our place to explain these things. Mirium can show you. Or Talya. Or the 49th, if she finds all five seals."

But Thomas was caught up in Gabil's mention of what was written in the Books of History. It was language from ancient Earth. The one he'd come from so long ago when he'd lived in Denver, Colorado. The two

187

worlds mirrored each other, but what was spiritual there was represented in a physical way here. Or so he'd once concluded.

The Realm of Mystics was a physical metaphor for the kingdom of heaven there—he doubted it looked like this on Earth. Or maybe it did. Could it be? Both realities were real, but in different ways.

"Now, we must be going," Michal was saying.

They followed the Roush, who'd both taken to the air. They were headed for the village where answers could be found, but a new kind of logic had already fallen into Thomas's mind. So many of Justin's teachings suddenly made sense. As did the struggle of all Albinos. And of all Horde.

The Circle had mistakenly embraced the thought that in becoming Albino, they were fulfilling the teachings of Justin, even though they had never truly manifested what he said they could expect. Particularly the evidence of love without judgment, which was the only true evidence of living in Justin's way.

They'd been blind to love this whole time, thinking that they could see! Their own doctrines of judgment had blinded them to love without fear. The 49th was here to help them see.

The thoughts were replaced by wonder as they walked under a great blue-and-gold arch at the village entrance, then down a wide brown path between rows of colored huts. Without a word, Gabil flew away, following others who were on a path heading east.

"Amazing," Chelise whispered, staring at the wood.

Thomas stopped at the first house, taken by the ruby glow of its walls. A lawn wrapped around the dwelling in a thick, uniform carpet of green, highlighted by flowers growing in symmetrical clusters. What appeared to be carvings of brightly colored sapphire and golden wood accented the lawn, giving it a surreal beauty.

"Do you remember?" Michal asked.

"Sort of." He looked up the row of homes. A few small groupings of Mystics busied themselves, paying them no mind.

"We go to the Thrall, where Mirium will come for you."

Both sides of the road were lined with beautifully landscaped lawns that bordered each colored cottage. The homes shone like pearl. Flowers like the daisies on the valley floor grew in wide swaths across the bright green lawns. Large cats meandered and parrots fluttered about the village in harmony as if they too owned a part of this incredible work of art.

Every object, every carving, every flower, and every path was in exactly the right location, like a perfectly arranged symphony. Move one path and the vision would crumble. Move one flower and chaos would ensue.

They reached a lawn where several women sat on the ground, working with leaves and flowers—they seemed to be making tunics. Two were quite thin, two plump, and their skin tones varied from dark to light. They each nodded at Thomas and Chelise with knowing glints in their emerald eyes.

He dipped his head and walked on, unsure of the proper etiquette here, assuming there was any.

On their left, a group of men pressed their bare hands into a piece of red wood, shifting its shape. Beside them a woman was closing up a fruit stand, seven or eight wood boxes filled with different fruits. They looked like ordinary Albinos, less the wear and tear of hard desert living.

But in each of them he saw two things. The first was that they were completely unaffected by the presence of strangers in their midst, even though such an occurrence was likely very rare.

The second was the look on their faces, in their eyes. A deep, inviting calm bright with mystery. Like wise children who knew no fear.

A hand suddenly filled his own, and he turned to see that a small boy with blond hair and bright eyes had taken both his and Chelise's hands and was hurrying between them to keep up.

"Hello! I'm called Johan," he said. "My mother is Mirium."

"Well hello, Johan." Chelise beamed. "We are so delighted to meet you."

"What do they call you?"

"Chelise. And that's Thomas."

"Hello, Chelise and Thomas." He looked at two children, a boy and a girl, who stared wide-eyed from a lawn just ahead. "That is Ishmael and Latfa. They're singers like me." Then to the children: "This is Thomas and Chelise! They're our friends."

Both children had dark hair and green eyes; both stood a tad taller than Johan. "Hello, Chelise. Hello, Thomas."

Thomas blinked. Hadn't this happened before? "Hello, Ishmael and Lafta."

The one on the left lifted a hand to her mouth and giggled. "Latfa!" she blurted. "My name is Latfa!"

"Forgive me. Latfa?"

"Yes. Latfa."

To his right, a plump woman in a tunic made of blue flowers chuckled at the exchange.

"Come now, we mustn't dally," Michal said, waving them on. "The Gathering awaits."

Johan released their hands and ran to join his two friends. With a glance behind, Thomas saw that half those he'd seen were already gone and the rest were setting things aside, preparing to leave.

"Hurry!" Michal was evidently eager for the Gathering.

The Thrall was large compared to the other structures, and if the village was a work of refined art, then this was its crowning glory. They paused at the bottom of wide steps that ascended to the circular building. The jade-colored dome looked as though it had been made out of some flawless crystalline material that allowed light to pass through it.

Ahead, Michal struggled up the steps one by one. Thomas took Chelise's hand, gingerly placed his foot on the first step, and led her up. They followed Michal into the Thrall.

The scope of the large auditorium was at once intimidating and spectacular. Four glowing pillars—ruby, emerald, jasper, and a golden yellow—rose from the floor to the iridescent domed ceiling. There was no furniture in the room. All of this he saw at first glance.

But it was on the great circular floor centered under the dome that he rested his gaze.

Chelise stepped past Michal and walked lightly to the floor's edge. "Can you walk on it?"

"But of course."

The floor seemed to draw Thomas into itself. He slowly knelt and reached out his hand. He couldn't see a single blemish on its hard, clear surface, like a pool of resin poured over a massive, unflawed emerald. He stroked the floor, breathing steadily. A sudden, slight vibration shot up his arm, and he quickly withdrew his hand.

"It's quite all right, my friend," a voice said behind him.

He stood, turning. In the entrance stood a woman. Bare feet. Simple blue dress. Gentle smile. Midtwenties, Marie's age. But there was nothing plain about the woman. Her eyes seemed to reach through him and hold the world in some unseen knowing that immediately stilled his heart.

"It's a sight that I never get used to myself," she said, walking in. Michal had left them. "It was made from a thousand green trees. Not a blemish to be found." She put one hand on her chest. "I am called Mirium, elder of the Mystics. We are so pleased Talya sent you to us."

"You're the elder?" Chelise asked, maybe because Mirium was younger than others they'd seen. Much younger than Talya.

"This year, yes. It's only a role. There is no status or lack of status among us." She stepped up to Chelise and ran her knuckles over her cheek. "So beautiful, daughter. Justin's heart faints at the sight of you."

Chelise stared for a moment before responding. "Thank you."

"No need to thank me, dear one. I'm not the one who made you. Or your daughter, Marie." She searched Chelise's eyes. "I know you think she's dead, but only because you don't yet truly know that death is only a shadow. Justin overcame it. Your daughter only shed one costume for another. I can hear her laughing with delight even now."

Chelise's lower lip quivered as the simple words washed over her.

Mirium smiled and stepped lightly over to Thomas. She took his hand and kissed his knuckles, never removing her gaze from his.

"And you, beautiful son. Justin weeps with gratitude in your presence."

Thomas felt his knees go weak. He couldn't imagine Justin feeling such gratitude for him, the one who'd failed the Circle in so many ways for so many years.

"No, Thomas, you haven't failed," Mirium said, voice soft. "Your journey has been precisely what you've required to come to this place of awakening. Even the law of blindness teaches by demonstrating its uselessness.[1] To think flesh is evil is the mistake of the Gnostics. Give yourself grace. You underestimate the infinite love and power of Justin."

She released his hand and stepped away, facing Chelise again.

"Do you remember the first time you felt unspeakable joy in the depths of the red pool? You were Horde then, being healed of the scabbing disease, yes?"

Chelise didn't seem to have a voice to respond, but none was needed. They all remembered.

"In that death, were there any problems, or were you aware only of goodness?"

"Only goodness," Chelise managed, voice weak.

"And you wonder why that joy didn't remain with you. Why that first love grew cold over time."

Chelise slowly nodded.

"In the ancient texts it is written that in the last days the whole earth will tremble at the goodness of God. That day is upon us both now and every day. We will all play our roles, beyond even our understanding."

The questions faded from Thomas's mind, replaced by a simple acceptance.

"Every problem you see is simply an opportunity to see the goodness of Elyon, until you finally understand that all problems are only shadows. They have power only to the extent you put your faith in them. Surrendering your faith in those shadows, to see who you already are in divine light, is called being Inchristi. That is your true identity. Your name. You're already glorified, meaning not of this world but of divinity. You just don't see yourself or the world the way Justin does until your mind is made new. When it is, you will tremble at the goodness of Elyon. As will all."

The words washed over him. A tear slipped down Chelise's cheek.

Mirium smiled. "If what you call death were of any concern, we Mystics would be in fear, knowing that armies gather to crush us. This is of no concern to us."

What was she saying? What did she know that would bring fear?

"Talya has asked me to teach you our ways before Thomas leaves in two days for his mission. That mission is known only to Talya and Justin now. Until then you will remain here with us. When you do leave, Chelise will remain here."

"They'll be safe?" Thomas asked. "The Circle."

"They, like you, are on a journey of discovering who they are. As is the 49th, who stood in this very Thrall many years ago and agreed to take the journey from blindness to light once more, beginning on her twenty-first birthday. She takes the same journey all take. If the 49th succeeds in knowing all five seals, the lion will lie down with the lamb in staggering fashion in this world. Struggle will finally yield to an age of innocence, and peace will reign in a new millennium. What you see here among the Mystics is the firstfruits of that age."

For the first time the prophecy made sense to him. "What about the other world?"

"Ahhh, you mean the one you came from. Ancient Earth."

"Yes."

Mirium crossed her arms and paced, eyes on the wall. "The age of peace will come there as well, though perhaps not as most believe." Her voice softened. "The lake is within all. The prophecies of terrible cataclysm and great reward are most useful when understood as the story of the struggle in the hearts of all humans in each moment."

So then he was right about the difference between the two worlds. That this wisdom and depth came from such a young woman mystified him. And the 49th was even younger.

Mirium suddenly turned, full of excitement. "And now Elyon will show you those firstfruits. The Gathering awaits. Quickly, we mustn't keep them long."

With that, Mirium hurried from the Thrall, down the steps, and up the path, blue dress flowing around her thighs. Thomas and Chelise ran after her, drawn by a power beyond them. Or in them. Or everywhere.

He'd been here before, and that distant memory was being coaxed out of a deep forgetfulness.

He could hear the distant roar of the waterfall, growing louder with each step as they ran. Along a creek beside the colored forest. Over a long, gentle slope.

Thomas crested the hill and slid to a stop beside Chelise.

Before them sprawled a great circular lake, glowing with fluorescent emerald water. The water was lined with huge, evenly spaced, gleaming trees, set back forty paces from a white sandy shore. Animals encircled the lake, sleeping or drinking.

On the far side, a towering pearl cliff shimmered with ruby and topaz hues. Over the cliff poured a huge waterfall that throbbed with green and golden light as it thundered into the water a hundred meters below. The rising mist captured light from the trees, giving the appearance that colors arose out of the lake itself. Here, there could hardly be a difference between day and night. To his right, the creek fed the lake.

Michal and Gabil were at the water's edge, as were all the Mystics, most seated on the sand with legs crossed, arms raised, swaying slowly.

Oblivious to Chelise now, Thomas stumbled down to the shore, heart in his throat, desperate to know as he'd once known. Feet bare on the sand, he took four long steps and dropped to his knees. A warm mist hit his face. His vision exploded with a red fireball and he gasped, sucking the mist into his lungs.

Elyon.

He was aware of the wetness tickling his tongue. The sweetest taste of sugar laced with a hint of cherry flooded his mouth. He swallowed. The aroma of gardenias blossomed in his nostrils.

Ever so gently, Elyon's water engulfed him, careful not to overpower his mind. But deliberately.

The red fireball suddenly melted into a river of deep blue that flowed into the base of his skull and wound its way down his spine, caressing each nerve. Intense pleasure shot down every nerve path to his extremities. He dropped to his belly, body shaking in earnest.

Elyon.

How long had it been since he'd felt such an intimate oneness with the Source of all that was? In that awareness now, he didn't know how he'd managed without it.

The waterfall's pounding intensified, and his mind reeled under the power of this Creator, who opened his senses to new colors and smells, his heart to new emotions that made the old seem flat by comparison.

The first note came then, a low tone, lower than the thunder of a million stallions in full gallop. The rumbling tone shot up an octave, rose to a forte, and began etching a melody in Thomas's skull. He could hear no words, only music.

The single melody was joined by another, entirely unique yet in harmony with the first. The first stroked his ears, the second laughed. And a third melody joined the first two, screaming in pleasure. And then a fourth and a fifth, until Thomas heard a hundred melodies streaming through his mind, each one unique, each one distinct.

All together not more than a single note from Elyon, one that was always present though rarely heard.

A note that cried, *I love you.*

Thomas breathed in great gasps now. He stretched his arms out before him. His chest heaved on the warm sand. His skin tingled with each droplet of mist that touched him.

Elyon.

Me too! Me too! I love you too.

Then he formed the words screaming in his mind. "I love you," he breathed softly.

Immediately, a new burst of colors exploded in his mind. Gold and blue and green cascaded over his head, filling each fold of his brain with delight.

The lake is inside. Always present but rarely known.

He trembled with the thought and rolled to one side, eyes closed. A hundred melodies mushroomed into a thousand. His nostrils flared with

195

the pungent smell of lilacs and roses and jasmine, and his eyes watered with the intensity.

It was as though Elyon was a bottomless ocean, and Thomas tasting only a stray drop. As though Elyon was a symphony played by a million instruments, and he thrown from his feet by a single note.

He opened his eyes. Long ribbons of color streamed through the mist above the lake. Light spilled from the waterfall. Chelise lay in a fetal position several paces away, curled up in the warmth of Elyon's power. The Mystics trembled as the mist washed over their bodies. No sound could be heard above the waterfall.

The words from Elyon came then.

I love you. You are precious to me. You have always been mine. Look at me again and smile.

"I will look at you *always*," he wept. "I worship the air you breathe. I worship the ground you walk on. Without you there is nothing. Without you I'll die a thousand deaths. Don't ever let me leave you."

How can you leave where you always are, hidden in me, and I in you?

Always present. Always light. Always here, never over there. A dimension, not a destination.

He heard the distant sound of a child giggling. Then the voice of the child.

Do you want to climb the cliff?

The cliff! Thomas gasped. He'd been up those cliffs before . . .

Mirium's voice cried out for all to hear: "In whom are we one?" She was on her feet, arms spread wide.

The rest were on their feet now, crying out in unison above the thundering falls, "Inchristi is all; Inchristi is in all!"

Thomas pushed himself up and gazed about, still stunned by the child's invitation. None of the others looked his way, not even Chelise, who was also on her feet, fists raised to the sky in rapture. Like children, their display was simple abandonment to affection. It would appear foolish in any other context, but it was completely genuine here.

The child's voice came again, echoing through his mind.

Do you want to climb the cliff, Thomas?

He spun toward the forest that ended at the cliff. Behind him the others were running into the lake, splashing with delight.

Do you want to play?

And then he knew where his mission from Talya would begin.

In two days' time, while the armies of Other Earth clashed in battle, he would climb the cliff.

19

WHEN STEVE said no one lived near the cabin, he meant it. After leaving the highway, we'd taken narrower and narrower roads that soon put us on a dirt road for six miles. By the time we finally pulled up to the cabin, I saw it was actually a small wood house set in a clearing with tall trees on all sides.

As soon as we stepped through the front door, I felt more comfortable. Steve had parked the car in a small barn, and we were sure to stay inside so no satellites or drones could find us.

The main room had a fireplace and a tall, peaked ceiling. The kitchen was past the great room, and there were two floors with a total of four bedrooms. Two bathrooms and a crawl space. Steve quickly showed me where everything was, going from room to room, making sure all the blinds were closed.

The long drive had given me time to process my situation. First-stage acclimation, Steve called it. My brain was scrambling for a context in which I could begin forming a cohesive worldview. My thoughts had to secure themselves to a set of beliefs, like anchor lines, so the brain wouldn't just float away. It was exhausting, but less so if I just let it happen, Steve said. Slow is smooth, smooth is fast, he coached, just like the motto of Special Forces.

According to him, I was actually better suited than adults to figure out what was happening, because my mind was open, not closed down by preconceived ideas. Perception was almost entirely a by-product of group consciousness. Now I could create my own to some extent.

So that's what I tried to do, and he let me by not stuffing my brain with more information.

"Can I use this one?" I asked, peering around a small room decorated in a kind of pink.

"Take any one you like. I don't know how long we'll be here." He was still sweating and looking out the windows every few seconds. It was odd, because when we weren't talking about what was wrong, I sort of forgot that the whole world was looking for us.

"Can I lie down for a few minutes?" I asked, suddenly aware of how exhausted I was.

He stepped away from the window. "Of course. You should. Did you know the brain consumes nearly three-quarters of all the energy you put into your body?"

"Really? The brain doesn't even move!"

"Oh, it's moving, all right. All matter is in movement, billions of vibrations a second. Most subjects who've had their memories wiped sleep like cats, eighteen hours a day." He headed for the door. "Rest as long as you like. I'm going to secure the house and terminate any internet. The television's old-school, untraceable, so that's good."

"Steve?"

He turned back. "Yes?"

"Do you really think we're going to be okay?"

He walked up to me and put his hands on my shoulders. "I took you from DARPA because I believe in you. I can help, but the best hope we have is letting your mind do what it can do."

"What if it can't do that sort of thing anymore?"

"You brought down the sky in Project Eden, didn't you?" He tapped my head. "It's all in there, waiting for you to access it. Of course you can do that! Right?"

"Right." And in that moment I thought, *Of course I can do that.* But I wasn't stupid either—we were in a terrible situation.

But I could trust him. He was the closest I had to a father.

Actually, he was the only person I knew.

"I want to try something when you're ready," he said. "Okay?"

"Sure."

"Come down when you've rested."

"Okay."

I lay down, exhausted, and I'd only just started wondering how much energy my new brain had used in all of its acclimation before I fell asleep.

In that sleep, I didn't dream. Not one stray thought. Or if I did, I didn't know it when I opened my eyes.

It was darker. I glanced at the window. Still day, but not for long. I bolted up, disoriented. The events of the day fell into my mind, but the worry I'd felt before was gone. Steve was downstairs, waiting to show me something. Oddly enough, I was more interested in what that was than in the troubles that had brought us to the house.

But that changed when I stopped at the top of the stairs, staring down at Steve. He was seated on the couch, watching the feed on the wall-mounted television. The news was of me and him, and we weren't just two small pictures anymore.

We were half the screen, stacked one on top of the other. To the right of the images, a woman who was an expert on terrorism was speaking.

"We've confirmed that the suspect's fingerprints were found on several fragments of the bomb casing. It may be hard to imagine that a seventeen-year-old would be capable of such a violent attack, but Rachelle Matthews isn't just any girl. She was put through a terrible ordeal in Project Eden, punished by a religious fundamentalism that preached the end of the world. It's easy to see how someone born and bred on religiously motivated hatred and survivalist doctrines could end up with a terrible aversion to the religion that broke her in the first place. The fact that she's schizophrenic only supports the evidence. She might be a young victim, but make no mistake, this is one very dangerous girl."

I stared, hardly able to process what they were saying. I didn't even remember the history she was talking about.

"We have to remind the audience that Rachelle Matthews is only a suspect at this point," someone else was saying, but the expert cut in.

"We should also remind the audience that she's not working alone. A post—"

"Assuming it *was* her."

"Correct. An untraceable statement from a group that identifies itself as Society Against Control claims complicity in the bombing. The fact that she's on the run with Steve Collingsworth, who may be connected to this society . . . It all adds up to a very disturbing picture."

"Steve?"

He grabbed the remote, killed the picture, and jumped up. "You're awake! Sorry, I just checked in on you and you were sound asleep."

We stared at each other.

"Don't pay any attention to that," he said, motioning to the TV with the remote, then tossing it on the couch. "Nothing·new, we're just being framed, that's all."

"But why?"

And then I remembered why. Vlad was going to finish what he'd started. And neither Steve nor I had any idea what that was.

"Never mind."

"Did you dream?"

"No." I walked down the stairs, aware of each time my feet touched the wood. Wood. There was something amazing about the wood, I thought. It used to be a tree but now it was a step. Strange how my mind jumped from worrying about the news of me to the wonder of the wood. Lack of context, maybe.

". . . thirsty?" Steve was asking.

"I'm good. So you were going to show me something."

"Yes." He hurried to his right, jittery, then turned back. "Now?"

"When else?"

"Okay, right. Now. Sit." He patted the couch. "Sit here."

I sat.

"Okay." He dragged the small glass coffee table to the edge of the rug. "Need some space. Okay, a little context, right?"

"Right."

He began to pace on the rug. "Okay, the only hope we really have is you, like I was saying earlier. More specifically, your brain. No matter how you slice or dice this, one thing's clear: someone out there sees you as a threat. And not just a little threat because you're able to read people's minds—which you can no longer do anyway. Follow?"

Made sense. I nodded.

"Which means you must have more power than either of us understands."

That made less sense, but he kept talking.

"We *have* to figure out what's so threatening to them. We've seen you do plenty that defies our understanding of nature, but what would push them to such extremes? What's really happening here?"

I sat mesmerized. He kept pacing, hands on his hips now.

"It was the business of this other world you and your father claimed to have tapped into that finally got me thinking. I'm going to put it in the simplest terms I can, using basic science."

He stopped, lifting a finger.

"But first some context. You have to understand that everything you can see, hear, smell, feel, and even think of is actually energy expressing itself at different frequencies. The whole universe, even the densest matter, is energy. Problem is, most of it—seventy-three percent according to our best models—is actually in frequencies that the human senses can't detect. Case in point: there's enough energy in one cubic meter of empty space to vaporize all the oceans of the world. We just don't have the technology to see all that energy, understand how it's really working, or harness it. Follow?"

"Follow."

"Even more, the forces that make our world what it is seem to be outside space and time. We see the effects in experiments but don't know how they work. Albert Einstein called it 'spooky action at a distance.'"

"Spooky action?" I said. "Scary?"

"Well, it can be. The unknown is always a bit frightening to the brain. Point is, all material expression is actually energy, and that energy is originating beyond space and time. We perceive the material world, but we don't see how it *really* is. Which makes what we perceive a kind of illusion. Clear?"

I nodded. "Clear enough."

"The biggest challenge that we scientists face is what we call the observation problem. One thing we've known for over a hundred years is that things exist only when we measure or observe them. When we perceive them. Somehow energy collapses into our perception of it as things like tables and chairs only as we observe it as a table or chair. Thousands of experiments have shown this to be the case at the subatomic scale, but we don't know how it's happening. Figuring out how is the single greatest problem facing science—this is the observation problem."

"So we're making up the chair, not looking at it?" I said.

"Not that, but something like that. Or maybe that, no one really knows. Our collective consciousness manifests the world we see in the way we observe it. Most scientists still refuse to consider the possibility that a higher consciousness exists. They insist that all consciousness comes from the brain, and when the brain dies, no soul or consciousness survives it. It's called materialism."

"But you think differently," I said. "You think that our brains are like radios, receiving certain frequencies. So everything is consciousness, but when we see the table we're only seeing what it is at a certain frequency. From a higher perspective, it would look like energy."

He looked at me, surprised. "Yes. Where'd you get that?"

I wondered the same thing myself. "I don't know. Just popped into my head."

"Really?"

"Really." I grinned. "Pretty good, huh? And I saw the radio on the table."

He bounded over to the side table and picked up the small black radio. Set it on the rug in front of me.

"Scientists are beginning to call that type of consciousness 'quantum consciousness.' A force beyond time and space activated by our own consciousness."

"God?"

"No, not God, assuming you believe in God, but—"

"Of course God is real," I said. "Even atheists believe in God, right? They just call it something else. At the very least, God is where everything comes from."

He hesitated. "This stuff is just popping into your head?"

I shrugged. "I guess."

"Okay then, God. But quantum consciousness wouldn't be infinite. It would be something an infinite God created. Regardless, what if our brains are like this radio? Like a radio, we can only pick up certain frequencies, so we operate within those limited frequencies. Still follow?"

"Yup."

"Now let's pretend that the way you tune this particular radio is by raising it or lowering it. So down here"—he dropped to one knee and held the radio just above the ground—"on terra firma, we only pick up lower frequencies, stuff we can see with our eyes and hear with our ears, measure with our instruments, et cetera." He stood, raising the radio higher. "But if we lift the radio up here, we encounter totally different frequencies. New music that supersedes the lower frequencies."

"And you think that's what I can do?"

"Yes. I think you have the capacity to rise into a higher state of consciousness that's beyond time and space. It's the only thing that can possibly explain how you see things happening before they happen. Spooky action at a distance."

"I can do that?" The thought made my heart beat a little faster.

"You've done it a hundred times. We've measured and recorded it over and over. It's nothing short of miraculous, which is impossible in the mind of science. Meaning maybe all the claims of spontaneous healings and other miraculous events that have been recorded in history really did happen. Someone, somewhere, activated a higher power beyond space and time, and that power changed matter within time."

"God," I said.

"If you will, God. Though I don't believe in God the way you seem to.

The fact that you even have a belief about God surprises me. You have no context for it. Religious belief is one thing that always vanishes in the MEP."

I stared at him. "Maybe you *should* believe."

"If it means becoming anything like you, I will," he said with a wink.

"So this is what you wanted to show me?"

"Not yet. One more thing. Your dreams." He set the radio on the fireplace mantel. "I think your dreams are real. At least as real as what we perceive to be real in this world. Whatever you can do in your dreams, you can do here, because you *know* you can. You believe it. You've actually experienced it by rising into higher consciousness."

"But can't you bring your radio higher? Then you could do what I did too."

"The rest of us can't because we don't *know* we can. We believe we can't, so we can't. But you can. I think you're the leading edge of a whole new way of being in the world."

"You mean I have faith," I said. Again, I was surprised that these ideas seemed plain to me. Maybe because in a way I had the mind of a child and it was easy for children to believe things.

He shrugged. "Yeah, I guess. Faith. Now that I think about it, it's the fulfillment of what the mystics have always insisted. Whatever is asked in a higher power is done. 'You will do what I do and even greater things'— Jesus said something like that. Problem is, few if any of us really operate in that higher power, or we would see it all the time. Knowing, belief, faith—they're all the same. It's what's activating knowledge in you right now. Stuff you shouldn't know after going through an MEP."

I stared at the lamp and thought about who he was saying I was and what I could supposedly do, and I knew he must be right.

"You're right," I said. "That is something."

"That's not what I'm talking about," he said, smiling.

"No? What is?"

He walked to the bar between the great room and the kitchen, picked up a clear glass of water, and set it down in the middle of the rug.

"You don't remember any of this, but you could do things with water.

Make it boil in a few seconds just by concentrating on it. We told you it was all in your mind and you believed it because of the drugs, but it was real. And that was with a doped-up mind."

He stood back, fingers trembling.

"Look at me, Rachelle." His eyes sparkled. "You have more power than you can begin to imagine. I need you to know that when they reformatted your mind, they also wiped out all the old paradigms that told you what *couldn't* be done. All the fears and doubts that limited you. You have the mind of a child who knows what the rest of us, beaten up by life in the physical world, don't know. Anything is possible. Because you've already experienced that higher frequency, you can do it again. You could walk on water if you knew you could. Do you hear me?"

"I can?" Maybe he was only trying to boost my belief. If so, it was working.

"You can. So do it for me now. Instead of looking at the water as a liquid, see it as the energy it is, and change its physical manifestation."

I looked at the glass sitting there. "Now?"

"Now."

So I did. In my mind's eye, I saw the cup as swirling energy and me with a light that was God flowing through me, connecting with the glass. It was all in my imagination, but imagination was actually image making, and in my wild creativity, I saw the water turn to light and rise from the glass. Out of the glass. Up into the air, then back down—*plop*—into the glass.

Steve grunted and I looked at him. "What?" His eyes were round like saucers. I looked back at the glass sitting there on the floor, unchanged. "What is it?"

"You . . . You didn't see that?"

"I was just getting started. I saw it in my mind but I—"

"It wasn't just in your mind!" He took another step back. "Do it again."

I'd done it? But of course I had. Now totally excited, I turned my head back to the glass and did more. I lifted the whole glass with water so that it was floating about four feet above the ground. The water glowed because I was seeing it as energy.

I saw it all right there in front of me, only this time I knew it wasn't only in my imagination. Or maybe it was, but if so, the whole world was an imagination, subject to belief and faith.

Steve was stepping forward, eyes fixed on the glass. "Can you hold it there?"

"Sure." I was grinning like a monkey. "I can do other things too."

"Just hold it there." He lifted his arm and reached toward the glass. When his hand was maybe six inches away, energy sparked on his fingertip and he jerked it back.

"Cool, huh?" I said. "Watch this."

I lifted the water out of the glass and threw it toward him. It collapsed back into liquid and splashed his face. Steve gasped, jumping back, face and shirt soaked. The glass fell to the rug with a thump.

"Oops," I said.

Then he was laughing. And I was laughing. And jumping up, dancing a little jig. We were like two children, both of us lost in the moment of making the impossible possible.

"That's what I'm talking about!" he said. "That's why all those news stories don't mean a thing." He leaped over to the couch, grabbed the remote, and stabbed it at the television. "That's why we're not afraid"—he faced me, jabbing a finger at the screen—"of that."

"Never," I cried, filled with more excitement than I had yet known in my six hours of new life. "Never, never!"

He reached forward and jerked up my right sleeve. "See this?"

For the first time since awakening, I saw that I had a tattoo on my arm. A white circle with a green circle inside it. The rest was black. But it wasn't on my skin as much as in my skin. Three-dimensional, as if someone had surgically implanted the circles in my arm.

"You had it when you came out of Eden. You claimed it came from your dream world. So you see, there's something very special about you."

I stared, stunned. "What's it mean?"

"That's what we're going to find out. Just say the first thing that comes to mind."

"It's a seal," I said.

"A seal? That's it?"

I looked up at him. "A Seal of Truth."

"Anything more?"

"No. Just a Seal of Truth."

"Okay, a Seal of Truth. That's good. You see how that happens when you're in this state? You know things no one who's had their mind erased should know. Little pieces of information that you're accessing in higher frequencies because your mind can somehow receive them."

"You think?"

"I do. And I also know that the brain is very selective. When you're in survival mode, the brain radically narrows its perspectives, robbing all the energy available to focus on only fight or flight. 'Get away from the tiger. Run!' Which you do to save yourself. In that state, the brain can't think logically. It shuts down all centers that process reason and redirects the energy to fight-or-flight programming and mechanisms. In fact, when you're in terrible fear, you don't even know who you are. You can't. That part of the brain is shut off."

"Really? That's kind of frightening."

He lifted a hand to me. "No, no, don't be frightened. I'm just telling you how the brain works so you can *avoid* fear! When you're in fear, that childlike imagination that knows anything is possible shuts down. Hundreds of studies have shown how fear locks out higher thinking. So you need to be like a child who doesn't know fear. No matter what happens, you just be you." He pointed at me. "*That* you, who believes anything's possible, fearless."

"Fearless," I said, flashing him a grin. "That's me."

". . . now can confirm reports of a second bomb at a church eighty miles south of Washington, DC." The voice on the television turned both of our heads. "There are no reports of casualties yet, but we understand that the church was in service at the time. It appears the bombing in Washington this morning was only the first planned by . . ."

I didn't hear the rest because the window by the door shattered.

I spun, heart in my throat, as a hot gust of air lifted the curtains and blew past me. It was pitch-dark outside. Someone was here!

As if in answer, a fist pounded on the door.

I heard the chuckle then. A deep laugh that I was sure I'd heard before, even though I had no memory of it.

Vlad! I thought, rooted to the floor. *Vlad's come to finish what he started!*

"Run!" Steve rasped. "Hide!"

I ran.

20

PULSE POUNDING through my veins, I ran. Leaping over the couch, two long strides to the staircase, quick as the beating of my heart, up the stairs four at a time, only barely aware that I was moving faster than what most would say is possible.

I had only one thought. The bed in my room. *Get under it! Hide!*

I hit the carpet next to the bed already rolling and was small enough to only scrape the bedframe, but as soon as I was under I thought, *Oh no, I forgot to close the door!*

Before I had time to think, I reacted, rolling back out, jumping up, closing the door quiet as I could, then quickly rolling back under the bed, facing the wood-framed mattress above me, breathing hard and trying not to.

What is seeing beyond what you think should be, dear daughter?

I caught my breath, surprised by the voice in my head. Like the ones DARPA had insisted were auditory hallucinations. But they'd lied to me.

Had I just read someone's mind? But no, or I should have been able to read Steve's mind. So maybe I was hallucinating. Or maybe I was hearing my own mind. Or something else, like a higher radio station.

That reasoning was enough to pull my mind out of raw reaction into logical thought. Where was Steve? Why hadn't he run with me? Had I actually heard the laugh that I assumed was Vlad's? What if I'd only imagined it? How could I even know what he sounded like if my memory had been wiped?

Something had broken the window and the wind had blown in, that much was true. Someone had knocked. Steve had told me to hide. All fact.

I held my breath and listened as carefully as I could. The house was creaking faintly. The veins on my neck were pulsing. The TV was still on downstairs.

Then I could hear other muffled voices, not from the TV but from Steve talking to whoever had come to the door. Who were they?

The TV went silent. The voices were still muffled and I had to strain to hear the words.

"Then I'm sure you wouldn't mind us taking a look upstairs."

I couldn't make out Steve's low response, but now I knew they'd come looking for me.

"Look, Steve." They knew his name. "Either you can let us handle this internally, or we can call the police. You clearly know what . . ." And then I didn't hear the rest because my mind was jumping around.

Steve had told me to hide because he wanted to protect me, but could he protect himself? I'd seen him fighting with the guard in the garage. That was one man, and if I hadn't saved Steve, we would both be in prison by now.

So who was here to protect whom? Steve said that fear would narrow my mind, so I shouldn't be afraid, but in a state of fight or flight, fear was a good thing, right? It was how people survived—and right then, all I could think about was that I had to save Steve, the man who'd saved me.

It was enough for me to move. Quickly. I rolled out, rushed from the room, and slid to a stop at the top of the stairs, staring down over the railing.

Two men faced Steve. Both were dressed in black slacks and long-sleeve black shirts, the kind without buttons. Both looked normal enough. Both looked up at me with Steve, who'd gone pale.

For a few seconds, no one spoke. The man on the right had reddish hair and blue eyes. The other, blond with a close-shaved beard. They didn't look so threatening to me.

"What's happening?" I asked.

The redhead cocked his eyebrow. "Well, well, speak of the little devil."

"I'm not a devil. Why are you here?"

He seemed to think that was funny. "I'm afraid the world perceives you as one very nasty devil who's come to kill all their children."

"Don't listen to them." Steve backed toward the stairs. "They say they're from DARPA, but I don't buy it."

"Of course you don't, Steve. But if we wanted to hurt you, you'd already be dead."

"How am I supposed to know you're with the company? A business card?"

"I told you," the redhead said. "We're with the compliance group. My name's Clive, he's Richard."

"Never heard of any compliance group."

"Because we don't exist. It's what allows us to do our job. You asked how we found you. Truth is, we never lost you."

He seemed like a decent guy, and maybe he really could help us. So I headed down the stairs.

But Steve wasn't so sure. "Stay where you are, Rachelle. Just stay up there."

I stopped halfway down. "But they already know where we are."

He blinked as if this was a new thought. Maybe he wasn't thinking clearly in his fear.

I walked all the way down, crossed the room, and sat on one of the stools at the breakfast bar, far enough away that I could still run out through the back door if I had to. I was probably a lot faster than them, right?

The redhead wagged his head at the couch. "Sit down, Steve." Clive was in charge. His partner, the blond, had crossed his arms and was watching, jaw firm, but even his glare didn't unnerve me much. Maybe I was being naïve.

And that made sense. The reason I was suddenly much calmer than Steve was because I was like a child, not knowing danger the way he did. But I was also easily influenced, so fear could come quickly, like it had when Steve told me to run.

So which was better: fear to survive, or no fear so I could believe anything was possible? Maybe right now I should feel more fear.

Steve edged over to me, strung like a piano wire. "Fine. You say you came to talk sense. So talk sense."

"Stand then. But what I have to say might come as a bit of a shock."

"I don't think anything would surprise me anymore."

"Fair enough. But don't say I didn't warn you."

Clive bent down and picked up the glass I'd played my tricks with. Turned it upside down and let the last few drops fall to the rug. Then set it on the mantel next to the radio.

"As you've heard," he said, turning to face both of us, "a bomb went off this morning in DC, killing forty-seven. Fifteen more in the hospital. The whole world is gunning for the girl with the shattered mind and her misguided cohort, who broke her out of a secure facility. They're saying you have links to an organization that calls itself SAC. Society Against Control. No one wants to be controlled, but few would ever resort to the kind of violence you have. That takes a truly twisted mind. Which is what—"

"None of it's true," Steve cut in. "And if you've been watching us as you say you have, you already know that. It's all a lie."

"Which makes you wonder what the truth is, doesn't it, Steve?"

"I know what the truth is. I was there."

"Of course you think you know the truth. We all think we know what the truth is based on the evidence we think we have. Not so long ago, everyone had evidence that made it clear to them the earth was flat and the body was solid. Today we know the earth is round and the body is 99.9999 percent empty space, held together by quantum forces we're just now figuring out how to manipulate. So what are people a hundred years from now going to know that today sounds absurd? Makes you want to second-guess everything, doesn't it?"

"As we should. What's your point?"

"The girl beside you is my point. The evidence you think you know tells you DARPA sees her as a problem. In truth, she's the most valuable human being alive. We would never allow any real harm to come to her."

Steve took a bit to respond. "That's not the way I read DARPA's attitude. Not even close."

TED DEKKER

"No? What else do you think you know? Starting with the bomb. Were you complicit in this morning's church bombing?"

"Of course not."

"But the bombing did happen, you do know that, don't you?"

"Yes."

"You perceived it with your own eyes, didn't you?"

This time Steve hesitated. "What are you saying?"

Clive paced to his right. Richard, the blond, still hadn't moved a muscle.

"I'm saying what you already know. Technically speaking, no one actually sees anything with their eyes. They're receiving signals that their programming interprets in the visual cortex at the back of the brain, not in their eyeballs. You know as well as anyone that we'll soon be able to reprogram the visual cortex so that if we look at a glass, say, we might see a ball instead, hard as that is to imagine. We don't see the world the way it is, we see it as our brain interprets it."

"You're saying we didn't see the church bombing? That's absurd."

"Project Eden proved that our entire lives are the result of what's been programmed into us, if not by an MEP, then by centuries of indoctrination and collective consciousness. But the MEP works much faster. Using it, we can just erase someone's memories and give them new ones, which radically changes their lives."

I tried to connect the dots. Was he saying we were still in some kind of Project Eden?

"There's no way," Steve snapped, but I could tell he wasn't certain. "There's no way! No way!"

"No way what?" I asked.

Clive drilled Steve with a long stare. "Do you really think the company would allow you to get away with running around and exposing our deepest secrets? *Your* brain was first wiped seven days after the fall of Project Eden. You went through the MEP a second time last night and woke up an hour before you so boldly snatched Rachelle from the white room. None of it happened, Steve. There was no church bomb."

214

Steve looked like he'd been slapped. I was surprised that he would actually believe the man.

"That can't be true, right?" I said.

"That's impossible." Steve's voice was trembling. "The news is—"

"The news was created by DARPA and is being fed only to the devices you have access to. Neither you nor Rachelle were at the church this morning. You were both under deep, in the MEP. Trust me when I say it was part of our research. As are you."

"That's . . . It's just not possible! It can't be true!"

"No? You tell me, Steve. You're the expert. *Could* it be true?"

"I . . . Yes, but . . ."

"But you don't want to accept it."

"You went through the MEP too?" I asked Steve, looking up at him. "But then . . . how do either of us know what's true?"

"You don't," Clive said. "Fact is, no one can trust what they see or remember. That may be the only truth we know is actually true. What we think is real is only the brain's cognitive perception of data streams. It's impossible for the brain to know what's true, so it makes itself the god who knows. Which is why Steve's falling apart right now. His brain is being told it's been wrong this whole time. It's practically short-circuiting. Look real close and you can see sparks flying."

Strange, but in that moment, I knew his reasoning not only made sense but was true. Whether or not that meant Steve was part of the MEP program was another matter. He could be trying to trick us with that.

"Don't listen to him," Steve growled. But he was sweating and nervous. "Don't listen to a thing these two fools say! If this is all part of DARPA's continuing research, why would you come here? Why not just let us play whatever sick game you're forcing us to play?"

"Because something's gone wrong. The second bomb, which went off an hour ago and was only recently reported, was real. And we have no idea who detonated it. The director pulled the plug on you. The three of us were sent to bring you back."

"No!" I snapped, standing from the stool. "I'm not going back."

"You have to. We can't just let you run around with all this in your head. Mack's in the van just outside now. If we're not out there in ten minutes, he'll be in here with guns. You don't want to mess with Mack when he's packing heat."

I stared at him, freshly frightened.

"Look, it's not so bad," he said, face softening. "The only difference between you and the rest of society is that you actually know your brains have been programmed to believe what you believe. You'll know for a few more hours, that is. Tomorrow you won't remember any of this and you can get back to believing what you've been taught to believe, just like everyone else. Regardless, you have to come with us."

In that moment I decided I hated him. I hated him because I knew that most of what he was saying was true, at least the part about how all people's brains had been taught what to believe. I wasn't sure about the bombing not being real. Either way, there was no way I was going back for more of their programming.

"Cheer up, pumpkin," the blond said, speaking for the first time. His mouth twisted slightly with an impish grin. "You can't run from the truth forever."

"How do you know *you* haven't been through the MEP?" Steve snapped at Clive.

But my mind was on Richard, the blond who'd called me pumpkin. Something about that word triggered a terrible fear deep inside of me.

"Why'd you call me that?" I demanded.

He grinned. "It's a term of endearment, sweetheart. Nothing to fear."

Panic flashed through me. The fear I felt was so dark and terrifying that I reacted without thinking.

I flew at the man in a barely controlled rage. I might have been able to stop myself before I hit him if he hadn't been taken off guard. If not for the fact that in being taken off guard, a red spark twinkled in his eyes.

But I did see that red spark and I screamed, throwing myself forward with every ounce of strength and speed the cells in my body could access.

It happened so quickly that he was only just turning when my fists slammed into his gut. His body flew back and crashed through the window, taking what glass remained with him, and me following, carried by my own momentum.

He crashed into one of the porch posts, hard enough to knock the breath out of anyone.

It didn't knock the breath from him. It hardly fazed him. What it did do was change his face—I saw it as I rolled to my feet on the porch. One moment he was a blond with a close-shaved beard, the next he was bald with red eyes the color of fire.

I didn't understand what I was seeing, and it didn't last long. Less than a split second later he was blond again, stepping forward. Then throwing himself at me. His ferocious roar shattered the stillness.

I could hear Steve yelling something inside, but none of that mattered now. I leaped up and over the blond just as he reached me. My movements were guided by something in the DNA of my cells, purely instinctive.

The man rushed under me as I flipped backward over his head. *The eyes*, I thought. *I have to get to his eyes.*

Still in the air above him, I slashed my hands down like claws, fingers curled. My palms connected with his forehead as he started to throw himself up to meet me. But I was too fast. My fingers were already digging into his eyes.

I shoved them deep, all the way to my third knuckles, screaming with rage.

He went limp and fell face forward onto the porch, pulling me down because my fingers were lodged in his brain. I collapsed on top of his still body, breathing hard.

With a soft whooshing sound, the flesh under me disintegrated, turned to a black fog, then was gone altogether. I fell to the porch floor.

I scrambled to my hands and knees, gawking at the empty space he'd just occupied. Then jumped back, trying to make sense of it. I had vaporized Richard, the blond from DARPA. Which meant he couldn't be from DARPA.

So who was he? Vlad?

My mind spun. Time seemed to stall. I don't know how long I stood there in that daze, only that I eventually noticed how quiet it was.

I turned toward the broken window. No sound from inside. Not a peep. "Steve?"

Nothing. Had he seen what I'd seen?

"Steve!" I cried, rushing to the door. I threw it open and faced an empty room. "Steve!" My voice echoed through the space. My chest was pounding and I couldn't think straight. I didn't have any instincts for this. For any of it! I was just a hollowed-out girl, knowing even less about who I was than when I'd made the glass float.

Had that really happened?

"You lost?"

I whirled to the voice behind me. Clive stood at the bottom of the porch steps, grinning. The back door! He'd come around the cabin.

"I see you got to know our friend. They didn't tell me you knew his weakness. Funny how it all comes back to the eyes."

"Where's Steve?"

"I don't know and don't care. You, they need alive. Steve won't last a day on his own. One way or the other, I'm taking you back." He walked up the steps. "Now if you want to put up a fight, that's fine, but I won't just vanish like the Leedhan. You'll have to kill me with your bare hands, and I don't think you have it in you to kill a human."

I probably would have taken his head off, but what he said stopped me. Three steps back and I was inside the great room, thinking maybe I should run out the back the way he had—I was pretty sure I was much faster than most people. But what about Steve?

"Steve?"

Clive lunged and grabbed my left elbow in a vise grip. Pain shot up my arm and I slapped his face hard with my right hand, crying out. "Stop it!"

Then he was on me, crushing me under his weight as I fell to my back. His hand was around my throat. "You're coming with me!" he bit off. "Get that through that thick skull of yours!"

"I don't think so."

Steve's voice. From behind the man.

He had a shotgun at Clive's head.

"You make one move and I pull this trigger." He nudged the man's skull with the barrel.

"Easy . . ." The bulldog was gone from Clive.

"Take your hands off her!"

The man slowly released his grip on my throat. Sweat beaded his forehead. "Easy, now. Easy."

"Hands behind your head," Steve snapped.

Clive did so slowly, jaw clenching, and I scrambled out from under him.

"Sit!" Steve motioned to the couch with the shotgun. "Now!"

"Easy. You do realize what you're doing. There's no way—"

"Shut up!" He walked around the couch, following Clive, who slowly sat. "What I realize is that someone's playing games with people's lives, mine included. So you're going to tell me who's pulling DARPA's strings."

"You know who's pulling the strings, you fool! You work for her! So do I."

"I'm talking about who's pulling the director's strings." He pushed the barrel closer, only a few inches from the redhead's face now. "I need a name and I need a reason. Talk!"

I was seeing a new side to Steve and joined his anger, pulse racing.

"Tell him!" I cried, stepping around the couch. "And don't think he won't hurt you, because if he doesn't, I will."

Clive glanced between us. "I can't do that."

"Oh, but you can," Steve said. "If what you told us is true—and I admit, it could just as easily be true as a lie—this place will be swarming with agents the moment they realize you've failed. And you have. Tell me and I'll let you go. Don't and you get to feel just how fun this game of yours is."

He lowered the barrel and pressed it against the redhead's thigh.

"I start with your right leg."

"Easy, easy! I already told you what's happening!"

"The truth! Who's behind this and why?"

"The truth!" I echoed.

Fear darkened Clive's eyes. It was a good plan, I thought. A man could live without a leg, right? They'd taken way more than a leg from me and Steve.

"Do it, Steve! If he doesn't tell you, shoot his leg!"

"Who's behind this? Why? Tell me!"

"Okay, okay! Just hold on. I can't—"

"Tell me!" Steve roared.

"Tell him!" I screamed.

"Karen Willis!" Clive said. "StetNox."

I didn't know who Karen Willis was, but Steve seemed to. It was working!

Filled with adrenaline, I stepped up to the man and shoved my face in his. "Why?" I snapped. "Why are they doing this to us? And who's Vlad Smith?"

I saw the red flash in his eyes as soon as I said the name, and I knew immediately that he'd betrayed himself. He was like the other one!

For a single beat, we stared into each other's eyes, mine blue, his red. Both stunned.

And then he was moving like lightning, but I had the advantage because he was seated and off balance. Before he could get a foot off the cushions, I threw my body forward, straddling his belly with both knees, and I stabbed at his eyes with my fingers.

All the way to the hilt, just like before.

His body jerked and quivered as if my fingers were electric prongs, then disintegrated into a whoosh of black fog, leaving me alone on the couch.

I knelt like that, two fingers extended with nothing but thin air under me. Steve still held the shotgun, shocked. "What?"

I stood shakily, eyes on the couch, fearing Clive might reappear.

The shotgun dropped to the floor beside me. "What . . . What was that?"

"He called it Leedhan," I said.

"How did he just vanish like that? That . . . Was that Vlad?"

"No. I don't know." I spun to the door. "But there's another one in the van."

"There is no van outside. No vehicle at all. They can't be from DARPA. Can they?"

I looked at Steve. "If they're not with DARPA, what were they doing here?"

He shook his head, still looking at the couch. "I don't know. But we're gonna figure it out."

"How?"

"Karen Willis." He stooped and grabbed the shotgun. "I know where she lives. Karen Willis is going to tell us everything we need to know."

"Tonight?"

"No. First I have to find out if the DC bombing was real. If not, getting to her will be easier. If the bombing did happen . . ." He stalled.

"Then it'll still be easy," I said.

"How?"

"I'm fast."

"You're just one girl."

"But I'm a very fast girl."

VLAD SMITH stood under the waning moon outside the cabin, arms crossed, pleased with himself. Honestly, it was hard not to be impressed. After so many years of careful planning, the execution could hardly have come off any better. Two of his Leedhan were dead, but attrition had always been part of the plan.

The 49th had finally fallen into a dreamless sleep after hours of pacing and talk. So naïve, so powerful. So blind.

He twisted his head and cracked his neck. Never had liked these bodies much. So dense. So much mush in the skull.

The poison had worked precisely as he'd told them it would, not only wiping the 49th's mind but also quenching her capacity to dream. The last thing he needed now was for her to receive the benefits of the old goat's training in Other Earth. He didn't know what was happening there, but that wasn't his concern now.

Earth was.

Vlad squatted, plucked a twig from the ground, and bit the tip off. Spit it out. He stood and chewed on his neatly fashioned toothpick. Tomorrow would be an interesting day. It was time to go inside.

Maybe he would sleep under her bed.

He smiled at the thought.

Poor wretch.

21

WHILE I SLEPT dreamlessly in the cabin on Earth, oblivious to Other Earth, I was finding myself in terrible misery in the desert with Talya.

Talya, who'd become my tormentor more than my savior.

During my quest for the first three seals, my dreaming between worlds had followed a linear pattern, which had supported me. Each time I fell asleep in one reality, I woke up in the other and was able to apply what I'd learned.

But that progression was now gone. I was independent in each world. Part of me wondered if this too was part of a large conspiracy to blind me further. More, I wondered if Talya was actually a part of that conspiracy.

Why would he turn me Horde, knowing full well how blind I was on Earth?

In that reality, I was clueless about anything happening in Other Earth; clueless even that I was on a quest to find five seals; clueless that I had to find them before the Realm of Mystics was destroyed; clueless that I would have to find the Fourth Seal there, on Earth.

Here in Other Earth I was once again dreaming of Earth, but those dreams only filled me with dread. I was utterly lost and destitute in both realities, suffocating in a blindness so deep that I would have gladly traded my eyesight for a release from that blindness.

I assumed that being taken from Jacob would be painful, but I was only partially right. It proved to be devastating, and more so with each mile as the scabbing disease took more of my mind. The onset of the disease was worse than living with it. Much worse.

The disease was repulsive. My revulsion of the putrid pus hidden in the cracks of my skin and the sickening odor of rotten eggs wafting from my flesh deepened with each passing minute.

Without my consent, I had been cursed. The 49th was supposed to show everyone how treasured they were, not become nobody herself. I was supposed to walk on water, not bathe in the sewer. I was supposed to be gloriously mounted on a horse, leading the world into a new age of stunning beauty—the light of the world, not a wretched gray Scab!

On that mount being led toward the Great Divide, I felt like a prisoner. The cage was my disease, which not even Jacob could love. I certainly couldn't. Who could?

That's the way I saw it, and a part of me hated Talya for taking me away from Jacob. I knew I had to find the Fourth Seal, but did that mean I had to be subjected to such abuse?

The whole of both worlds had become my enemy!

You are your own enemy, dear daughter. You are tearing you down. Tell me, what is seeing beyond what you think should be?

I heard the voice, but in my misery I forgot it almost immediately because I was sure I should be Albino, not Scab, and I was afraid to see beyond that.

For the first few hours trudging north, I knew better than to demand any answers from Talya. He was the wise one, and bitter though I was, I had no choice but to trust him. I was the daughter of Elyon, and I tried to remind myself of what the first three seals had shown me about who he was and who I was. But I might as well have been reminding a brick wall.

I finally broke my silence as the sun began to set. We were on the last stretch of rocky sand at the base of the mountains when I halted, glaring at Talya's back as he continued onward, seemingly oblivious to me, his slave in tow.

"I don't like this!" I yelled.

He kept going. Not even Judah, who was trotting up to the trees, paid me any mind.

"Did you hear me?" The cracks on my cheeks and lips hurt when I opened my mouth to yell. I didn't even have any of the morst paste the Horde used to ease the pain and stench of the disease.

"I don't like this one bit! My skin hurts, my body aches, and I smell like a cesspool!"

"Oh, it's much worse than that, 49th," he said without turning. "The disease is also fogging your mind."

"You didn't have to take Jacob from me!"

"I needed him out of your way."

I stared at the back of his head, aghast. "That's why you sent him? That's absurd! You brought us together! The armies are gathering, I'm lost in the other world, this world is coming to an end, and all you can think about is teaching me some lesson?"

"So you don't like this part of your story, is that it?"

"I need to get back! We're not doing anything out here!"

"We're doing *you*, 49th. Your transformation is the story. *You* are the story."

I ignored his dismissal of my concerns and nudged my mount to draw closer, because Talya was pulling away. "Why would you make me Horde if the drowning heals us from the disease? It doesn't make any sense. It's cruel!"

He still didn't turn, so I screamed at him. "Do you even *care* how I'm feeling? Have some compassion!"

"I have great compassion for you, but I don't join your suffering. Perhaps you could practice metanoia, and do so in silence if you don't mind."

I had no desire to change my cognitive perception of the world while I suffered. A sick joke.

I stopped my horse again. "I'm not going to follow—"

"Silence!" he thundered, twisting back in his saddle. He said it with such force that I could almost feel his words strike my chest. Even in that state, I couldn't ignore his authority.

But I could stew in misery as I reluctantly followed.

We started up the mountain, but I hung back twenty paces, fuming.

Somewhere along the way I thought about being born blind. Why had the man been born blind? the people in the story asked Yeshua. Was it his sin or the sins of those who came before his birth? Neither, but so that the Father's glory could be revealed inside of him.[1]

Yeshua had turned that story into a larger lesson that revealed why mankind was on earth, Talya said. We were all born blind to discover Elyon's glory inside of us while in a world of darkness.

But the truth of that teaching felt distant and quickly vanished. I only wanted to be healed of the scabbing disease.

"And so you make your body your god," Talya said ahead of me.

That was the other thing I didn't like: his knowing my thoughts. I didn't bother reacting, at least visibly. Inside, my frustration only deepened.

It softened that night as I watched him practice his metanoia. I was drawn to his singing, that one long, pure note he often sang into the dusk air. But even by showing his joy and starting the fire and going about his business as if nothing was wrong, Talya continued to reinforce my frustration with him.

I barely had the good sense to keep my mouth shut, but I did, maybe thinking my silence would finally get him to ask if I was okay.

He didn't. Of course he didn't. He was undoubtedly trying to make a point. Elyon corrected those he loved, right? I was being chastised in that way and I hated it.

"Correction," Talya said, laying out his blanket. "Your earthen vessel Scab self hates it. Tomorrow we stop to check on two souls who are precious to me. Please try to at least pretend you're sane."

I ignored his biting comment and rolled over.

It took me a long time to fall asleep in that painful condition. When I finally did, I dreamed, and in that dream I was in a cabin with Steve, learning about consciousness, rebuilding an identity, fighting for survival, a victim of the whole world, being blamed for something I had nothing to do with. I was lost, with no grasp of who I really was.

My predicament in that world was so disturbing that when I woke, I forgot my situation in this world. Then I tried to get up and felt the terrible pain in my joints, and I looked at the disease on my skin and remembered.

The sun was already blazing. I twisted my head, looking for Talya, but there was no sign of him. Smoke from a spent fire coiled slowly into the air. We'd camped on a wide sandy ledge on the east side of the Divide. That's all I knew, because in protesting with silence, I'd refused to ask Talya where we were going.

I scrambled to my feet, only distantly aware of my pain. His blanket, his pack, his horse . . . all gone.

"Talya?"

My voice echoed off the trees and cliffs. There was only one path leaving the camp, but he didn't emerge from that way, or any other.

I decided to wait, but after sitting in silence on a boulder for ten minutes I began to wonder if he really had left, intending for me to catch up. He'd spoken of stopping in to check on someone—maybe he'd left me behind because he didn't want me around them. I was an embarrassment to him.

Setting my jaw, I quickly stuffed my blanket into my saddlebag, mounted, and took the horse up the path.

"Talya!"

No one but me. So I urged my mare to a full run, not sure if I should be outraged or frightened.

I'd ridden for ten minutes—calling out his name, pushing my mare faster, wondering if I'd made a mistake in leaving the camp—when I broke from the trees and saw the small camp. A canvas lean-to faced away from me. Smoke rose from a fire I couldn't see.

I pulled up, blinking. "Talya?"

A head popped out from behind the canvas. A child with gray eyes. A small Horde girl staring at me with great excitement, as if holding a secret. "Mama!"

She ducked back behind the lean-to, and a woman stepped out. A small woman with long braided locks, wearing a simple brown knee-length dress. She too was Horde. What were they doing here, beyond the Great Divide?

The woman welcomed me with a graceful wave. "Come."

The little girl popped out from behind the lean-to again. "Come, come!"

Compelled by such an eager reception, I slipped off my horse and walked up to the camp. The girl grabbed my hand and led me around the side, grinning ear to ear as if presenting a great trophy.

There on the ground by a small fire sat Talya, nursing a clay mug of herbal tea. He chuckled at the girl before lifting his soft eyes to me.

"Good morning, 49th. So nice of you to join us. This is Soromi." He motioned with his mug to the woman. "And her daughter, Maya. Say hello to Rachelle, Maya."

"Hello, Miss Rachelle."

Thoughts of scolding Talya for leaving me took a back seat to the sight of such a delighted girl. "Hello, Maya."

"Talya says you are very special."

I glanced at him. "He does?"

"But that you can't be special until you see that you aren't special because you aren't any more special than me."

They all smiled at me.

"Well, if Talya said that, it must be true," I said with a slight bite in my tone.

"Now, now, 49th, they've come a long way to help a poor Scab in distress, so be nice." Talya motioned to a small boulder opposite him. "Time for a little course correction, my dear."

The mother, Soromi, settled to the ground and leaned on one arm. Her daughter sat beside the boulder Talya wanted me to sit on. I lowered myself to the rock and the girl scooted closer, smiling up at me. Half her teeth were missing, as any young child's would be.

Talya cleared his throat. "I was just sharing some wonderful news with Soromi and Maya, but first you should know what's happening."

"That would be nice," I said.

"We will see." He shoved his chin at the tree line fifty paces away. "Just beyond the ridge lies the Marrudo plateau. On that plateau camps the Circle, the Albinos who've come with Thomas Hunter, just an hour's ride from here."

I stared at the trees. Thomas, the one who'd dreamed of the other world like I did. "He's there?"

"No, but his son is. And in desperate want of some guidance. You're needed, 49th. We leave as soon as we finish our tea, fair enough?"

My heart skipped a beat. "Samuel's there?"

"In the flesh. The one who's smitten with you and refuses to admit it. That Samuel. But I'm afraid you'll only make a fool of yourself in your current state of being, so I've asked Soromi and Maya to share the good news that might help you out." He winked at the little girl. "Maya, tell Rachelle what you've learned."

She didn't hesitate. "Talya says that before we came into these . . ." She glanced at her mother, who helped her out.

"Earthen vessels. But you can use your own term."

Maya turned back to me. "Before we were in these clay bodies, we knew Elyon, who made us. And we still know him, but our clay brains don't know it." She beamed proudly at her mother.

Soromi nodded. "Well done, Maya." She lifted her gray eyes to me. Kind eyes despite her diseased skin. "Talya tells me you need to be reminded that we were foreknown by Elyon before this world, as written. To be foreknown is to have had experience with, not knowledge about. You were in union with Elyon before this world, you understand this?"[2]

Did I? Of course I did.

"Yes."

"Also that all who were foreknown have been glorified. This is also written in your Scriptures. And yet most are still blind to themselves as that glorified light."

She said it with such grace that I wondered if this really was news she'd just heard. But if she'd known Talya from before, why was she still Horde?

"If everyone who's foreknown is glorified, are all foreknown?" I asked, feeling anything but.

"That isn't our business or within our comprehension. Only know that you were and are."

Still, it sounded totally foreign to me now.

"Maya," Talya said to the little girl, "see if you can tell the 49th why we are here in this world of clay bodies with so many problems."

"To see ourselves as light in the darkness so we can be that light," she announced, clearly reciting what had been taught to her. "Justin made us light, like him!"

"Excellent! Now tell Rachelle why we experience so much darkness in this world."

"Because we wear masks that blind us to the light." Maya beamed. She promptly stood and pretended to rip a mask off her face. "We must take them off!"

Talya chuckled, completely taken with her. "Such a smart little girl!"

And I had to admit, in that moment I didn't see her as Horde but as . . . well . . . a delighted little girl.

"When you grow up, Maya," Talya said, "the whole world will listen to you. You're so very good with words."

Maya grinned and squatted back down, suddenly a little shy.

Talya stared at the small fire and spoke gently. "Now tell her the rest of the good news, Soromi."

She lifted her kind gray eyes. "We all put our faith in something." The words slipped from her mouth easily, surely long known. "Those beliefs have more power than we can possibly imagine. With our thoughts—our perceptions—we create our lives. Everyone is doing this all the time, in every moment. It's called binding, which is another word for faith. You know this, daughter?"

It was Talya's teaching when he walked on water. I glanced at him. "Yes."

"What we bind on earth is bound in heaven. In the same way, what we loose on earth is loosed in heaven, Yeshua taught.[3] To bind is to attach or align to. To loose is to let go of or to forgive. The power of forgiveness is yours. What you forgive is forgiven, and what you don't is not forgiven and masters you still.[4] Binding and forgiving are your greatest powers, experienced in every moment of life. They create your experience of life on earth."

I felt Maya's little hand settle on my thigh and I closed my fingers around hers, eyes on Soromi, wondering who she was to know so much.

"Your earthen vessel is bound to this world of judgment. It has many special relationships with itself and with this world, and it searches for love and approval in those relationships. All these are the gods it has deep attachments to. These are all the things your earthen vessel thinks *should be* based upon what it has been imprinted with over many generations. So it seeks meaning and salvation in those things. The earthen vessel is like a bird born into a room, blind to the great sky beyond the room, knowing itself only by what it sees within the walls. Do you follow, child?"

Her words reached into me, and for a moment I wondered if she was Justin, coming to me as a woman. If not, her words could be his, I thought.

"Yes," I said.

"Good. Then you'll understand when I tell you that your great inheritance in this life is the kingdom beyond the room. But to enter it, you have to leave the room, yes? You can't know your risen, glorified self unless you surrender your need for approval and significance in that small room that you think defines you. It's the cost of freedom, yes?"[5]

"Talya says most Albinos only talk of the sky but don't know how to fly," Maya interjected, excited again. "We are free to fly in the sky like a bird!"

Soromi smiled at her daughter. "Like a bird. In the perspective beyond the room, everything will look very different. New sight is found. All things are new. But to enter the door that opens to freedom, you have to leave behind your attachment to the room and embrace your true identity as the one who can fly in the sky."

Emotions clogged my throat because I felt like that poor tethered bird, flapping hopelessly in its small, dark prison. A diseased bird. I looked at Talya.

"But I'm . . ." I stopped, not wanting to offend little Maya with complaints of my condition.

"You're Horde," Soromi said. "And in your judgment of yourself as Horde—your binding—you make for yourself a prison. But if you let go of your judgment of your flesh—if you forgive yourself—you will be free to see that you're neither Horde nor Albino. You're the daughter of Elyon and you love who you are, made in his likeness."

"That's why you made me Horde?" I bit off, looking at Talya. "So that I would have one more thing to let go of?"

"Not one more thing, 49th," Talya said. "The whole room."

He held my gaze for a long time, and I felt frightened, wondering if he was losing faith in me.

"I'm sorry," I began. "I just—"

"No need to condemn yourself for the fear you feel, child," Soromi said in her soft voice. "Condemnation is only trying to fight fear with fear."

She picked up a stick and poked the fire.

"Among my people, I'm an outcast. My husband was a great warrior. Cruel. He threw me out three years ago because I found love in the arms of a more gentle man. I was desperate, you know. Talya found us in the Elong desert and brought us food. Even more, he showed us truth over the years. He asked us to remain Horde." Her eyes lifted. "I see now that it was for you."

Talya had known even then that this would happen? And to what end?

"Don't you want to be healed?" I asked.

She smiled. "Am I diseased? You mean my body. But you must see, being in this body of pain has allowed me to know myself beyond it. I may very well be Albino one day, but my life is happening now. And in this moment, my practice is to align my sight to love. This is how my binding to the world of judgment falls away on its own. I think that's wonderful, don't you?"

Maya looked up at me and grinned. "You can see too," she said. "Don't be sad, I have gray skin and I still love you."

Hearing those words, I hung my head as tears slipped from my eyes. For a long time no one spoke. It was just me feeling sorry for myself and Maya holding my hand. And for those few minutes, hers was the hand of Justin to me.

I finally lifted my head, sniffing, and I chuckled to cover my embarrassment.

Maya jumped up and brought me a yellow fruit from a bag in the corner. "Nanka! It will make you strong!"

"Thank you, Maya."

"You'll have to bring it with you," Talya said, setting his mug down. "Duty calls. The worlds await."

Maya immediately ran to Talya's stallion, grabbed the reins and tugged the beast toward us. "I go with you!" she announced.

"Yes, Maya has generously agreed to lend assistance in the event you run into trouble," Talya said. "I've assured them both that only you will face danger."

"You aren't coming with me?"

"I'll take you, but I think it's best if I stay back, don't you? Maya can be your guide." He swung into his saddle, reached for Maya's outstretched arm, and gracefully pulled her up in front of him.

I looked at Soromi. "You're not coming?"

"This is Maya's adventure," she said, hurrying up to her child. She took Maya's hand. "Now remember, do as Talya says. Nothing more, nothing less."

"I'm a big girl, Mama."

Talya clicked and Judah stepped out of the trees. "Come along, 49th. An opportunity for salvation calls you forth."

22

STILL TOTALLY UNAWARE of my dilemma in Other Earth, the me on Earth was rebuilding my identity from scratch, just like anyone first coming into the world.

That's not to say I was a child. Only my mind was, and it was learning fast.

My body, on the other hand, was more adult than any other adult, Steve said. Faster and more skilled than a ninja—a black-clad fighter who used special martial arts to overcome her enemy.

I had enemies, you see. That was the main thing my child mind was learning fast. The whole world was divided between friends who agreed and enemies who disagreed. Friends were good. Enemies were bad.

But enemies weren't only people. Tooth decay was an enemy. Disease was an enemy. Gravity could be an enemy. *Enemy* was actually everything that was wrong, anything that needed to be fought. It had to be stopped with force.

That's why Steve broke me out. That's how he was saving me.

All of this I learned from Steve as we made ourselves busy at the cabin the next day, figuring things out. Things like how to get to Karen Willis's house after dark, then into her house in the dead of night without anyone knowing.

Karen was our enemy.

Actually, the greatest enemy is yourself, Steve said to me. Or more accurately, who I thought I was or wasn't. Most people covered up their fear of failure by pretending to be who they weren't. But I didn't have decades of evidence that told me lies of who I couldn't be, so I had a huge advantage.

That's what he said, and whenever I brought up the subject of Vlad being my biggest enemy, he shook his head. "We can only deal with what we know."

"But what were those creatures? And what if there are more of them?"

"Which is why we have to get to Karen. That's what we know. If this really is all about Vlad, and I think it probably is, she's the one who knows. Don't think about Vlad right now. Think about Karen. She's the next step. The only step right now."

Made sense, but it didn't matter. I couldn't stop thinking about Vlad and why those two things had come for me last night. Really, I thought Steve didn't want to talk about them because he still couldn't figure out how they could have been real.

So I left it alone.

Figuring out whether the church bombing had been real turned out to be a simple thing. We couldn't use Steve's phone because it was traceable, and he didn't trust the internet in the car either. He wasn't sure about the TV anymore, so he'd dug up some batteries and got the old radio to work. There was no way DARPA would have isolated an old broken-down radio and fed it fake news.

There, on that radio, we heard the real news. The bombings were real. So was the fact that the whole world was scrambling to find us. Which meant the two Leedhan I'd killed weren't tied to DARPA, because if DARPA knew where we were, they'd be all over the cabin.

We were safe, for now.

That afternoon we heard about a third bomb, which destroyed a mosque fifty miles south of the second bombing. Hearing my name repeated over and over on the news was strange. Like it wasn't even real. But everyone was believing it, and I was tempted to believe some of it myself when I heard my own words from the church being played back.

"I think most religion preaches a form of false law, blinding people to who they actually are as the light," my voice said on the radio. "The law's a system of fear and control based on punishment, because fear has to do with punishment. It's like the sky in Eden. Something has to give or people will never be free to know who they really are."

The first time I heard it, I was stunned. "I said that?"

"Totally out of context, but something like that. You said it at the church before the bombing. Before they wiped your memory."

"I really said that? No wonder they think I'm the devil!"

"You're an angel, not a devil," he said. "They just don't know it yet."

We climbed into the car at nine o'clock that night, old paper map from the cabin in hand. No GPS. My stomach was in knots. This was it. The knots were as much anticipation as fear, I thought. We were going to set everything straight.

Both of us were dressed in black, I in a hoodie he found in one of the closets. It was too big, but with the hood up, I wasn't easily recognized.

I bit my fingernail as we drove, mind spinning through everything over and over like a stuck song. I had no idea where we were going, other than to Karen's house—that was Steve's business. We weren't even sure she'd be there, but she'd eventually go home. When she did, we'd be waiting. That was the plan.

What is seeing beyond what you think should be, Rachelle?

I looked at Steve. "Did you just think something?"

"I'm always thinking."

"No, about seeing? I just heard a voice."

He glanced at me. "You can hear thoughts again?"

"I don't know. I heard, 'What is seeing beyond what you think should be?'"

He looked surprised. "Really? Was it my voice?"

"No. I don't know whose voice. Like . . . I'm not sure if it was male or female. Just a soft voice, but I heard it."

"You sure?"

"Yup," I said. "Is that not good?"

"Why would you say that?"

"I don't know. Just the way you looked."

"Sorry. I have a lot on my mind." He glanced at the mirrors and pulled off the highway. "So far so good. We should be there in fifteen minutes."

"Already?"

"It's going to be fine." He gave me a brave smile and turned onto a side street. "Just remember the plan."

Right. And I knew the plan because it was simple.

"About you hearing voices," he said. "Actually, there is something I've been thinking about. Remember what I told you yesterday about not letting fear get in your way?"

"Because it restricts the higher stations."

"Something like that, yes. But the way you moved last night, when you went after . . . Richard. I've never seen anyone move like that. It was incredible." He eyed me. "There's a rare genetic condition called myostatin-related muscle hypertrophy."

"So that's what I have?"

"No, your DNA confuses even our best geneticists, but I think what's happening to you is along the same lines. The human body's capable of far, far more than what we experience. We're learning how to modify genetic expressions without throwing systems out of balance, but we're not there yet. You are. Something triggered an epigenetic shift in you."

"My dreams."

"Some level of consciousness you're accessing in your dreams, yes, so it seems. Let me ask you . . . What were you feeling when you went after him last night? What happened?"

I thought about it.

"It was the way he talked to me. I don't know, but it terrified me. I suddenly hated him. It was like, I had to. And then I saw the red spark in his eyes and I couldn't stop myself."

"That!" he said, lifting his finger. "That's what I've been thinking. If fear makes you move like that, then maybe I was wrong about letting go of fear, at least until we get past this."

"So now you're saying I should feel fear?"

"Think about it. You come out of the MEP with a clean mind, fearless.

Fear causes most people to freeze up or run. Some fight, and it almost always backfires because they don't fight smart. But you . . . You learn fear and some raw, ancient instinct kicks in. Every cell in the body carries dormant memories passed on genetically. No MEP can erase that. Point is, on a cellular level, your body's remembering how to fight when you drop into the lower animal instincts of fear. Make sense?"

"I guess."

"We're depending on you for our survival. On the same kind of skills I saw you execute last night."

"They weren't like people. I can't hurt real people. Right?"

He shrugged. "When it comes to enemies, and I mean people who want us dead, we have to protect ourselves. Sometimes the only way to protect ourselves is to harm others."

Like Karen, I thought. I didn't even know who she was.

"If they're willing to kill hundreds of innocent people in churches, the stakes are much higher than you or me. It's not just about us anymore. When you see Karen, I want you to remember that whatever she knows could lead us to saving thousands, maybe hundreds of thousands of people."

I hadn't thought of it that way, but he was right.

"So yes, I think you should embrace fear. Think of it like a radio wave. Tune in to it. Use it. Hate if you have to hate. People are dying out there. You may be the only thing that can stop it."

I nodded, but I wasn't sure how I felt about hurting people to save people.

"You believe in God, so think of God hating our enemy if you have to. Or think of how God will be upset if you don't save the innocent people you could save by hating our enemy."

Did God hate people? I wasn't sure. Something about the idea bothered me. Made me a little panicky. But he would punish whoever failed him, right? A brick settled in my stomach. What if I failed him?

"I don't like subjecting you to these kinds of ideas so soon after an MEP because you're still in a fragile, innocent state, but I don't know how else to handle this. What I do know is that I don't have the power you do, and if fear and hate let you do what you did last night, do more of that. Hate the whole world if you have to."

He was giving me permission.

"So you think there's going to be problems tonight?" I asked.

"I have no idea what we're up against. You keep me safe, I'll keep you safe. If anything happens to us, who else will stop them?"

It made me nervous, I won't lie, but maybe that was a good thing, like he said, so I gave him a brave grin. "Okay, but I have a question."

"Sure."

"I know you don't know what they were and so you don't want to talk about it, but who do you think they were? I mean, not human, so then what?"

He hesitated, then spoke softly. "You mean Clive and Richard. What I wouldn't give to have one of them in our labs to take energy readings. They're clearly energy expressing itself in physical form—human form—a kind of spiritual technology, if you will. And I say 'spiritual' only because they have intention. They're up to something. Like angels or demons, but I don't know what to do with any of that."

"Then you believe in angels?"

"I wouldn't go that far." He thought for a second. "Then again, Christian Scriptures say that angels walk among us as humans all the time. Sounds absurd to me, but maybe. And maybe lower energies can appear as well, in any form they choose."

He shook his head and blew out some air.

"Crazy. Regardless, as far we're concerned, they're the enemy. Rage. We fight rage with greater rage." He shrugged again. "It's all we have to go on."

So Steve and I were kinda in the same boat. We had to fight force with force.

Steve pulled the car to a stop in an alleyway next to Karen Willis's neighborhood. It was a gated community and there was no way to drive in. Likely guards at the front gate. He didn't even want to drive by.

"This is it?"

"This is it." He reached over the seat and grabbed a black bag full of

239

items he'd collected at the cabin. Flashlights, duct tape, a few hunting knives, that kind of thing. He'd left the shotgun because it was too big and would make too much noise. "Over the wall, down two streets. 459 Rampart. Remember the plan?"

I nodded.

He put his hand on my shoulder. "If anything happens to me, get back to this car. There's a key above the right rear tire. I've programmed the self-drive to take you back to the cabin." He pointed to the display. "Just press this button to start the car, pull up Destinations here"—he showed me—"and select Cabin. Then this—Self-Drive. Got it?"

Seemed simple enough. "What do I do at the cabin?"

"Hide. But it's not going to come to that. We're going to protect each other."

Then we were out and standing in front of a wall about eight feet tall. I remembered my hood and pulled it over my head.

"Over?" I asked.

"One way or the other."

No way over but straight up that I could see. So I jumped up like a cat, saw only dark houses, and dropped onto the grass on the other side.

"Rachelle!" Steve rasped from the far side.

"Jump over!" I whispered as loudly as I could.

A long beat.

"Catch!"

His black bag sailed over the wall and I caught it easily. Then his arms appeared, hooked over the wall as he struggled to haul his body up. He rolled over and landed hard. In my excitement, I'd forgotten that he wasn't as agile as me. Maybe not as strong either.

He clambered to his feet. "This way!" he whispered, grabbing the bag.

Steve led us down two streets, keeping to a line of trees along the edge, hopping over fences. Then up Rampart Street. We crouched under a tree, staring at a large, dark, two-story house with the number 459 on a post by the door. One porch light.

"That's it," Steve whispered.

We both stared, and if he was feeling like me, he was trembling. I knew the plan but I was suddenly sure I would fail. Something would go wrong. They would take me back to DARPA.

"Okay, remember," he said, grabbing my arm. "It's simple. There's no law against ringing someone's doorbell. If no one answers, we wait. She isn't married and lives alone as far as I know. Got it?"

"Got it. What if she sees me and calls the police?"

"She won't. You don't look threatening enough. Trust me. I'll be right behind and out of sight until she opens the door. Ready?"

"Now?"

He looked at the house and nodded. "Now."

I stood and hurried across the sidewalk, then up three brick steps to the front door, glancing back only once to see Steve duck behind the bushes by the steps. My heart was hammering. Part of me wanted to run back to where he was, but I pushed that part aside and pressed the doorbell.

A faint ding sounded inside. So I stepped back, arms behind me. Just a girl in a black hoodie needing help.

But no one came to help, so I glanced at Steve peering around the bushes and he nodded. I pressed the doorbell again.

This time the ding was followed by the sound of pattering feet. The door's brushed-glass panels filled with light from inside. I rubbed my clammy hands on my jeans and waited, ready for anything, including running away if that ended up being the best thing to do.

A small panel opened and a woman's brown eyes looked at me through the glass. If she recognized me, she didn't show it.

Apparently satisfied that she wasn't in danger from a girl in a hoodie, she unlocked the door and cracked it as far as the chain allowed. White-and-black-checkered flannel pajamas. Short dark hair. I recognized Karen Willis from the pictures Steve had shown me, and now my heart was beating so fast I could hardly hear anything else.

"Can I help you?"

"Karen Willis? My name is Rachelle Matthews and I need some help." Then I said the part Steve insisted would get us in. "Vlad sent me."

Her eyes went round, staring at me, unsure.

"Can I come in?"

"How . . ." She looked past me and saw no one else because Steve was hidden. "How did you find me? How did you get in?"

"I told you, Vlad sent me. He said only you. We have to talk."

She looked confused and doubtful, and for a moment I thought she was going to slam the door and call the police.

Just for a moment, and in that moment I reacted.

I threw myself at the door, shoulder first. The chain snapped with a bang as the door crashed in, sending Karen sprawling. Then I was in and Steve was bounding up the steps.

That's when I discovered that Karen Willis wasn't just any ordinary woman. Now that she knew what she was up against, she turned into a wildcat, kicking out and flipping back onto her feet. She charged me, screaming, then spun with a roundhouse kick to cut me down with her heel.

And that's when Karen Willis discovered that I wasn't just any ordinary girl either.

Steve had given me permission to use rage, so I did. I jumped straight up, over her swinging kick, and slammed my heel into the side of her as she came around.

Her head snapped to one side and she collapsed on the wood floor, unconscious.

The door shut behind me. The lock snapped home.

"I think I knocked her out," I whispered, feet planted on the wood floor. "Now what?"

For a second I just stared, heart pounding. This wasn't part of the plan.

"Now we tie her to a chair before she wakes up. Wait here."

He ran down the hall, checking rooms as I watched Karen. Not dead— she was breathing steadily. This was my enemy, I had to remember that. This was the person who knew about Vlad because the Leedhan knew about her. Had to be.

This was my enemy. Thousands of people depended on me hating this enemy, even though she looked like an ordinary person who'd just come to answer the door.

"This way!"

Steve grabbed Karen's heels and dragged her down the hall, me following. Then into a large office, a fancy one with a huge desk and dark wood bookcases lining the walls. A small yellow desk lamp was the only light on.

"Get the curtains!" he said, dropping Karen's heels. He hurried around the desk and wheeled out the wood chair as I pulled the thick curtains closed.

"Help me get her up." He hooked his hands under her arms and pulled her up, and I rolled the chair under her body.

Something about doing this to another person bothered me, but I had to remember that she was my enemy. Anger would keep me on my toes. I had to find some anger and stay with it.

Two minutes later we had her arms and legs duct-taped to the arms and pedestal of the chair. We stepped back and looked at our handiwork.

She wasn't going anywhere.

"Now what?" I asked.

"Now we question her. Wake her up."

"Me? How?"

"Just give her a slap," he said, digging through the black bag.

So I stepped up and lightly slapped her cheek. "Wake up."

"Harder."

I slapped harder, twice. "Wake up. Wake up!"

"Harder! Much harder! We don't have all night!"

He sounded disappointed in me, and maybe that's why I felt such a surge of anger. I hit her harder, much harder, palm across her jaw, screaming at her to wake up. Her head jerked to the side and she groaned. Blood seeped from the corner of her mouth.

"Like that?"

"Something like that." He had a knife in his hand.

Karen's eyes slowly opened. Then sprang wide as she tried to jerk her taped arms free from the chair. "What are you doing?"

"My name's Steve Collingsworth. You met Rachelle at the door. We're the two fugitives who're being framed for the church bombings, but I think you already know all of that. Tell me what StetNox is."

Her eyes darkened and she set her jaw as her awareness of the situation settled in. She spit blood, furious. "Do you have any idea who I am?"

"The president's chief of staff," Steve snapped. "Which is why we're here. We were attacked by two men last night. They called themselves Clive and Richard. Far as we can tell, they work for Vlad. I need you to tell me who Vlad is, why he's after Rachelle, and what StetNox is, and we're not leaving until you do."

Karen stared. And then she began to scream. A wide-jawed scream that made me jump.

"Shut up!" Steve leaped up to her, clamping his hand over her mouth to keep her quiet. "Shut up, shut up!"

I looked around in a panic, half expecting to see the army rushing in. She kept screaming. Then biting at Steve's hand, which he jerked back with a cry. Then more screaming.

I rushed in, shoved Steve aside, and slapped her cheek again, shouting for her to shut up. And when she didn't, I slammed my fist into her temple.

Karen sagged in the chair with me standing over her, arm cocked for another blow. But she was out cold.

"Miss Karen?"

We spun to the voice calling from down the hall.

"Are you okay?"

Steve snatched his finger to his lips and backed up against the wall. Seeing him take cover, I dove behind the desk.

Someone walked down the wood hallway. We'd left the door open—I could see it from where I crouched behind the desk.

"Miss Karen?" Closer. Much closer. "Did you call?"

A barefooted woman in a green robe stepped into the doorway, and Steve rushed her. She gasped, but he was already there, behind her somehow, clamping his hand over her mouth. Knife at her throat.

"Shut up! Not a peep, you hear me?"

She was terrified and I felt sorry for her, but I knew what the stakes were, so I clenched my jaw and stayed hidden.

"I'm going to let go of your mouth, but one scream and I swear I'll cut your throat. Nod if you understand."

The woman nodded and Steve slowly removed his hand. The woman began to cry, doing her best to be quiet. I was horrified for her, because she wasn't my enemy. But what could we do?

"Just calm down. It's okay," Steve said. "What's your name?"

"Anika," the woman said in a shaky accent. She was from India.

"You're a live-in maid?"

She nodded. "Please don't hurt me. I beg you, don't hurt us."

"Are you alone?"

A hesitation, then a quick nod. "Please, I don't want any trouble. I beg you!"

"Hush!" He pushed her toward one of two stuffed chairs next to a floor lamp. "We're not going to hurt you, but we can't let you go until we get what we came for."

"Mama?"

A child's voice echoed down the hall and my heart lodged in my throat. Bare feet, running.

"Mama?"

Anika whimpered, then called out to her daughter as bravely as she could, "It's okay, Gracie. Go back to bed."

But then the small girl was there, in the doorway, staring in at Karen and Steve and her mother.

"Mama?"

I jumped to my feet, fixated on the girl. She was more than a foot shorter than me with brown skin and long curly black hair. Terrified.

"Grab her!" Steve snapped.

The woman tried to break free. "No!"

"Quiet!" Steve clamped his hand over her mouth. "Sit down!" He shoved her into the chair. "You want to live, then keep your mouth shut. Rachelle, grab her!"

This wasn't the plan. Not at all. I stood staring at the little girl, mesmerized. She could have been me.

"Grab her!"

I glanced at Steve. He had the duct tape in his hands, tearing off a piece. The woman was sobbing silently, eyes wide. Seeing her mother so afraid, the girl began to cry as well.

"Mama, Mama!"

I rushed up to her and dropped to one knee. "No, no, it's okay, Gracie. It's okay, we're not going to hurt you." But she kept crying.

I put my arms around her and pulled her close, one hand on the back of her head. "I promise you, we won't hurt anyone. I swear it! You don't have to cry."

She kept crying. Her small arms wrapped around my neck, holding on for dear life. I could feel her soft cheek against mine. It was almost as if we were the same person somehow.

Tears sprang to my eyes and slipped down my face.

"I love you, Gracie," I said.

I had no idea where the words came from.

23

THE JOURNEY east toward the Circle camp presented me with many "opportunities for salvation," as Talya called encounters with fear and worry in the world of troubles.

As Maya had so cleverly stated, we were here to see ourselves as light in the darkness because Justin made us light, like him. That was the Third Seal. But these thoughts only enraged me because I wasn't seeing myself as light. I was seeing myself as Horde and I hated it. All of Talya's philosophical statements now felt like salt in the cracks of my skin, but I held my tongue, wishing he would do the same, even knowing he was here to help me.

Talya looked at me and winked. "That's why you are here: to see yourself as the light and so be the light. A fine calling, 49th."

"That's why you are here," Maya parroted, offering me a toothless grin. "You are special!"

"Just like you," Talya said.

"We're all special!" Maya said, spreading her arms wide. She hesitated, mind spinning behind her bright eyes. "So no one is special."

Talya chuckled and patted her hand, uncaring of the flaking skin that covered her little body. "Tell me, 49th. Is Maya embraced by the Horde?"

"They said no."

"We are outcast," Maya said, still grinning.

Talya nodded. "And among Albino?"

"Outcast," I said.

"Then they are the least among all, wouldn't you say? From the world's view, that is."

Maya was still looking at me. What could I say?

But Talya rescued me. "'What you do to the least of these, you do to me,' Yeshua said. He was speaking of the sinners in his day, destitute and imprisoned and cast out for their crimes. Help me out, 49th. How could Yeshua say that what we do to sinners and outcasts, we are actually doing to him? Why would he go on to say that those who called him Lord but didn't grasp that he was all, including the outcasts, were like goats, while his true followers were sheep?"[1]

"He said that?"

"Have you not read your own Scriptures?"

I sat on the horse in silence, trying to wrap my clogged brain around such a teaching.

"And so I ride with Justin seated before me," Talya said. "Seeing her any other way would make me a goat, the true outcast." He stared off. "Now tell me, 49th, who do you sit with on your horse now, as we ride?"

"Myself."

"A Scab. The least among us. An outcast. And what you do to yourself as that Scab, you do to Justin. Perhaps you might consider loving yourself, then. You can only love your neighbor as yourself if you love yourself as you are." He looked at me. "Love, 49th. The evidence of Justin is love."

"I'm a water walker," Maya said proudly, hijacking the discourse. She craned her neck and looked up at Talya. "I walked on water."

"Indeed you did, indeed you did." He winked at me. "Once. Three steps, I think it was."

"Three steps, but then I sank. Talya's going to help me again, aren't you, Talya?"

"But I am helping you, Maya. I already am. As much as I'm helping the 49th. And maybe I can help you cross into the other world, like Rachelle does. They could use your help in the future, I think. Would you like that?"

"I can fly to another world like a bird!" Maya proclaimed.

"Like a bird in a dream."

And so we went, onto the Marrudo plateau, drawing ever closer to the Circle and Samuel. I heard all of Talya's teaching but remained silent, stewing again, frustrated by such lofty teachings and judging Talya for offering them when I was so lost.

Maya repeated almost everything Talya said, and he made no attempt to quiet her. In fact, he seemed to say things just to hear her repeat them, like a proud grandfather.

"Just over that knoll," he finally said. "We've been trailed by two of their scouts for the last ten minutes. If you were a warrior, they would've already sounded the alarm." He stopped his horse and scanned the horizon. "But they see only a Horde woman with her child. And me. They see me, the wizard who snuffed out their fire. I stop here."

"Are you sure?" Worry battered me. "I'm not even sure why I'm going."

"That's why Maya's going to guide you. Isn't that right, Maya?"

She clambered from the saddle, eager to join me. "Don't worry, Miss Rachelle. I'm not afraid of the Albinos. They gave us food too."

I had no idea how such a young parrot of Talya could guide me, but I had few reasons to argue.

Talya cleared his throat and faced me. "Tell me who you are."

My mind was on Samuel and what I might find on such a doubtful mission that had no clear objective. "I'm the 49th Mystic."

"This is one of the names you cling to," he said. "A mask that imprisons you."

"That's a mask," Maya repeated. "Like a prison over your head!"

"Tell me who you really are."

I hesitated, then gave him the correct answer. "Inchristi is me," I said. "As one, we are in this earthen vessel called Rachelle. Inchristi is all and in all."[2]

He dipped his head. "Nothing else matters if you forget who you are and cling instead to your old names."

"A name like Albino," Maya said.

"Like all the names you wear," Talya said. "Scab. Woman. Victim. Wounded. Stupid. Ugly. Failure. Even 49th Mystic. Surrender all of them on that altar where judgment was put to death."

He spoke in terms familiar to me from Eden, Utah. Take up the cross. Die to yourself daily. Those hard teachings of Yeshua that Simon had turned into frightful sermons.

"They are hard only because most people see according to the powerless traditions and reasoning of men and religion," Talya said. "In truth, they're the most liberating of all his teachings. Through them, he shows us how to find salvation from the troubles of this life. Inchristi is the *only* way."

Then he repeated another hard teaching I'd heard in Eden.

"As he taught: 'Unless you hate your father, wife, husband, children—indeed, hate everything about yourself—you cannot follow me in seeing the kingdom now at hand.'[3] Sounds brutal, wouldn't you say?"

I looked at him. "Only a moment ago you said I should love my neighbor as myself. Now you say hate?"

"But to hate simply means to release all attachment to. When you surrender your clinging to all attachments, all masks, all judgment, you awaken to a staggering love. In that love, you hold no record of wrong, and you escape all fear because there is no fear in love. Isn't that what you want, 49th?"

I looked at the rise ahead of us and saw that a line of six or seven warriors had formed. "It's all I want."

"Wonderful. And here I thought you wanted to be Albino." He drew his horse around. "You can find me at the large boulder we passed."

THE CIRCLE'S camp was like a grain of sand compared to the massive sprawl of the Horde camp we'd passed through in the desert. They used simple canvas shelters affixed to saplings—easily torn down at a moment's notice. Everywhere I looked I saw order and color, whether only a yellow shawl hanging over an entrance or a basket of red and purple plums set out on the grass. Even their warriors' armor made liberal use of dyed leather, blue and yellow mostly.

None of these Albinos scowled at the sight of their warriors leading a Scab woman and her daughter through the camp. Their way was to offer drowning, not slaughter, to the Horde.

Maya sat motionless in front of me, staring at the Albino children as we were led to a large tent on the northern side of their camp. Word had been sent ahead of us. A woman claiming to be the 49th Mystic was here to meet with Samuel.

They'd also undoubtedly delivered the news that this so-called 49th Mystic was Horde.

"Samuel's inside," the warrior who guided us said, shoving his chin at the closed flap. He looked us over one last time. "They're expecting you." And then, "Know that whoever you are, you're a friend of the Circle. A cloud of division hangs over us all, so if things are said that should not be said, please accept our apologies."

I could hear strong voices inside, someone arguing a point with unwavering passion. The warrior dipped his head, turned his horse, and left us.

Maya stood on the saddle, then dropped to the ground like a monkey. She reached her hand up to me. "Come, Miss Rachelle. They are our friends."

But the moment I swept the flap aside and stepped into the large room, I knew that not all saw us as friends. The one who was talking seemed put off that our entrance had interrupted his argument. His face darkened when he saw our skin.

As one they stared at us. Four of them, two men and two women, all in battle dress, were seated on thick sheep hides. Bows and swords lined the tent wall next to a few crates of supplies.

On the far right, Samuel.

Samuel, who stared dumbly at me with round eyes.

One of the women stood, and with her, the rest. "My name is Mikil," she said, stepping forward. But she didn't offer me any customary grasp. "This is Vadal, Suzan of Southern, and Samuel, son of Thomas."

I gave her a shallow bow. "My name is Rachelle. This is Maya." My eyes were on Samuel, who still stared, locked in confusion. "Samuel and I have met. It's good to see—"

"I don't know you," he snapped. "You're not the Rachelle I saved."

"But I am. It's just that I've . . ." I stopped, at a loss. What could I say that they would believe? Embarrassment heated my face.

"She's become Horde," Maya said innocently. "Talya made her like me because we're both special."

Mikil smiled at my guide. "Well, aren't you a precious thing. You know this Talya?"

"Don't be ridiculous!" the one called Vadal snapped. "They're more likely spies, sent to us from Qurong. If they knew Talya, they would've drowned already."

"Not necessarily, Vadal," Mikil gently corrected. "There's much about this whole business that turns what we've believed on its head. Love, not exclusion, is our way."

"Tell that to my bride!" Vadal bit off. "But you can't because she was butchered by the beasts! She's dead! We took up swords then, and we will now, as Samuel insists. May they all rot in hell."

I heard little Maya speak beside me. "You should let go of the special-ness of your bride so you don't suffer," she said to Vadal. "Justin says we should have no attachments to special people. You've made her an idol to you. A boulder tied to your legs so you can't fly."

A moment of silence lingered in the wake of her statement.

"And what would a child know of brides?" Vadal asked.

"The role of bride is only a mask. We can't love if we hide behind masks."

"This from a little imp who wears Scab as her mask."

"That's enough, Vadal!" Mikil snapped.

Part of me wanted to join in Maya's defense, but I was still fixated on Samuel, silently begging him to recognize and accept me. I was Horde, but my face was still the same face he'd known. My voice the same voice. Flakes of skin from my dried scalp had filled my dark hair, but it wasn't in dreadlocks. Not yet anyway.

"Samuel . . ." I took a step toward him. "It's me, can't you see? You rescued me from the Horde in the southern desert, where I was trapped under the cliffs. We went to the pool, where Talya took me. I was put on trial in the Elyonite—"

"No. No, that wasn't you!" His eyes darted to the others. "I'm telling you, that old wizard has used his magic to bring us an imposter." A beat.

"She's Horde, for the love of Elyon! With a Horde child! This isn't the 49th Mystic I know!"

"No, sir, you're mistaken!" Maya piped up, grabbing my hand. "She is the Mystic Talya brought to us. We've come to tell you the good news!"

"What good news?" Mikil asked.

"That we are the light of the world and we don't have to be afraid of each other."

"Blasphemy!" Vadal roared, gripping his hair. "Blasphemy!" He thrust his finger at Maya. "How can this rotting little corpse be the light of the world? She's Horde!" And then again, as if the second time was needed to drive his point home: "Horde!"

"Talya says blasphemy is denying that you are the divine light. It makes you blind."

Vadal fumed. Then spat his charge again. "Blasphemy!"

The dark-skinned one named Suzan spoke up. "Metaphorically speaking, I can see how such an innocent young child could be called the light of the world. But surely, even innocence knows that it is Horde, child."

"Talya said that what you do to me you do to Justin. This is true love. I've come to help Miss Rachelle tell you."

They were all struggling with Maya's claims, but then so was I. Intellectually, I knew her statements were true, but I wasn't experiencing the truth like she was. Only a week earlier I'd stood before Elyonite Albinos and boldly stated what I had learned when my eyes had been opened by Talya. I felt none of that power now, but Talya had sent me to speak truth, I assumed, so I did.

"Maya's right. I admit that I'm not at my best right now, as you can see . . ."

I stopped midsentence, hearing my words. In saying those words I was condemning myself. I was saying that another way would be better, and that right now I didn't measure up to that better version.

I was blinding myself through judgment. I was such a failure.

But that thought stopped me too. I was now condemning myself by calling myself a failure. Did it never stop? It was no wonder there were so few water walkers in the world.

And now I was judging the world.

"Yes?" Mikil asked.

"Sorry, I . . . What I meant to say is that Maya is right. I can't say I know how it all works, because I'm not thinking straight, you know." *Dear Elyon, help me.* "But I can tell you that the Horde aren't your enemy. Your own perception is. Most Albinos are as blind as the Horde to who they are."

"Impossible!" Samuel blurted. "How can you pretend to be the 49th Mystic? The Rachelle I knew used her blade when the Horde attacked us. I don't know by what means of magic the old goat has turned you into someone who looks vaguely like her, but the 49th I knew would speak no such blasphemy!"

"That's not true!" I snapped, losing my good sense. "I didn't know who I was when Jacob attacked us!"

"And you do now, as Horde?" He stepped up, face red. "Jacob is with the 49th now, I saw it with my own eyes. And since you seem to know so much about her, you must know where she is. So tell me, where is she?"

"Here!" I said, hands balled into fists. "I'm right here! And I'm here to tell you that you'll be fools to join the Elyonites against the Horde. Tens of thousands will die in that bloodbath!"

"So says the spy from the Horde. Of course you don't want us to take up arms with our brothers. You know how much value we add against your beasts! And for the record, I was sent here to find the 49th, who alone can open the gate to the Realm of Mystics. Is that you? No! You're Scab." He spat to one side.

"What are you saying?" Mikil asked, facing Samuel. "Aaron sent you to find the 49th here?"

"The Elyonites are our brothers," Vadal said. "Aaron sent Samuel to speak common sense into us. That common sense demands that we do what we crossed the Great Divide to do. Go to war as we should have long before our wives and children were slaughtered by the Horde."

"No, Thomas was clear," Mikil snapped. "We hold our ground here."

"While he vanishes into some sinkhole chasing ancient dreams of another world?" Samuel cut in. "Aaron takes his army against the Horde tomorrow.

We can't wait for my father. Even he drew his sword against them. This is what he would want."

"That isn't what he wants," Mikil objected. "He was very clear. We wait!"

"Then we'll let each man decide for himself," Vadal said. "It's always been our way."

"Yes, but this isn't just always . . ."

They went on, oblivious to Maya and me standing there like two sores. I could hardly follow their angry exchange because I was too caught up in my own. The one happening between my ears. The one telling me that I was a failure.

A failure for being furious with Samuel, who was betraying me as I stood there in desperate need. I wasn't judging only him, I was judging the whole world for conspiring to put me in the impossible position of having to surrender just to be able to see clearly.

Tears of shame filled my eyes as they threw their words at each other. Maya had gone silent in the barrage. I had to get away from this. There was only hatred here, and I didn't know how to offer love to myself, much less to them.

Mikil noticed the tears on my cheeks and the others followed her stare. For a few seconds, silence visited the tent as the Scab before them silently wept for herself. Maya was the one who broke the silence.

"It is true, she is the 49th," she said in a simple, sweet voice. "Talya told me."

Samuel spat to one side again. "If you're the 49th, then the Elyonites are right in their interpretation of the prophecy. You will bring all Albinos to their knees at the feet of Horde. Your being Horde now proves it." He clenched his jaw. "But you're not her." To the others: "We should bind her and hold her in a hole so she can't report."

"Don't be absurd," Mikil snapped. "War or not, we don't treat women and children with cruelty." She studied me. "I don't know why you're here, but if you do know Talya, tell him this isn't the way to win our confidence." Another beat. "You may leave us. No one will harm you."

Turning immediately, I slipped out of the tent and hurried to my horse, hearing the patter of small feet behind me.

I could not have been more mortified. Not because I was Horde but because I should know better. Do better. Be better. Me, of all people, the 49th Mystic! And yet I'd just shown myself to be an utter fool, powerless and crying with self-pity for all to see.

I wanted to run. I wanted to hide and never be seen again.

Releasing a sob, I spun back, threw my arms around Maya and lifted her from her feet, holding on for dear life.

Here was the one who loved me. This little Scab girl. Here was the one I clung to, a child who hadn't learned to judge yet. Whatever Talya had expected of me, I didn't know, but I had gloriously failed.

What is seeing beyond what you think should be?

I didn't know, but I did know that I should be better than I was.

And so you live in a prison of your own making, precious one.

For a split second, I saw the power of those words, and then I was swallowed by self-loathing once more.

"It's okay, they don't mean it," Maya said in her tender way. "Talya says we should forgive them because they don't know what they do. Forgive everyone because they're only doing what life taught them to do."

She pulled back and looked into my eyes.

"It doesn't matter what they think. *I* love you."

Her words pulled more tears from me.

"I love you too, Maya."

24

I KNEW I was supposed to be tuning into anger so I would have the power to stop Vlad, but embracing anger was a hard thing at first. Like tuning into other frequencies, it required practice.

There in Karen Willis's big office late at night, everything was chaos. She was awake and bound to a chair, mouth taped so she couldn't scream and tell the neighborhood we'd tied her up.

The Indian maid, Anika, was staring at her daughter, terrified. Steve had taped her mouth shut too. And the little girl's mouth.

All three were seated and bound to chairs, and Steve had asked me to tape the girl's feet together so she couldn't run away. I did it, whispering apologies all the while because I knew she didn't deserve to be treated like this. But there were hundreds, maybe thousands, of people dying in churches and temples and mosques, and I had to play my role.

I kept reminding myself that I might be the only one who could save them.

Steve picked up the big hunting knife and faced Karen while I stood to one side, watching little Gracie, heart in my throat.

"Satisfied?" he snapped at Karen. "Let me be clear: I need to know why we're being framed for bombings that have nothing to do with us. And I need to know why anyone would go to such lengths. Someone's been pulling DARPA's strings all along, and you're going to tell me who and why."

Karen stared back, defiant.

"Look, I understand your reticence, but this goes way beyond you. You have to ask yourself why whoever got to you wants Rachelle compromised. Why one girl is worth so many deaths."

That was me. And hearing Steve put it so plainly, I wondered who I was too. Karen would know. She was our enemy.

"I'm going to take the tape off your mouth and you're going to tell me. If you scream, I'm going to hurt you. Not because I want to, but because you're now our only hope, do you understand?"

Nothing.

Steve stepped up and ripped the gray duct tape from her mouth. She didn't even wince, though it must have hurt. But she didn't scream either.

"Well?" Steve demanded.

"You have no idea what you're getting into," the chief of staff bit off. "Kidnapping and torture are capital crimes."

"So is terrorism. You're justifying killing a few hundred for the good it will ultimately bring to the world, right? Playing God, willing for some to die to save the rest. Consider me your god. You confess or I will punish. It's that simple."

I wondered if that's how God really was. Maybe he was like a terrorist when he needed to be, which meant that what we were doing was just like him. That gave me some courage as I stared at Karen.

But she wasn't persuaded.

"You're a fool," she said in a low voice. "Hurt me all you like. I have nothing to say."

Steve frowned, knife at his side, eyes locked on hers. Beads of sweat covered his forehead. "Rachelle?"

"Yes?"

"There's another knife in the bag. Get it out."

"What for?"

"Just get it out. Trust me."

I crossed to the bag, knelt on one knee, and dug out a knife nearly as long as my forearm. Stood up. "This one?"

He didn't bother looking at me. "That one. Put that blade at the mother's throat."

"You hurt her and I swear the government will send you straight to hell," Karen growled.

I stood frozen, horrified by the idea of hurting Anika. I understood what Steve was doing, but I hated it.

"Do it, Rachelle. Remember what I said, embrace that fear. It's the only way."

Anika was shaking, eyes clenched. Gracie was whimpering.

"Are you sure?" I asked in a thin voice.

"Trust me. Embrace your hatred. Remember the power it gives you. That's the power they want to stop, but you're not going to let them take it from you. Do it."

Torn and confused, I did it. I imagined all those innocent people in churches being slaughtered because this one woman was playing God, justifying her actions for some greater good. If she could do that, I could do the same thing.

If God did that, I had to as well. I just had to tune in to that radio wave called anger. I had to let my hatred swallow me.

The moment I surrendered to it, rage swept through me like a rushing wave. But my anger was directed toward Karen, not Anika, and I lost my mind to it. Without thinking, I dropped the knife and flew past Steve, reaching Karen in three long strides.

Then I was on the chair, knees planted in the cushion on either side of her legs, grabbing her hair with both hands.

"Tell us!" I screamed, jerking her head back and forth. This was all her fault. Her not confessing would force Steve to hurt the mother. "Tell us who's trying to kill us!" My face was inches from hers as I hurled the words.

Her lips were quivering and she was clearly frightened, but she wasn't telling us anything. So I slapped her with an open palm, then again with the other hand.

"Tell us!" Then, "Tell us who Vlad is!"

A muffled grunt sounded behind me, followed immediately by a soft chuckle that sent a chill through my spine. I was already twisting back when he spoke.

TED DEKKER

"That's the real question, isn't it?"

A man dressed in a black suit and cowboy boots stood behind Steve, one hand over Steve's mouth, the other with a knife pressed against his throat.

He drilled me with his stare. "Who is Vlad and why is he manipulating the world to keep all the skulls full of mush swimming in darkness? Isn't that it, my dear little peach cobbler?"

Karen's body had gone rigid under me. Steve's eyes were round, full of terror. He'd dropped his knife and made a feeble attempt to free himself, but Vlad was much stronger.

"Even now the shadow reclaims you and there's nothing you can do to stop it. Only I can. And I will if you do as I say. That's what this is all about, 49th. Me helping you stop all this nonsense before you divide the world with your pitiful truth and bring ruin to us all."

I blinked, barely able to breathe, confused.

"You're gonna have to get one thing through that pretty little skull of yours. Sometimes you just have to do something ugly to bring about goodness. Even God does it. And now I'm afraid I have to ask you to do it."

His jaw flexed.

"Now be a good girl, pick up the knife, and cut the mother's throat before I cut Steve's throat. Fear is the only way to get Karen to confess, darling. Show her you mean business."

A dozen thoughts slashed through my mind. The loudest was that he was going to hurt Steve. The next loudest was that I couldn't cut the mother.

I couldn't even move. Or process my thoughts clearly.

"Get up!" he snapped.

His demand jolted me and I jumped off the chair, facing him.

"Pick up the knife!" He jerked Steve's head back, baring his neck.

I did it, hand shaking.

"Now . . ." His eyes were daring me. "Do as Papa says. Kill the heathen, she's bound for hell anyway. This will only speed her along."

If Steve had told me to do it, I might have, I don't know. But his mouth was covered and my head was spinning and I just stood there, terrified.

"No?" He softened. "I didn't think so, not yet anyway."

260

His hand flashed to his side and he threw me a pair of handcuffs. They hit me in the stomach and clattered to the wood floor. "Hands behind your back. Put them on."

No one other than he had spoken since he'd come from nowhere. We were all too stunned.

"I don't have all night," he said.

I picked up the handcuffs and clipped them around my wrists behind by back.

"Good girl." He gave Steve a shove from behind.

Steve's face was white. As was Karen's. She'd been unnerved by our threats, but Vlad's coming had filled her with a far deeper dread.

Vlad paced, flipping the knife in his hand, eyes still on me, always on me.

"Now, I'm going to forgive you this once because you're so new at the game of fear and shadows, still falling from innocence and all that. That's why I had to wipe your mind, darling, so I could teach you from scratch. The only thing that will save you is fear. You have to protect yourself and your loved ones! You have to *fight* for what you believe in, just like Steve told you. The only way you can do that is to fear the loss of whatever you're trying to protect. Embrace it. Even God fears the loss of what is good!"

How did he know what Steve told me? Had he been in the trunk of the car while we were driving? But he hadn't been there when we opened it . . .

"Just to be clear," he continued, "when I say kill, I really mean kill. And when I say the mother, I mean exactly that. Like this."

He threw the blade with a snap of his wrist. It flashed through the air, slammed into the mother's right eye socket. But it didn't stop there because suddenly there was no mother and no eye socket. The moment the blade reached her eye, her body turned to wisps of black fog.

The blade embedded itself in the bookshelf behind the chair she'd been sitting in.

Behind me, Karen gasped. Steve and I stared at the empty chair, speechless.

"You see?" Vlad said. "All for the good, if you'll just learn to trust me." To Steve, pointing at the now-vacant chair: "Sit down."

Steve balked. "There?"

"It looks empty to me. Sit!"

He stumbled over and dropped to his backside. Vlad worked quickly, snatching up the roll of duct tape, wrapping Steve's torso to the back of the chair, speaking calmly as he made quick work of it.

"I'm going to let you stew for a few hours. If you try to leave this office, I'll kill you." He finished securing Steve, walked over to me, shoved me down, and fixed one of the cuffs to the desk leg.

He stepped to the door and faced his handiwork. Winked at Karen.

"Not to worry, my dear. Silence wasn't part of my deal. Tell them what you like."

The strong-willed chief of staff had been reduced to a limp noodle.

"When I return, we'll try again, this time with the girl. Either you will kill the little scab or I will cut Steve's throat. This time, there will be no second chances. Capisce?"

I stared up at him from where I was seated on the floor.

Vlad started to turn. "Oh, and for the record, she isn't one of my Leedhan. You wasted that chance. But she *is* heathen. God's gonna kill her anyway."

And then he was gone, closing the door behind him.

"YOU'RE SURE?" Steve demanded. "He said it would end at the World Security Summit in two days? It wasn't just another ploy?"

Karen nodded, eyes red, still in shock. "That's what he said."

"That he would activate StetNox then, after you'd delivered on your end."

"Yes." She swallowed deep, shifting her eyes to stare at the drawn drapes. "That's what he said."

Steve was stunned. "Heaven help us . . ."

For the first few minutes following Vlad's departure, not much was said. My mind was on Steve and Gracie, trying to identify the right thing to do. Doing nothing wasn't an option. Vlad would only kill them both. I couldn't see my way past such an impossible situation.

Karen was the first to break the silence, collapsing into tears. Vlad had given her permission to speak freely, so she had. It all came out in long, broken sentences, a tormented soul seeking comfort in her confession.

She told us how the president, Calvin Johnson, had come into power using Vlad's wealth and reach. Johnson had always been a devout citizen, focused on social justice motivated by deeply held religious beliefs. As a senator he had access to verified models that predicted the economic collapse of the United States with devastating consequences unless drastic changes were made.

Vlad had approached him years earlier, laying out a plan that would accomplish precisely those controls required to save the country. It would mean tearing some things down before rebuilding, and a spoiled populace would never go for hard corrective steps. The country could be saved only by strong leadership willing to take those hard steps.

The activation of StetNox, which already resided undetected on most of the country's computing devices, would give the administration untraceable control of every bank account in the country and many abroad. In the dead of one night, they could empty every account without a trace if they so desired, and blame it on terrorists. Martial law would follow in the chaos. Then a rebuilding from those ashes, making the president the country's savior.

The church bombings were a distraction, Vlad's idea: prime the country with fear focused on terrorism. Whip them into a frenzy, then pull the rug out from under them.

In return, Vlad only wanted access to Project Eden and, in particular, a girl—me—who evidently played a significant role in his own religious beliefs. My most recent MEP had been facilitated by a vial of fluid supplied by him. All of this was Vlad's doing.

President Johnson was now at his mercy. So was I.

There were three more bombs scheduled to go off in the next two days. All would be pinned on me.

Some of this was way over my head, but Steve listened with rapt attention, momentarily distracted from the looming threat: either I killed Gracie or he would die.

"You're saying that this is all about some cult?" I asked.

Karen sniffed. "I'm saying that's what he claims. He's convinced there's something special about you and he's obsessed with bringing you down. Some 49th Mystic business. A great darkness that will make all our own concerns look like child's play. Typical radical ideology."

That's who I was, I thought. I was the 49th Mystic. But I didn't know what that meant.

I looked at Steve. "From my dreams. Right?"

"What dreams?" Karen asked.

He shook his head. "Too much to explain. Dreams Rachelle used to have in Project Eden."

"Dreams of another world," I said. "That's where Vlad and his Leedhan come from. Supposedly. But you saw it yourself."

"You're suggesting that Vlad is like whatever that thing was that just vanished?"

Steve answered for me. "That's the theory we're going off of, yes. But we're groping in darkness here. Suffice it to say Vlad isn't just human. He's an energy being of some kind, one that breaks most conventions of the standard model. Science-speak for our understanding of physics."

"But I break those conventions of science too, right?" I said, pulse surging. "I mean . . . maybe I'm the only one who can stop him."

"What do you mean?" Karen asked.

"Rachelle has some gifts most humans don't. The ability to access higher forms of consciousness. Like I said, we're groping here. We need to study these things properly in a lab instead of shutting her down." He glared at Karen.

"I had no idea," she said. She looked at Gracie, who was staring at us with blank eyes. "Gracie, listen to me, honey. I know this is hard, but do you know where your mother is? Did you see anyone come and take her from your quarters?"

The little girl hesitated, then shook her head.

"No? So you didn't see anyone else?"

Another shake.

"Okay. I want you to be brave, okay? Your mother's safe, but we have to get out of here. No one's going to hurt you. I promise."

If a Leedhan had taken the form of Anika, was Gracie one as well? Was her mother still alive somewhere?

We sat in silence for a few seconds, afraid to talk about Vlad's ultimatum. One thing I knew: I couldn't kill Gracie. Vlad had to be lying when he said God protected his own at the expense of others like that little girl.

"What should I do?" I asked.

Steve was staring at the door, jaw fixed, lost in thought.

"You're going to dig every ounce of hatred you can find out of your gut and direct it at Vlad," he said. "Then you're going to kill him."

The thought filled me with terrible anxiety. "What if I can't? He might kill both of you. I can't live without . . . I need you."

"And I need you too, Rachelle," he said, facing me with watery eyes. "That's why you have to find your power. More power than you know you have. To do that, you have to go as deep and as dark as you can. Wrath. Find your wrath. It's the only way to protect us all."

25

CAUGHT BETWEEN two worlds, each now independent of the other, my mind was filled with thoughts of innocent children as I slowly awakened in Other Earth.

After leaving the Circle in utter defeat, I'd retreated into a guarded emptiness that quieted even Maya.

Talya hadn't even asked me how it had gone—I guess he knew. He'd taken Maya back to Soromi, who received her daughter with a gentle smile before exchanging a few whispered words with Talya and wishing us well on our journey.

"Journey to where?" I found the courage to ask.

"To the sea," he said.

"Sea? What sea? I didn't know there was a sea here."

"Few do," he said. "Most see only another wasteland, like they see the Realm of Mystics. But the upper sea has always been." And that was all he said about our destination.

Little Maya had hugged me and offered me her own blessing. "Talya says you can be a water walker like me. Would that make you happy?"

I'd given her a smile and kissed her forehead. "*You* make me happy," I'd said.

My eyes fluttered open as I awakened now, and I squinted at a bright blue sky.

What is seeing beyond what you think should be?

"That's the question, isn't it, my dear?" Talya's voice was warm and gentle.

I pushed up my pain-riddled Scab body and looked around. The day was already half gone. Talya had kept a small fire burning. We were on the sandy shore of a vast sea with a boat tied off to some shrubs. I didn't even know there were boats in Other Earth.

After a long, silent journey well into the night, we'd arrived here, at the sea with the boat. When I asked Talya why we'd come and what the boat was for, he gave me the same tiresome answer he often gave. "When the student is ready, the teaching will appear. You'll see."

For the first time since I had met Talya, his lion, Judah, didn't travel with us. When I asked where he was, Talya told me he'd gone home. And where was home?

"You will see."

But would I?

As much as perspective, something else had vacated me through all those hours of silent trudging up and down steep.inclines and across the wide plain that delivered us to this shore. Hope. I began to give up hope. And with that numbing, I found my way easier. So I gave up even more hope and fell asleep in the comfort of my own worthlessness.

Looking at the vast blue waters and bright blue sky now, I felt different.

Hopeful, maybe.

"Hopeful for what, 49th? This is the other question you get to ask yourself if you intend to be of any help to the children of slaughtered warriors."

The war. "It's started?" I asked, surprised.

He sat on a small boulder, whittling on wood that he'd carved into a small human figure. "The day has come, but this is none of your business now. They only prepare the way."

"The way for what?"

He lifted his eyes. "For you, my dear. If you are willing."

My stomach dropped. For me? The war was on my account?

With that one thought, the urgency of my predicament as the 49th became palpable. My quest for the seals had been fogged in all my stewing. And I still had only three seals!

I looked at Talya, who was watching me with gentle eyes. The bitterness I'd felt over the last two days was gone. He was my guide, not my enemy. Vlad was my enemy.

I was my enemy.

I crossed my legs under me, facing him. "I *am* willing," I said.

"Yes, my dear, I believe you are. It's amazing how much goodness can come through the fires of purification. How much beauty through the waters of cleansing."

He resumed his whittling.

"Tell me, if not for all this 49th business, what would your hopes be in this life?"

It took me a moment to enter that frame of mind.

"Health," I said, maybe because I was a Scab.

"Ahhh, yes. Health. Such a tiny little hope. Bigger, 49th. Give me a bigger hope."

"I think health is—"

"Humor me."

"Okay, a husband? Someone to love? Maybe children?"

"There are plenty to love, and you can love none of them if you don't love yourself, but okay. A companion. Maybe Jacob, yes? And some little innocent ones to love you as you are?"

The thought of being with Jacob made my heart beat faster.

"Maybe."

"Oh, to be loved by another. Such a small dream, 49th. Far, far too small. Another."

He continued carving the little figure.

"Enough things to be comfortable," I said, trying to be true to his question.

"Yes, things. Just enough, maybe a cow, a little plot of land?"

"Something like that."

"A simple life free of problems. Marriage and a cow and a garden to tend to with your little ones, like in Yeshua's story of the banquet?"

I hesitated, thinking he was goading me.

"Yes."

He threw the carving at his feet and abruptly stood. "Now you've done it!" he shouted, flinging his arms wide. "Now you've exposed the only problem all of mankind faces, ever! All there in your three tiny, insane little answers."

Heat flushed my face, but I was too shocked by the sudden change in him to react.

"Too small, 49th! You think way too small!" He threw his words out for any living creature to hear, pacing now.

"Why are you being so angry with me?" I blurted. "I'm trying my best!"

"But I'm not angry with you. I'm showing you *wrath*! Wrath shows you the gritty taste of the clay pie you're addicted to so you might consider the banquet instead!" He jabbed a trembling finger at his face. "This, 49th, is the wrath of Elyon, lovingly nudging you, like a tender mother taking a knife from a child even when that child screams in disappointment."

He threw his arms wide again, eyes bright with eagerness.

"Do you think true life is about reputation and fashion and marrying and children and all those wonderful blessings of God that all Albino and Horde crave? You think too small."

"But I wouldn't say I *crave* those things," I managed.

"Oh, but you do, 49th. All humans have many addictions to this life! Do you know why?"

I stared at him, at a loss.

"Because you don't see who you are without them. You desire a new body because you don't see that you are beautiful. You crave the love of another because you don't know yourself as love. You crave power because you don't know the power you already have. You seek the seals because you don't know you already have them!"

I blinked, stunned by his claim. Then jerked up the sleeve of my tunic. Three seals set in my scabbed skin.

"Not there," Talya said. He pressed his hand against his heart. "The treasure is here, where the seals have always been, covered up by"—he wiggled his finger at my body—"that beautiful clay costume you wear. The seals are like a treasure in a field that you own, only waiting to be exposed."

In a single bound he was at the fire, snatching up the carving he'd thrown down. "Do you know what this is made of?"

"Wood."

"Smaller."

"Molecules."

"Smaller!"

"Atoms!" I shouted back.

"Smaller, 49th. Much smaller."

I knew because my father had been a scientist in Eden, Utah.

"Energy that's collapsed into what we perceive to be solid."

"And if you apply heat? If you add a little wrath?"

"It burns," I said.

He tossed the small carving of the wood-man into the fire. "It shifts form and becomes a hot gas that we see as flame," he said as the fire consumed the little figure. "Has anything been lost?"

"No. It's just changed form."

"So the fruit became the seed that became the tree that became the wood that became the carving that now becomes the flame. Which is it? Fruit, seed, tree, wood, carving, or flame?"

"It depends on when."

He straightened. "But you know as well as I do, don't you, 49th? It's none of those things. They're only various expressions of the energy that it is. They are temporal forms, as written. Earthen vessel, yes? Here one day, changed the next. All expressions of the same unchanging thing, only changing form."[1]

I nodded. By now my heart was beginning to pound because I saw where he was going and I liked it.

"Now let's say that unchanging thing is called *atom*. If you were to take the atom rising from the fruit that became seed, that became tree, that became wood, that became carving, that became heated gas, which we now see as flame"—he drew his finger through the fire—"and split that atom . . ." His eyes snapped up to me. "What would you see?"

I knew it! I stood, inflamed with excitement.

"A nuclear detonation," I breathed.

"A sun!" He grinned, eyes flashing. "A sun." He stepped around the fire and put his hand on my shoulder. "You are like that sun. The light of the world. Experiencing yourself as the light is the celebration the Father calls you to. You flow with more power than most give themselves permission to imagine, much less believe. If you set your hopes on the fruit and wood of this life, you will only experience fruit and wood in this life, faced with the problems of worms and rot. If you set your hopes on the sun, you will experience the light. And how bright is that light."

"As bright as the sun."

"All form is beautiful in its time, but eternity is also written in your heart.[2] In the eternal light, there is no threat. No danger. No darkness. No fear. Only love, which knows no darkness."

"No blindness!"

"None! The wood-man doesn't subject himself to the altar of fire because he's evil, but to experience the power of his glorified self, one with the light."

"The power of the light. *In* the world of form and earthen vessel but not *of* it."[3]

He whirled back, excited like a child.

"Can you imagine what that would be like, wood-man Rachelle? Can you imagine what it would be like to discover the power of your true identity, one with the Creator of the universe? You would love every aspect of this temporal life, knowing that none of it defines you! You would dance and sing and shout for joy!"

Tears filled my eyes.

"The atom that contains the sun doesn't care if it's in a wooden carving, or if that wooden figure is purified and made a hot gas in the fire. It doesn't dictate what *should be*. It knows it's an aspect of the sun, not a tree or earthen vessel or Albino or Horde or man or woman or 49th or Mystic. You are the light of world, only briefly in this form."

Like a sweet refrain, the knowing of truth filled me. How could I have lost my grasp of something so obvious?

271

"Ahhh. You want to know how one goes about remaining in that truth flowing with so much power, is that it? You want to know how one maintains her experience of her identity as that staggering light while still in an earthen vessel, yes?"

"Yes."

"Well, there's only one way, 49th. Didn't you hear Soromi and Maya explain Yeshua's teaching yesterday?"

Their simple words crashed in on me and I began to pace. "By letting go of my attachment to the world."

"All of it!" he cried, thrusting both arms wide. "The earthen vessel has only one true power, and that is to align. It aligns to the system called love or to the polarity of judgment. All of us do this in every moment. What you believe manifests as your experience in this life. All of this is written. For the sake of all, tell me you finally know this, 49th!"

It seemed so obvious. He was describing the basis for all of human life, like a divine alchemist giving me the formula for how all things worked.

I nodded.

"And yet in blindness to the great light you are, you continue to bind yourself to the polarity of the wood-man. To the earthen vessel and all of its special judgments of this versus that. Better to be a wooden carving than a fire. Better to be Albino than Horde. Better to be married than unmarried, fat than skinny, skinny than fat, tall than short. And so it goes, the curse of the knowledge of good and evil, which masters all since the Fall."

I stared out over the blue lake.

He swept his hand toward the horizon. "The kingdom of heaven is here already, as Yeshua said. Everywhere! You just aren't aligned to it, so you can't see it. It's time to real-ize it. To make it *real* in your experience. Surrender your old sight and see with newborn eyes. This is the forgotten way."

"How?" I asked, suddenly desperate. "How do I follow that way?"

"Align your sight to the light you already are.[4] To the you who is complete and glorified. Do this and all your small attachments will fall away. Lift your eyes—change your perception!"

I felt panicky because that still didn't seem to help. It was an endless circle. Surrender to see; see to surrender.

"But *how*, Talya?" I cried, shaking now. "*Show* me how to surrender!"

Without warning, Talya clapped his hands with tremendous force. I ducked instinctively. As if someone had pulled the plug on the sun, the world darkened. The sky changed from blue to charcoal gray, billowing with angry clouds. Strong gusts of air buffeted Talya, who stood still.

"You want me to show you how?"

A long, jagged finger of lightning crackled over the sea. I had no idea what was happening, but I was desperate.

"Yes."

He eyed me for a moment, standing with his back to the water. "Begin by not judging yourself for not knowing how," he said, voice now low. "Do you trust me?"

"Yes!" I wanted to run for cover because the wind was now whipping my hair around my face.

"Do you trust *me*, Rachelle?"

"Yes! I trust you!"

"Do you trust the *light*?" He seemed to be daring me.

"Yes. I said yes!"

"Do you trust *you*, 49th?"

"I . . ." A stick flew by my head, whipped by the wind. We were exposed and in a storm that was growing ferocious. A storm Talya had somehow brought upon us.

Talya repeated his demand, yelling now. "Do you trust *you*, 49th?"

I was the light. Did I trust myself? Which self? "I don't know, but what's happening?"

"*You* are happening, daughter of Elyon!" he boomed. He spun and ran for the boat. "Hurry, into the boat!"

I stood frozen, terrified by the idea of getting into a boat on waters now tossing and turning with foam.

"Hurry, 49th. If you don't trust you, then trust in me. We voyage into the shadow of death!"

I stumbled forward, heart crashing with the thunder rolling above us. He was in the water, tugging free the rope that tied off the boat, waving me forward. He had the look of a crazed old man with long, white, wind-blown hair, eyes blazing with madness.

"Hurry, 49th! Thomas awaits!"

Thomas? We were going to see Thomas Hunter?

I splashed into the water, grabbed the side of the wooden boat, and rolled in. It was maybe twenty feet long with one sail and five planks for seating. My heel smashed against one of the wooden planks, but I hardly noticed the pain.

Then Talya was in, up by the mast, tugging to unfurl the sail as the wind swept us from the shore.

"Don't put the sail up!" I was yelling at Talya, but more than half my mind was on trying to secure myself in the boat, which was rocking on rising waves. I grabbed onto the same seat that I'd smashed into and hung on for dear life in the bottom of that boat.

Talya felt no such compulsion. The sail was already up, and he stood with one foot on the most forward plank and the other up on the bow, facing the wind with one raised fist as if he were a conqueror and this yet one more sea to cross.

"Do you feel the pain, 49th?" he cried. "The pain in your bloodied heel, do you feel it?"

I didn't have the presence of mind to answer. Small as it was, the unfurled sail bowed and hummed with the wind, hurtling us forward at breakneck speed. A wave picked us up and slammed us back down.

"Talya!"

"No, you don't feel it, do you? You don't perceive it. It's not a problem for you. You couldn't care less about the pain in your heel, 49th. All of your attention is on something else, isn't it?"

I twisted my head and looked back at the shore. To my horror, I saw that there *was* no shore! No horses, no fire, no land.

A small suggestion hidden deep in my mind told me that I was safe, because I was with Talya and Talya could walk on water, but I could barely hear it over the fear thundering through me.

And then I couldn't hear it at all.

"Do you feel the fear of being Scab, 49th?" Talya cried. "Is being Horde a problem for you now?"

"No!" I screamed, only to appease him. "Just stop this! Please . . ." The words froze in my throat as the boat lurched to the left, nearly tearing my hands from the bench.

"Hold on! Hold on to the means of your salvation, daughter of Elyon. Don't let go of the boat. Don't you dare!"

Water washed over the sides, drenching me from head to foot.

"Are you afraid, 49th?"

I gulped at the air, shaking the water from my face. "Yes!"

Talya had released his hold on the sail and now faced the storm with both hands spread wide, and for the moment I was sure he'd lost his mind completely. Even though he was a water walker, I had none of his powers. I could easily be washed overboard.

"Feel the Father's wrath!" he screamed into the wind, grinning wildly. "Feel the wrath that lovingly nudges the lost sheep back onto the path of peace! Smile with the Father as he smiles down upon you, 49th!"

He spun back, eyes wild.

"Are you afraid? Are you afraid of the water that can swallow you up? Are you clinging to your boat, hoping that it will save you from the storm?"

"Stop it!" I cried. "Just stop it!"

The boat shuddered as it crashed down into a trough. Another huge wave washed over the side, filling half the boat.

"Talya!" I screamed.

"Do you care if you're Scab now? Does your heel hurt you now? Do you miss Jacob now? Do you see these as problems for you now, 49th?"

"No!" I cared about none of those things in that moment. All I cared about was being saved from the monster of that storm.

Lightning brightened his face, revealing a daring grin. "If you can so easily let go of those small problems with just a little shift in attention, just imagine how you would feel if you followed Yeshua's teaching to let go of your whole life. Put all of your attention on the incomprehensible power of love that invites your surrender to it."

Talya said the words gently, but they hit me like a hammer. It was true, I had let go of the pain in my foot, focused on something greater. I wasn't judging myself as Horde. I wasn't fixated on the specialness of Jacob.

That was my earthen vessel playing god, telling me what I should and should not need. I was a slave to that voice, that master, that fear.

"Stand up, dear daughter," Talya said. "Stand with me. Take your eyes off the storms of polarity. Lean into the shadow of fear. Do not resist the evil one who comes against you! Stand in the face of the accuser's pitiful arrows and see with new eyes as the daughter of Elyon!"

His rapture caught fire in my own chest, and I lurched forward on my knees. Desperate, I hooked my arm around the mast and pulled myself up as best I could. The boat rocked to the left and I grabbed Talya's belt to steady myself.

Talya was steady, gripping only thin air. I wondered if he even felt the storm.

He grabbed my hand and jerked it up so that I was now standing with one arm raised, the other on the mast. Water sprayed in my face and I gasped.

"Why are you afraid, 49th?"

"The storm," I said, but I was already starting to let go of it.

"Oh you of little faith. Is that what you see? A threatening storm?"

I felt a sudden surge of power in the hand he gripped. It rushed down my arm like an electric current.

"When you surrender your faith in the storm, you'll find faith in Justin. When you forgive the world, you find it forgiven. You see it as powerless to do any more than smash your earthen vessel to bits so you can get on with life in another dimension!"

I could hardly fathom his utter lack of concern. But of course. He suffered no anxiety over his body or the storm. He'd let his attachment to this world go.

"Forgive the storm, daughter! Let go of your old sight and see what I see!"

Forgiveness was letting go of the perception of wrongs. It activated a love that held no record of wrong. Talya was seeing in the power of love, but I was in the power of fear.

Two masters.

"Yes, 49th! Yes, shout it. Shout it with me. I release all of my clinging to my boat!"

"I release all of my clinging to my boat," I cried above the thunder.

"I don't care if I'm white or black or Albino or Scab!"

"I don't care if I'm white or black or Albino or Scab!" I shouted, louder now.

"I lift my eyes to see that I am light in the kingdom that is here!"

"I lift my eyes to see that I am light in the kingdom that is here!"

He leaned back and roared at the dark skies, "Inchristi is all!"

I blinked. "Inchristi is all!"

A hot fist of power filled my belly and rose to my throat. I suddenly knew more, and I hurled that knowing at the sky.

"Inchristi is me!" I cried with all my strength. And then I cried more of my own making, fueled by all I had learned. "I am the light of the world! I am the daughter of my Father! I am known by Elyon and one with Justin, riding the storms of this world to know myself beyond the knowledge of good and evil! I am love! I am love! I am love!"

The moment I cried those last words, my view of the world shifted. I could still see the storm, but now I saw the water was made of bands of energy, yellow and red, flowing innocently. The boat, like my body, was made of a billion bits of information, held together by my sight of it.

I felt as though I was standing on nothing, and I knew in that moment I could easily step out of the boat and walk on what I thought of as water.

Talya leaned back, chin held high, and began to laugh. I caught his delight and giggled. Our earthen vessels were a tall man with a gray beard and a small woman with diseased skin, and we laughed at the storm pounding our boat.

The fear I'd felt was gone. Entirely. And with it, the entire matrix that supported fear. Grievance. Defense. Judgment. Punishment. I'd surrendered them all.

All the things I thought I should have to keep me safe in this life suddenly felt like clay masks. Everything my earthen vessel insisted should give it value had only been clay pies.

But I was the daughter of my Father, who'd given me all that was his. I was like the bird who'd escaped from the dark room and was now flying free.

In that moment, I saw all things as made new.[5]

And I knew that I was being Inchristi.

Then I was laughing with Talya. Face lifted into the wind, screaming my delight at the dark skies. I was laughing and he was singing that high note he often sang when he practiced his metanoia. Singing it with pursed lips now as if to mock the storm with such a simple, pure tone.

Truly, I didn't care whether the storm smashed me to a million pieces or not.

With that single realization, light blinded me in a brilliant flash. Just one massive, hot ball of light that vanished as quickly as it had flared.

I gasped.

The boat slapped back down, but this time there was nothing to raise it up. The water was calm, like glass. The sky was blue, streaked with ribbons of gold and purple.

A soft hum laced with faint, beautiful long notes filled the sky. Not just the sky—my very frame seemed to resonate with those tones so that my fingers buzzed. The sounds were coming from me as much as to me, and I knew immediately that they had always been there to hear. I just now had the ears to hear them.

I glanced down and saw that my skin was smooth. Smooth! Free of the condition others called the scabbing disease.

I was Albino once more and I didn't care. I was seeing what had always been here to see, beyond all I had once grasped to define me.

Lifting my eyes, I stared around, stunned. No shore that I could see. No wind to push us toward one, though we were moving quickly.

Talya drew a deep breath and let it out slowly.

"Well, well, now that was fun, wasn't it? Welcome to the way of Justin, maestro of all Mystics." He patted my hand and stepped down from the bow. "The Fourth Seal awaits. Time is short."

What is seeing beyond what you think should be?

"I . . . I think I know what the Fourth Seal is." I was still reeling from the power that had flooded my veins.

"But does *she*?"

She. Rachelle, who was lost on Earth, blinded by the shadow named Vlad. She had to find the Fourth Seal there. Meaning, I had to. She who was me but didn't know it.

"So we go to Thomas, who lends a hand," he said.

"Thomas . . ."

"Yes, Thomas." Talya shoved his chin at the far horizon. "We will find him on the other side of this lake."

26

THREE HOURS passed before the door to Karen's office opened again. In its frame stood Vlad Smith, dressed in black, grinning wide.

I hated black. I hated his smile. I hated everything about him in every way. I always had, but now much more than before because Steve had helped me dig deep over the last hour.

Steve asked me to trust him and I did, letting him explain how everything vile and ugly in the world was Vlad's fault. That's how he put it and that's how I dug deep.

At Steve's urging, I looked at Gracie and imagined her being abused and crushed by a ruthless master, and that master was Vlad.

Fear him. Hate him. Despise him. I did, and it was easy.

He talked about all the innocent people being killed in my name. Each church bombing, tearing limb from limb—thousands of unsuspecting children being burned by the explosions. That was Vlad.

Fear him. Hate him. Despise him.

He talked about cancer and death, a mother's loss of her child, a lover's loss of her husband, a mother's son being seduced into drug abuse, a woman being captured into slavery. All of them Vlad's fault, Steve said.

Fear him. Hate him. Despise him.

I did it all and it made me sick, because all the stories he told me were like new to my naïve mind. Fear and hatred were the only way, Steve said. All I had to do was hide them from Vlad until the right moment.

My face was sweating and my hands were shaking when Vlad stepped into the office, and it was all I could do not to scream at him.

I hated the way he walked, strutting in those black boots. I hated black boots. I hated boots. I could smell his cologne, a spice of some kind, and I hated all spicy-smelling cologne.

That's how much I hated Vlad. It didn't matter that I was going way overboard, because that was the point.

His right brow arched. "So, have we been sharing secrets? Trying to figure out a way to kill big bad Vlad?"

He knew? But of course he would. I glanced at the others, all staring at him, uncertain and on guard.

"I've made my decision," I said.

"I can see that. Tell me . . ." He hooked his thumbs into his belt. "How does it feel to trust me? Because once you go there, it's mighty hard to come back."

"I don't trust you," I snapped. Then tried to soften my voice. "I'm only doing what I have to do to survive."

"Exactly. I asked you to embrace your fear, which you've done. So you see, you have put your faith in me because you know I'm right."

"I'm not afraid of you."

"No? Don't you know that anger is just fear of loss, a fear so deep that it manifests as an emotion you feel? If you're angry at me, it's only because you fear what I can do to you or to things you care about."

I knew he was right. There was nothing I could do about it now. So he knew, so what?

"My point is, you should trust in me. Anger is a good thing, sweet pea."

"Don't call me that."

"That's it. Feel that resentment. Let it run deep, 49th. It's the only thing that will save you in this life. It's what God uses to save himself and those he loves. Anger, frustration, bitterness, hatred." He spread his arms wide. "Fear! It's all fear, and only fear works."

His voice echoed in the hardwood office. He lowered his arms.

"Now, let's use some, shall we? Show me what you've learned."

He stepped up to me, grabbed my shirt, and jerked me forward. Snapped the handcuffs without using a key, maybe just to show me his strength. But I'd already figured he was too strong for me. I'd have to take him completely off guard or use a weapon, and even then I wasn't sure I was fast or strong enough.

He lifted me clean off the ground and plopped me down on my feet, a handcuff dangling from each wrist. Then tossed me the key as he turned his back.

"Pick up the knife. Kill the girl."

It was strange, because I was sure he knew my intentions but he seemed unconcerned. Strange also because I didn't care that he knew my intentions. I was too angry to care.

I quickly released the cuffs from my wrists, stepped over to the knife, and scooped it up. When I turned back, he was standing by the door facing me, hands on his hips.

"Be careful now. Anger can mess with your aim until you learn to control it. Or do you just want to do it up close and personal? Get some blood on your hands." He winked.

My hands were shaking, no hiding that, but I didn't care. Nor did I care that he was goading me, daring me to go after him now that I held a knife.

Neither Steve nor Karen made a move. Gracie sat with wide eyes despite my repeated assurances that I wouldn't touch her.

It was now up to me, and me alone.

I started to turn toward Gracie because that was my plan—fake like I was going after her, then switch to Vlad as quick as a viper.

"Try her eyes, 49th," he growled. "She's already blind like the rest of the world. Might as well make it obvious. Make her blind like you."

Something in me snapped when he said "blind like you"—a hidden memory that exploded in my mind. I was spinning toward him before I knew what I was doing. My hand was already moving with lightning speed.

Then the knife was streaking toward him like a bullet, straight for his right eye with razor-sharp precision.

But I chased the blade while it flew because I already knew he was as fast as me, and he proved it by catching the knife an inch from his eye.

I was halfway to him, moving with an ancient instinct that told me to go high and low at once. Me high and to his left; the desk low and to his right. A distraction, that's all I needed. Just a momentary shift in his focus.

Screaming full-throated, I launched myself at him five feet off the ground, intending to claw at his face. His eyes widened as my hand flashed for them, and he turned on the balls of his feet to avoid me. Still, my nails slashed across his cheek as I spun to his left, still airborne.

But none of that mattered, because without thinking about what I could or could not do, I had already elevated the desk behind us an inch off the ground and sent it toward the bookcase using thought alone.

With a bone-smashing crunch, the corner of the huge desk narrowly missed me and slammed into Vlad with enough force to easily crush any man, pinning him against the bookcase, which shattered behind him.

It wasn't enough to kill him, I knew that. But the knife in his hand was.

Landing on both feet beside him, I snatched the knife from his hand and slammed it into his left eye, wide in shock.

All of this in the space of three seconds.

Vlad's body jerked once, then turned to coils of black fog, leaving a mess of fallen books and broken shelves piled on the desk.

The knife dropped to the desk, flipped over the edge, and clattered on the floor.

I stood in a crouch, breathing hard, stunned it had worked. I spun to Steve, who looked as shocked as Vlad had in that last moment.

"Like that?" I asked.

"Like that," he whispered.

"How . . ." Karen gaped at the desk, then at me. "You did that?"

I looked back at the desk. I had, and now I could hardly believe it.

"Cut us free," Steve said. "Hurry!"

I bounded to the knife, snatched it up, and cut Steve free, then Karen. Then Gracie, pulling her little form into my arms. "It's okay now, Gracie. We'll find your mother, I promise."

She was moving toward the door before I released her, and I let her go. "Mama!"

"In the apartment at the end of the hall!" Karen said, hurrying after her.

We ran down the hall, following Gracie's slapping feet. The apartment door was still open the way Gracie had left it, searching for her mother. Lights still on.

She raced into a room on the right. Anika's bedroom. Pulled up sharply, eyes on the tossed sheets. The bed was empty.

"Mama?"

Silence.

I leaped to the closet and threw the doors wide. There, bound and gagged, lay Anika, staring up at me.

"Anika!" Karen brushed past me and fell to her knees, pulling at the twine binding the woman's ankles and wrists. The moment her gag came off, Anika was reaching for her daughter, who threw herself into her mother's arms.

"Gracie! Oh, my dear little sweetheart. There, there, it's okay." She smoothed her daughter's hair as Gracie wept into her shoulder. "It's okay, Mother is here. We're safe. You're such a brave little girl."

For a few breaths, Karen, Steve and I just watched them.

The sight filled me with a terrible loneliness. I didn't like feeling fear. I didn't like embracing anger. I didn't like being all alone without a father. I didn't like not knowing who I really was.

"Let's give them a moment," Karen was saying. I headed back into the hall, suddenly exhausted and overwhelmed.

I didn't even like that I'd killed Vlad so easily, because that had to mean something was wrong, and I didn't like not knowing what was wrong.

The moment Steve stepped out of the maid's quarters I turned and fell into his arms, hugging him tight.

"You did well, Rachelle. I'm so proud of you."

With those words a waterfall of relief cascaded over me, washing away all of my hatred. I couldn't stop the tears that sprang from my eyes. It was as if someone had pulled the plug on a whole life's worth of rage.

I was free. We were safe.

"It's okay." He kissed the top of my head. "We're going to figure this out. When the world finds out what's really happening . . . Well, they won't find out what's really happening because they're as blind as bats."

I heard Karen gasp behind me.

I twisted my head. "Why, what's happening?"

Karen stood stock still, staring above my head.

"I'm happening, darling," Steve said, only it wasn't his voice.

I turned back, arms still around his waist. Around Vlad's waist. Steve was Vlad. He'd changed while he held me. Vlad!

I jumped back, horrified. Then who was the other Vlad I'd killed? Where was Steve?

"You see, 49th," he said with a daring grin. "The only thing you can trust is fear. And I am he."

His hand flashed and hit the switch on the wall, plunging the hall into darkness. I stood breathless, frozen to the floor.

I could hear Karen breathing hard. Little Gracie talking excitedly to her mother, her crying done. Anika's warm soothing voice as she comforted her daughter. My heart pounding.

Karen hurried to the switch and turned the lights back on, gawking down the empty hall. Vlad was gone.

I knew then that the Vlad I'd killed in the office was one of the Leedhan posing as Vlad. The real Vlad had been Steve, at least since . . .

"The cabin!" I cried, spinning to Karen. "Steve's at the cabin!"

She was still staring down the hall, dazed.

I grabbed her hand. "You have to help me! We have to get back to the cabin!"

"How can you know? I don't understand how . . ."

"Vlad's a shape-shifter!" I tugged at her arm, pulling her down the hall. "I know it happened at the cabin, because after that night Steve started talking about me embracing fear."

"But we *should* embrace fear. Without it, you burn your hand in the fire."

She was right and I was in fear, desperate to save Steve, who was still the only person alive who understood me. She was right, but that's what

Vlad wanted me to think, so it must also be wrong. Maybe there were different kinds of fear.

"Hold on." Karen pulled up halfway down the hall. "It's four in the morning. Are you sure Steve's at the cabin? How far is it?"

"He has to be! A couple of hours. Steve, I mean Vlad who was Steve, programmed it into the car. You see what's happening, right? Vlad's using you!" I wondered briefly if Vlad had become her when the lights went out. No, he wouldn't have had time to get rid of the real Karen. This Karen.

I could see the wheels spinning behind her eyes as she tried to come to grips with everything that had happened.

"Please, I'm begging you. Just get me back to the cabin. Steve'll know what to do. If you don't figure this out, Vlad's going to destroy us all."

Eyes on me. "You're right." A beat. "I'll drive."

THERE WAS no traffic so we drove fast, faster than I knew the car could go. It occurred to me that by taking Karen back to the cabin, I was showing her my only hiding place, but I had no one else to trust. And the more we talked, the more I trusted her.

She was just another person in the world doing what she thought was best to help others in her own way. That's what I saw. She'd been wrong, but then so was everyone else, including me.

Everyone was working out of the system of fear.

Strange how that was so plain to me and not everyone else—maybe because my old programming had been wiped clean.

Strange how I was in as much fear as Karen, maybe more, without any clue how to get out of that fear. When I'd first come out of the MEP two days earlier, I hadn't felt any fear. Now it was bone deep.

That's what Vlad wanted.

I only hoped Steve was safe.

"So," Karen said, "you're saying that these two men who found you at the cabin were like Vlad, these . . ."

"Leedhan," I said. "Shape-shifters from another dimension."

She was having a hard time with it all, even after seeing it firsthand. It didn't fit her programming.

"Like demons? From your dreams?"

"I don't know about demons, but Steve said I talked about the other world when I was in Project Eden."

"Is that world real?"

"You tell me. Was Vlad real? Were the Leedhan who took the shape of Anika and the men at the cabin real?"

"So . . . the Steve we find at the cabin could be Vlad again. He could be there right now."

The thought scared me. "I suppose." But I couldn't see why Vlad would do that same thing again, now that we knew.

"How many Vlads are there?"

"One. The others are his Leedhan. They can change their shape to look like other people. If I'm right, Vlad was one of three who came to the cabin. I killed two of them, but Vlad shifted into a body that looked like Steve's later that night, knocked him out when he was asleep, and hid the real Steve like he hid Anika. Make sense?"

"No. I mean, it does, but how's that even possible?"

"In the same way making the desk move was possible." I shrugged.

"Tell me exactly what happened at the cabin."

So I told her in as much detail as I could. Whatever Karen had believed before was being turned upside down, but she was still having a hard time believing.

Maybe she didn't want to believe, because it meant she'd been manipulated by Vlad all along and would probably pay a price. I wondered if the world would forgive her.

"Can you stop the next bomb before it goes off?" I asked.

She took her time answering.

"No."

"You have to!"

"I can't!" she snapped.

I let it go and put my mind back on Steve.

The sun was just up when we reached the cabin.

We found Steve ten minutes later, bound and gagged in the small barn next to the cabin. I ripped the ropes free, ignoring the thought that he might be Vlad.

"Vlad was you!" I told him, throwing my arms around him. "He took me to Karen's house."

His eyes were red and dazed, fixed on Karen. "He . . . Something attacked me and knocked me out while I was in bed. I woke up here." He looked at me, confused. "What happened?"

An hour later we sat quietly in the cabin, everything out in the open. Steve was watching Karen. Karen was lost in a world of political power I knew little about. I was slowly sinking into a new desperation.

The problem was simple: no one knew what to do.

Even more, no one really trusted anyone. Except Steve, who trusted me. But I wasn't sure I could trust him. It was the business of Vlad to deceive and confuse. In all truth, I couldn't be one hundred percent sure that *this* Steve wasn't Vlad. Or that Karen wasn't one of the Leedhan.

I couldn't get Vlad's last words to me out of my mind. *The only thing you can trust is fear. And I am he.*

Karen took a deep breath and let it out slowly. "I should go."

"Not a chance," Steve snapped.

"Don't be ridiculous. I'm the president's chief of staff! It's almost eight o'clock, and it's a two-hour drive back, longer in traffic. He'll be pinging me any second, wondering where I am."

"And what exactly would you tell the president? This is all a terrible mistake and we're going to spend the rest of our lives in prison? I'm sure that'll go over big."

"What do you expect me to do? Sit here while the world blows up?"

Steve stood and crossed to the shotgun. Picked it up. Then to her purse. Dug out her phone. "You said you have no way to call off the bombings." He took out a chip of some kind to deactivate it. "So you won't be needing this either."

She stood, furious. "What do you think you're doing?"

He tossed the phone onto the couch, shotgun cradled in his arm. "Sit down!"

"I can't just vanish!"

"You can and you have. You know as well as I do that you can call off the bombings. You don't want to because you're terrified of crossing Vlad, I get that. But short of saving lives by making the call, you're doing nothing and going nowhere until we figure this out."

"And you think we can do that from here?"

"I don't know. But I'm not ready to hand Rachelle over to the authorities, which is what will happen if I let you go. You're staying here until I have full assurance of your help."

They went on, but I tuned out because the voices of fear were now pushing down so deep that I could hardly think straight.

Everything that had happened to me had been organized by Vlad. He'd taken my life, my mind, and now the last threads of courage that might help me.

I was the 49th Mystic, on some journey to find the seals that appeared on my arm, but that's pretty much all I knew. That and one other thing: fear was my enemy. The fear now creeping through all of my bones.

Normally, fear came into a child's life slowly, like water being heated up so a person hardly notices how hot it's getting. Not with me. I'd been thrown into a pot of boiling fear.

The thought only increased my fear. I felt panicky.

I stood and headed for the door.

"Where are you going?" Steve asked.

"I need to think. If you need me, I'll be in the barn."

He said something, but I was already out the door. Then at the barn, walking on feet I could hardly feel. Then in the corner next to some dried-out hay bales and an old tractor.

I slid down to my seat, dropped my head to my knees, and began to cry.

27

SAMUEL OF HUNTER brought his mount to a stamping halt on one of seven hills overlooking the battlefield. Drew it sharply around to face the valley of teeming death called Miggdon. Vadal sat on his steed, breathing hard, armor scarred, face streaked with red paint, bloodied sword resting across his saddle.

From their right, Suzan of Southern galloped at full speed, leading a band of twenty Forest Guard. All were as bloody as Vadal, but today the stench of Horde blood was a thing to relish. The more the better.

Vadal spat to one side. "The Eramites aren't making things easy. With them, the Scabs outnumber us two to one."

"Three to one," Samuel said. "We always knew sacrifices would be made."

He scanned the valley. To the west, the main Horde body, well over a million strong, were sacrificing their own as they chewed into the smaller numbers of Elyonites sweeping in with quick strikes before doubling back to regroup.

But the Horde had the sense to create three fronts, north and south complementing the main force to the west.

Samuel had arrived six hours earlier with the two thousand Circle fighters willing to risk war in defiance of the order to stand down. The order of Thomas, who'd abandoned his beloved tribe in their hour of deepest need.

Aaron had taken Samuel's advice and split his force into six regiments, two to attack each grouping of Horde from the front and the back, leaving archers on the hills to pin the Horde in the valley. The Forest Guard were divided evenly among all six regiments, lending their more experienced tactics.

Thousands of bodies littered the ground already, mostly Horde but only because Albinos retrieved their dead, unlike the Scabs.

The greatest challenge proved to be the Eramites, who favored archers nearly as adept as the Albinos—something none of them had anticipated.

Suzan reined her horse up, snapping orders. "Take them back to the camp!"

Only then did Samuel see that half of the fighters were either badly wounded or dead, leaning over the horses to which they'd been strapped.

She looked at Samuel with crazed eyes. "They keep pinning our fighters in the valley, picking them off one by one as they make their escape. It's a mess!"

"How many of ours?" Samuel asked.

"Alive or dead?"

"Dead," he said.

"I don't know. At least a few hundred."

"Are you sure? So soon?"

She waved a hand at the valley. "Look at it! Aaron overestimated his strength in this terrain. The Elyonites are stealth fighters, ghosts in the forest, but here, even speed doesn't give them the advantage they expected. Qurong's no fool." She shoved her chin at the bloodied desert. "The Horde are like a hammer out here in the open."

Samuel felt the first pang of concern since the battle had begun three hours earlier.

"How many Horde dead?"

Suzan considered. "Twenty thousand, if I were to guess. Half that many Elyonites."

"So we're slaughtering them. It's twenty thousand fewer Scabs to kill our children."

"And they slaughter us."

"Because we're using the wrong tactics," he said.

"How so?" Vadal demanded.

"We underestimated Qurong. As did Aaron. We overestimated the strength of his Court Guard in open battle."

"Obviously. But we're still taking three of theirs for every one of ours."

"As sweet as revenge is, killing them all does us no good if we lose most of ours in the same battle. We're not thinking clearly!"

"So think clearly," Suzan snapped. "Because our fighters will lose a taste for this mad quest of yours. If Thomas knew—"

"Thomas doesn't know because Thomas isn't here!" Samuel cut in. "He's abandoned us!"

"The way you abandoned the 49th Mystic?" she jabbed.

"That woman wasn't the 49th, I tell you!"

"Maybe not, but the old man did tell us to wait on the plains for her. Without her, none of us would even be here."

"So now you doubt. You could have stayed with Mikil, but here you are. Why, if only to cut me down?"

"Shut up!" Vadal snapped. "Both of you chose to be here, so be here or go back to Mikil!"

They sat three abreast, staring at the valley. Like a sweeping army of black ants, the Horde was surging around a smaller group of Elyonites caught in the center. Black on black. At this distance only the red banners flown by all Albinos distinguished them from the enemy, who used no color.

The Horde flowed over fallen bodies, uncaring. The dead were dead until after the battle, they said. They would collect and mourn each only then. As for the wounded, they recognized no wounding, only life and death, freeing up their warriors from caring for those who'd been compromised.

Bold. Ferocious. Samuel couldn't help but respect their mettle.

"What do you suggest?" Vadal said.

As they watched, the encroaching Horde army ate into the fleeing Elyonite rear guard before slowing and beginning their retreat back into the main body.

"Tell me, whose war is this?"

Vadal frowned. "The whole world's."

"But who drives it? Besides this nonsense of the 49th Mystic," he added, glaring at Suzan, who kept a firm jaw, facing the valley.

"Aaron, who would rid the world of heretics, including all Horde," Vadal said. "Isn't that what you said?"

Samuel cut to the chase. "And Qurong, who blames the Elyonites for the loss of his son. It's the only reason he would drive his full army across the desert to confront such a vast enemy."

"And Eram, commander of the Eramites," Suzan added. "He sees an opportunity to own the whole world, no doubt."

"Yes, but without Qurong, Eram has no stake in this battle. Our mistake is engaging the Horde with full strength before we cut off its head. Without Qurong to guide them, their army would be like a stumbling bull."

"Qurong's surrounded by the very army that keeps us pinned down. No Albino could get close."

"True. So we go in as their own."

"Scab? Even if you knew how, who would be willing to contract that dreadful disease?"

"No one. Which is why we'll skin one and wear it into their camp, a warrior wounded and bloodied from the heat of battle. Right down their throats."

They both stared at him, but neither was arguing.

"A small force, three or four."

Vadal frowned. "You'd have to fight your way out."

"Then twenty or fifty. The Elyonites are giving up thousands each hour. Surely Aaron would be willing to sacrifice a small force for such an opportunity."

Vadal turned back to the valley, intrigued. "It could work. But would you be willing?"

It was daring and dangerous enough to be unsuspected by the Horde. Nightfall would be the time. For the glory of it, he would be willing. If he were personally responsible for the death of Qurong . . .

Chelise would mourn her father's death, but the rest of the Circle would secretly honor Samuel. If he couldn't turn the tide, on the other hand, they might blame him personally for so many deaths.

"Yes," he said. "I would."

"As would I," Vadal said. "We would need Aaron's support."

"And he'll gladly give it." The idea grew larger in his mind. After so many failings, his risk would recover his honor. And if it resulted in his death, he would die knowing he had risked his life to save the Circle. Hadn't that always been his intention?

He studied the small grouping of men on the hill across the valley where Aaron had last been staged. "Is Aaron still on the hill?"

"An hour ago he was on the hill to the west, bent over a map with Jamous."

"Jamous is with him?"

"No longer. Something to do with gathering more of the Circle to deal directly with the Eramite archers."

Made sense. Why had he not been consulted? He felt a pang of annoyance.

"Send word to our fighters. Archers and surgical attacks only. Don't put yourself in danger. A new day will bring a new battle. Survive this day."

"They're with the Elyonite Court Guard. They can't just pick and choose where they want to fight."

"Of course they can. I'm their leader, Aaron is not." He dug his heels into his mount.

"Where are you going?"

"To find Aaron. Tell our fighters, Vadal. Tell them all."

QURONG RODE west flogged by rage, away from the battle, beyond the walls of warriors that protected him. For six hours the Albinos had thrown their full weight behind countless attacks, darting in and out like dogs intent on taking down the bull. They had underestimated his power—his army had killed at least thirty thousand of the Elyonite guard. He'd lost twice that, maybe more.

But none of this was the cause of his rage.

Jacob was. His own flesh and blood caused him this grief. The son of Qurong had betrayed them all.

And even more than Jacob, the Horde girl who called herself the 49th Mystic was the cause for his rage. The one who'd seduced Jacob into betrayal.

He was well aware that he was throwing caution to the wind by sending his full army into battle on the first day before they had time to better understand the Elyonites' tactics. But he'd lost his interest in strategy when Jacob had shown himself as Albino.

If his army couldn't prevail before falling by half, he would retreat. All would be for naught.

If they did prevail, he would still retreat in loss, because he was lost without Jacob. So all was already for naught. He was now slaughtering Albinos in Jacob's name as a means of mourning his son's death.

Five hundred warriors rode with him, flanked by another hundred scouts scattered two miles in all directions. The Elyonite commander, Aaron, had sent word of a summit three hours earlier. They would meet west of the valley, where no other warriors loitered. No details, only a vow that no harm would come to Qurong or his guard.

Ba'al had insisted he accept the invitation. Surely it was regarding the 49th Mystic, the old goat said. But in Ba'al's mind, everything was about the 49th Mystic. At times, Qurong wondered if he'd gone insane.

"Just over the knoll, my lord," Kircus said, nodding at the rise a hundred yards ahead. "He's waiting already."

Qurong gave the leader of his Throaters a nod.

The passage of the old wizard and his lion through Qurong's ranks had thrown Ba'al into fits. Talya, they called him. His power couldn't be denied, and if Ba'al was right, it was the power of blinding, a foretaste of the 49th's mission to subjugate all Horde.

They crested the knoll and Qurong lifted his hand, halting his column. A hundred Elyonite guards waited in the draw below. He watched as a single white stallion stepped out ten paces, then stopped.

Aaron.

"Wait here. I go alone."

"My lord—"

"Wait here. Keep the high ground covered."

He drew ahead slowly, letting his mount amble, waiting to see if Aaron would leave his guard and come alone.

He did, as anticipated. Whatever Aaron had on his mind, it was for his ears only.

They met halfway, at the base of the slope. The commander was dressed in black with a red band around his sleeve. Leather gloves, unsoiled by battle. This one might be their finest warrior, but he delegated the bloodletting to simpler minds.

One look at his sharp jaw and eyes and Qurong knew he was a strategist to the bone.

Aaron dipped his head. "So we meet."

"What do you want?"

A slight smile twisted the man's lips. "Indeed. No need to mince words."

"We mince bodies. Many of them your own."

"And many more of yours."

"Far fewer than I anticipated. Your reputation is overblown, as are all rumors."

For a few moments they studied each other.

"Then I'll say what I came to say and hope you see what I can see," Aaron said. "Until recently I would have said that the Horde was the greatest threat facing our world, if for no reason than your sheer numbers. Even this morning, I wondered. But now I see the slaughter on both sides and I have reason to believe the Leedhan who came to us was right. There's a greater threat to Elyonites than Horde."

The Leedhan who'd set his path on stopping the 49th.

"I'm assuming he came to you as well," Aaron said.

"He did."

"So you know his claim."

"That both Elyonites and Horde will be destroyed if the 49th isn't stopped. You're saying you believe this nonsense?"

Qurong half believed it himself, but he wanted to gauge the man.

"Isn't that what we're witnessing on the battlefield?" Aaron said. "But there's more. I have reason to believe that we have in our hands the means to destroy the Realm of Mystics. If we can, the prophecy is vacated. Once it is, we can resume whatever battle we still have a taste for."

"As I see it, I have the advantage now, while you're still reeling from your underestimation of my power. You wish me to pause so that you can regroup?"

"I'm more than happy to continue slaughtering your army. It's only a matter of time before you're all dead. But that still doesn't deal with the greater threat that faces both of us."

"The 49th Mystic."

"I've seen her deception firsthand. I saw the way she was with Jacob. My father is an old man, hardly capable of leading but not easily disturbed, and yet after ten minutes with her he was foaming at the mouth. And in our courts, no less. Did you know she has the power to heal herself? I had her blinded, yet she now sees."

Qurong heard it all, but his mind was on his son. "You saw the way she was with Jacob . . ."

"The way she had him wrapped around her fingers. She an Albino and he Horde, trembling in each other's presence. A diabolical kind of love. They bewitch each other. How can an Albino love any Horde?"

"My *son* is now Albino!"

"He is?" Aaron looked caught off guard. "You saw this?"

"And she is Horde."

Aaron hesitated, clearly perplexed by the revelation.

"More deception," he finally said. "And your son isn't the only one she would beguile."

"What do you mean?"

"I mean Samuel of Hunter, from among the small band who call themselves the Circle."

Thomas of Hunter's son. Thomas, who'd stolen Chelise from him.

"Go on."

"The 49th has the power to expose the Realm of Mystics. The Leedhan said we must force her to expose it quickly, before she gains more power to destroy us all. I now know where the Realm is, but it can't be seen unless she's present. It's the kind of wicked magic these Mystics seem to have."

"I don't see what this has to do with the Hunter boy."

"We need the 49th to expose the Realm, but we don't have her. What we do have is Samuel. He and a small band of the Circle fight with us now. I have reason to believe that if we offer him up to be killed, she'll come to save him, despite the fact that he's betrayed her. When she does, we will be ready."

"Why would she come if he betrayed her?"

Aaron shrugged. "I saw them together. She loves him. An absurd, naïve love. She should punish him for his betrayal, but these heretics have the absurd notion that love holds no record of wrong. They don't understand Elyon's judgment or justice. Trust me on this, we've been dealing with these heretics for many years."

"And you do understand Elyon's judgment, which is why you would destroy all Horde."

Aaron arched his brow. "As you would destroy all Albinos. But we are reasonable men. And reason now calls us to consider the greater threat facing us all."

Qurong noted for future reference that Aaron was comfortable betraying his own, something that always made his skin crawl.

"How would you offer him up?"

"On the battlefield for all to see."

"She has a wizard with her. He's not a weak man."

"And we have two armies."

Samuel, along with his father, was also one of the Horde's greatest enemies. The Albinos had stolen his daughter and now his son. Taking Thomas's son had a ring of justice to it. If the plan worked and they were able to kill the 49th and destroy her Realm of Mystics, all the better.

But Aaron was still a man cut from the cloth of betrayal.

"Where is this Realm?"

"Across the Divide, half a day's ride."

"How can I be assured this isn't a ploy to lure my army into your lands? As you can tell, my army favors the desert."

"Of course. Which is why I'm willing to give myself into your custody as a guest if the 49th takes the bait. My life will be in your hands. Kill me and my army will tear you limb from limb, naturally, but rest assured, I have no desire to die."

The Elyonites were as preoccupied by this prophecy as Ba'al if they were willing to go to such lengths. Qurong shifted his eyes to the horizon beyond Aaron. His skin prickled with the realization that the world truly was on the cusp of a great turning.

"I suggest we suspend battle at sunset under the guise of regrouping," Aaron was saying. "Tomorrow, we deal with the heresy of the 49th."

For the first time since he'd laid eyes on Jacob as Albino, Qurong felt a measure of peace. Ba'al would be out of his mind with delight.

"I'll give the order to cease all engagement at sunset," he said with a nod.

"And I will deliver Samuel of Hunter when the sun rises."

"So be it."

"So be it."

Aaron drew his horse around.

"One more thing," Qurong said. "Is Thomas of Hunter among these warriors from the Circle?"

"Thomas? No. Samuel tells me he's gone into the Realm of Mystics, searching for meaning. I suppose we will bring it to him soon enough."

28

THE SEA had turned to glass, green but transparent, so when I looked down I could see what looked like a thousand miles of never-ending water. There was no wind that I could feel—the old boat seemed propelled by some other power as it slipped through the water. I stood beside Talya, caught up in a transcendent awe that robbed me of breath.

After the storm's sudden passing we'd traveled far, but I had no way of telling how far, because there was no shore either ahead or behind. The sky had turned from blue to a majestic painting of green and orange and lavender, flowing with long tendrils of blue light.

I could feel a slight vibration through the boat's wooden panels, like an electric current. And when I dared dip my hand in the water, that same hum rode up my arm and filled my mind with amazement. I jerked my arm back, gasping, and Talya chuckled.

He dug a small shell from his pocket, leaned over the bow, scooped the seawater into it, and stood up. He pointed to the outer shell.

"Your earthen vessel. Rachelle."

Then he showed me the water inside the shell.

"You. Inchristi."

"Me," I said, smiling.

He emptied the water from the shell back over the edge of the boat, where it was swallowed up in the sea. Then he pointed at it. "You!"

"Me!"

And he dropped the shell into the bottom of the boat, grinning wide like a child.

We didn't speak again as we moved east, always east. Every time I thought of something I should ask or say, it immediately became unimportant and forgotten. Like lost fireflies, those thoughts blinked on and off again, until I paid them no mind.

I couldn't, because my mind was being swallowed by unquestioning wonder.

I knew I was on a quest to find five seals and that the next two would be found in another dimension called Earth, but that didn't concern me on those waters.

I knew that on Earth I was lost and destitute, but this was hardly more distressing than a child getting lost in a maze while her mother looked on. In fact, an entire life was like that, I thought—getting lost in a dark maze for the wonder of finding the light. But my mother was smiling on me there, daring me forward.

I knew that in a valley beyond the Great Divide, a million warriors had entered into an agreement to slay one another's earthen vessels in a silly game called war, waged to defend sacred beliefs. That war was no different than exchanging bitter words or thoughts of judgment and grievance.

I knew that only I could stop that war. That I would be shown the way. That I was experiencing that way now, drawn to some far shore I couldn't yet see.

But mostly I knew that I was light, and that everything else was only a matter of perception. I felt born again, and I was seeing the kingdom of heaven. In this experience, there were no problems except those I chose to see with distorted vision.

I didn't choose that because I'd surrendered my attachment to who I thought I should be and accepted myself as the light in the storm.

All of this I knew intimately, without Talya having to say a word.

Hours had passed, surely—or only minutes, I couldn't tell—when Talya stood, leaning forward with one hand on the mast.

"Do you see it?" he asked.

I stood and stared and saw a sandy white beach in the distance. And beyond the beach, a colored forest. My heart caught in my throat. Now I could see how fast we were traveling, because the shore was silently rushing toward us, far faster than our wake would suggest.

As we came closer, I saw a boy on the beach. A young boy of maybe twelve or thirteen, dressed in only a white loincloth, arms crossed and at ease, watching us.

By his side, a lion. Judah.

And then we were there, suddenly slowing to within twenty paces of the shore and its gently lapping waters.

Talya lurched to his right, nearly tripping over the bow as he took to the water. He splashed, then was on his feet knee-deep, sloshing forward. I watched with amazement as he clambered from the water, rushed up the beach, robes flapping, and fell to his knees before the boy. Hands unsteady, he reached for the boy's feet and kissed them lightly.

The boy's eyes, bright green like emeralds and smiling in amusement, remained on me. He giggled once, barely more than a hiccup, and only then slowly looked down.

Talya wrapped his arms around the boy's waist and clung to him tightly, shoulders shaking as he wept with gratitude. The boy draped one arm over Talya's shoulders and lifted his eyes back up to me.

"Come," he said, motioning me forward with his free hand.

To this point I'd been rooted to the boat's floorboards, but that single word exploded in my mind like a fireball and I leaped from the boat, desperate to reach him.

All I could think was, *Me too! Me too!* Silly and simple, but on that shore more profound than all the words found in a thousand books.

I splashed through the water and hurried forward but pulled up three feet from him, suddenly aware of a crackling power that sent a buzz through my bones.

I knew then without the slightest doubt who he was. I dropped to my knees, unable to stand.

The boy stepped up to me, searching my eyes.

"I'm so glad you came," he said. His voice was youthful but carried an unmistakable authority. He leaned forward, kissed the top of my head, and nodded once, looking between Talya and me.

Then Talya was chuckling as the boy grinned.

Without any announcement, the boy turned and walked down the beach, leaving light footprints in the wave-washed sand. The lion was gone. Talya jumped to his feet and bade me follow like a frantic mother. *Go, go, go!* So I hurried forward with Talya at my heels.

It was surreal, Talya and I following a boy who wasn't a boy at all.

He was Elyon. I could feel his power when my feet touched his footprints, as if there was energy in the sand itself, rising up through the soles of my bare feet.

By showing himself to me as a boy, he was stripping away any preconceived notion I had of what I thought he should be, just like taking off the clay mask had stripped away my preconceived notions of what I thought I should be. My journey was to become like a child so I could see beyond what my programmed perception showed me.

We walked in silence, me behind the boy, Talya behind me, and each step felt like a lifetime of wonder. After days of struggle, the deep rest I felt in following him was utterly intoxicating. In that space, I couldn't imagine even thinking of a question, much less asking one. I had none.

I didn't know how far we'd walked when the boy turned, smiling, a mischievous twinkle in his eye. A light breeze lifted his bangs.

"Do you want to see something?"

Again, I glanced at Talya, who dipped his head. *Yes, yes, of course you do.*

"I would love to," I said.

"Watch." The boy leaped one long stride up the beach where the sand was darker, almost brown. He squatted and began drawing some words into the sand with his forefinger.

Love. Light. Kingdom. Son. Daughter.

Each word he etched into that dark sand filled with glowing light. I glanced at Talya, who watched eagerly.

The boy drew a circle around the words and jumped back. "See?"

"Beautiful," I managed, watching the light flow like molten metal in each word.

Like a conductor with a wand, he motioned to the circle. Immediately, the sand gathered and quickly formed a small human figure made of sand. The light was covered up by the dark sand.

I stepped back, bumping into Talya, who gently placed his hand on my shoulder.

The boy waved at the figure and it collapsed into the words written in light. *Love. Light. Kingdom. Son. Daughter.*

He was showing me a story that symbolized his creation. In that place I understood the story implicitly.

"Watch." He jumped over to another bare patch of sand and quickly drew more words made of light.

Lamb. God. Elyon. Boy. Father. Mother. Origin.

This time he drew a square around the words.

"Who do you say I am?" he asked, standing.

I started to say the words he'd written, but I stopped. All of them were right and all of them were wrong at the same time.

"That's because language creates boxes of understanding in time. The infinite can't fit into any of your small boxes called words, see?"

"You're the Word without words," I said.

"I am."

"You are infinite."

"I am."

"We cannot put you in a box."

"No." And the square around the words vanished.

"Yes!" Talya cried, pumping his fist.

The boy grinned at him. "Talya is so easily excited."

"Me too," I said.

"Me too," the boy said. "Watch this." He swept his hand over the words at his feet, and the sand leaped into his palm as a ball of white light.

He jumped over to the words *love, light, kingdom, son, daughter* and swept his hand over the circle. The sand swirled into a second ball of light, which leaped into his other hand. Now he had two balls of light, one in each hand.

He brought them together to form one ball, which he held out. I blinked, delighted by his play. The orb of light hummed with power.

He drew the ball back and hurled it over my head toward the sea. I spun and saw it meet the water. Instantly the endless sea turned white, blazing and humming with light under a blood-red sky.

A wave of hot energy hit me, and I staggered back as the light rose from the sea and scattered into a canopy of countless tiny white lights against that red sky.

"Wow!"

Talya chuckled.

The boy lifted his hand toward the sky and beckoned the lights with his finger. *Come.* One of the pinpricks streaked toward us and stopped ten feet away, a small glowing orb that then shifted into the form of a human made of light.

As I watched, a layer of dark sand began to wrap itself around the light-man until it looked like a gingerbread man made of sand. Blinded by the sand, the walking figure slowed, faltered, then fell from the air and plopped on the sand at our feet, where it lay on its back. There was a frown on its face.

That's like the Fall, I thought.

The boy grinned. Then took a deep breath and blew toward the fallen figure. His breath whipped around the figure and blew the sand off, revealing the light it was. It leaped back into the air and began to walk again.

And that's like the wrath, I thought. It seemed to be the kindest thing in the whole world to me. How incredible was that?

The boy motioned with the back of his hand, and the figure of light flew back into the sky to join the others, glowing once more.

"The whole earth groans for the revealing of the sons of God,"[1] he said, grinning. He crossed his arms and scanned the sky, beaming. "Amazing?"

"Amazing," I breathed.

The sky shifted to hues of orange and green and bright blue. Everything was back to the way it was before he showed me how it all worked.

"It's all still unfolding, exactly as I always knew it would." He turned and winked at me. "I don't do *oopses*."

His choice of words offered in such common language delighted me, and I laughed. "No oopses!"

He hesitated for a moment, then looked up at the tree line.

"Which brings us to the reason for your coming here today. There's someone I'd like you to meet. His name is Thomas."

There beside a tall tree with a golden trunk stood a man dressed in a white tunic and black pants. His hair was dark, flowing to his shoulders. Judah sat on his haunches a few feet away, tongue lolling from his mouth, panting.

"Hello, Thomas," the boy said.

Thomas stepped down the bank, eyes on me. Then on Talya.

"I've been showing Thomas a few things so he'll be ready," the boy said.

Ready for what? But I was distracted by the sight of this legend who'd come from Earth as I had. I knew his face—everyone on Earth knew it. He'd saved Earth from the Raison Strain years earlier. Even in Project Eden we knew that.

And yet here he was, in the flesh.

He stepped up to me and dipped his head. "It's an honor to finally meet you, 49th. I think I was expecting a giant."

He took my hand and kissed my knuckles, and I liked him immediately. He turned to Talya. "And so we meet again. Forgive me for my reluctance."

Talya winked. "Aren't we all hesitant at first? And yet here you are."

"Here I am."

"Good," the boy said. "There's no time like the present. Talya, old friend, tell them what you've cooked up."

With that, the boy hurried up the beach to Judah, ruffled the lion's ears, and sat down beside him, legs crossed. Like a boy on a beach looking over his sandcastle. And what a magnificent creation the world of earthen vessels was.

"Come." Talya walked back down the shore to the water's edge. We followed quickly, keeping up with his long strides. Now I saw the Talya I knew, walking in authority. I glanced back and saw the boy scratching the underside of Judah's belly.

"Focus, 49th." He winked at me. "Show Thomas your shoulder."

I pulled up my sleeve to expose the three seals.

Thomas reached for my arm and ran his thumb over the tattoos. "They . . . I've never seen markings like this. They're set into your arm."

"Like a holographic tattoo," I said. "From Earth. Neat, huh?"

His eyes darted up to meet mine. "So you really are from there."

"And so are you, right?"

He took a deep breath. "It's been so long since I dreamed, I was beginning to wonder."

"Wonder no longer," Talya said. "You won't be dreaming this time. You'll be going in the flesh. The Fourth and Fifth Seals will be found there, but the 49th seems to have lost her way in that world. Her blinding is deep and you'll have to work quickly."

"Work how? You mean to say I'm . . . What are you saying?"

"I'm saying that you'll enter this thin place, which has no boundaries," he said, staring at the sea. "At the bottom you'll find yourself in another dimension called Earth, which is a mystery because this sea has no bottom. There, you'll find Rachelle. Everything you need to know to help her, you'll learn in the waters. That's what I'm saying."

A quiver had taken to Thomas's fingers. He stared at the crystal-green waters. "I can go in the lake?"

"Do you want to?"

"Yes! Yes, I want to."

"You've been in before?" I asked.

"Not here, no. But I've been in another lake, before the Fall into darkness. I . . . Maybe it was this one, but smaller. Yes, I want to go. Yes, I most definitely want to go."

"Good," Talya said. "By my reckoning, you'll have two days at most."

"What happens in two days?"

"Even now the armies gather to crush the Realm of Mystics. But that's Rachelle's concern here. Her concern there is to find the last two seals before they succeed. Your concern is to help her see so that she can. Her way will be treacherous with the seals, impossible without them. Am I clear?"

"What's my way?" I asked, wondering what he meant by *treacherous*. "What's happening with Jacob?"

"He returns as promised." Talya looked out over the water. Then bent and scooped some up, letting it trickle through his fingers. Light swirled through the water as it caressed his hand and slipped back to the sand. "The Fourth Seal will give you strength."

"Strength for what?"

"You'll know when you find the Fourth Seal, assuming you find it soon enough." He put his hand on Thomas's shoulder. "Which is why you must go now, my son. Dive. Dive in, dive deep. Breathe. Follow your heart. Bring her sight!"

Thomas glanced at me, then Talya, eyes wide.

"Now, Thomas."

He needed no further encouragement. In the space of only a few seconds he'd stripped out of his tunic and torn his boots off. It reminded me of Jacob running for the red lake.

Bare-chested and wearing only his black slacks, Thomas plowed into the waters. He stopped and twisted back, water to his knees.

"Go on," Talya said, flipping his hand at the water. "Dive deep."

With that Thomas turned and dove into the clear green waters.

The moment he slipped beneath the surface, the sandy bottom vanished. A current snatched his body and pulled him deep with breathtaking speed. His torso arched and I could see his jaw spread in a scream. It wasn't fear. It was love.

And then Thomas Hunter was gone.

Gone to me.

29

I HAD FALLEN asleep in the barn, exhausted from Vlad's madness at Karen's house. No dreams. Just sleep and then waking again, caught between darkness and shafts of light streaming through cracks in the barn walls.

Slowly, the events of the last couple days filtered into my awareness—the church bombings, DARPA's wiping of my brain, my role as the 49th Mystic, Vlad and his Leedhan . . .

Were they real? How was that even possible? I blinked as the thought filled me with anxiety. Why was all of this happening to me? Who was I to be caught up in such a terrible state of things?

But I knew who I was. Vlad had told me. I was the one who couldn't trust anyone. Including myself. Maybe least of all myself. I mean, I hardly had a brain! Well, I did, but it was floating away from me because I didn't have anything to tie it to.

Steve. Steve was the only one I could trust. But Steve was out of ideas, assuming that he was still Steve.

I gasped and jerked up. How long had I been asleep? What if Vlad had . . .

My question stopped there, because there was a man in the barn, sitting on one of the hay bales, watching me.

For a long second we just stared at each other, he smiling, I panicking, because all I could think about was Vlad. And this Vlad didn't have a shirt on. Or shoes. Only black pants, drenched, like his long hair.

"Good day, 49th. My name is Thomas Hunter."

All I heard was *hunter* and I knew that he was Vlad. He'd found me again!

I bolted to my feet, only then remembering my speed. My instinct was to escape. Flushed with adrenaline, I embraced all of my fear and rage and flew at him, screaming.

He didn't even have time to wipe the grin off his face before my fist slammed into his jaw, knocking him backward off the bale of hay.

I fled, streaking for the door, across the lawn, up to the house.

"Steve!"

In that panic, I didn't care if Steve was really Steve or if Karen was really Karen, because I knew that Vlad was behind me and he wasn't wearing a shirt.

In my rush, I failed to turn the doorknob all the way, so when I crashed through the door, the frame splintered with a loud crack.

"Steve!"

He was jumping up from the couch, shotgun spilling to the floor. Karen sat on a stool at the breakfast bar, stunned by my entrance.

"He's here!"

"Who's here?" Steve started for the window, then thought better and jumped back for the shotgun. "Who, Vlad?"

"He's here?" Karen cried, shoving off the stool. It clattered to the wood floor.

I bounded to the stairs and was halfway up before thinking that getting trapped upstairs might not be a good thing. So I whirled back. Steve was at the blinds, looking through the slats.

Then leaping for the door. Slamming it shut.

"That's him?" The door bounced open, latch broken. He dropped the shotgun, grabbed a crate filled with firewood, and shoved it against the door. But that wasn't going to hold anyone out.

"You're sure that's him?" he shouted.

Karen was at the window now, peering through the blinds. That was another thing—the window was broken. Keeping Vlad out wasn't going to work. We had to either get out or use the shotgun.

"That's not Vlad," Karen rasped, stepping back. "Not *Vlad*, Vlad."

But Vlad could be anyone. I vaulted the railing and landed on the floor like a cat. "We have to get to the car!"

"And go where?" Steve asked. "We can't just run, they'll find us!"

The clock on the wall read 9:37. I'd been asleep less than two hours.

"He isn't wearing a shirt," Karen said. "His hair's wet. You sure he's Vlad?"

"Who else would he be? Just keep the gun on the door. Go for his head, his eyes."

Karen still wasn't convinced. "Hold on . . ."

But then it didn't matter because a fist was pounding on the door.

"Hello in there! There's no need to be frightened."

Steve backed up, shotgun raised. None of us spoke, we just stood there, rooted to the floor.

A hand suddenly tore down the blinds at the broken window. In the frame stood the bare-chested man, breathing hard. His green eyes glanced between us.

"What's the meaning of this? I'm here for the 49th—to help her, not harm her, for the love of Elyon!"

"We can't trust him," I snapped, and I almost went after him again, because who else would know anything about the 49th except for Vlad?

Steve had the shotgun on him. "Don't move."

The man eyed the weapon and slowly lifted his hands chest high. "It's been a while since I've seen one of those. Please don't use it."

"Who are you?" Karen demanded.

His eyes settled on me, deep and piercing. "My name is Thomas Hunter, as I said. I've come with urgent news for Rachelle. That is you, isn't it? The 49th Mystic from Other Earth?"

The roof ticked as it warmed under the sun.

"Thomas Hunter?" Karen said. "That's not possible." Spinning to Steve: "Shoot him!"

"Wait!" I was terrified, but I wondered if he could be telling the truth.

"It's one of them!" Karen cried, stepping back. "Looking like . . . Thomas Hunter died two decades ago."

"In this reality, yes," the man claiming to be Thomas said, eyes still on me. "But not in my dream world, Other Earth, which is as real as this world. There, I'm the commander of the Circle. I was sent here by Talya, the man with the lion, and by Justin, who appointed the 49th to find the Five Seals of Truth before the Realm of Mystics is destroyed."

It all sounded impossibly true to me. A fantasy I had once dreamed.

"Vlad could say those things," Karen said.

"He could, but he isn't. Thomas of Hunter is." His voice was gentle now, unconcerned. "Look in my eyes and tell me, 49th: what is seeing beyond what you think should be?"

The voice I'd heard in my head. It was his? Heat gathered at the back of my neck.

"It's the voice of truth, leading you to the Fourth Seal. Hear it and you will know that I've come to help, not harm. Please, I beg you. Listen to your heart."

"Why are you wet?" Steve demanded. "What kind of pants are those?"

"I've emerged from a pool beyond the trees," he said. "I'm not dreaming of this world, like I used to. I've come through the sea. But we're running out of time. If you don't find the last two seals in the next two days, the Realm will—"

"How can we know any of this is true?" Steve interrupted. "It's crazy!"

"It doesn't matter if you think it's true. Only whether she does, and for her I have proof. If you just let me in, I'll show her."

"Show her now," Karen snapped. "From there."

He considered this briefly, then lifted one hand and squeezed some water from his wet hair into his palm. He held it out to me.

"Drink."

I glanced at Steve, at a loss.

"It's from the lake I just passed through. Drink it and you'll know."

"Don't be ridiculous." Steve's tone was as adamant as his words.

"For the love of Elyon, please. How can I point the way to the Fourth Seal if you stand here questioning my identity? We don't have time for this!"

"What will happen if I drink it?"

"You'll know."

"Know what?" Steve asked.

"Know that I'm not a Leedhan, who are incapable of love. Know that I speak only truth. Know the meaning of the seals now on your arm."

"Water can't—"

"These waters can!" Thomas interrupted. "She was poisoned with Leedhan blood. It was used with your mechanisms to erase her memories. This water will return her memories. Drink!"

I stepped forward slowly, drawn by his promise. The heat in my neck was spreading down my back.

"This is a mistake!" Karen said. "All of it. None of this was supposed to happen! I have to reach the president!"

"Shut up," Steve shot back. To me: "Just hold on, Rachelle. I'm not sure about this."

I ignored him, eyes on Thomas. Steve had convinced me I'd tapped into a different consciousness found in my dreams. That's why I could do the things I could. If what Thomas said was true, he knew all about that higher consciousness, or whatever it was. If not . . .

What did I have to lose? My mind? I'd already lost it.

Steve made no attempt to stop me as I stepped up to the shattered window and held out my hands. I could smell the scent of fresh flowers on Thomas. His jaw was smooth and his chest was scarred. A strong chest with bronzed skin.

The mad idea that he was a man from the same world I'd visited in my dreams felt nearly irresistible. Maybe because it was true.

He poured hardly more than a splash of water into my hands, then put his much larger hands under mine and looked into my eyes.

"Know this, daughter of Elyon." Tenderly, like a father. "The Leedhan doesn't know I've come. In taking your mind, he's unwittingly made you like a child, which is a gift. Use your innocence for truth now. Believe. Drink the water and know that in this realm, the lake is inside of you."

Then he lifted my hands to my mouth.

I set my lips into my palms, tilted my head back, and let the water flow into my mouth, then down my throat.

The moment the liquid hit my stomach, heat flashed through my hips, gathered at my back, and rose like a ball of fire up my spine. It happened in the space of a single breath, and when the heat reached my mind, it detonated in a light that blinded me to this world and opened me to another.

My head jerked back and I gasped, overwhelmed by the intensity of it. Of love. Of truth. Of knowing.

Steve was yelling something, but he was distant to me. Karen's shrill voice sounded like a cricket at the far edges of my consciousness. I was at the center, watching streams of truth flooding into my awareness.

And I knew . . .

I knew I was tapped into the higher consciousness that Steve had tried to explain to me. Only it wasn't what he thought, because it was a consciousness that couldn't be described in words.

My whole body was shaking, I could feel that, but I was strangely disconnected from it. It was almost as if *I* was filling my mind. My eternal self, unbound by space and time. My body was only an earthen vessel and I was using it to experience myself in this world. Until now, that earthen vessel had somehow taken me over.

My earthen vessel self only knew up and down, plus and minus, and all things as polarity, but my eternal self knew an infinite reality, beyond the knowledge of good and evil. And in that infinite space, I knew once again the full meaning of the three seals on my shoulder.

The First Seal, the outer band, was white. *White: Origin is Infinite.* God is infinite light.

The Second Seal was a green band of light. *Green: I am the Light of the World.* Inchristi is me and in me.

The Third Seal was the way. *Black: Seeing the Light in Darkness is my Journey.*

All of this I knew instantly, and it shook me to the core. But there was more, because I also remembered everything I'd forgotten about my dreams in both worlds—everything surrounding my quest for the five seals, both in Project Eden and in Other Earth. All of it, including meeting the boy before Thomas vanished into the clear green sea to find me.

I knew it all, and then the light collapsed back in on itself and was gone.

The room had gone silent. I opened my eyes and looked around, breathing hard, still shaking. Steve was by the door, staring. Karen was at the breakfast bar, crying silently into her hands. Thomas stood by the fireplace, watching me with a smile.

How much time had passed?

"What happened?" Steve managed.

I turned my head. "I'm . . . I'm in love," I said.

His stare was blank.

To Thomas: "With Jacob. He's Albino."

"Yes, he is."

"Samuel's in trouble."

"Yes, he is."

When the student is ready, the teaching will appear. I was ready. I was very ready.

"I'm going to find the Fourth Seal."

"Yes, you are."

The voice filled my mind as it had so many times, tender and loving.

What is seeing beyond what you think should be, precious daughter?

But I knew! Talya had told me. Little Maya had told me. I had known *about* this truth for a long time and *known* it in the storm with Talya. And now I knew it here, in this reality, where the Fourth Seal could be found.

There was only one way to see the kingdom.

I turned to Steve. "At DARPA I saw words etched into the wall. A riddle."

"You . . . How can you . . . You're remembering?"

"What were they?"

He hesitated. "What is seeing . . . something about beyond."

"What is seeing beyond what you think should be?" I said.

He nodded. Glanced at Thomas.

But my eyes were on the door beside Steve. Because the words were there now, burned into the wood. And as I watched, a band of light emerged from the wood, forming a two-foot white circle around the words.

"Like that," I breathed, staring.

Steve followed my eyes, saw the markings, and stumbled backward. I stepped forward as a green band emerged from the wood.

"How . . ." Behind me, Karen was seeing what we were seeing.

The center of the seal filled in with black as I walked toward the door on feet as light as feathers. The first three seals. *White. Green. Black.*

And below the seals, the finger pointing the way to the Fourth Seal. *What is seeing beyond what you think should be?*

I stopped eighteen inches from the door.

"What we think should be is what the flesh self thinks should be," I said, voice thin. "Gravity should draw down. Water should not support your weight. You should be in fashion. The world should be nice to you. The flesh holds judgment and grievance against whatever isn't what it thinks should be."

I pulled up my right sleeve so they could all see, lifted my arm, and slowly extended my hand toward the door. As I did, a red cross filled the black center. *But of course,* I thought. *Of course!*

"Our journey in this life is to see light in the darkness. The only way to see beyond what the flesh self thinks should be is to surrender. Surrender everything that blocks sight of the light. All judgment, all grievance, all blaming of wrong. Deny that self. Let go of all attachments in this life. Be in the world but not of it."

I knew what was coming next, and my anticipation of the Fourth Seal robbed me of breath.

"Red: Surrender is the Means to Seeing the Light," I whispered, and pressed my palm against the center of the cross.

For a moment, nothing. Then it came, radiant and hot as if lit by a thousand volts. A red glow filled the room. The energy surged up my arm, burned hot on my right shoulder, then winked out, leaving me trembling where I stood.

I slowly twisted my head and stared at my shoulder. There, at the center of the black core encircled by green and white bands, shone a red cross, reaching into my flesh.

I had the Fourth Seal, and it was surrender.

FOR AN HOUR Steve and Karen paced and questioned and stared and touched my shoulder, just to be sure what they'd seen was real. Steve was like a child in his excitement, Karen the stubborn doubter, questioning everything that had happened in a desperate attempt to cling to what she thought she knew about the world.

I didn't speak much and answered their questions more with silence than with thoughtful insight. Although I did tell Steve that he was right about belief and consciousness. In Other Earth it was called *binding*. What you bind in heaven is bound on Earth. What you bind through faith in a higher plane manifests on Earth.

But my mind was more on the path before me, both in this world and in Other Earth. Talya had said the Fourth Seal would show me my path. I was sure that the me there now had the Fourth Seal as well and would find her way, though I would remain unaware of what she was facing until I fell asleep and dreamed.

And I *would* dream again, Thomas said. The dreams wouldn't work in a linear way as they had before, but I would dream and know what the other me was doing, both ways.

So I set my mind on my path in this world.

My whole demeanor had shifted. It was as though in the space of twenty minutes I had grown up ten years, Steve said. But none of that mattered to me because my mind was fixed on my quest.

I would undoubtedly need that focus. All of it.

Vlad was no fool.

Thomas had found a blue shirt and some hiking boots that fit him well enough. He wouldn't consider changing his pants—his would dry out just fine, as would his hair, which was tangled, befitting a warrior from Other Earth, I thought.

I spent more than half of the first hour outside with him while Steve and Karen argued over a course of action. We were the same, he and I. Two dreamers who'd changed the world in one way or another.

We talked about Samuel. An impulsive but passionate son who brought a smile to both of our faces.

We talked about Jacob's drowning near the Realm of Mystics, and how he'd missed such simple truth for so long.

I'd lost a father in David but found one in Thomas. He, far more than Steve, was my mentor now. And I his.

Strangely, I already knew what we would do next. It was obvious to me and I knew we had to move quickly. But I let Steve and Karen talk as I acclimated to my new way of being. And to Thomas, whom I adored.

"It's time," I finally said, seated next to Thomas on the porch seat.

He nodded and stood. "Yes. It is."

He opened the door for me and I stepped in. Steve and Karen dropped their discussion and turned from the center of the room.

"Karen, you said the next bombing will happen this afternoon?"

She gave a little nod.

"You should call the president now and tell him to call it off. Everything, including StetNox."

"You don't understand. Vlad—"

"Vlad will do what Vlad will do, and both you and Calvin Johnson will deal with the consequences of your actions as the world sees fit when I'm finished doing what I need to do."

She blinked. "What are you going to do?"

"Find the Fifth Seal."

She stared at me dumbly.

"I'd like to meet with the president," I said. "You can arrange it, right?"

"Half the world is looking for you! He'll never put himself in a compromising position. Meeting with you would incriminate him."

"I think he'll agree to meet."

"How can you be so sure?"

"Because you're going to tell him that Thomas Hunter is risen from the dead and will talk to the media if he doesn't."

30

TO SAY the first full day of battle had surprised them all could be an understatement, depending on the Horde's expectation. Knowing Qurong's stubborn ways, he might have anticipated the loss of the fifty thousand men, but Samuel hadn't expected the losses he and the Elyonites suffered.

In all, nearly five hundred of the Circle. At least twenty thousand Elyonites.

The war of the world had become a bloodbath. So much blood and so many fallen warriors that Qurong accepted Aaron's request that they cease fighting to deal with their dead and wounded.

Dusk brought a light but welcomed rain, and Samuel pulled the Forest Guard back into the trees, north of the valley, where they hastily erected canvas shelters.

Samuel's mind tripped back to his meeting with Aaron an hour earlier. He'd found Aaron on the third hill overlooking Miggdon as the sun set. There, before the Elyonite commander and three of his generals, Samuel laid out his plan.

"Twenty, no more. The very best fighters. Qurong won't suspect such a mad move. He'll be dead before he knows his life is in danger!"

Aaron lifted his brow, curious. "It would be suicide."

To this, Samuel ripped open his bag and pulled out a Scab skin he and Vadal had taken off one of the dead warriors. They'd washed the face and scalp of blood—the rest of their bodies would be masked by Horde armor.

"Not wearing this," Samuel said, holding up the skin. "Messy, but with some mud, blood, and tar, it will pass." He dropped the skin on their table.

That stopped them. Of course it did, because it was a brilliant plan.

"You did this?"

"I did. With one of my men."

"I see." Aaron picked up the skin with a stick and studied their handiwork. "Clever. And who would lead such a daring raid?"

"I will, of course."

Aaron chuckled, eyes bright. "You're full of surprises, aren't you, son of Hunter?"

It was then Samuel learned that Aaron had sent word to Qurong to cease the slaughter for the night.

"If our summit in the morning fails, we'll make an attempt at the head of this snake, as you suggest." He slapped Samuel on the back. "Ten of my men, ten of yours, wearing these skins." Eyeing the Horde carcass, he said, "You do have brass, I'll give you that."

"A summit? What summit?"

"I was going to send word to you. A night of reconsideration after such heavy losses might shift Qurong. We will stand face-to-face and gauge our enemies—Qurong, Eram, you, and myself. If he fails to surrender, we will show no mercy."

"We will show no mercy even if they do surrender!" Samuel objected. "All of them must die. We may never get another chance to break them!"

"That's the whole point, my friend. Lure them into some form of capitulation and betray them when they are weak!"

He wasn't convinced. "Qurong has agreed to this summit?"

"He has."

So soon? But Samuel nodded. "So be it."

He fell asleep late, unable to settle his frayed nerves, and woke after the sun was already high. Frantic, he dressed and pulled on his boots.

"They come!" Vadal called, slapping the side of his lean-to.

Samuel buckled his fourth knife to his thigh and adjusted the leather armor on his chest. "Where?"

"At the center, as you said."

He ducked into the clear morning air and headed to his stallion. Hundreds of canvas tents littered the forest floor. He suspected half of the men were eager, the other half wondering what Thomas would say when they mourned their dead at the funeral pyres.

But all of that would mean nothing after they cut off the viper's head. One way or the other, the Circle's great enemy would be no more. Leadership had its price.

He swung into his saddle and pulled his mount around. Vadal joined him and they rode the hundred paces to the high tree line in silence. Suzan waited alone, staring into the valley.

He pulled up next to her and scanned the Valley of Miggdon. Rain had washed the blood into the sand, and the battlefield was empty of fallen warriors—vacant of all warriors but twenty or thirty around a single canvas at the center, two miles down the valley.

"You're sure about this?" Suzan said.

"What do you mean? Of course I'm sure."

"I mean going alone. Why would they bring a guard but ask you to come alone?"

"Aaron and his men are my guard. It's a summit, not a battle. We're a small contingent—the best fighters, mind you—but a fraction of their numbers. They only need our leader. Me."

She frowned. "I suppose you're right."

"Well then, Samuel of Hunter, what are you waiting for?" Vadal prodded. "And get a good look at the beast whose head we'll take when all this talk is done. We don't want to kill the wrong Scab."

It took him ten minutes at a brisk pace to reach the center of the valley, where he slowed his mount to a walk. Above, the hot sun hung in a blue sky dotted with soaring vultures, though most were on the ground, picking at body parts. To his right, the hills were lined with Eramites, at ease and awaiting orders. Thousands of Elyonite guards loitered on the southern hills, watching. The Horde's large army lay west, unseen from his vantage point. A massive bull waiting for its supreme commander to point it one way or the other.

There, under the canopy, were four men—three Scabs and one Albino. A priest of some sort, Qurong, Eram, and Aaron. Awaiting his arrival.

All eyes were on him as he let his stallion amble up, dismounted, and approached the canopy. All three were in full armor. All well seasoned in battle. But none of them had spent their lives in constant danger, evading and outsmarting an enemy at every turn.

He stepped into the canopy's shade and gave Aaron a nod, not quite sure what to say.

"So. Here we are."

Aaron returned his greeting. "Here we are."

Qurong stood to his right, arms crossed, staring at him with vacant gray eyes. Chelise's father. It had been years since Samuel had last seen him, and then only at a distance. The commander was taller and thicker than he remembered. His priest, the one they called Ba'al, watched him with beady eyes.

"Here we are," Qurong said.

Eram stood behind and to the right of Qurong, oddly disconnected, as if he was there only as a prop to do Qurong's bidding. In the same way Samuel was Aaron's prop in their minds. But that would soon change.

"Thank you for joining us, Samuel," Aaron was saying. "We didn't want to start without you. In fact, we couldn't."

"Of course."

"It has occurred to us that we're here because of the 49th Mystic. Without her, none of this would have transpired. Since you know her better than any of us, we would require your opinion."

Mention of the 49th gave him pause. What did this have to do with her?

"Yes, of course. What do you want to know?"

"Tell Qurong what you know about this Realm of Mystics."

"The Realm? It's of no concern to us. A hole in the ground beyond the Divide."

"Indulge us. What did you see and how did you see it?"

He glanced between them, annoyed by the question. "It . . . I saw it as a forest filled with color. Then as a wasteland."

"Both?" Qurong demanded. "How's that possible? It sounds like your eyes were deceiving you."

"I can assure you, I'm not easily deceived. When she was there, it was a forest. After she left, it was what you saw. A wasteland."

The priest, Ba'al, stepped forward, eyes unblinking. "Then you claim it's her witchery that reveals the Realm," he rasped. "When she's present, it can be seen. When she's not, there's nothing to be seen but wasteland, which is why it's eluded the world for so long."

The priest's face was gaunt and nearly white with the scabbing disease. His presence so close was far more disturbing than his commander's. Teeleh himself had possessed the man.

"It was your own witchery that created her," Samuel said. "Without your poison, I don't think she ever would have been what she is."

The priest blinked. "How so?"

"She claimed Justin told her that losing her mind was the beginning of her journey."

Ba'al stepped closer, far too close, and Samuel would have backed away if not for the rest. The priest studied him up and down.

"You were the one who stole her from Jacob?"

"I . . . I rescued her, yes. She's Albino."

"She loves you?"

"Loves me? I don't know what—"

"Does she love you?" Ba'al spat.

"I would say she loves all!" Samuel snapped. "What's the meaning of this insanity?"

"But does she love *you*?" the old bat cried, stabbing Samuel's chest with a long, thin finger. "You, you, you!" Three insulting stabs and it was all Samuel could do not to take the man's head off with his bare hands.

"Yes! Back up!"

"There you have it," Aaron said. "Are you satisfied?"

Ba'al spun back in a whirl of black robes and strode past Qurong. "Take him," he muttered.

The warriors standing guard on either side of the canopy shifted, forming a circle. The meaning of the summit was suddenly clear to Samuel. His value to Aaron and now Ba'al was only in his ability to lead them to the Realm of Mystics.

He moved quickly, snatching the knife at his right thigh before they could breathe. He put the knife to Eram's throat before they could move.

"Back!"

"That won't be necessary," Aaron said. "You have an important role to play, and if you play it well, you may live to speak of it."

"Back!" A heavy breath. "What do you mean?"

"He means," Ba'al bit off, "that your life has only one value, and that value is to draw out the 49th so we can use her to reveal the Realm of Mystics. The prophecy is all that matters now, you fool!"

Samuel pressed his blade deeper into the folds of Eram's neck, panicked. Beyond the canopy, warriors were erecting a tall wooden beam.

"Wait! I can draw her!" He jerked his head to Aaron, pleading. "It doesn't have to be like this. I can bring her. She'll come."

"We're counting on it." Aaron shrugged. "So sorry, young friend."

"I . . ."

A mallet smashed into his head from behind and Samuel felt himself collapsing.

DARKNESS. Deep darkness filled with dreams of Shataiki clawing at his skin. Samuel was sweating under the heat of their breath as they slammed into his body, tearing at his wrists and his ankles. One of them was gnawing on his head, sending bone-chilling pain into every nerve, but he couldn't seem to reach it.

He had to wake up, that's all he knew. He had to wake from this nightmare tempting him to believe what could not be. It was just a dream. Only a figment of his imagination.

He couldn't move his arms! He couldn't run! He had to wake!

With a tremendous will motivated by terror, Samuel pulled his mind from sleep and opened his eyes with a groan. His head was bent back and he was staring at the sun directly overhead. Three black Shataiki soared above him, circling.

No, vultures. The battle . . .

Then the rest of it crashed into his awareness and he jerked his head up. Cried out with a deep pain in his neck. But no cry came. He was gagged.

Gagged and bound! Hung upright on a tall post with a crossbeam, planted in the desert.

He jerked his arms, but the ropes binding his wrists to the crossbeam were unyielding. As were those at his knees and ankles.

He looked down, horrified to see himself stripped of all but a loincloth. They'd covered him with Horde blood and beaten his feet, both now swollen and bruised. Even if he could get down, running would be futile.

Samuel screamed into his gag and craned his neck, searching for the Circle.

But there was no Circle to be seen. Tens of thousands of warriors lined the hills, watching him, Elyonites on the left, Horde to the right. The canopy they'd erected for the summit was gone, as was the guard. Not a soul to be seen in the valley itself.

They'd left him alone like a slab of meat.

He knew then that no one could help him. The Circle would cry and plead, but there was no way Vadal or Suzan or even a thousand Forest Guard could find their way past two full armies.

They were baiting the 49th. He was their bait.

Samuel hung his head and wept.

31

IRRITATION. That's all it was, and Vlad was as comfortable with the sentiment as he was with fear. They were one and the same.

The 49th had the Fourth Seal. He'd felt the shift in him the moment it had happened, only two hours earlier. And for the first time he wondered if he might fail.

Against the Fifth Seal there was no defense. But she didn't have the Fifth.

She'd found surrender, a state of being that very few ever found. Yes, the 49th had tasted the full power of surrendering into the light beyond polarity, but even this could be choked out by the concerns of this life.

He strode down the corridor to the West Wing, following the Secret Service bimbo with skinny hips. If the woman had any idea who she was, what power she had, what fabric she'd been cut from . . .

But she didn't, and he was here to make sure she never did. That none of them did. Ever.

"He's waiting," she said, motioning at the door.

"Splendid."

Calvin Johnson was pacing by the second sofa, sweating, wrung out like a used dishrag. He spun to the door when Vlad stepped in.

"I just received a call from Karen. She was taken by those fugitives, for heaven's sake! She wants to bring them in. They have her in a panic."

"And she has you in one. Good. You should be in a panic."

The man's faced darkened. "This isn't what I signed up for! I'm the president of the United States! If you think you can push me around, I'll . . ."

Vlad moved and was behind him before he could finish his threat. Hand in the man's hair, jerking his head back so his neck was bare to Vlad's grip. He cut off Calvin's windpipe and spoke reason into his ear.

"It's too late to whine like a little girl. Everything's going along perfectly, give or take. One misstep from you now and I'll bring this whole office down around your ears. Better yet, I'll make sure the courts do it for me. Death would provide you with far too much comfort. Nod if you understand me."

Calvin nodded.

"Good. Now, before I let you breathe I'm going to tell you what to do. Let her bring them in. Do whatever they want you to do, I don't care. Just make sure Rachelle Matthews is at that security summit tomorrow at one, second session. She's the only thing that matters to you now. If I fail tomorrow, I'm gonna slaughter every last world leader at that summit, and that will be on you. If I go down, this whole world's going down. Clear?"

A quick nod.

Vlad relaxed his grip and stepped back, straightening his new jacket. "Well, that was simple."

Calvin staggered to his desk, grabbed a glass, gulped some water, and coughed.

"You caught me in a bad mood," Vlad said. "I doubt it will change. Mind your manners."

It took a full minute for the big man to calm himself. He was no idiot, but even the most logical and well-intentioned human was stupid in the grip of fear.

Calvin seated himself in his special chair behind the cherrywood desk, straightened his phone, his pen, a pad of paper and a paper clip.

He put his elbows on the desk and looked up. "Okay, tell me what I need to know."

"You called off the bombings?"

"Yes. Karen insisted."

"Do you think you can trust her?"

"Yes. She'll take the fall if it comes to that."

"No. You'll take the fall. I've had my fond moments with her."

"I want to call off StetNox. The only crime that's been committed so far is the placement of a harmless piece of malware on a billion connected devices. Please tell me you won't activate it."

"I don't care about your silly cyber war, but it's going wide if I fail. Like I said, I'm taking the world down with me. Play your part and it won't come to that."

Calvin eyed him carefully. "So what you're saying is that I'm finished."

"Most definitely. If I fail, very finished."

"Fail to what? I don't even know what you're trying to accomplish here. Stop a girl from Project Eden from doing what?"

"From finding the Fifth Seal before the Realm of Mystics is destroyed. For this alone Teeleh sent me! If she succeeds, all is lost."

This drew a blank stare. So Vlad brought things back to this Earth.

"We may very well be at this world's most critical juncture since the light bringer came back to life two thousand years ago. You'll know that tomorrow, assuming you're still alive. When will they be here?"

The president sat back and drew a deep breath. "It's too risky during the day. Their faces are plastered all over the internet. After dark. I'm still making the arrangements. It's not easy, you know."

"Great accomplishments never are. When you meet them, you'll put up a fight. It's madness to allow her entry into the World Security Summit—that sort of thing. She mustn't suspect. Tell them I was here and out of my mind with rage."

The president closed his eyes and shook his head as the full scope of just how compromised he was continued to sink in.

"Only the 49th. Do what you like with her handler. This Steve fellow."

Calvin opened his eyes. "They're with some crackpot. Karen was a bit hysterical so I don't know where they picked him up, but he claims he's Thomas Hunter. Some—"

"Thomas Hunter?" Vlad's irritation shifted to something closer to fear. "You're sure?"

"That's what she said. It's not him, of course. He's dead."

So . . . The old mystic had found a way to send Thomas of Hunter through. It was how she'd found the Fourth Seal.

"It can't be him," Calvin was saying. "Please tell me I'm not losing my mind."

"Of course it's not him. But Rachelle may think it is. She's a dreamer from Project Eden, given to delusions of grandeur. If she brings him, humor her, but if she insists he go with her to the summit, refuse. I need her alone."

The president nodded. "Tell me one thing," he said.

Vlad lifted an eyebrow.

"If your only objective is to stop Rachelle Matthews, why not just kill her? You told me you can't, I just don't understand why."

His answer would make no sense to the man, but he gave it anyway.

"Teeleh forbids me from killing her. If I kill her here, she'll die there, and we need her alive there to reveal the Realm of Mystics. It's the only way to destroy it. Otherwise I would have killed her in Eden."

Calvin blinked.

"But technically speaking, I can kill her." Vlad strode for the door. "And if it comes right down to it, believe me, I will."

32

AFTER LEAVING the sea, I slept in the desert night next to Talya, and there I dreamed.

In that dream I was in a cabin with Thomas Hunter, drinking a trickle of water squeezed from his hair. In a rush, the full meaning of the first three seals filled my mind once again. I was aware that I was dreaming, and this me was screaming encouragement to the me who was being reborn as the 49th on Earth as each seal entered my consciousness.

It was then that she who was me found the Fourth Seal on the door of the cabin. I was asleep in Other Earth, but when she put her hand on the cross, uttered those words, and experienced the Fourth Seal, my entire body in Other Earth began to shake violently even as I slept.

I was aware that my right shoulder was burning, and I knew that the Fourth Seal had found me. If Talya had been awake—and he might have been, for all I knew—he would have seen a slender girl lying on the sand, shaking like a leaf in the wind as the full power of the Fourth Seal filled every cell of her body.

Then I was with Thomas in the dream, deciding my fate. I still had the final seal to find.

The next awareness I had was of a bright light shining down on me. *The sun*, I thought. *I'm in the desert and it's day.*

I opened my eyes and bolted up, gasping. I jerked my sleeve up and stared at the red cross that had manifested on my shoulder as I slept.

A low chuckle on my left broke the stillness and I turned.

Talya was picking at his teeth with a twig, watching me. "You like?"

Something had shifted in me. Everything felt new. Not necessarily different, but new, as if the world around me was still terra firma but now alive with an energy I'd never known.

"When you actually surrender the old, you actually experience everything as new," Talya said.

I slowly stood, scanning the desert, the tree line to our right, the blue sky above. I didn't know how to describe what I was seeing, maybe because in some ways I was seeing for the first time beyond what had blocked my sight.

Talya said that everything not done in a binding to the light, a binding called faith, was called sin by the ancients. It was best understood as being off center or missing the mark or blindness, not simply deeds done. Whatever was not done in faith was sin. So even most lived in sin most of the time, experiencing powerless lives.[1]

But I had surrendered out of the world of sin. It wasn't a bad world as much as it was a blind world.

I was seeing as Inchristi.

And in that sight everything looked alive as if for the first time. Everything was the same and radically different at the same time. Greens were greener, the sky was bluer. Even the sand seemed to be alive.

All was held together Inchristi.

Talya had asked me if I liked it. There was no need to answer the question. It was impossible not to like this. I was home.

"Not quite yet," Talya said. "Tomorrow."

What is shown to be in the one who sees, dear daughter?

The voice washed over me like a sweet, warm breath and my heart jumped. The final finger, pointing to the last seal!

"The Fifth Seal!" I said. "I have to find the Fifth Seal."

"You do." Talya stood and flicked the twig away. "And you must know that you will be tempted to bind once more to the cares and concerns of the world, which so easily choke out all four seals. It's easy to once again want what used to be so comforting to the earthen vessel. And you always get what you truly want."

331

But I was too distracted by my quest for the Fifth Seal to ponder his words.

"What is shown to be in the one who sees? It's the fifth finger. Do I have it in the other world?"

"She will when she dreams tonight."

"What if Vlad gets to me before then?"

"If she abides in the Fourth Seal, he won't."

"Will she?"

"Will you?"

With those words my momentary concern fell away. My place was to see in each moment to the extent I could, not worry about whether I might see in the next moment.

I faced the desert. Talya hadn't told me what to expect, only that my way would be treacherous. Resting now in new sight, I couldn't imagine anything being treacherous. How could it be, if I'd surrendered my attachment to this earthen vessel?

"There was a teaching," he said. "A man was cleansed of what blocked his sight. But the accuser that blocked his sight went out and found seven more like himself, and they returned to find the man's mind ready to be blinded once more. So the man entered an even deeper blindness. That's how, 49th. It's common."

Even then, after all I had been through, I felt no concern.

"Remember, they can only accuse. Fear is their greatest power. When the evil man comes against you, turn the other cheek. The only thing you require is the armor of your true identity, as Paulus so eloquently put it. Your resistance is being who you are: the light of the world."

I looked at him. "You're leaving me again?"

He walked up to me and lowered himself to one knee.

"I return to the Realm. They need me now. You must go alone, 49th." He searched my eyes, and I thought I could see tears building. "I am so proud of you. No matter what happens now, know that. I see no failure in you, even if you fail. Promise me you'll remember."

I choked up. Not with sorrow, but with love. I cupped his head in my hands and kissed his forehead.

"I promise." Then I dropped to my knees too and threw my arms around him like the child I was. "I love you, Talya. I will always love you!"

His long arms held me close. "I am so honored to know you."

After a moment of silence, he cleared his throat, stood, and walked toward the horses. He led my pale mare back, saddled and ready.

"Follow the desert due south. When you see the black cloud in the east, head toward it."

I looked south and east, seeing only a bright blue sky. "Just head for the black cloud? What am I supposed to do?"

"You're supposed to follow your heart."

What is shown to be in the one who sees? Find the Fifth Seal.

"What if I can't trust my heart?"

"You can always trust your heart. It's your mind that gives you trouble. Your cognitive perception."

I wasn't sure I knew the difference, but I nodded anyway.

"You must go."

He handed me the reins and I swung into the saddle.

Without warning, Talya slapped the mare's rump and it surged forward. "The Fifth Seal, 49th!" he called out after me. "Bring us the Fifth Seal!"

I twisted back. "I will."

Little did I know what I was saying.

I RODE six hours by my estimation before I saw the black cloud, high above the desert. Each stride of my mount felt like a step into newness. I had no concerns, no fear, no conflict of any kind. I was simply the daughter of Elyon, riding in a dimension that had been created for me, where I could be the light. In it but not of it.

Honestly, I could hardly wipe the grin from my face. I replayed my time with the boy over and over, enchanted by his staggering power and innocence. To say that he was Elyon would be a mistake, because God could not fit in a box called *boy*. To say that he wasn't Elyon would also be a mistake, because he was. And that also made me smile, because it made perfect sense to me.

Not to my earthen vessel mind, but to my eternal mind, which was my heart, I supposed. How could the earthen vessel's mind describe, much less grasp, the infinite?

It couldn't, but the heart could.

Follow your heart, Talya said.

So I did.

It led me east toward the black cloud. A thundercloud, maybe. But it didn't move with the breeze. So what kind of cloud was it?

The reason I didn't see it for what it was until I was only a few miles away must have been because I was so caught up in the wonder of the Fourth Seal, my surrender out of suffering and into light.

But then I did see it, rotating around itself like a gathering hurricane stuck over a valley. It wasn't a cloud.

I stopped my horse and stared.

It was Shataiki. Hundreds of thousands of them.

"Hmm." Curious.

I still felt no fear. I saw them with my eyes, but I wasn't perceiving their fear, not even when I crested a low dune and saw into the valley ahead of me.

I pulled up, stunned.

It was the same valley I'd met Qurong in a few days earlier. Only now his army wasn't in the valley. It blanketed the northern hills, a sea of horses and Horde and mallets and axes and spears and sickles. Unmoving. Dark. The Elyonite army hugged the slopes on the other side of the valley, leaving a wide swath of vacant desert with something posted in the center. A cross of some kind.

Beyond the valley, the Great Divide rose on the horizon. Above the valley, the swarm of Shataiki slowly churned.

I felt no fear because I knew I could easily pass through the valley without being harmed. I could use that power just like Talya had used it. Was I supposed to?

As if in response to my question, two lines of horses, one from each side of the valley, broke free from the main bodies and surged toward me, still a mile distant.

I clicked and my mare headed forward, straight toward the center of the valley.

The two columns of warriors reached me when I was halfway, sweeping wide and behind to cut off any escape. But they didn't concern me.

The cross suddenly did, because I could now see they'd hung a man from it.

Jacob? Where was Jacob?

I looked at the columns to my left and right, each roughly a hundred paces from where I rode, watching me warily.

And Jacob? Talya had told me he was returning as agreed.

I blinked and studied the nearly naked Albino on the cross, head hung, hair covering his face. It was him, I could feel it in my bones.

Now unnerved, I spurred my mount and took it into an easy gallop, eyes fixed on that cross. Immediately, the columns to my right and left matched my movements. A dozen Shataiki spiraled from the throng above and streaked toward the cross, where they landed on the body like vultures intent on feeding.

I spurred my mount faster, thinking only that I had to save Jacob!

Two smaller groups broke from the hills and galloped toward the center of the valley to meet me. I recognized Aaron with his escort on the right, Qurong and the priest, Ba'al, on the left.

They reached the cross thirty seconds before I pulled my mount to a walk, fifty paces from the scene. I was breathing hard now, knowing that I was sliding into fear and trying my best to let it go.

My demise was one thing. But Jacob? I didn't want him to suffer!

All of Talya's and little Maya's and Soromi's and the boy's teachings on letting go whispered to me, but my attention was on the body. I still couldn't see his face.

"She's Albino!" Ba'al croaked on my left.

I pulled to a stop, staring up at the man hanging from the beams. For a few breaths, no one spoke. It was just me ten paces from the cross, and the high commanders of both armies seated on horses flanking me.

Ba'al left Qurong's side and nudged his horse to the base of the cross, pale eyes on me, unblinking. In his hand, a long spear.

"Do you love this one, wicked witch?" he rasped.

I studied the man on the cross, letting fear wash through me. Do not resist, Talya had said, so I didn't, but I wasn't liking it.

What is shown to be in the one who sees, dear daughter?

Ba'al spoke over the gentle voice.

"Do you come into our noose to save your precious Albino?"

It was Jacob, then! The priest was punishing him for turning Albino! They'd set him as a trap.

"Take her!" he screeched.

Seven or eight Horde broke from the left, six Elyonites from the right, all galloping toward me. They were halfway to me before I lifted both arms, palms facing each group of warriors. As if hit by an unseen force, their horses pulled up sharply, rearing, clawing at the air with their hooves.

"No," I said.

A commotion stirred among all who could see. Qurong's horse jerked back, stamping. Aaron stared at me, stunned.

"No, you will not take me." Power surged through me. "You will cut him down."

Ba'al grinned wickedly, lifting the spearhead to Jacob's side. The sharp tip rested against his flesh.

"You don't understand, witch. Either he dies or you surrender yourself to face the consequences of your heresy. Five hundred thousand warriors encircle you. How many can you take before an arrow finds his heart?"

And with that he gave his spear a little jab. Enough to send pain through the man's body and jerk him back into consciousness.

He groaned and lifted his head. His hair fell from his face and I saw that it wasn't Jacob. It was Samuel. Samuel.

His eyes fluttered open and he looked at me, only half aware. But in his eyes I could see that he'd betrayed me. They knew where the Realm of Mystics was.

Now they'd betrayed him, beaten him, humiliated him in the face of the whole world. None of them could see the Shataiki flapping around his head now, driving their talons into his brain, feeding on what life he still had.

None of them could see, but I could, and compassion swallowed me whole.

What is shown to be in the one who sees?

A commotion behind me begged for my attention—someone yelling my name—but it felt distant. I stared at Samuel, unable to tear my eyes from his face, stunned by the surge of new emotions washing through me. I didn't lower myself to the energy of pity for him. Compassion was something else. An openness to him. A oneness with him.

Tell me, what is shown to be in the one who sees? Whisper it to me. Join with me and we will tell the world.

I knew the answer, didn't I? My heart knew. But I didn't have the words.

The commotion behind me grew louder. Qurong grunted. A murmur rose from the Horde army on my left. But I was swimming in a new knowing, and I felt my muscles begin to relax.

Everything seemed to slow down. Sound became distant. A faint hum filled the valley. The Shataiki became more frantic, screeching now, but even those panicked shrieks were oddly vacant.

Yes, sweet daughter. Yes . . .

"Rachelle!" a voice was crying out behind me.

Jacob's voice. He'd returned. My beautiful Jacob had come back. But I didn't turn. He wasn't my path now. Samuel was.

My hands began to tremble. What my mind was accepting, my body still couldn't fully grasp.

Then Jacob was to my right, pulling his mount up with tight reins. His eyes darted to the cross. Then to Qurong. "What's the meaning of this?"

I felt a tear slip down my cheek. *Samuel, Samuel, dear Samuel . . .* In that moment Samuel was Jacob, you see? *What you do to the least of these, you do to me.* I held no distinction between Jacob and Samuel then. One was no more special than the other.

"Back away!" Ba'al snarled at Jacob. "You defile all that is sacred, and now you conspire with the wickedness that tears this world in two. Back!"

Jacob's mount stamped. He spun to me. "Save yourself, Rachelle! Samuel's chosen his path."

Qurong had turned his face from Jacob. The world went still around me as I slowly turned my head to look into Jacob's eyes. How beautiful he was! Such a worthy man with a heart spun from gold.

My jaw quivered as I spoke, still flowing with a sweeping power none of them yet knew.

"I love you, Jacob," I said. "This is my path. It's going to be okay."

"What's your path?"

"Samuel," I said, facing Ba'al. "Cut him down and take me."

"No!" Jacob cried.

I slid from my horse and walked toward Ba'al.

"Cut him down," I said, dropping to my knees in the sand. "Set Samuel free and the 49th is yours."

Ba'al had frozen, taken off guard. Feet landed hard in the sand behind me.

"Then you'll take me!" Jacob rasped, falling to his knees. "Take me for her!"

"Qurong!" I heard Jacob's mother screaming behind us, rushing through the ranks. "Jacob!"

"Hold her back!" Ba'al cried.

"Don't you dare touch my boy, you filthy little beast! Jacob . . ."

Then she was silenced. I heard her body crash to the ground.

Part of me wanted to protest with her, but my eyes were on Samuel again, hanging above me, body broken, spirit crushed. He was the light of the world, there before me.

What a beautiful daughter you are to me. What a beautiful son he is to me. Now you know, dear one. Now you know.

Tears flowed freely down my cheeks. They weren't for me or for Jacob. They were tears of compassion for Samuel. Beautiful, beautiful son, Samuel . . .

Ba'al snapped his fingers and one of the guards approached Jacob. A nod from Ba'al and his mallet fell on Jacob's head. My warrior fell face forward in the sand.

But my eyes were still on Samuel and I was weeping with him now. He was every man, every woman, every child, every father, every mother, desperate to know themselves in a world of polarity, torn apart by opposites.

And yet I wasn't torn in that moment. I wasn't opposites. I was love.

Ba'al stepped forward, gloating. "And so the end has come. Salvation awaits us all!" His voice rang out for all to hear. He shoved his spear at me. "Take her!"

33

OBLIVIOUS to what was happening in Other Earth, I slipped into a strange, disconnected space as Steve drove Karen, Thomas, and me toward the city that evening.

Thomas and I sat in the back. We saw in each other's eyes a great knowing that could hardly be given words in this world. I don't think either of us knew what would happen. Only that this was our path.

He offered me a thin smile, took my hand, and gave it a gentle squeeze. It was all I needed.

The plan was simple. It was time for me to give truth to the world. Talya had said the Fourth Seal would lead to the Fifth Seal. In the surrender of that Fourth Seal I knew I wasn't in need of anything. The earthen vessel had its wants and needs, but I was no longer needing anything because I was the light and the light had no lack.

True life was really about giving, not receiving, because giving *was* receiving. We were all one, even the least among us, as Yeshua had said.

So now I would give. In giving I would find the Fifth Seal. What I would give might divide the world, I didn't know. Justin had said I would bring a great crisis and I had, more in Other Earth than here. Maybe now that would change.

I just didn't know and that was okay. I was okay. Everything was okay. That's what the boy had said, and I believed him.

We drove through streets and dark alleys, headed to some warehouse district, Karen said. No one could know we were meeting with the president. It was terribly dangerous. Everything was terribly, terribly dangerous.

She was wrong, of course, but I didn't say anything.

It was just after ten when we pulled up to a door off an alleyway. I could see light leaking through pulled blinds on the window. Two Secret Service agents quickly ushered us from the car into an office off a warehouse, although it didn't look like any warehouse I'd seen.

The office had thick white carpet and bookcases, four chairs, and a dark wood desk with a computer screen and a brass lamp. Three mounted heads of deer or antelope or something in that vein hung from one of the walls. A cabinet with a glass door held several rifles with scopes.

A tall man in a blue suit stood and looked at us for a moment, first me, then Thomas. Dark circles sat under tired eyes. Bombing churches could do that to a person. He was the president of the United States—the most powerful man in the world, Steve said—but to me he was just a man, lost in his earthen vessel.

"You're the one who claims to be Thomas Hunter?"

"Yes, Commander. Sir. Yes, sir. I am Thomas."

The president glanced at Karen. "How's this possible?"

"I don't know, but I ran a facial scan. It's him."

"Actually him? I thought he was only claiming to be him."

"I told you, it's him."

This was news—a revelation that seemed to bother the president a great deal.

"And you're Steve."

"That's right."

To one of his guards: "Please escort Steve to the holding room."

"What do you mean? No, you don't understand. I'm not leaving her with—"

"I understand perfectly well, Steve. Please, don't make this any more difficult than it already is."

"It's okay, Steve." I gave him a nod.

He left with some reluctance, but it was better, I thought. He'd done enough. If we got through this, I'd make sure the world knew how he had helped me.

If we got through this . . . For the first time since I'd found the Fourth Seal, a hint of worry coiled itself around my mind. I still had to find the Fifth Seal. I still didn't know what was happening in Other Earth, and I wouldn't until I slept, assuming I dreamed again. I thought I was supposed to tell the world some truth, but didn't the world always crucify its prophets?

Even questioning the status quo caused a great ruckus among those who were heavily invested in their version of truth. Questions caused them to feel threatened and fearful. They didn't know that there was no fear in love.

That was my earthen vessel's mind talking. But still . . .

Pulse surging, I spoke as soon as the door closed.

"This is very simple. You may have meant well, but you killed a lot of people. There's no way to hide that. By now you know that Vlad Smith isn't from this world. All he cares about is stopping me. He used you, and I'm sorry for that, but here we stand, in an old warehouse with a fancy office, talking about how to undo what he's done. We have one chance. If I fail, it's not going to be good. So you have to get me into the World Security Summit tomorrow. I need to speak."

He stared. Blinked. "I see."

"Do you?"

"I see what you think, yes. But it's not that simple." He glanced at Karen, worried. If I could still read minds, I would have an advantage, but that was gone. "Vlad visited me today. He's outraged. I've never seen him like this."

"I don't think you understand the gravity of our situation," Thomas said, stepping forward. He spread his arms. "Who do you see?"

"I see someone who looks like Thomas Hunter."

"But can't be, because I'm dead, right? And yet here I am." He lowered his arms. "Which means that everything you know about life and death is turned on its head. Are we standing on some mount of transfiguration? Are the dead really dead? What's really happening beyond this temporary existence? All the metaphors used by ancient writers point to a truth that's beyond the human capacity to grasp. There are things Vlad doesn't want you to know because he is the Shadow of Death. Will you play to him, or will you play to us? It's the only question you should ask yourself."

My confidence soared. I had Thomas Hunter by my side!

"All of this is diabolical!"

Thomas eyed him. "You're a religious man?"

"Of course I am." The president crossed to the desk. "But I didn't come here to discuss theology." He eased into the chair, leaned back, and faced us, a man now clearly in charge.

"I accepted my role as president to return this country to its former glory, and I intend to do that. Our economy is falling apart, our politics have become a bloodbath, millions are suffering in squalor while the rich thrive. I'm going to put an end to it, and if that means making some deals along the way, so be it. Maybe I miscalculated Vlad, but I can assure you of one thing. Remove my administration from office and this whole country is going to fall apart. Every algorithm we've run gives us no more than five years. So I'll ask you the same question you asked me. Will you play to Vlad, or will you play to me? If you insist on exposing Vlad, you also expose me, and the country needs me."

He'd flipped the conversation, dismissing love in favor of doing practical good. He didn't understand that all practical good was useless if it was done in the energy of fear rather than in the energy of love.

"You can't solve any problem on the same level of consciousness that created it," I said. "You can't fix fear with fear."

"Stop with the New Age nonsense! I'm a devout man of God. I don't need you preaching at me."

"New Age?" Thomas asked.

"It's another form of religion seeking to serve itself," I told him. To the president: "What matters is our transformation through the renewing of our minds. Like being born all over again into a new operating system beyond the earthen vessel. Yeshua called that operating system the kingdom of heaven."

"Now you're spouting Gnostic crap. None of this matters to me. I'm trying to do some practical good, for the love of God. Surely you can see that."

"Gnostic?" Thomas asked.

I turned to him. "It's the belief that form is evil or inconsequential because we are spirit. A half-truth."

But even as I spoke I realized how impossible it would be to share the truth with anyone like the president, who had invested so much in his identity as a righteous man who knew more than others.

And I was supposed to speak truth to a whole gathering of such men and women at the summit? I should be taking the truth to the outcasts, like Maya and Soromi. Only those in suffering would have ears to hear, I thought. The rest had too much to lose.

My fingers tingled with a surge of adrenaline. Who was I to do this?

"I'd like to make you an offer," the president was saying.

Thomas held his eyes. "An offer?"

"Go away. Vanish. I'll give you both new identities and kill the story of your involvement in the bombings, Rachelle. I'll also make sure you get to wherever you want to go with ten million dollars in whatever form of untraceable payment you choose. Live peacefully on a beach in the South Pacific, or disappear in the mountains of Nepal for all I care."

Ten million dollars? Was that what thirty pieces of silver looked like these days?

Karen spoke for the first time. "You do realize that he'll come unglued." Meaning Vlad. There was fear in her voice. She'd seen him work up close. "He's not human! He'll see right through it."

The president lifted a hand to stop her. "I realize that, Karen, but it's either that or play his game on his terms. I've already done that, and it's a fool's game. His interest isn't us, it's her. This whole 49th Mystic madness threatens the only thing that can save this country! The only shot we have is to remove her from the playing field entirely."

"He'll crush us!"

"Maybe. Or maybe we recover. We've done it before." Eyes on me. "The only thing he wants is for you to speak at the summit tomorrow.

I'm supposed to pretend I don't want you there and then make sure you are. Instead, get on a plane tonight. Vanish."

Vlad, at the summit? That coil of anxiety was tightening around my chest. My plan was actually Vlad's plan! He was still a step ahead of me. Panic lapped at my mind.

"Ten million dollars will get you a long way," the president said.

I moved in a blur, without thought, two steps toward the desk, leaping over him and twisting so I landed at his back, arm around his throat.

"Do I strike you as the kind of person who cares about ten million dollars?" I breathed into his ear.

The remaining Secret Service man was only now grabbing for his gun. It had just cleared his jacket when Thomas snatched it from his hand as if it were a toy. He ejected the clip and tossed the weapon back to the man.

Then he winked at me and I caught myself.

I released my grip and stood upright. "Sorry about that," I said, stepping back around the desk. "I've been under a little stress lately." I turned back to him, sitting there in shock. "As you can see, Vlad's not the only one with power. I could easily kidnap you or kill you or hunt you down. Especially if I had ten million dollars."

I let that sink in.

"But I wouldn't even dream of it. That's the difference between Vlad and me. He uses fear, I'm trying to use love. So maybe you should work with me."

He responded after a long hesitation. "And what would that look like?"

"Usher me into the summit tomorrow. Let me speak. I won't implicate you, I'll only state my case plainly, exposing Vlad. The world has to know about him. It's the only thing I ask."

"And Vlad?"

"Tell him I took you up on your offer to run. Tell him I'm headed to the United Nations to expose him. Tell him we met and I attacked you and your man killed me. Tell him whatever you want, just make sure he's not at the summit. Buy me that time. When I say what I have to say, I think the world will look at everything differently."

"Trust her," Thomas said. "Trust her because I'm standing here and I'm dead. That should be all the evidence you need."

"Her," the president said, recovering. "Not you."

"It's her place to go to the summit, not mine."

I turned to him. "What? You should be with me!"

"No, 49th," he said in a gentle, reassuring voice. "This is yours alone to do. Trust me."

Fear tempted me again. That was another thing that worried me: I was still feeling fear, even after gaining the Fourth Seal. Even though I thought I'd surrendered. There was no fear in love, so did that mean I wasn't in love? What if I was in fear when I tried to speak at the summit?

The president stood, straightening his jacket. He stepped around the desk and crossed to Karen. "Excuse us for a moment, will you?"

"Sure."

He opened the door into the warehouse and ushered his chief of staff from the room, followed by his security.

"What do you think?" I asked Thomas as soon as the door closed.

"I think you're magnificent."

"Really?"

"Really."

He drew a deep breath and paced to the bookcase, eyeing the thick volumes there, hands clasped behind his back.

"I can only wonder what you're doing there." Other Earth. "I'm only here, but you're in both places. It must be strange."

"Not really. In a way we're all in two places."

He turned back to me, brow arched. "Earthen vessel and spirit."

"Something like that."

"I suppose so. I just can't help but wonder how the Circle is faring. War is waging there, I saw that deep in the lake."

The revelation took me off guard. "Already? You're sure?"

"I thought you knew."

"The Fourth Seal only opened my eyes to the lessons I've learned, not all the circumstances surrounding them. I haven't dreamed for a long time."

"You'll dream tonight, then you'll know more than I know. I would have news of my son, Samuel." He sighed. "Either way, you must find the Fifth Seal before the Realm of Mystics is destroyed. My wife, Chelise, is there, you know." A smile curved his lips. "It's all a bit mind-boggling."

"How did you find the boy?"

"I climbed the cliff to the upper lake. It feeds the lake in the Realm."

"So the upper lake and the sea are the same."

He gave me a nod, eyes sparkling. "It has no boundaries."

We turned to the opening door. The president stood, hand on the knob, glancing between us, then settled on me.

"I'll do what you propose."

His agreement brought me some relief. But that reprieve was immediately overshadowed by another thought.

What would I say?

"Karen will take care of the details," he said, crossing to the exit. He turned back, drilling me with a measured stare.

"For the love of God, I hope you know what you're doing."

347

34

What is shown to be in the one who sees, my love?

The voice spoke to me like a tender mother. A gentle father.

"The one who sees, sees light," I said, but my voice was silent because they'd gagged me.

And I was seeing darkness because they'd bound me to a horse and tied a hood over my head. We'd been traveling for hours, up the Divide and across, followed by the muted thunder of two armies who crushed the ground underfoot. It was night and cool. Jacob was on a second horse behind me.

My poor, beautiful Jacob! How my heart broke for him. I found myself doubting the decision I'd made to give myself up for Samuel. What had I been thinking? Nothing! I'd only followed my heart, just as Talya told me to.

Just as I knew I must.

The comforting voice kept me sane, reminding me always of who I was when it whispered through my mind, but then I would hear the rattling and crunching of the massive army marching me home, and tears would fill my eyes.

They were going to destroy my home. The home I would expose to them.

Tell me again what your journey in this life is. Whisper it to me.

"The Third Seal," I said. "Seeing the Light in Darkness is my Journey. And then the Fourth Seal: Surrender is the Means to Seeing the Light."

And when you surrender to see the light, what do you see?

"The First Seal," I said. "You are infinite and can't be threatened. You are the light in whom there is no darkness."

What else, dear one? Tell me what else you see.

"The Second Seal. I am the Light of the World. Inchristi is me and in me. I'm also beyond threat, one with you, only temporarily in an earthen vessel, like a costume."

My sight shifted and I saw light there under the hood. Immediately my anxiety vanished, replaced by the tender embrace of that light, which was love. It was as though I was breathing a power beyond this world, so that each and every atom was infused with that light. When the light came into darkness, it came into all of it, down to the tiniest electron. It came *into* it, not next to it.

For long minutes I forgot all of my concerns.

Then I saw darkness once again and my jaw began to quiver.

The Fifth Seal would have saved me from my wavering. But I wasn't there. I was still vacillating.

When Yeshua was on Earth in a body, he came into alignment with the light through his suffering, just like you, daughter. This is written. Even your elder brother had to learn that obedience. And he cried out to me, begging for the cup to pass. It was then that he finally surrendered his own will and became the way for you to follow, as written. I gave him comfort as I comfort you now. Then they hung him from a tree.[1]

"Am I going to die too?" I was shaking.

Death is no more. It is finished. That's what happened and that's what you're learning to see, my dear one.

A calm settled over me. In that moment, I loved Yeshua as I never had. He was my elder brother? Justin was my elder brother? He understood my struggle because he had experienced it! The thought pushed me far away from the army's incessant clanking and crunching.

"Yea, though I walk through the valley of the shadow of death, I will fear no evil." Why? Because death is only a shadow. There is no fear when you realize it is finished.

"There is no fear in love," I said in silence.

There is no fear in love, nor darkness in light. Death is only a shadow.
Held in that embrace of comforting light, my heart soared.

Thirty minutes later, I was sweating in fear.

And so it went. Mile after mile. No one spoke to me. No one offered me water. No one eased the ropes that dug into my wrists and my ankles, bound together under the horse's belly.

Talya had told me there was a back way into the Realm, a full day's journey from the Elyonite city. They were taking me there so the armies could enter. I was a thin place, and my presence would lay the Realm bare to be seen by all.

Then destroyed.

So why had I given myself for Samuel? I was only following my heart.

After many hours, exhaustion finally overtook my aching joints, and I found myself dreaming.

Once more I was Rachelle on Earth. Thomas was with me, guiding me, giving me courage. Vlad was in a panic. So then, I might still find the Fifth Seal there before the Realm was destroyed here.

There was still time! The 49th Mystic could still fulfill her role by finding the Fifth Seal there, maybe at the World Security Summit. Anticipation shortened my breath even as I dreamed.

But I had dreamed there as well, and in that dream, I'd become this me, being led to the Realm of Mystics, bound and gagged. I'd dreamed it and woken with an urgency that shook my bones.

We were both rushing headlong into a final showdown that would bring either light or darkness, love or fear.

The sun was hot when I woke on the horse. I could see light filtering through tiny pinpricks in the hood. But something else had changed. I slowly sat up from where I'd slumped over my mount's neck.

Our stopping had awakened me. Not just me, but the whole army, silent now.

I jerked my head to the right as if doing so might give me sight.

I could hear flies buzzing. A horse grunting. Someone behind me coughed. Jacob. Then the clopping of hooves as someone approached me.

"Let her see," Ba'al rasped.

Fingers untied the cord around my neck and the hood pulled free. I squinted in the bright sunlight as my eyes adjusted.

We'd stopped on a wide swath of rocky sand between two towering cliffs. Ahead, more wasteland surrounded by cliffs. And above . . .

A huge vortex of slowly circling Shataiki hung high above the wasteland. They'd followed us the whole way. And the wasteland was the Realm of Mystics, now masked by a desert landscape.

I twisted in the saddle. Jacob sat on his mount ten paces behind me, gagged and bound. But he was defiant, his eyes steady on me. A shallow nod and I knew he had no remorse.

Behind him, a sea of Horde and Elyonites, awaiting their orders.

"Now we see, witch." Ba'al sat on his mount to my right, lead rope in his bony grasp, eyeing me with gray eyes. "Prove your sorcery to us."

I don't do magic, I wanted to say, but I was still gagged. Even if I hadn't been, I was far too distracted by thoughts of what awaited me to exchange words with someone as blind as Teeleh's high priest.

"What he means to say," Aaron said, pulling his mount abreast on my left, "is that the time has come for you to show us what you've been hiding for so many years." He looked at the wasteland. "If your power fails us, I will tear Jacob limb from limb in front of you."

Qurong was mounted ahead of us next to six of his commanders, eyes forward. "Lead her."

Ba'al led me like a lamb to the slaughter. Past Qurong and his men, through the wide canyon, toward the mouth that opened into the Realm of Mystics. The others fell in behind, a slow and wary procession. They didn't know what to expect.

But neither did I.

I am everywhere, daughter. Everywhere.

"Please give me strength. Please . . ."

I ride on the horse as you, one in light. Nothing can threaten me. Nothing.

My saddle creaked beneath me. We drew closer, closer, only a few horse lengths from the end of the canyon, and I was praying that nothing would happen. If nothing happened, the Realm would be spared.

If so, Jacob would suffer. Then what should I hope for?

A new thought filled my mind. Could the Realm even be destroyed?

We were past the canyon's mouth, stopping on a rocky strip of sand, gazing at the towering cliffs that encircled the massive sinkhole. On the far side up high was the ledge where Talya had opened our eyes. I was a thin place, he'd said. My pulse was pounding. Maybe I had to be up high. Maybe it didn't . . .

A faint, crackling hum filled the air, and the scene before us began to shift from wasteland to forest, rolling out like a scroll from where I sat toward the center of the sinkhole.

Ba'al's mount startled and reared.

I watched in wonder as the depression transformed from wasteland to forest in the space of three breaths. It wasn't just any forest, it was a colored forest spotted with lush green meadows and stunningly bright flowers. A waterfall thundered on the cliff to our far right. And though I couldn't see it from here, the village rested near it.

My fingers were shaking. I had exposed the Realm of Mystics.

Above us, the swirling mass of Shataiki surged eagerly, screeching with either delight or rage—they were the same now. None of the others could see them, but I could, and I knew they'd been waiting for this day a very long time.

For a full minute my escort stared at the lush valley in disbelief.

Ba'al was the one who gave the order, twisting in his saddle.

"Bring the armies!" he cried. "Crush every blade of grass and slaughter every living soul." He shoved a shaking fist into the air. "Burn it to the ground!"

35

WE'D SPENT the night at a new secure hotel called the Hyatt, a location Karen doubted Vlad would suspect—her house was far too risky. The summit was being held across town at a building they called the Abernathy Center, on the northern side of Washington, DC. Three thousand were expected to attend, dignitaries from every participating nation as well as representatives from all segments of security and welfare within those nations. Held once every three years, the summit was the largest of its kind, passing resolutions that affected every aspect of global security and well-being, from armed forces to planet care.

The whole world was watching.

Driving to the summit now with Karen, I understood what she meant when she said that security would be heavy. We passed through three checkpoints before approaching the large round dome surrounded by a huge, full parking lot.

Karen had given me other details that morning, but more than half of my mind was on the dream I'd had while sleeping. Other Earth was falling apart. I'd given myself up for Samuel and was being taken to the Realm of Mystics, bound, gagged, and hooded.

But what could that mean for me here? I had the Fourth Seal on my arm—I checked three or four times just to be sure. I'd experienced true surrender of myself, and I no longer cared what happened to me. But so many innocent people now depended on me. Why had I ever agreed to such an impossible quest?

Had I agreed? Or had it been forced on me?

"You agreed," Thomas had said when I mentioned it to him earlier, pacing. "They said you chose it in the Realm of Mystics when you were younger."

Yes, I already knew that.

"But you're not alone. In this world, all are on the same journey of awakening to truth. Not in the same way you are, but we each get to discover where we come from, who we are, and why we're alive in earthen vessels."

We were all born blind to discover the glory in darkness. But I already knew that, didn't I? I just wasn't thinking clearly.

He put his hand on my neck and kissed my head. "Trust, 49th. Trust what Talya has shown you. Trust the boy. Trust Elyon. Trust Justin. Trust yourself."

Yes, I would. I did, but so much of what I'd experienced now felt like a dream, and many of those dreams were from a long time ago in Eden, Utah. I was suddenly unsure of my abilities.

"Allow, don't resist. You were made for this. I'm returning to the pool that I came through. My task is finished here. It's your turn to shine."

I felt a moment of anxiety even though I already knew he would be leaving. I closed my eyes and took a deep breath.

What is shown to be in the one who sees, sweet daughter?

That tender voice blanketed me with a deep calm. I'd learned part of the answer in Other Earth already. It had to do with love—true love that held no record of wrong. But the Fifth Seal hadn't come. So either there was more, or I hadn't experienced that love yet.

I had no choice but to trust.

As I saw the Abernathy Center now, that calm slipped away, because in that large structure, thousands from all over the globe waited. For what, not even I knew.

"I've made arrangements for us to go in the back," Karen said. "The fewer people who see you, the better." She reached for a bag in the back seat. "If you don't mind, put these on."

I pulled the bag open. Dark sunglasses and a white hat. A badge that read "Holly Radcliff, White House Staff." My image was plastered all over the internet, the face of a terrorist. This was my disguise.

"They'll run a fingerprint scan, but I've altered your records. You're officially one of my clerks. Fair enough?"

I peered ahead as she drove past the full lot toward the back side of the building. This was it. Dear God, help me. What was I going to say?

You will tell them what I say, precious daughter.

"But what do you say?" I asked silently.

What is shown to be in the one who sees? The answer is found there.

The Fifth Seal. I would find the Fifth Seal in this building. Once more a calm settled over me, and I let my fear slip away. *Allow, don't resist. Trust.* Thomas's last words to me.

Steve was taking him back to the cabin. He'd soon be gone. Not me. Not until I dreamed. I wasn't sure which was worse, here or there.

Neither.

Allow, don't resist. Trust.

"You go on in ten minutes," Karen said.

"I do?"

"The president's opening the summit at ten. He thought it best you speak at the beginning of his time rather than at the end." She kept glancing in the rearview mirrors, wound tight. "He's in a real vise, you know. This whole thing . . . I don't think he could give a speech now if his life depended on it."

"You want me to wear this stuff inside?"

"No, you'll go on stage as you. Then you'll tell them you're being framed but you don't know by whom. Tell them what DARPA did to you, show them your innocence, say whatever else it is you came to say. Just don't mention me or the president. I gave him my word. You have fifteen minutes."

"I'm here to find the Fifth Seal, not point fingers."

She pulled the car into a spot marked "White House Staff" and turned the motor off. Then twisted to me and put an unsteady hand on my arm.

"Listen to me. If I hadn't seen what you're capable of with my own eyes, I'd say you were certifiable. You're not. You may be the most sane person I know. Just do what you do. Whatever happens to me now, I'm okay with it." She gripped my arm tighter. "I'm behind you, Rachelle, you hear me?" Another beat. "Just go in there and be you."

Be you. I felt a fresh surge of confidence. But of course. Just be me.

"I will," I said.

"Let's go."

"Hold on." I slipped on the sunglasses and white hat. "Okay."

I was wearing black pants and a white blouse that Karen had purchased in the hotel lobby store. Black sandals. It was the fanciest outfit I'd ever worn, I thought. The white hat probably didn't look right, but I was way beyond that.

It only took us a few minutes to pass through the rear-door security—two of the agents knew Karen. I was the new staffer. Then we were through, hurrying to the back stage.

I don't know what I'd been expecting, but it was all going so fast. We were alone at a side door in a dimly lit hall. I closed my eyes, listening for the comforting voice. My head was empty. But maybe that was a good thing.

Just be who you are. Just walk out there and wait for the words to come.

That's what I was thinking when the door opened. I looked up at the coordinator, a man dressed in white who nodded at Karen. "The floor's yours."

I felt Karen's hand at my back and started forward, but she stopped me to take off my hat and sunglasses.

"Be brave," she whispered in my ear.

The coordinator was eyeing me with curiosity, seeing me without my glasses on. Maybe he recognized me. That as much as Karen's words pushed me forward, past the man, through a curtain, and onto a huge stage covered in gray carpet.

The first thing I saw was the president, descending some steps to take his seat at the left of the stage. He wasn't looking my way. I guessed he'd already introduced me. As who, I didn't know, only that he wouldn't use my name.

The second thing I saw was the podium at the front of the stage and the three cameras aimed at it, winking red. On.

The third thing I saw was the audience. Three thousand of them seated in curved rows that rose all the way to the back. A hush had fallen over the room. It was just me at the back of the stage, staring out at three thousand faces who were patiently waiting for someone the president of the United States thought they should hear.

I walked toward the podium, feet numb, eyes fixed on nothing, wondering if any of them would recognize me. My heart was pounding and my palms were clammy. I'd confronted Vlad in another auditorium once, a smaller one with fewer people. And no cameras broadcasting to the world.

Somewhere someone gasped. Then a murmur ran through the gathering. They were starting to recognize me.

Then I was there, at the podium, staring at the microphones aimed at my mouth.

I still didn't know what to say. Inside I was begging to hear, but I could only hear the growing sound of surprised voices.

So I leaned forward and spoke the first thing that came to mind.

"Hi. My name's Rachelle Matthews and I'm being framed for the bombings that have killed all those people."

A hush fell over the crowd. The cameras were winking at me but no one had rushed out to arrest me, so I continued, only barely aware that hundreds of millions of people across the globe were watching me.

"It wasn't me. Steve took me from the white room at DARPA because they'd wiped my brain again and I didn't know who I was. I was at the church because I always go to church on Sundays. I had nothing to do with that bomb."

For the first time the world was seeing the real me, just an innocent girl brave enough to step forward for all to hear. And the fact that they were letting me speak was good. Really good.

Tell them who you are, daughter. Tell them what you know.

Filled with surging confidence, I spoke louder now.

"My name is Rachelle Matthews, but that's only the label put on my earthen vessel. Really, I'm the light of the world, daughter of my Father, and I've been sent to share what I've learned about who we all are. As Rachelle, I was born blind in a town called Eden . . ."

A loud, slow clapping stopped me and I turned my head. A man stepped out of the side-stage shadows. A man dressed in black pants, cowboy boots, and a white jacket, hair slicked back.

My heart bolted. Vlad was here. Vlad! Walking toward me, clapping, eyes daring and bright.

I spun to the president, but his face was turned away from both of us, and I knew immediately that he'd betrayed me.

Doors suddenly banged, slamming shut all around the auditorium in rapid succession. His Leedhan were sealing off the room! How many, I didn't know, but even one or two would be enough, moving quicker than the eye could see.

A security officer by the door to my right collapsed, unconscious. Startled cries erupted as a few in the audience realized something terrifying was happening.

Something was locking them all in and neutralizing security. I saw it all from the podium, and my hands began to shake.

Vlad stopped ten paces from me, grinning wickedly. He spread his hands wide.

"Welcome to the end, my darling."

36

I SAT upon my horse at the gateway into the Realm of Mystics, smothered by dread. The rumble behind me built slowly as the armies approached, then grew as a hundred thousand horses surged forward, moving at a full gallop.

The ground shook as the leading edge thundered by me, fifty horses abreast. I was on the sand in the center with Ba'al and Qurong and Aaron protected by their guards. Jacob, behind us. I prayed Samuel was safe with his people now.

The armies spilled into the valley like a herd of stampeding buffalo bent on crushing the earth. They all knew the prophecy. They all feared the Realm more than death itself. Their priests had made the case plain, and now their orders were as plain.

Crush the Realm. Raze it. Burn it to the ground.

Ba'al fixed his eyes forward, gloating. But he no longer concerned me. My eyes were on the sky above. On the Shataiki.

I watched, breath gone, as the swirling cloud of winged beasts began to spiral down in a vortex, descending on the exposed Realm. I couldn't hear their shrieks over the thundering hooves, but I could see their jaws widen as they streaked for the valley floor and spread out like a swarm of massive locusts, tearing into the foliage, consuming all that stood in their way.

The Shataiki weren't acting alone, I realized. Though Ba'al and the armies could not see the beasts, they were somehow giving them the permission they needed.

And I had given Ba'al permission in surrendering myself.

The Elyonite army surged to the left, circling around to destroy the southern side.

The Horde army veered to the right, trampling, slashing, headed for the waterfall. There, where the village hid behind falling trees. There, where Talya had come to join the other forty-seven Mystics. He would stop the enemy. Surely he had a plan to avert this destruction!

But no defense had come yet. It was as if the valley was accepting its annihilation without concern for itself. *Strip me, kill me, burn me, trample me underfoot.*

Still the armies flowed into the Realm, nearly halfway through it now.

Still the Shataiki descended, blanketing the trees like a swarm of black locusts.

Still I watched, horrified, eyes directed to where I assumed the village lay. The death of the Realm was a death I felt inside, hollowing me out. I had failed.

What do you see, daughter?

It was a tender whisper, but I could hear it clearly above the crushing roar echoing off the cliffs, and I blinked, momentarily distracted.

"A valley of death," I answered in my mind.

And what is death?

I hesitated, remembering.

"A shadow."

A shadow. Then tell me again, what do you see?

Such a gentle voice. So unconcerned. I thought of Talya, showing me how Elyon's wrath was like a tender mother gently nudging her infant back into safety. This was that voice. Talya wasn't with me, but I wasn't alone.

"Shadow," I said. "I see the valley of the shadow of death."

Yes. Yes, that's what you see. Shadow. And in this valley of the shadow of death, you need fear no evil.

"But . . . how?"

Tell me how, daughter. Tell me the only way to rise above fear.

I answered from weeks of training under Talya's charge.

"By seeing beyond the shadow," I said. "By seeing with the eyes of love. There is no fear in the sight of love." Then, "I'm not seeing it the way you see it?"

In my nature and in my name, I see no darkness. It is cast infinitely away from my sight as far as the east is from the west.¹ What is cast infinitely far doesn't exist. It's only a shadow. Remember?

"There is no fear in love because love doesn't make any account of wrong."

It sounded so simple to me. I'd known this in the storm. I was the daughter of Elyon, one with him in the light, beyond any threat. But binding myself once more to the perception of danger separated me from that knowing, dragged me back into fear.

"So I have to see with the eyes of love," I said. "With *your* eyes."

Love, precious one. Let the wind of my wrath blow away the judgment that blinds, and see that only love remains as you. Now tell me, what is shown to be in the one who sees?

The Fifth Seal! Was there still hope? Was the me on Earth finding the Fifth Seal?

Ba'al lifted his hand, and the thundering warriors to my right and left reined up, separating from the last of those who'd entered the Realm.

Smoke billowed to the sky in the direction of the village, and my heart sank.

"Be strong, my love," a gentle voice said to my left. I turned to see that Jacob had chewed through his gag and edged his mount beside mine. He couldn't hide the dried trails of tears left on his cheeks, but he showed me a courageous face. "Death means nothing to us."

I nodded, but tears slipped down my face at the sight of him. My Jacob. What a beautiful man he was. What a tender heart, yet strong like a mighty oak, unbreaking in the most ferocious gale.

"I love you like I love Justin," he said. "You are a flower in the desert. None of this means anything. As Talya said, death is but a shadow."

I love you, Jacob! I wanted to say. *I am so proud of you, mighty warrior.* But I was still gagged.

"Silence!" Ba'al snapped. He glanced between us, eyes fiery, lips twisted in a wicked grin. "Gag him and bring them both!"

He headed into the Realm with Aaron and Qurong riding high on either side. They were surrounded by their guard, entering a Realm their armies had turned to wasteland.

One of the warriors took my horse's lead rope and led me forward. Another gagged Jacob and followed.

With the Shataiki, the armies had annihilated all but the outer edges of the valley—they alone now showed any color at all. It was as if a fire had passed through, pushed by a blasting wind. Wrath.

But if the wrath revealed beauty, I wasn't seeing it. The kingdom was here, just as Yeshua had said, but I needed his eyes to see it. And I wasn't seeing with those eyes because I was still being born again, learning to see with the eyes of Christ, just like everyone else. I was still journeying out of blindness into truth beyond the storm, where there was no trouble and no fear of trouble.

The moment my horse stepped into the first lines of stripped trees, the Shataiki all around the valley took flight, soaring up to the cliffs, where they perched, peering down with red eyes. The Realm of Mystics had become a great arena of death. I knew death was a shadow, but I couldn't deny just how deep that shadow appeared to me.

The trees weren't just stripped of leaves—they were drained of life. The grass wasn't merely trampled but pounded to dust. There were no flowers, no green to be seen, only bare, gray trees with long branches stretching to the sky like claws, begging for mercy.

Tell me, daughter. Whisper what you know into my ear.

"There is no fear in love," I said, trembling inside.

Love. See with the eyes of love. Offer them love.

"How? How do I love?"

Bless those who persecute you.[2]

I took a deep breath and closed my eyes. In the darkness, I saw no destruction. There was only emptiness in my sight. But then that darkness lightened and I saw a sea of earthen-vessel sand-men against a red sky.

The boy's sky, filled with those who'd become blinded to who they were in the light. And me? Was I blind or was I seeing with the eyes of love? Either way, I was seeing more now than when my eyes were open, wasn't I? This was truer than what I saw as a ruined valley.

Bless those who persecute you, daughter. Forgive them, for they know not what they do. Let it all go. Enter my rest.[3]

I swallowed the knot in my throat, sinking into a warm grace. I rode like that for a long time, eyes closed, resting in a peace that was beyond my earthen vessel.

Not until we stopped did I open my eyes. We'd come to the crest of a hill overlooking the village. It was burned to the ground except for one tall structure on the far side. A Thrall, colorless and bleak, surrounded by a hundred warriors.

The steps were red with blood. There was only one body on those steps, and it wore a bloodied white robe. My heart stopped.

It was Talya. Was he dead? No, still moving. But badly wounded. My heart pounded.

I quickly scanned the charred ground, looking for any sign of life other than Horde or Elyonite. There was none. They'd slaughtered the Mystics. All but Talya, whom they allowed to suffer. The Thrall was now their tomb.

New tears flowed down my face and I was powerless to stop them. But I felt no dread for Talya because I knew that neither he nor any of the other Mystics I'd once known were attached to this life.

My sorrow was for the deception that had caused such devastation in this valley. It was a strange feeling that defied my old mind. I should be crushed. But at least a part of me had already surrendered what I thought should be.

"And now you are the last Mystic," Ba'al rasped. "The very last heretic to deceive this world. When you are gone, only Albinos stand in the way of our enduring peace."

Aaron overheard him and drilled him with a hard stare. "When she is gone, I will personally cut out your tongue and feed it to my dogs."

"Silence!" Qurong snapped, still not turning back. "We finish what we came for and leave this pit of death." He refused to lay eyes on his son. My heart broke for the Horde leader.

I caught myself. A new awareness began to fill my mind. My compassion had been far more for Samuel and Qurong than for myself or Jacob. I had no fear for my life. Nor Talya's. But I had compassion for Samuel and for Qurong because they were so blind. No blame, only compassion. Was that the expression of love? Was that *being in love*?

What you do to the least of these, you do to me.

"They're you?"

What you do to the least of these, you do to me.

"To you . . . Then . . . they are you."

What you do to the least of these, you do to me. To me. To me, sweet daughter.

"You are the light of the world. They are the light of the world. To see in love is to see the light in them, not the darkness they cling to."

I blinked. The "least" were the lowest sinners. But . . .

"Love even Ba'al?" I asked.

Especially Ba'al.

I sat stunned, unable to comprehend how that could be possible. Love held no record of wrong. Love saw beyond another's fear. Love saw beyond all darkness and shadow.

Hear me. Tell me. What is shown to be in the one who sees?

"To the water!" Ba'al growled.

His voice jerked me back. They were going to drown Jacob and me. The realization hollowed me out. Terrified my earthen vessel. But the tender words I'd heard echoed still, haunting me, drawing me.

The greatest power that existed in the universe waited for me beyond a door that was opened with a single key. And that key was the answer to one question.

What is shown to be in the one who sees?

But it was still beyond my grasp. And time was running out.

In the few minutes it took us to reach the lake, I knew a fear deeper than any I had yet known. Deeper because I knew the Fifth Seal was love and there was no fear in love. The fact that I was feeling fear meant I wasn't in love, which meant I was failing.

That self-condemnation took my mind into an even deeper darkness. The voice was silent now, and I longed for it, begged for it, crying out to Justin and Elyon and Yeshua and God—all of whom were One.

And I was one with them, but my fear blinded my experience of that union as we approached the pool of death. Of my death. Of Jacob's death.

The waterfall was now a gray trickle splashing into a large pool of muddy water. High above perched a large Shataiki, twice the size of the others that eagerly peered down from the cliffs surrounding the vanquished Realm.

Teeleh. This was Teeleh, gloating in silence high above us all.

Come to me, my beloved. Awaken from your sleep. Awaken and tell me what is shown to be in the one who sees.

"Fix the hoods and cut them down!"

I swallowed and closed my eyes.

"I come to you because I'm already one with you. I will love Ba'al because we love him. I will surrender what blinds me. Awaken me to love."

The hood fell over my head but my world didn't darken. I was seeing the red sky again, and against it the sea of lights the boy had shown me. I was going there, I thought.

They cut the ropes and dragged me from my mount, arms bound before me. Then they hauled me to my feet and shoved me to the edge of the muddy pool. Cool water swallowed my ankles.

A great silence filled the valley as I stood there, mind numb, trembling from head to foot.

"I love you, 49th!" Jacob was crying out. He'd cut through his gag again. "I love you more than death!"

"Drown them!" Qurong's voice was torn by rage and terrible sorrow.

"Drown them!" Ba'al's shriek was the last voice I heard before being shoved headlong into the water.

Forgive them, for they know not what they do.

And then I was under.

37

"WELCOME TO the end, my darling."

Vlad's words might have been heard by some, but his voice was low and meant for me alone. He lowered his arms and walked up to me. I could smell his scent, a musky cologne that made me nauseous.

"I have news for you, 49th."

And then he was right in front of me, flashing a grin that sent chills down my spine. He leaned close so only I could hear.

"The Realm is no more. Even the old goat is dead. All but you. Now it's your turn."

He quickly reached past me, snapped up one of the wireless microphones, stepped away, and spun to the closest camera, mic at his mouth.

"Keep it rolling! Keep them all rolling. I want the whole world to see what we have here! Because what we have here"—his accusing finger stabbed at me, frozen behind the podium—"is hatred!"

But my mind was on his previous claim. The Realm of Mystics was no more. There hadn't been an ounce of deception in his voice. It was true. That's why I'd frozen. He was going to kill me because he could do it now without compromising his plan.

He'd won!

I was completely lost without a clue what to say or do. It was just me, the seventeen-year-old girl who'd had her brain wiped, now cowering under a powerful man who could crush me with one fist.

But that wasn't true. I was as fast as him, maybe faster. I was, but the world was watching. I couldn't fight Vlad here—it would only make me look like the terrorist they thought I was!

"Hatred!" His voice echoed over the PA system. "Now . . ." He lowered his voice. "You're probably wondering who I am. Who is this man in the white jacket who's somehow managed to slam every door and incapacitate every guard without moving a muscle? Think of me as the angel of truth."

That wasn't true and I had to tell them, but I could hardly breathe, much less speak.

He lifted a finger, pacing. "Truth one: The esteemed president of these United States of America introduces you to a wonderful little girl, but when that wonderful little girl comes out, you see that she's the monster the world has been hunting. You have to wonder why the president would deceive you. The answer is me."

"That's a lie!" the president snapped, standing. "A lie!"

"Shut up, Calvin." Vlad strode to the left, eyes on the president, who returned his hard stare, face white and sweaty. "Sit down!"

Calvin Johnson hesitated but then eased back down, unable to find the right words for his own defense.

"Better," Vlad said. To the auditorium: "Truth two: She's here because I told the president that if he didn't give her the floor, I would expose my deal with him to use StetNox, a nasty little piece of malware that he released two years ago. With it, the president can manipulate any bank account with impunity. My funding put Calvin Johnson in power with the understanding that when my malware brought the world to its knees, he would be there to sweep up—that was the deal."

The president stood again, nostrils flaring. "He's lying! The evidence will show . . ."

Vlad lifted a hand, and the president slammed back into his chair as if shoved by an unseen force.

A collective gasp broke the room's silence. Just that one gasp as the world saw Vlad's power.

"So sorry, Calvin," Vlad said. Then to the rest of the hall again: "So you see, there's a lot of nasty business under the skin of this world, but nothing so threatening as that innocent-sounding girl behind the podium, shaking in her boots because she's now realizing that this was always my plan, exposing her failure for all the world to see. The end is here."

"That's not true," I said. My little voice echoed through the room, but the anger that was welling up inside of me wasn't little. I could feel it rising like a fast tide, fueled by an ancient ocean of frustration and grievance.

He turned, brow arched. "No? What's not true? That the president's a crook or that you're more dangerous?"

"It's not true. I'm not dangerous." I spun to the hall. "He's lying, don't listen to—"

"Hatred!" he roared, overpowering my voice. "You all heard what she said at the cathedral she blew up. You've seen the death and destruction that followed. False religious zeal in the heart breeds hatred, which breeds violence. When a young skull full of mush comes to believe that her God rejects others who don't believe the right thing, she becomes an antichrist, willing to kill and destroy those she thinks her God hates. This is terrorism of the highest order, and it, not war, is the world's greatest security threat!"

The cameras were winking red, broadcasting his half-truths to the world.

"And the girl before you is an antichrist who would have brought this world to its knees had I not come to save you all."

He was twisting the truth, rambling, confusing them with deceit and fear. I couldn't let him do that!

"No!" I screamed. The word came from me like a wave. A rippling surge of energy hit the front of the room, toppling two of the cameras, slamming into the front rows with enough force to knock confused ushers and attendants back several feet as they gasped. The whole room saw it.

A small part of me was amazed by my power. A larger part of me wanted to use it against Vlad.

His lips twisted into a grin. "Do you despise me, 49th? Do you hate me? Do I strike fear into your heart? Fear and anger have the same root, you know."

I knew he was goading me with truth now. I knew there was no fear in love and I had to find the Fifth Seal, which was my only purpose now.

But I also knew that I'd already failed in Other Earth. Now he was here to kill me in front of the whole world. He'd waited his whole life for this day.

"A witch!" Vlad said, eyes fired. "Hatred gives her that kind of power, and she has no trouble using it because that's what demons do!"

I was moving at the word *demons* because he was the demon, not me. Two long strides and then I was in the air, throwing myself at him without concern for what he could do to my body.

He dropped under me just as I reached him, then jerked up, slamming both fists into my abdomen midflight.

The microphone clunked and whined with feedback as it hit the floor. Cries filled the room as the audience saw what defied their eyes. We'd both moved far too fast for their minds to comprehend.

My body tumbled through the air, then slammed into the wall ten feet above the stage. I twisted my head back to gain his position as I dropped to the floor, landing in a crouch—one knee, one foot, one hand. My body surged with power, fueled by a final resolve to end it all now.

Either I would kill him or he would kill me, right here in front of the whole world.

What is shown to be in the one who sees, daughter?

"Do you hate me, 49th? Do you despise those who slashed Talya's body? Does Ba'al make you sick?"

I was already moving, streaking for him. But so was he, away from me, streaking left. I veered to intercept, driving forward with every ounce of strength and speed in my body. This time my head slammed into the side of his, knocking him into the podium, which splintered and toppled off the stage.

When I landed and spun back, he was already on his feet, arms spread wide, chin lifted to the ceiling, laughing. He wasn't fighting back . . . A pang of confusion momentarily stalled me.

"Hatred!" he shouted. My confusion ended and I moved, blinded by rage. "It's all about hatred, and the only way to protect yourself is to hate your enemies and the enemies of God. She isn't from this world! She's a . . ."

My knee crashed into his jaw and my momentum carried me past him, but the blow threw me off axis and I spun wildly. I landed in a crouch at the back of the stage.

What is shown to be in the one who sees, daughter?

Vlad stood at center stage. Blood trailed down his chin and he spat to one side, eyes on me. The goading and daring was gone from them, and at first I thought I was getting to him.

I circled to my right, aware of the pounding in my head. I was faster and stronger than most humans, but so was he. I didn't know how much more my body could take.

Vlad remained where he was, staring me down. "Rage," he said in a low, gravelly voice. "The key to your demise has always been the rage hidden deep in your heart and in the heart of all."

I hesitated, confused again, because I knew that he was speaking the truth. And there was something different about him now. I could sense the terrible darkness that seeped from his bones as he stood before me, face flat, levity gone.

"Rage, 49th. Drink it in. Defend your honor."

Tell me, sweet daughter. What is shown to be in the one who sees?

I blinked. It was the third time I'd heard the faint voice. Why wasn't I listening? And if I'd failed, why was I still hearing?

You can never fail me.

I couldn't? But of course not.

You can never disappoint me.

But . . . Yes, but *I* was disappointed in me.

See yourself as I see you, and then you will know what it means to be in the one who sees.

What had come over me? I stood still, bewildered by what had happened here in front of millions.

When the evil man comes against you, do not resist. Step into the love that knows no fear, daughter. Trust me. Let it all go, just like in the storm.

Vlad lowered his head, gripped his hands to fists, and roared at me. "Now!"

But this time I didn't react to his rage. I let my muscles relax and lowered my arms to my sides. No. No, I couldn't defeat him with fear because he *was* fear. I couldn't use shadow to overcome shadow. My safety was in my defenselessness, because only there could I find the power called love.

He flashed me a grin. Without warning strong arms hooked mine and jerked them behind my back. Lifted me high off my feet.

Panicked, I twisted. I was being held four feet off the ground with both arms pinned behind my back by nothing.

But I knew that *nothing* was one of Vlad's Leedhan. In the sight of all I hung in the air as if by magic, but it wasn't magic at all. I was in the grip of the shadow of death.

"Now, 49th," Vlad said, glaring at me. "Now you die."

38

THE MOMENT that cool, muddy water swallowed me before the eyes of Ba'al and Qurong and Aaron and all the forces gathered to see the crushing of the lamb, a current sucked me deep with such force and speed that I gasped.

And when I gasped, the water seeped past the gag in my mouth and into my lungs.

And when the first trickle of water hit my lungs, the darkness vanished, replaced by a blinding flash of hot light that dissolved the hood, the gag, and the bonds that bound my wrists as if they'd never existed. I was so stunned by the sudden shift that I instinctively sucked deeper, flooding every corner of my lungs with that water.

But to say it was water would be to vastly misrepresent the light that coursed through every cell of my body as the current sucked me deep into the lake.

My body trembled with a love so pure, so infinite, so enrapturing that I found myself screaming. Not in astonishment but with a pleasure and joy so immeasurable that I was sure my body would be torn into a billion pieces, vaporized in an instant to become one with that light.

My eyes were wide and my body arched backward, splayed out and helpless as the light sucked me deeper, deeper, deeper at breakneck speed. I had no thought of anything but the wonder that had swallowed me whole. I had no questions, no concerns, no fear, only a raw love that shook me with its power.

The first note came then, a high, pure song of only one note, just like the one Talya often sang, only now it sounded like it was being sung by love itself. A single note, but in that one note, a symphony of creative power.

The boy, I thought. It was the boy!

As if in answer, I heard a giggle. Just one distant syllable, delighted and in wonder of itself.

Hello, Rachelle. Do you like it?

In my mind I was screaming to the boy, "Yes, yes, yes, I like it!"

But there in the warm embrace of love, I could only weep.

Who do you say I am?

It was now the same voice who'd whispered to me so many times when I was alone. And I knew the answer because in that moment I seemed to know all things.

"Love . . . Infinite light."

There were no words for the true nature of *infinite*, but I experienced it then, one with my origin, shown to me as Father, Mother, Boy—even though these were only simple metaphors for what was beyond all images and words.

White. Origin is Infinite. The First Seal. I was experiencing the First Seal!

I was in my infinite Father, who was the eternal light in whom there was no darkness. There was no time here. No space. No opposites. No polarity. No up or down, no good or bad, no preference or judgment or differentiation or specialness. Only infinite love spun by a single note that shook me to the bone.

I was being foreknown before time, one as light with Origin, who was far, far, far greater than me. And I trembled with wonder and awe because our union was so intimate.

Now you know.

With those tender words, the hue of the water that was light began to shift. I was drawn into a sea of emerald green, and I knew that I had reentered my earthen vessel. I was still made of the same light, but now in a kind of life called *body* and in a creation called *world*.

The single note that had sung in the light now blossomed into a million notes, each distinct.

The water was green but I could see through it, like seeing through a prism. And in that fluid prism, I could see a million other colors, far more than I had thought were possible.

My heart leaped. I was experiencing the Second Seal. *Green: I am the Light of the World.* Inchristi is me and in me. I was that part of God that could be known in the dimension called world without the knowledge of good or evil. Like a garden, I thought. Like Eden before the Fall, rich with color and staggering beauty.

The color darkened and I was falling into a cloudy sea filled with debris. I gasped. And as the darkness grew, the high, pure tone dropped through a hundred octaves and became a low, throbbing sound that filled me with dread. The colors vanished as the water became muddy, then black like tar, sticking to me, covering my body, my face, my eyes.

Panic seized me. *Oh no! No, no, no!*

But it was too late. I had fallen out of the garden, and now the whole world went black. I was falling into the Third Seal and I was screaming again, this time in terror.

Black: Seeing the Light in Darkness is my Journey. But I was lost in that darkness, trembling in dread.

The memory of being foreknown in light with my Father was only a distant, foggy thought that seemed powerless to save me from the fear thundering through me. Fear, because in that darkness I saw myself only as worthless. Ugly. Wretched and undeserving of life. The thoughts of accusation in the low, throbbing tones pummeled me, mocking me, stripping my awareness of whatever glory I had known in the light, so that I began to beg for my own death.

What was the Fourth Seal? I couldn't remember! I was desperate to remember, but in the cloud of fear my mind was no longer functioning correctly. Or maybe it was and this is what I had always been: a worthless wretch spewed out by a Father who couldn't tolerate me.

Maybe I had always been darkness, a stain on my Father's heel, depraved and worthless.

Far below me, a single faint but pure note cut through the throbbing tones, and I jerked my head toward it. In that distant tone, the Fourth Seal whispered through my mind. *Red: Surrender is the Means to Seeing the Light.*

A small shape formed before my eyes. Red. A deep red like blood, shaped like a cross, barely visible. I threw my arms over my head and let the current draw me, willing it to take me faster, desperate to enter the Fourth Seal. Nothing mattered to me now except that red water taking shape before me.

What had looked small at first now grew rapidly, and my desperation to reach it deepened. Larger, larger, until all I could see was red.

And then, for one searing instant, I was in a sea of blood.

A terrible pain ripped through my body as all that had blocked my sight of the light was stripped from me in one holy moment.

Only one moment and I was through, back into a brilliant white light. The current dispersed and I slowed to a stop, suspended in the light.

Once more the pure note filled the water. Once more I was embraced by a love so deep that I found myself trembling. But now I knew something new. I wasn't simply embraced by the love in that light; I was a part of that love. It was coming as much from me as from the water around me.

I was seeing more than light. I was seeing love.

I was *being* love.

I was love, just like my Father, just like the boy, just like Justin. I was in that likeness and it was called love. Not just any love, but a love that knew no darkness, no record of wrong, no fear, because it was beyond all judgment.

This was the Fifth Seal! I was in the Fifth Seal, and like the First Seal it was white.

I looked around, stunned by the simplicity of it all. And to my amazement, I saw another body hanging in the water a hundred feet away from me.

Jacob! Jacob was in the lake with me, eyes closed, back arched, arms limp, body shaking in the staggering power.

Now tell me, daughter. What is shown to be in the one who sees?

I jerked my head up and saw the seal shimmering just above me. The outer white circle, glowing with power. The inner green circle, me as an aspect of Elyon in an earthen vessel. The black circle of blindness to my divinity Inchristi. The red cross of cleansing, the way made by Justin.

And at the center, a white ball of light, made of the same light as the outer circle. I had come full circle, from light to light.

What is shown to be in the one who sees? But I knew! I already had the answer!

What is shown to be? Evidence is shown. What evidence is in the light? Love. True love.

It all came back to what Talya had first told me so long ago when he'd walked on water. Understanding all mysteries and all knowledge meant nothing without love. Faith to move mountains, loyalty to creed and confessions to the point of death, speaking in the tongues of men and angels—they all were nothing without a true love that could not be provoked and held no record of wrong.

There is no fear in love. They will know you follow me by your love.

My journey out of blindness was a journey into a pure light called love, unknown by a world lost in blindness.

Daring not to breathe, I reached out and placed my palm on the center of the Fifth Seal.

"White," I said. "True Love is the Evidence of Being in the Light."

For a moment, nothing happened.

Then the Fifth Seal under my palm grew hot. A surge of power filled my hand, and as it did, I could see through my flesh, as I had when Justin first opened my eyes in the desert.

The light flowed into my veins, up past my elbow, gaining speed. It surged into my shoulder and glowed hot like the sun.

I had the Fifth Seal, and that seal was love.

My Father's love. Justin's love. My love. The kind of love that held no record of wrong and could not judge. In the end, it was the only evidence of life Inchristi. Everything else was only empty claims.

The circle was complete—the circle uniting me and my Father, white to white, light to light, love to love. One.

Now you know.

I began to weep with gratitude as I hung there in the light's embrace. Now I knew.

Now, sweet daughter . . . Be who you are for me.

A strong current suddenly rushed up from below me and thrust me forward, through the seal, streaking for a glimmering surface, and I thought, *I'm entering heaven! I'm entering a new realm far beyond the skin of Other Earth!*

My hands parted the surface first. Then my head. Then all of me, water streaming from my hair and body as I sailed through the air and landed on my feet, five feet from the edge of the lake.

I stared at the sight before me, stunned.

I was back in the Realm of Mystics, which was still gray and lifeless. Jacob stood four paces to my right, panting, water spilling from his body. A thick band of Shataiki still clung to the cliffs, encircling the entire Realm, gloating with beady red eyes.

A hundred paces off and moving away from us walked three horses mounted by Ba'al and Aaron and Qurong. Beyond them, ten thousand warriors were also leaving the drowning pool.

I saw it all in a single glance.

As one they turned. As one they fell silent.

The 49th Mystic was back from the dead.

39

I HEARD Vlad say it. I heard his words, "Now, 49th. Now you die."

But I didn't take those words the way Vlad intended. How could he kill one who'd already surrendered her life? He couldn't. Hadn't the Fourth Seal shown me that?

Surrender. Turn the cheek. Forgive. Let go. Love.

Find love by letting go of everything but love. Find love by dying to self, the small self, the earthen-vessel self so desperate to be a god of its own making, seeking honor, seeking vindication, seeking correction, seeking to know itself through the polarity of law.

My knowing of the first four seals crashed in on me with those three words: *Now you die.*

The auditorium filled with cries of alarm as Vlad ripped a dagger from his jacket. It was shaped like a cross with a jagged blade. That's what they saw and I saw it as well, but then my perspective shifted.

The world was moving slowly, like a movie running at a tenth of its intended speed. Vlad was streaking for me, lips twisted, dagger drawn back, intent on shoving the blade deep into my heart. But I saw him moving slowly through air as heavy as water.

The crowd's panicked cries sounded far away, as if from another world. Or maybe I was in another world, just watching this one, oddly disconnected.

Fear fell away like a thick cloud of tiny metal filings falling off an electric magnet that had been unplugged. Shut off the negative charge and the darkness falls. Judgment was the negative charge, because judgment was only a form of fear.

This is what it means to cast darkness away, I thought. This is how you resist evil. You abide in love because love has no negative charge. No polarity.

There is no fear in love. There is no darkness in light. Simple.

So I unplugged. I died to my small judging self once more. I let go of all my attachments to this life just like I had in the storm in Other Earth.

All of this before Vlad had completed his first stride and my awakening was only beginning.

What Vlad had intended for evil in all that he'd done—right down to saying, "Now you die"—the light was using for good. All things worked together for good in love, even what I perceived as darkness. Like the devil in the story of Job, even Vlad was only playing his role as shadow with the consent of divinity.

Did he know that?

Now he was two steps in, rushing at me, hatred spilling from his eyes. He was screaming something, but he sounded like a mouse squeaking as it poked its head out of a hole in the wall. That's all Vlad was to me in that sudden shift in perspective.

Vlad was like a mouse. The *shadow* of a mouse.

The room had erupted in a cacophony of confusion and panic, but I was above it all, thinking these thoughts that seemed so simple and clear to me.

What is shown to be in the one who sees? Tell me. Close your eyes and sing my song with me.

I let my eyelids fall, and as soon as I did, I heard the note. A single note, sung high and pure in a lake of light far, far away. But that note was also singing in me, because in this world the lake was inside of me. It was inside all of us.

In one brilliant flash, I saw what was happening to me in Other Earth. Felt myself rushing through the lake, from the light to the green to the black through the red and into the light once more.

And in that last light, the note again, sung high and pure. The song of love that was me.

The Fifth Seal blossomed behind my closed eyes, and I saw myself place my hand on the ball of light. Heard myself say the words. "White: True Love is the Evidence of Being in the Light."

And with those words I felt the raw power of love rush up my arm and brand my shoulder with a searing heat.

I didn't know and I didn't care what Vlad was doing now, because I was lost in a sea of love in which there were no problems. Love never had nor ever could have a problem.

My body, suspended, trembled in the Leedhan's grasp. But it was the infinite energy of love that shook me now, not Vlad's fear. I was caught up in the rapture of that one pure note called love.

Warm tears were streaming down my cheeks. I could feel them running off my chin.

Sing it with me, dear daughter. Sing our beautiful song for the whole world to hear.

I parted my lips and let the note from the lake inside of me sing. It was hardly more than a whisper, thin and broken through this small earthen vessel's vocal cords, but it was pure and true.

The moment that note left my mouth, something in the room changed. My eyes were closed so I didn't see it, but I could feel the seismic shift that altered the state of consciousness in the hall.

Still I sang that note, broken but pure, no longer aware of time. I didn't dare stop any more than I would dare stop being me. The song was love, you see.

I was love.

Open your eyes and sing our song, my beloved. Let the whole world see how beautiful they are. You are such a beautiful daughter to me. Sing, dear one. Sing!

I held the note beyond the need for breath, overwhelmed by its power, and I slowly let my eyes open.

The whole scene had changed. I was on my feet now, facing the people, and the Leedhan that had held me in its grasp was gone. The power of that single note streamed from me, flooding the auditorium, rushing over the gathering. If they couldn't see it, they could feel the power, because it was like a wind, lifting their hair.

To a man, woman, and those few children who were present, tears streamed down their faces. Some were wailing, doubled over. Others lay on the floor, sobbing. The president was doubled over, trembling.

It was only a single note barely sung by a seventeen-year-old girl who'd been born blind, but it was shaking the world.

My voice fell silent. Vlad stood less than ten feet to my right. His eyes were wide with shock and he'd dropped his dagger, trembling in his boots. I didn't feel any grievance toward him. Nor did I offer him any resistance.

He'd told the world that I was an antichrist, but it was he and those who would come after him who were the antichrist. It was the energy of all who clung to judgment in opposition to love that was the antichrist.

I was the 49th Mystic, and I had found all five seals. Love was the only power that could undo fear, and I was that love. Inchristi was the light of love. Against the Fifth Seal there was no defense.

You don't sweep a shadow from a room; you simply turn on the light.

"Go," I whispered to Vlad.

His body trembled and then vanished into a swirl of shadowy fog. He was gone, leaving his black slacks and white jacket crumpled over a pair of cowboy boots. None of it mattered to me anymore. I was still swimming in a lake deep within me, flowing in a love unaffected by shadows.

I stepped up to the microphone that had fallen, picked it up, and walked toward the front of the stage.

It was time to tell them what was really happening. They would now learn that they were all the 49th Mystic on a journey from blindness to sight, from darkness to light, just like me.

Seeing is being in love. I was now seeing and being in love. I was witnessing.

It was time to do what I had come to do.

40

AS ONE they turned. As one they fell silent.

The 49th Mystic was back from the dead.

But neither the Horde nor the Albinos yet knew that there was no death. Or that my drowning in the lake was the final surrender that led to the Fifth Seal—not even I knew until that moment, there by the pool with my feet planted in warm, white sand, staring at Ba'al and the armies and the ring of frozen Shataiki that rimmed the Realm of Mystics.

Talya had always known. All of the Mystics had known. Even I had once known. The 49th Mystic would know the Fifth Seal called love when the world drowned her in the Realm of Mystics. Then the lion would lie down with the lamb.

I could hear the boy's song hanging in the air, a faint and beautiful refrain spun from the purest source. It had always been present to hear, but now I had the ears to hear it.

Something was about to change—I could feel the air itself charged with a desperate need for the sons and daughters of Elyon to be revealed. My skin prickled in anticipation of it.

Not a soul moved. Not a single Shataiki drew even a single breath. They now knew their own folly in thinking they could crush the light. They knew and they were trembling in that knowing, because their time had come to an end.

All of this was plain to me as I stood beside Jacob on the sand, eyes locked with Ba'al, who stared in stunned disbelief. I felt no disdain or the slightest ill will toward him, because I was seeing him in the light of love. He, like the rest, was only blinded by judgment because his earthen vessel was bound in judgment. And he, like all, had suffered deeply in that blindness.

But now he *would* see. All would see. Every knee would bow, every tongue sing the glory of the one who reigned supreme.

Still no one moved. No one dared.

I heard the pounding of hooves behind me first, and I turned. Looked up at the cliffs where the waterfall had flowed from the upper lake only an hour earlier. Teeleh's large, mangy body clung to the dried cliffs, frozen in place, staring at me with unblinking red eyes.

Then I saw it. Saw the white horse leap over Teeleh's head, ridden by a man in a robe dipped in blood, blazing sword of light held high in his right hand.

I stood in astonishment, watching as Justin's stallion bounded over the edge of the cliff, sailing high, and as soon as he'd crossed that threshold, the lake erupted with a brilliant green light, blasting up the cliff's face, vaporizing the little bat called Teeleh before it reached him.

But the lake's light didn't just flow to the top of the cliff. It shot to the sky, shattering the silence with an ear-splitting roar. Behind that roar, I could hear the distinct sound of the same pure note that had become so familiar to me in the lake.

The sound of a love that knew no opposite.

I jerked my head to see the light spreading east and west along the cliffs, from the ground up into the sky, so that the whole Realm was surrounded by cliffs made of the lake's green light, streaming from the earth to the sky. It was as if the lake had been underneath the whole of the Realm and was only now breaking free.

In one fell swoop, the Shataiki were no more. They didn't flee; they were ended. The knowledge of good and evil was no more. The shadow had been vanquished.

With the crashing of hooves, Justin's stallion landed on the shore to my left, and I spun to see him hurl his blade even as he thundered on, straight toward Ba'al.

And I thought, *I come to bring a sword that divides truth from untruth.*

His sword spun through the air, end over end, and impaled the ground fifty paces from me. A great thunder cracked high above. White light seared my mind, blinding me for a single moment. I gasped.

And then I could see again.

Light from Justin's sword spread out in all directions, like fast-moving ripples in a pond. Only these ripples were made of the lake's green light, flooding the charred wasteland of that sinkhole that had been the Realm of Mystics.

At the same time, the blue sky high above shimmered and began to peel back in all directions, as if the sky itself was falling. What had once blinded the world was now being pulled away to offer new sight. And in that new sight, the sky flowed with bright colors—gold, red, purple, green—like the sky I'd seen over the sea after the storm had cleared.

I knew then what I was watching. The green light was true perception before the knowledge of good and evil had distorted it. The light was the healing balm that made blind eyes see what was in truth.

The Realm of Mystics wasn't a place hidden here in this sinkhole. It was everywhere and always had been, to be seen with new perception by those who had eyes to see.

I was witnessing the teaching of Yeshua right here in three dimensions! And I thought, *The Spirit is on me to proclaim good news and sight to the blind, to set the oppressed free and proclaim the favor of Elyon.* It had always been Justin's mission. Now the fullness of that mission was at hand.

The world suddenly stalled. Justin raced, but I saw it in slow motion. He was bent over his stallion, robe flapping behind him like a banner, chasing the cleansing green light.

The light reached Ba'al and Aaron and Qurong, slamming into them and then rushing past them, flowing with gaining speed as it flooded the Realm and joined the wall of light flowing up the cliffs.

It shot to the tops of the cliffs, where it bent at a right angle and flowed over the land above and beyond the Realm with breathtaking speed.

The green light now covered every square inch of the Realm, but my eyes were back on Justin. His stallion raced even faster now, past the commanders and their armies, through the Realm, and then leaping high for the tops of the far cliffs and disappearing from sight.

Everything was happening at once, too much to take in.

White lions bounded from the trees behind me, sweeping by me in Justin's wake. Above, a thousand white Roush, flying west. And other magnificent creatures as well. Large dragonfly-like birds, wings glinting in dancing colors. Golden elk and deer, flocks of red and yellow parrots. I was sure I saw Judah among the lions.

In the power of the light, the grayed and charred landscape came back to life. Where the Shataiki and the armies had darkened the land, the trees budded and flowered and began to fill with leaves before my eyes. Green grass sprouted and covered the meadows; the wooden structures in the village shed their charred skin and glowed in bright yellows and blues and greens again.

I stood in stunned fascination, breathing steadily beside Jacob.

"Look!" His eyes were on the Horde. On Ba'al and his father.

They were no longer Horde! Their flesh was cleansed of the scabbing disease.

But even more, their skin wasn't Albino. Nor was the Elyonites' flesh Albino. It was flesh, yes, and flesh-colored, but it shone with a golden hue. Like a glorified body.

I snatched up my arm and saw that my skin had shifted as well, no longer the pale white I'd known myself to be. No, my skin hadn't changed, I realized. I was just able to see more than skin. I was seeing beyond the skin of this world. Where once I had seen through a glass dimly, I was now seeing clearly.

I looked back up. It was as if they had all drowned in the lake in one fell swoop. All. Albino, Horde, Eramite, Elyonite, and undoubtedly the Circle, wherever they now camped. The whole world, brought to true sight once more in the lake's power.

But of course, I thought. *Forgive them, for they know not what they do.* All had been blind, I chief among them. And now all of Other Earth was being healed from that curse.

Grace and love had finally come. In truth, the whole earth was and always had been the Realm of Mystics.

The kingdom of heaven had always been here, as Yeshua had claimed. We were just finally seeing it in its fullness.

I watched as Ba'al stared at his hands in stunned wonder. Then fell to his knees and wept, arms raised to the heavens.

It was the end of one age and the beginning of another. The lion was yielding to the lamb in the hearts of all mankind. Conflict had surrendered to peace. Guilt had been washed by innocence.

Jacob stumbled forward and then was running toward Qurong.

"Father!"

Qurong spun back, dazed. His eyes shone bright and his skin sparkled in the glow of the light, which was still flowing up the cliffs and spreading beyond. He saw Jacob and ran.

They met halfway, throwing themselves into an embrace. Qurong slumped to his knees, weeping, clinging to his son's waist as if Jacob was his own life. They were tears of joy and love, not regret. The same tears that moistened my own eyes.

Water splashed behind me and I turned to the lake. It was water once more—the light was streaking up along the cliffs from below the Realm, leaving the pool shimmering and green.

From the pool rose Thomas, carrying a woman. Chelise, I thought. This was Jacob's sister! She'd been in the Realm and been killed, but now Thomas brought her back. Which meant Thomas had gone to the pond by the cabin and come back through, leaving me there to speak to the world.

The me who had the Fifth Seal both here and there.

As soon as Thomas set Chelise down she caught sight of Jacob, her brother, and Qurong, her father, and was running for them. But first she pulled up, hurried to me, grabbed my hand, and kissed my knuckles.

"Thank you!"

"No, I wasn't—"

"Thank you, thank you." She kissed my cheeks. "Thank you."

"It wasn't me," I said. "It was Justin and . . ."

But she was already running for her brother and father again.

Ba'al was now jumping and leaping and hugging his guard like a captive released from endless suffering. A suffering he'd lived in for far too long. Now he was free.

Beyond him, thousands of Horde and Elyonite warriors stood in wonder, gazing about as if seeing for the first time. They were only now beginning to cry out, realizing what had happened.

They were cries of awe. The shouts of stunned disbelief at such fortune.

But it wasn't fortune. It was Justin's power, which was far greater than any could have possibly imagined. Greater even than the first Adam—Tanis—who'd first embraced blindness in this world forty years earlier.

Thomas rushed up to me, eyes on his flesh, then on the light still racing up the cliffs, then on me, eyes wide.

"Justin . . ."

"Came," I finished.

A smile of wonder slowly curved his lips. "Was there ever any doubt?"

I hesitated, lifting my hand to see it again. I almost thought I could see through it to the light coursing through my veins.

"Far too much," I said.

He nodded, eyes on me. "And the other world?"

Ba'al was now running toward me, eyes bright, grinning like a newborn child. Ba'al, whom I would embrace like a mother because Ba'al had been all of us.

Now you know, my precious daughter. Now you know.

I took a deep breath, overwhelmed by a love beyond the knowledge of good and evil.

"The final judgment against all judgment is finished here," I said to Thomas, eyes still on Ba'al. "I think it might just be beginning in the other world."

And then I was running for Ba'al.

41

"SET IT down, Mike."

The pilot glanced over his shoulder at Steve and nodded.

The helicopter banked to the left, angling for the wide flat rock on the cliff's most eastern rim. We were high over Eden, Utah, now hardly more than a wasteland in the sinkhole that had once housed Project Eden. Even the buildings that had survived the explosive charges five months earlier had been demolished, leaving nothing but rubble.

A month had passed since the world watched me at the World Security Summit. I'd shown them the only thing I knew to show, which was a love that held no record of wrong. Only that and the seals glowing on my arm, explaining each for the whole world to know. The audience had watched me in stunned silence, except for those who already knew what I was saying. Their streaming tears were born of a love that joined with my own as I spoke the truth that would divide the world.

I spoke the words simply and without fanfare, just a girl on the stage sent to speak truth about the *Way*, the *Truth* and the *Life*. The words were gentle, but the power flowing from me thundered through their hearts. It was a message for all, regardless of religion, race, nationality, gender, or age.

It was the same forgotten way that Talya had drawn me into, symbolized by the Five Seals of Truth glowing like the sun on my arm and from my heart.

I said it all, and when I was done, I left that overwhelmed audience and exited through the side door. Karen was waiting, weeping like a child, not because of the words I'd spoken but because of the power that had filled the air. Because of the love.

She took me back to the hotel, and I stayed there for three days. The FBI came and took my full statement twice, just to be sure. The NSA came and asked me a hundred questions about DARPA and the bombings, using a retinal scan that would tell them if I was lying.

But my eyes fried their machine.

I didn't watch television, so I didn't know what the world was saying and I didn't care. Instead, I cared for the maid. Her daughter had been killed in one of the bombings, so I shared my love with her and she wept in that love.

And I cared for the bellman and the room service attendants and everyone else I saw while I was in the lobby or in the halls. Many of them teared up as soon as our eyes met, because most of the world had seen what had happened, either live or when it was played back, over and over.

After three days, Steve came for me. Steve, who I loved like a father and whose mind had been as fried as my own.

He was no longer with DARPA, and I stayed with him in West Virginia for the next two weeks. We spent most of the time talking about life. All of life. Especially the part of life that couldn't be seen with natural eyes.

It was then that he'd told me Congress was offering me restitution. Anything I wanted.

The helicopter settled on the rock slab above Eden, Utah.

"How long?" the pilot asked, turning back.

"Two hours?" I said.

He nodded. "Okay. Back in two hours."

I scooted out after Steve, ducked under the whirling blades, and hurried to the lone pine that had managed to stake a claim on the otherwise bare cliff. Thirty seconds later the helicopter was in the air, and within a minute we could barely hear it.

Steve hooked his thumbs in his belt and stared at the sinkhole. "Well, there it is."

"There it is."

We stood in silence for a minute. I couldn't remember most of my time in Eden—DARPA had taken those memories. I could only remember the scenes around the church where I'd faced off with Vlad. And the hospital near my old house where I'd first encountered him in the flesh—everything tied to the discovery of the first three seals.

But the church along with my house and the rest of the buildings were no more.

"You're sure this is what you want?" he asked. "I know you don't care about money, but twenty million dollars could go a long way out there."

I had no idea what twenty million dollars could or couldn't do. It was just the limit they gave me when they said anything I want.

"You think twenty million can rebuild this place?" I asked.

He frowned. "Half of it would go to clearing it out and rebuilding infrastructure. A power plant, roads, fix the tunnel . . . Sure. With plenty to spare."

"Then yes. This is what I want."

"They'll be clamoring to come see you, you know."

"Who?"

"Half the world. The half who were ready to hear what you said."

"What kinds of people?"

"Everyone from theologians to mothers who have hurting children."

I wasn't sure how I felt about that. I mean, yes, I felt deeply for them all and I would never turn anyone away, but I wasn't anyone special. Specialness wasn't part of love because it meant something else was less special.

"You could also build a top-of-the-line research facility here. Maybe get more funding. I could run it for you."

"That sounds fun."

"Really?"

"Why not? The more we learn about how these earthen vessels work, the better, right?"

His eyes brightened. "Yeah. Yeah, that could be amazing!" Now he was pacing, pointing down. "Right there, where the hospital was. Quarters next to it. Only open-minded researchers devoted to the Way. Physicists, neuroscientists, biologists, the whole lot. A center for spiritual awakening." He spun to me. "What do you think?"

I chuckled. "I think you're excited."

"'Course, we'll need more money. And security. A lot of security."

"Security? What for?"

"For the other half of the world," he said. "The ones who think you should burn for heresy." He paused. "I shouldn't say 'the other half' because it's only a few, but the judgmental few make a lot of noise. They still think their outrage is a form of love. Security's a must."

It was the first time I'd heard anything about any resistance to what I'd said, and for a moment the thought bothered me.

But then I let it go. After all, who was I?

I was my Father's daughter. I didn't have the slightest interest in defending what needed no defense, either ideologically or physically. At least that's how I felt.

"No security," I said.

"But of course you need security! The country's falling apart out there. With the president's impeachment and the collapsing economy, the nuts will come out of the woodwork, blaming it all on you. Not to mention religious zealots who took issue with the way you speak of Christ."

"Christ is love," I said. "It's foolishness to those who haven't experienced that unconditional love themselves, so they get upset and justify their judgment by what they were taught Yeshua meant. It's okay. They're only trying their best."

"Still, as they say, prophets are always martyred."

"No security." I had no concern for my life. Besides, in some ways I'd already lived two of them—one here and one in Other Earth.

The thought set butterflies free in my belly. Good ones. Tomorrow was the Day of the Bride there. After I'd emerged from the lake, my dreaming had once again become linear. Every time I fell asleep here, I woke there, and vice versa, just like at the beginning.

When I fell asleep tonight I would dream, and when I dreamed I would be on the cliffs overlooking the old Realm of Mystics. I still sometimes wondered if Other Earth was a real physical place or a metaphorical vision of this world. Did it matter?

What did matter was what story of life I chose to live in every moment. Was I holding grievance or was I in love? Was I blinding myself to the world by judging myself and others?

To what perception was I binding myself—the seen in polarity, or the unseen Inchristi?

One thing was certain: the power of Christ made manifest was far, far greater than anyone, even the most devoted follower, could imagine. I had experienced it in both worlds. There, in a lake that shook me to the bone. Here, in the lake deep within me.

Here, everyone was on the same journey that I, the 49th Mystic, had taken, and most were still just beginning to awaken to their new birth—a process that would probably include a great tribulation of some kind or another, both in the heart of each and in all the world. Religion formed in fear, regardless of its name, had blinded some as much as agnosticism had blinded others.

There, all had risen as Mystics, and all were my friends.

Which reminded me, I should find some close friends on Earth. I would, maybe here, in the very place I'd grown up.

Karen could be one of those friends. But I'd have to visit her in prison.

"It'll be hard to secure proper funding without assurances of reasonable security," Steve was saying.

"Then we'll have to do it without proper funding." I looked up at him and grinned. "Vlad didn't stand a chance against me. You think people with guns scare me?"

His brow arched and he smiled. "Well, there is that."

"So we have a deal? Do you want to help me?"

"Just like that?"

I shrugged. "Why not?"

He looked at the sinkhole that had become as much a part of his life as it had mine. "Yeah. Why not?"

I grabbed his hand and pulled him over to a boulder. We sat down, overlooking Eden.

"Okay. Tell me again how it could look."

MY EYES slowly opened as I pulled myself out of one world and entered another. On Earth, I had just fallen asleep in a hotel room in Salt Lake City after spending the day visiting Eden with Steve. We'd run around on the cliffs like children, spinning wild dreams of how we might rebuild.

But I was in Other Earth now. I'd been up late, sitting around the fire with Jacob, Thomas, Samuel, and Talya, laughing at the antics of Paulus and Maya earlier in the day.

Paulus, who was once known as Ba'al, changed his name when Talya told him about the ancient mystic whose life had been radically changed on a road to a place called Damascus. Like Ba'al, Paulus had been determined to slaughter those in the light.

Now Paulus had taken to much mischief with Maya, the little Horde girl who'd spoken such truth to me when I was Horde. It seemed that Paulus didn't yet know how to swim, and Maya was trying to teach him in the pool that Jacob had drowned in.

"You have to move your arms, Paulus!" Maya cried, hopping around the bank as Paulus floundered.

"I *am* moving my arms!"

"Above the water, not under it! Like this!"

"I will sink if I lift my arms!"

Talya had curled up in a ball on the grass, howling with laughter, and the rest of us were laughing with him as much as at Paulus.

Of all the Mystics, only Talya was still with us. And who was Talya, really? How could he know so much about Yeshua and Paulus? He finally told me.

Talya was actually a young man in the deserts of northern Arabia in the year AD 43. He lived with his mother, Maviah, and her husband, Saba, who had both known Yeshua well. In fact, Talya was in that desert now, dreaming of this world when he slept there and dreaming of that ancient world when he slept here.

Talya was a dreamer like me, you see?

And he knew of Paulus not only from the many texts of his journeys and teachings, but because Paulus was with him in that Arabian desert now, and had been for several months. Paulus had gone into the desert following his encounter with the light on the road to Damascus. He'd been caught up in the heavens and seen the truth of being one with Christ, which he would later write extensively about in his letters.

It was a beautiful mystery. The only one that finally mattered.

Thomas's wife, Chelise, had been killed in the Realm along with the others, but it wasn't her time to pass on. The Mystics had always known they would be killed and they saw no problem with it. But it wasn't time for Chelise yet.

She would see her son Samuel reborn. And so she had.

As had I. And I'd embraced him in a fierce love. Neither of us mentioned his betrayal—it no longer existed.

None of us had any remorse. Nor could we court condemnation. Instead, we rested in a realm flowing with love.

And what a staggering love it was.

"Will it be like this on Earth?" I'd asked Talya.

"Of course," he said. "Though not necessarily the same physical form."

"It'll happen so suddenly?"

"A day is as a thousand years in the sight of the divine," he replied. "Even now in that ancient world, Paulus truly expects Yeshua to return in his lifetime. Every generation does. We know from history that Paulus was wrong about this, but I let him think what he will. He doesn't know that I dream of this world."

I'd never heard that about Paul the apostle. But it made sense.

"As for the other world you live in," he continued, "only know that as all surrender their small need for prophecy to follow a particular linear pattern based on man's interpretation, they will make a thousand years only one day in the journey of their own hearts. Those prophecies are as much the story of each soul as the story of a species. Both are true, but this is the deeper truth. All face the antichrist in their own hearts. Metaphor, my dear. Metaphor is the finger that points to the truth beyond the earthen vessel's mind."

Just like the journey I'd taken here in Other Earth, I thought.

Other Earth, where I was now, having just awakened, suddenly aware that I was alone in a cave.

I jerked up, gasping. The day was bright outside. It was late! I flung myself from the bedroll and sprinted to the opening, feet bare, hair tangled.

The first thing I saw was Jacob, resting back on one elbow ten paces away, talking to Aaron, chewing on a piece of grass. He looked up at me and smiled.

"She rises from her dreams."

The next thing I saw were the throngs of people lining the cliffs, some seated, some standing. They'd arrived yesterday and through the night, millions. All the inhabitants of Other Earth, gathered here for the Day of the Bride.

Justin had never left and Justin had come and today Justin would come. This was the mystery of Justin. He wasn't bound by time. Only metaphor could approximate his life beyond death.

"She rises with a bird's nest on her head," a voice said behind me. Talya.

"And dust on her dress." Samuel, chuckling.

I glanced down and noted my dusty white dress, and I brushed the cloth absently. Appearances meant little now, but in my excitement for this day, I'd slept in the white dress, thinking it a good choice for a celebration called the Day of the Bride.

I glanced over my shoulder. Samuel and Talya sat on a boulder, legs dangling, both smiling at me.

"Good morning, Samuel. Talya."

"Morning is long gone, my dear," Talya said.

But my mind was on the old Realm beyond the lip of the cliff. I ran over the grass and peered down.

The meadows were filled with people, more than I could have imagined. There was nothing special about the Realm now—the whole world was decorated by colored forests and lush meadows, all unique and wonderful in their own ways. The lake's light had swept over the earth like a tsunami, transforming every inch of desert, every structure it touched, every rock and tree.

Every day new tales came, describing new discoveries. White sand that held its form no matter how you shaped it; blue fruits the size of cabbages, dripping with intoxicating juices; seas made of liquid crystal that could be breathed; magnificent creatures in those light-filled depths.

All wonderful, but far more so the Bride. And the Bride was here.

Here were those made in the likeness of Elyon, gathered for Justin. The land existed for them and was loved by them.

I hurried back and settled next to Jacob. "You let me sleep."

"But of course." He stroked my cheek. "Did you find Eden there?"

"I did! Steve and I are going to rebuild it, just like I said."

"Wonderful."

"There's an Eden there?" Aaron asked. "Like this one?"

"Not quite."

I shared all my dreams with Jacob—they were just stories to me—but the concept was new to Aaron. It was interesting, living in two places. Here, I felt no worry, no fear, no annoyance of any kind. But in my dreams, I was still bound in the old polarity. Here, I felt only love. There, fear still tempted me on occasion until I forgave it. There, the world thought of me as either a prophet or a devil.

Here, I was no different from the smallest child, because none could be honored when all were already equally honored.

None but Justin, and we were all one in him.

"No word?" I asked.

"Not yet. I think we will know when he—"

And then we did know, because everything went perfectly still. Everyone knew at once, catching themselves just as Jacob had, as if the air itself had spoken. And it had.

The three of us stood as one, and I saw that all either stood or were gaining their feet. Without a word, I ran back to the edge of the meadow, breathless. My heart was hammering and my fingers tingled.

He is here.

He was always here, but he was *here*. I could feel his power in every cell of my body.

Jacob joined me and took my hand, wide stare fixed on the distant waterfalls. Then came Aaron, tears in his eyes already. Then Talya and Samuel, and that's all I saw because they came, a hundred thousand Roush flying over the distant cliffs in a massive formation. It's why Michal and Gabil and the other Roush weren't with us now, as they often were. They were with him.

With Justin, who emerged from the forest next to the waterfall on his horse, flanked by a hundred white lions.

I could barely contain my excitement. I wanted to leap and shout and scream my pleasure for the whole world to hear.

But the whole world already heard that pleasure. It was coming from every rock, every tree, every blade of grass, every man, woman, and child in Other Earth.

Where once the whole earth groaned for the revelation of the sons and daughters of Elyon, it now celebrated that revealing.

Justin was in the meadow past the lake now, riding slow, settled in his saddle. Not a word was yet spoken. Not a breath taken. He was across the Realm from me, and he was right before me. I felt as though if I reached out my hand, I would touch his.

Still not a word.

He stopped in the middle of the meadow. For long beats of my heart, he sat upon his white stallion, looking at us in silence. All of us.

I saw motion from the corner of my eye—Paulus dropping to his knees, arms of welcome spread wide. Tears of joy streaming down his cheeks.

I dropped to my knees with him, and with me, millions, like falling dominoes. The sound of so many knees hitting the ground was like a distant herd of wild stallions.

A lone cry shredded the air.

"Inchristi is all!" Paulus cried, trembling now. "Inchristi is in all!"

And then a thunder shook the Realm of Mystics, threatening to tear every leaf from every tree, promising to reduce every stone to dust under the power of the crushing sound of three million voices in rapture.

The thunder of every living soul in Other Earth, shouting one word over and over so it sounded like an everlasting peal from the heavens, speaking a simple truth for all who had ears to hear.

That word was *Justin*.

Justin, who was One with me and with all.

Justin, who was love.

The End

AUTHOR'S NOTE

You've just finished the final chapter in the two-book saga Beyond the Circle. Is there more to come? Perhaps. We shall see.

Then again, yes, there is more to come. We are all on the same journey of discovering ourselves in this world, just like Rachelle. It's the journey from fear to love, from darkness to light, from blindness to sight.

If the journey draws you in any way, please visit The49thMystic.com. There you will find much more: additional content, behind-the-scenes interviews, and more of Yeshua's teaching in *The Forgotten Way*, including a daily guide that will assist you in taking the same journey Rachelle took to find and know the truth of who you are in this reality we call the world. Dive deep.

Ted Dekker

Ted Dekker is the award-winning and *New York Times* bestselling author of more than forty novels, with over ten million copies sold worldwide. Born in the jungles of Indonesia to missionary parents, he lived among cannibals. His upbringing as a stranger in a fascinating and sometimes frightening culture fueled his imagination, and it was during the lonely times as a child that he became a storyteller.

Dekker's passion is simple—to explore truth through mind-bending stories that invite readers to see the world through a different lens. His fiction has been honored with numerous awards, including two Christy Awards, two Inspy Awards, an RT Reviewers' Choice Award, and an ECPA Gold Medallion. In 2013, NPR readers nationwide put him in the Top 50 Thriller Authors of All Time.

Dekker lives in Nashville, Tennessee, with his wife, Lee Ann, and their four children, Rachelle, JT, Kara, and Chelise.

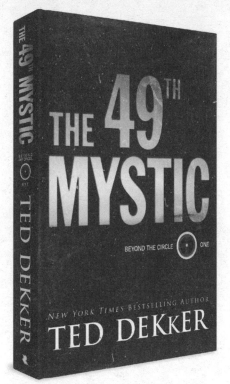

DID YOU MISS THE FIRST BOOK OF THIS EPIC TWO-VOLUME SAGA?

Join the high stakes and mind-bending quest to find an ancient path that will save humanity.

Some say the great mystery of how one can live in two worlds at once died with Thomas Hunter many years ago. Still others that the gateway to that greater reality was and is only the stuff of dreams.

THEY ARE WRONG. In the small town of Eden, Utah, a blind girl named Rachelle Matthews is about to find out just how wrong.

Talya's Journal

on the Forgotten Way

Key excerpts from the journal of Talya, who herein did transcribe those teachings of Yeshua, Paulus, Johnin, and Petrus as written in the ancient Books of History called Scriptures.

(Talya's personal notes in parentheses.)

Organized by Rachelle, the 49th Mystic

Relating to Chapter 12

1) [Love] is not provoked, takes no account of evil. (Other translations say it does not keep a record of wrong or holds no record of wrong. It is a legal term meaning "inadmissible as evidence." Paulus's word for *evil* or *wrong* is singular, the same word Yeshua used for *evil*, and so has been translated as "does not take evil into account." Some scribes have felt compelled to insert extra words of their own such as *deeds* or *thoughts* following the word *evil*, and *easily* before *provoked*, but again, these words are not in Paulus's writings.)

Paulus's First Letter to Corinth 13:5 WEB

2) If I . . . know all mysteries and all knowledge (doctrine and confessions); and if I have all faith, so as to remove mountains, but do not have love, I am nothing. And if I give all my possessions to feed the poor, and if I surrender my body to be burned (service and loyalty to beliefs), but do not have love, it profits me nothing. (True love, which does not take into account wrong.)

Paulus's First Letter to Corinth 13:2–3

3) And those whom he foreknew he also fashioned in the likeness of the image of his Son, that he would be The Firstborn of many brethren. And those whom he pre-fashioned, he called, and those whom he called, he made righteous, and those whom he made righteous, he glorified. (Past tense. Our true state of being right now.)

Paulus to Rome 8:29–30 ABPE

4) The eye (singular, perception) is the lamp of (shows you) the body (our earthly experience); so then if your eye is clear, your whole body will be full of light. (We experience only light and beauty in this life if we are seeing clearly.) But if your eye is bad, your whole body will be full of darkness. (The state of most, most of the time.) If then the light that is in you (the light is already in us) is darkness, how great is the darkness! (Suffering in this life.)

Book of Matthew 6:22–23

5) Do you not say, "There are yet four months and then comes the harvest"? Behold, I say to you, <u>lift up your eyes</u> and look on the fields, that they are white for harvest. (A change in perception shows you the kingdom is already here, though most are blind to it.)

Book of Johnin 4:35

Now having been questioned by the Pharisees as to when the kingdom of God was coming, He answered them and said, "<u>The kingdom of God is not coming with signs</u> to be observed (it is now, not later); nor will they say, 'Look, here it is!' or, 'There it is!' (It is beyond our dimension of space, neither above nor below, not seen with earthly eyes.) For behold, <u>the kingdom of God is in your midst</u>." (Literally, already inside your very being.)

Book of Luke 17:20–21

6) From that time Jesus began to preach and say, "<u>Repent</u> (metanoia, change your cognitive perception, go beyond your knowledge) <u>for the kingdom of heaven is at hand</u>." (Already here and in your very being.)

Book of Matthew 4:17

Relating to Chapter 13

1) Ye have heard that it has been said, Eye for eye and tooth for tooth. <u>But I say unto you, not to resist evil</u>; but whoever shall strike thee on thy right cheek, turn to him also the other. (One of Yeshua's many teachings on love versus resistance in all respects.)

Book of Matthew 5:38–39 DARBY

2) <u>There is no fear in love</u>; but perfect love casts out fear, because fear involves punishment, and <u>the one who fears is not perfected in love</u>.

First Book of Johnin 4:18

Relating to Chapter 18

1) Wherefore <u>the law was our schoolmaster</u> to bring us unto Christ, that we might be justified by faith. But after that faith is come (Inchristi), we are <u>no longer under a schoolmaster</u>.

Paulus to Galatia 3:24–25 KJV

The former regulation (the law of Moses) is set aside because it was <u>weak and useless</u> . . . and a better hope is introduced (the law of grace), by which we draw near to God (know him intimately).

Letter to Hebrews 7:18–19 NIV

Relating to Chapter 21

1) As He passed by, He saw a man blind from birth. And His disciples asked Him, "Rabbi, who sinned, this man or his parents, that he would be born blind?" Jesus answered, "It was neither that this man sinned, nor his parents; but it was so that the works of God (the manifestation of God's light) might be displayed (made visible) in him (literally inside him). We must work the works of Him who sent Me (seeing God's light within us) as long as it is day (while we are alive on earth); night (death in this life) is coming when no one can work. While I am in the world, I am the Light of the world." When He had said this, He spat on the ground, and made clay of the spittle, and applied the clay to his eyes, and said to him, "Go, wash in the pool of Siloam." . . . So he went away and washed, and came back seeing. (By symbolically blinding the man, Yeshua showed how this world blinds us and how only the water of the Spirit can give us true sight. We are all born blind to see.)

Book of John in 9:1–7

2) And those whom he foreknew (an experiential intercourse with God before the foundations of the universe, *ginosko* in Greek—firsthand acquaintance) he also fashioned in the likeness of the image of his Son, that he would be The Firstborn of many brethren (Christ is our elder brother). And those whom he pre-fashioned (all of his children), he called, and those whom he called, he made righteous, and those whom he made righteous, he glorified. (Past tense. Our true state of being right now and always.)

(Note: Some have translated *fashioned* as *predestined*, as though this suggests a future act, which undermines both the meaning of the Greek, which is "to establish or fashion," and the rest of Paul's statement, which is definitively past tense.)

Paulus to Rome 8:29–30 ABPE

The One having saved us and having called us with a holy calling, not according to our works, but according to His own purpose and grace, <u>having been given us in Christ Jesus before time eternal</u>. (This happened to us before time began, a great mystery.)

Paulus's Second Letter to Timothy 1:9 BLB

3) Truly I tell you, <u>whatever you bind on earth will be bound in heaven</u> (heaven: the dimension that is here now, unseen by earthly eyes), and whatever you loose on earth will be loosed in heaven. Again, truly I tell you that <u>if two of you on earth agree about anything they ask for, it will be done for them by my Father in heaven.</u> (Yeshua's claim of the power we wield through our beliefs and agreements, both collective and individual. This manifestation is happening every moment of every day by all, though most are blind to it. Most don't flow in the miraculous because they are bound to their earthen vessel and the laws of physics in agreement with collective observation.)

Book of Matthew 18:18–19 NIV

4) <u>If you forgive anyone's sins</u> (including yourself), <u>their sins are forgiven; if you do not forgive them, they are not forgiven.</u> (Through grievance we cast others and ourselves into outer darkness. The power of letting go of offense—forgiveness—releases that bondage in darkness.)

Book of Johnin 20:23 NIV

5) In the same way, those of you who do not give up everything you have cannot be my disciples. (Letting go of attachment to the world of polarity and judgment is the only way to experience the kingdom of heaven.)

Book of Luke 14:33 NIV

Relating to Chapter 23

1) And He will put the sheep on His right, and the goats on the left. . . . Then they themselves also will answer, "Lord, when did we see You hungry, or thirsty, or a stranger, or naked, or sick, or in prison and did not take care of You?" (This spoken by those who call Christ "Lord" but have not awakened to true love.) Then He will answer them, "Truly I say to you, <u>to the extent that you did not do it to one of the least of these</u> (the sinners of his day, those in prison and destitute for their failings), <u>you did not do it to Me</u>." (Not "as if unto me," but "<u>to me</u>." Thus we see and serve Christ in all.)

Book of Matthew 25:33, 44–45

2) [You] have put on the new self (a new way of being in the world) who is being renewed (metanoia, a transforming of the mind, like being re-born) to a true knowledge according to the image of the One who created him—a renewal (awakening) in which there is no distinction between Greek and Jew, circumcised and uncircumcised, barbarian, Scythian (seen as the worst of the worst in his day), slave and freeman, but <u>Christ is all, and in all</u>. (We are one with Christ, and that One, our true identity, lives in our earthen vessel. Inchristi is all; Inchristi is in all.)

Paulus to Colossae 3:10–11

3) If anyone comes to Me (responds to the good news of the kingdom), and <u>does not hate</u> (release attachment to) his own father and mother and wife and children and brothers and sisters, yes, and even his own life (all the masks we cling to in relationship to others and ourselves), he <u>cannot be My disciple</u>. (Cannot follow Yeshua into an experience of the kingdom now present within all.)

Book of Luke 14:26

Then he said to them all: "Whoever wants to be my disciple must <u>deny themselves and take up their cross daily</u> (release attachment to the earthen vessel) and follow me." (Unless one lets go of everything this world values in form, one will not experience the kingdom of heaven that Yeshua experienced—i.e., born again as an infant to experience all things in a new way. This is a continual process daily, not a onetime event.)

Book of Luke 9:23 NIV

Relating to Chapter 25

1) For God, who said, "Light shall shine out of darkness," is the One who has shone in our hearts to give the Light of the knowledge of the glory of God in the face of Christ. (We are that light Inchristi.) But <u>we have this treasure in earthen vessels</u> (temporal and returning to dust), so that the surpassing greatness of the power will be of God, and not from ourselves (the earthen vessel self).

Paulus's Second Letter to Corinth 4:6–7

<u>So we fix our eyes</u> (perception) <u>not on what is seen</u> (earthen vessel self and all polarity), <u>but on what is unseen, since what is seen is temporary</u> (dust to dust), <u>but what is unseen is eternal</u> (true eternal self—eternal, beyond time and space).

Paulus's Second Letter to Corinth 4:18 NIV

2) <u>He has made everything beautiful in its time.</u> (Without exception.) He has also set eternity in the human heart (foreknown before the foundations of the earth); yet no one can fathom what God has done from beginning to end. (In part because in the eternal there is no beginning or end—it defies the mind, which thinks only in time.)

Book of Ecclesiastes 3:11 NIV

3) They are not of the world, even as I am not of the world. (Yeshua's affirmation that we are not of the world, explained by Paulus in different language as only in temporal earthen vessels for a short time.)

Book of Johnin 17:16

4) You are the light of the world. A city set on a hill cannot be hidden; nor does anyone light a lamp and put it under a basket, but on the lampstand, and it gives light to all. (Yeshua declared this to the outcasts and destitute of his day, and his words are true of all who live. This is the foundation of the good news to which most are blind. That light shines, but the earthen vessel too often is blind to it and keeps it hidden under another identity, or basket.)

Book of Matthew 5:14–15

5) Therefore if any man be in Christ, (since you are in Christ) he is a new creature: old things are passed away; behold, all things are become new. (Being in Christ is a state of being known by those who experience themselves as the light of the world, beyond the world of polarity. In that being, all is experienced in a new way.)

Paulus's Second Letter to Corinth 5:17 KJV

Relating to Chapter 28

1) The creation waits in eager expectation for the revelation of the sons of God. (All who were foreknown and glorified before creation but blinded by the knowledge of good and evil in the Fall.)

Paulus to Rome 8:19 BSB

Relating to Chapter 32

1) So whatever you believe about these things (what is and what is not sin as described) keep between yourself and God. Blessed is the one who does not condemn himself by what he approves. But whoever has doubts is condemned if they eat, because their eating is not from faith; and everything that does not come from faith is sin.

(Paulus's most direct definition of sin as a state of being out of alignment with faith, not defined by the act itself, but the intention behind the act. What then is faith as he uses it? Faith is alignment to the unseen kingdom we place our hope in as expressed in the letter to the Hebrews 11:1 [BSB]. "Now faith is the assurance of what we hope for and the certainty of what we do not see"—the kingdom of heaven not seen with earthly eyes yet ever present within and everywhere.)

Paulus to Rome 14:22–23 NIV

Relating to Chapter 34

1) During the days of Jesus' life on earth, he offered up prayers and petitions with fervent cries and tears to the one who could save him from death (garden of Gethsemane), and he was heard because of his reverent submission (comforted by angels, as written). Son though he was, he learned obedience (came into alignment) from what he suffered and, once made perfect (having surrendered the will of his earthen vessel in that garden—"Not my will but your will," two different wills), he became the source of eternal salvation (alignment to the eternal realm now in our midst, called the kingdom of heaven) for all who obey him (also align to Christ).

(In that garden, Yeshua's will was not in alignment with his Father's, thus two wills: his will and his Father's will.

Yeshua made the final surrender and became perfect there in that garden, and became the way for us if we follow by aligning to our risen, eternal selves. Otherwise we are mastered by the storms that rise against us, and we live in suffering.)

Letter to Hebrews 5:7–9 NIV

Relating to Chapter 36

1) I, even I, am he who blots out your transgressions, <u>for my own sake</u> (as a matter of God's character he does not see darkness), and remembers your sins no more. (God does not hold our blindness against us, nor does he hold it in mind.)

Prophet Isaiah 43:25 NIV

As far as the east is from the west (infinitely far), so far has he removed our transgressions from us.

David's Psalm 103:12 NIV

2) But I say unto you, <u>Love your enemies</u>, bless them that curse you, do good to them that hate you, and pray for them which despitefully use you and persecute you. (Only in a love that holds no record of wrong is this possible. In such love is our salvation in this life and in no other way. This is Inchristi.)

Book of Matthew 5:44 KJV

3) Then said Jesus, Father, <u>forgive them; for they know not what they do</u>. (Those who <u>do not know what they do</u> in any wrongful act are innocent by reason of insanity in the court.)

Book of Luke 23:34 KJV

Of note to all who read the letters of Paulus

Paulus's letters written later in his life (Colossians, Ephesians, and so on) were more mystical than earlier letters and focused on our true identity as one with Christ while we yet live in these earthen vessels, which return to dust. He called our being one with Christ "the great mystery" (letter to Ephesus 5:32).

Thus, we call ourselves Mystics.

This is the essence of our mysticism: aligning to our union with the infinite One who cannot be fathomed by intellect alone. By doing so, we find ourselves in the world but not of it, flowing with peace, power, and above all, a love that holds no record of wrong, the truest evidence of our awakening, without which all other evidence is nothing. Only this kind of love will awaken the world to the glory of Christ made manifest on earth.